De Profundis

1905-2025
出版120周年纪念

－中英双语－

自深深处
DE PROFUNDIS

［英］奥斯卡·王尔德　著

梁永安　译

湖南文艺出版社
HUNAN LITERATURE AND ART PUBLISHING HOUSE
·长沙·

博集天卷
CS-BOOKY

这痛苦恒久、模糊而暗黑，直像无边无际

因 为 爱 比 恨 美 。

———

奥斯卡·王尔德

寄自雷丁监狱

1897 年 1—3 月

亲爱的波西：

经过漫长和徒劳的等待之后，我决定主动写信给你。此举既是为你着想，也是为我自己着想，因为我不乐于看到，在漫长的两年监禁期满后，还是收不到你写的一行字，或是得不到任何你的消息或口信（那些让我伤心的不算）。

你我那段命运坎坷和最可哀可叹的友谊已经随着我的身败名裂而结束，但往日的情谊仍常常在我的记忆里浮现。一想到自己心中那个曾经被爱充满的地方就要被厌恶、怨尤和鄙夷永远占去，我就满怀忧伤。我想，你自己心里一定也清楚，你与其未经我允许就发表我的书信，与其未问过我便把你的诗集题献给我，倒不如写封信给牢里孤孤单单的我，这会让我更加受用。不过，当然，那样的话，世人便不会知道你选择来回应或叫屈的是哀伤还是热情的言辞，是悔恨还是冷漠的言辞。

因为这封信不免会谈到你的人生和我的人生，会谈到过去和未来，会谈到一些美事如何变成苦事，以及一些苦事如何可能在未来变成欢欣，我毫不怀疑有好些内容会深深刺伤你的虚荣心。果真如此的话，你就应该把信一读再读，直至它把你的虚荣心杀死为止。假如你认为它对你的指控有不公之处，那就应该记住：若我们还有足够的清白可以受到不公指控，便应该感谢上天。假如信中有那么一段话能让你涌出眼泪，那就哭吧，像我们狱中人那样尽情痛哭（监狱的白天和夜晚都是专为眼泪而设）。哭是唯一可以拯救你的方法。如果你不这样做，反而跑去找令堂告状（上次你得知我在写给罗比[1]的信中数落你之后便是如此），让她哄你捧你，使你回复到沾沾自喜或自负的原有状态，那你就定然被毁。如果你现在找到一个借口，便很快会找到一百个借口，让自己安于当那个原来的你。你是不是到现在还认为（就像你在回信给罗比时说过的），我是把

---

1 “罗比”是罗伯特·罗斯的昵称。——译者注，后同

"一些莫须有的动机"加之于你？唉，我又怎会把什么动机加之于你！你的人生毫无动机可言，有的只是吃喝玩乐之思。要知道，"动机"是一种知性目标。还是说你会辩称，在你我交往之初，你还"少不更事"？但你的问题不在对人事懂得太少，而在懂得太多。少男年华犹如初露的晨曦和初绽的娇嫩花朵，但你很快被它那些纯洁清澈的光辉、它那些无邪的欢乐和希冀弃如敝屣。你用飞快的脚步从浪漫主义奔向了现实主义。阴沟和生长其中的东西让你着了迷。这就是当初你何以会惹上麻烦，找我帮忙，而我出于怜悯和善意，很不明智地（世人定义下的"不明智"）给予你帮助。你务须把这信好好读一遍，哪怕它的一字一句都可能像外科医生所用的火或刀那般，让细嫩的肌肤灼痛或流血。要记住，诸神眼中的蠢材和凡人眼中的蠢材大不相同。一个人即便对艺术流变或思想演进的种种一无所知，即便不懂得欣赏拉丁诗歌的华彩或元音化希腊语更丰富的音乐性，不懂得欣赏托斯卡纳式的雕刻或伊丽莎白时代的歌谣，照样可以充满最甜美的智慧。真正的蠢材是缺乏自知之明的人（诸神专嘲笑或加害这种人）。我有很长一段时间曾是这种人。你当这种人迄今已很长时间，别再当了。不要害怕改变。最要不得的缺点莫过于浮浅。凡经过悟明的都会归正[1]。也别忘了，这信中任何读了会让你惨戚的内容，我下笔时的心情要更加惨戚。那"看不见的力量"[2]一向厚待你。它容许你只是像看见水晶里的阴影那样，看见人生怪异和悲惨的形状。美杜莎[3]的脸会让人变成石头，但你被容许透过一面镜子看她。你一直都可以在鲜花丛中自由自在地行走，不像我那样，失去了整个充满声光色彩的美丽世界。

我首先要告诉你的，是我自责得厉害。以身败名裂者的身份穿着囚衣独坐在幽暗囚室时，我怪自己；在辗转反侧和睡睡醒醒的煎熬夜里，我怪自己；在漫长单调的痛苦白昼，我怪自己。我怪自己任由一段毫无知性成分的友谊主宰我的人生，任由一段不是以创造和沉思美丽事物为首要目标的友谊完全主宰我的人生。从一开始，你我之间便存在着巨大落差。你念中学时懒散度日，念大学时更甚。你不明白，一个艺术家，特别是像我这样的艺术家（一个作品质量仰赖强烈个性的艺术家），其艺术的发展需要以观念交流、知性氛围、安静、平和和孤独来灌溉。你对

1　这里的"悟明"指反省过去，悟明其中包含的意义。王尔德认为，这种"悟"可以让"不正"（wrong）归于"正"（right），其详请见下文。

2　"看不见的力量"似乎指命运之神。

3　美杜莎：希腊神话中的蛇发女妖，凡直视她的人都会变成石头。这里王尔德是把自己和波西的人生比作美杜莎，取笑波西对人生的悲苦无知无觉，冷眼旁观。

我写出的作品赞叹不已，你享受我每出戏剧首演之夜的辉煌成功和随之而来的盛大庆功宴，你也以（这是很自然的）身为我这样的杰出艺术家的密友自豪。但你不明白艺术创作需要哪些必要条件。我以下说的这个不是什么夸大修辞，纯粹是忠于事实的陈述：有你在我身边的全部时间里，我不曾创作出一行字。不管是在托基（Torquay）、戈灵（Goring）、伦敦、佛罗伦萨还是其他地方，只要有你在身旁，我便会灵感枯竭、创意全无。说来遗憾，在这段时间里，除了几个特定时段，你总是在我左右。

例如（这里只举众多例子的其中之一），在一八九三年九月，为了可以心无旁骛地写作，我特地在詹姆斯旅馆租了一间套房。事缘我答应过帮约翰·赫尔（John Hare）写一出戏，却过了交稿日期还没动工，被他不停地催。头一周你没来找我。你是因为你我对《莎乐美》译文的艺术价值意见不合[1]，负气不找我，光以写一些蠢信骂我为满足——这种事在你不是不常见的。结果，那周我写出《理想丈夫》的第一幕，连所有细节的润饰工作都全部完成，几乎可以直接拿来演出。但第二周，你又出现了，让我的工作近乎完全停摆。我每天上午十一点半便会到旅馆

---

[1] 波西把王尔德用法语写成的诗剧《莎乐美》译为英文，但译文拙劣，王尔德拒绝接受。这件事情在后面有更详细的记述。

去，以便可以不受打扰地构思和下笔（因为我家里虽然宁静，仍不可避免会受到打扰）。但我的如意算盘落空了，因为你总是十二点坐马车到来，抽烟和拉我聊天直至一点半，然后我又不得不把你带到皇家咖啡厅或巴克莱餐厅吃午饭。连喝利口酒在内，这顿午饭总是持续至三点半。饭后，你会到怀特俱乐部休息一小时，再在下午茶时间准时出现，一直待到要换衣服吃晚餐。我们要不是在萨沃伊饭店就是在泰特街[1]吃晚餐。你总要缠我到午夜，非得在威利斯餐厅吃过消夜才会心满意足，觉得一天没虚度。这就是我在那三个月所过的生活，天天如是，唯一的例外是你出国那四天。然后，到了游程结束，我当然又得跑一趟，到加来[2]接你回来。对我这样心性气质的人来说，这种处境既荒诞又可悲。

你现在应该知道你是个欠缺独处能力的人了吧？知道你天性上汲汲于占据别人的关注和时间了吧？你缺乏任何维持知性专注的能力。你无法培养出"牛津气质"真是一件憾事，也就是说，你从来无法优雅地掂量不同观念的分量，对什么问题都是武断地下结论又坚持己见。这一切，加上你的欲望和兴趣只在享受人生而不在艺术，不只对你

1　泰特街指王尔德家里，王尔德与家人住在泰特街。
2　加来：法国北部城市，往返英国的主要港口。

本人文化修养的长进具有摧毁性，也对我的艺术创造力具有摧毁性。每当我拿你我的友谊和我与一些更年轻朋友的交往相对比，便会感到汗颜。只有和约翰·格雷[1]或皮埃尔·路易[2]之类的朋友在一起，我才能说是真正在过生活（一种层次高得多的生活）。

你我的友谊带来了哪些可怕结果，这里暂且不说。目前我只想谈谈这友谊在其维持期间表现的质量。它给我带来了知性上的降格。你无疑也隐含着一点未萌芽的艺术气质，只可惜我认识你的时机不对（是太早还是太晚我也说不准）。每逢你不在左右，我的创作便会顺顺利利。例如，在上述提到那一年的十二月初，我成功说服令堂把你送出国，那之后，我重整我那支离破碎的想象力，人生也重归自己掌握，所以不但完成了《理想丈夫》剩下的三幕，还构思好甚至几乎写出了另两出类型完全不同的戏剧，一是《佛罗伦萨悲剧》（*Florentine Tragedy*），一是《圣妓》（*La*

---

1 约翰·格雷：著有诗集《银点》（*Sliverpoints*），与他人合著有《勒索者》（*The Blackmailers*），制作过一出在威尔士亲王剧院上演的戏剧。他也是《比亚兹莱的最后书信》（*Last Letters of Aubrey Beardsley*）的编者。盛传他和王尔德有暧昧。虽然有人主张《道林·格雷的画像》的主角以他为蓝本，但缺乏证据。他在一九三一年为王尔德写了一首挽歌，题为《主耶稣望向彼得》（*The Lord Looks at Peter*）。

2 皮埃尔·路易：法国诗人、作家，一八九一年创立文学评论刊物《贝壳》（*La Conque*）。王尔德把剧作《莎乐美》题献给他。

Sainte Courtisane)。可你突然回来了，在足以让我的幸福致命的情况下不请自来地再次出现。自此，上述两部作品便始终停留在未完成的状态，因为我再也无法重拾当初创作它们时的那种心绪。如今，你既已出版过一部你写的诗集，理应可以体会我所言不假。但不管你能否体会，这仍然是位居你我友谊中心的一个丑陋真理：只要你在旁边，我的艺术就会彻底被毁。一想到我曾任由你隔在我和艺术之间，我便无比汗颜和自责。你无法明白，你无法体谅，你无法欣赏，但我本无权指望你能够做到这些。你唯一感兴趣的是吃喝和闹脾气。你的欲望只是寻欢作乐——一些平庸或等而下之的欢乐。这些都是出于你性情气质的需要，至少你在想到它们的那一刻会觉得需要。我本该禁止你在未经邀请的情况下踏入我的房子或旅馆套房。我为自己的软弱毫无保留地责怪自己。一切只是软弱作祟。与艺术共处半小时比与你厮混一整天要让我有更多收获。在我人生的任何阶段，任何东西与艺术相比都微不足道。但就一个艺术家来说，软弱不亚于罪，因为软弱会瘫痪他的艺术想象力。

我还怪自己任由你把我带到经济上彻底崩坏的境地。我还记得，一八九二年十月初的那天早上，我与令堂在布拉克内尔（Bracknell）树叶渐黄的森林里对坐聊天。当时我对你本性的了解还甚少，因为你我有过的较长共处时间仅有两次：一次是我在你牛津的住处从周六待到周一，另一次是你在克罗默（Cromer）陪了我十天，其间我们一起打高尔夫球。我和令堂聊着聊着，话题自然而然地转到你身上。她指出，你的个性有两大缺点：一是虚荣心太强，另一是（用她的原话说）"对金钱的观念错得一塌糊涂"。我清楚记得我的反应是放声大笑。我万万没有想到，你的第一个缺点将会导致我身陷囹圄，第二个缺点将会导致我破产。那时的我认为，虚荣心是合乎年轻人佩戴的优雅花朵，至于"爱铺张"（我以为她指的不过是你"爱铺张"），我也完全没放在心上，因为我自己和家人从没有把精打细算和节俭视为美德。不过，与你交往了一个月之后，我便开始明白令堂的真正所指。你坚持要过一种挥霍无度的生活：你不断向我伸手要钱；你宣称你的寻欢作乐都要由我买单，不管我是否参与。过了一段时间之后，我在财政调度上便陷入了严重困难。最要命的是，你的挥霍千篇一律且无趣透顶，无非是把钱花在满足口腹之欲或类似的事情上。不时就着一张被葡萄酒和玫瑰花映红的桌子用餐的确是乐事，但你的不知节制破坏了一切品位与雅趣。你以毫不优雅的方式向我索取，得到之后又从不道谢。你养成了一种心态，以为自己有权靠我的供养生活。你的胃口越来越大，最后乃至于在阿尔及尔哪家赌场赌输了钱，第二天便直接发电报到伦敦，要我把你输掉的数目存入你的银行账户，然后当成什么都没发生过。

从一八九二年秋天到我锒铛入狱那一天为止，我与你一起花和花在你身上的钱超过五千英镑。而这还只是付出的现金，记账的部分未算在内。知道这些，你就会对你坚持过的是什么样的生活有一点概念。你认为我夸张吗？那让我算给你听听。在伦敦，我普通一天的普通花费（包括午餐费、晚餐费、消夜费、娱乐费、马车费等等）是十二英镑至二十英镑，换算下来是一周从八十英镑至一百三十英镑不等。待在戈灵那三个月，我的开销（当然含租金在内）一共是一千三百四十英镑。就这样，我人生拥有的每项财物一步一步迈向了破产管理人手中。真是可怕。在那时候，"简朴的生活和高逸的思想"[1]当然并不是你能欣赏的理念，但你的铺张浪费对你对我都是一桩丑事。我记得我平生最愉快的其中一顿晚餐是与罗比共进的，地点不过是苏活区（Soho）一家小小的餐馆，而且价钱是以先令为单位，不像与你共餐时动辄以英镑为单位。我第一本对话录（也是最精彩的一本）就是从那顿晚饭里得到的灵感。它的观念、标题、处理手法和表现方式全都是来自一

1　出自华兹华斯（Wordsworth）的《一八〇二年写于伦敦的十四行诗》（*Sonnet written in London*，September 1802）。

顿三法郎半的客饭[1]。但我不曾从与你共进的那些荒唐晚餐里得到过什么，有的只是太过饱腻和酩酊大醉的回忆。我老是迁就你的需求对你其实只有坏处。你现在明白了吧？因为我的迁就只让你更常索要——虽然不是每次都是出之以厚颜无耻的方式，但至少每次都是出之以毫不优雅的方式。有太多太多次，我在做东之时都毫无欢快或荣幸之感可言。你忘了你该做些什么。我不会说你忘了说些客套的道谢话，因为太客气会让亲密友谊变得拘谨。你忘了的是好朋友相处时应有的雅趣，是愉快交谈（古希腊人称之为 τερπυόυ κακόυ）的魅力，是所有能使生活变得可爱的贴心举动——它们就像音乐那样，可以让万物和谐，让荒芜或死静之处被旋律充满。虽然你也许会觉得奇怪，我明明已经潦倒不堪，怎么还会计较一种羞愧和另一种羞愧的不同，但我还是得老实承认，那么愚蠢地在你身上撒钱，任你糟蹋我的钱财，这让我加倍羞愧。因为此举不但害了我自己，还害了你；也因为我竟由于庸俗的花天酒地而破产实在让人不堪。老天生我是另有他用的。

但我自责最甚的是任由你把我带到精神高度荡然无存的境地。人格的基础是意志力，我却让自己的意志力完全

1　客饭：这里只是比喻他与罗比的餐资相当于一顿最平价的法国饭食。

臣服于你。这听起来有点不可思议，但真得不能再真。其中有几种原因，包括就像出于某种身体需要似的，你无休止地闹脾气，这让你的心灵与身体发生扭曲，使你变成一个别人不敢看不敢听的怪物；你遗传了令尊那种可怕的狂躁，这狂躁又驱使你不停写出一些让人反胃恶心的书信；你完全无法控制自己的情绪，不是突然像癫痫发作那样大吵大嚷，就是板起一张臭脸，久久闷不吭声。我在许多信中都提过你的这些毛病（你从不把我的信当一回事，到处乱放，不是掉在萨沃伊饭店便是其他什么饭店，被人捡去。其中一封还落到令尊的律师手中，被当作呈堂证供）。在那些信中，我都不无悲情地恳求你（如果你当时了解什么叫悲情自会看出），我会要命地屈服于你与日俱增的苛索，正是上述你的种种毛病所导致。那是小性子对大性子的胜利，那是以弱凌强的范例，而正如我在一出戏剧里说过的那样，弱者的专制统治是"唯一可持久的专制统治"[1]。

　　我的屈服是无可避免的。在人生的每种关系里，我们都必须找出相处之道（moyen de vivre）。与你的相处之道是：要么全听你的，要么放弃你，再没有第三个选项。出于对你的爱（哪怕是错爱），出于对你性情缺憾的极大怜

1　出自《无足轻重的女人》第三幕。

悯，出于我有口皆碑的好性情和凯尔特人怕麻烦的个性，出于艺术家对吵嚷场面和恶言相向的反感，出于我当时受不了别人恨我，出于我不愿生活的美被鸡毛蒜皮的事破坏——出于上述种种原因，我事事向你让步。一个很自然的结果就是，你的要求、你控制我的努力和你的苛索变本加厉，越发不可理喻。你那些最委琐的动机、你那些最低下的口腹之欲、你那些最平凡的激情对你来说变成了别人必须遵守的法则，而为了成全这些法则，有必要时甚至可以无所顾忌地让别人牺牲。因为知道大吵大闹总可以让你如愿以偿，你自然会（我相信几乎是不自觉的）无所不用其极，什么最难听、最下流的话都说得出口。但说到底，你并不知道自己汲汲营营的是些什么，不知道自己目标何在。出于盲目和无止境的贪婪，你吸尽我的才华、意志力和财富，占去我的整个存在。你把它拿走了。另一方面，在我人生最为关键和悲剧性的时刻，就在我要为我的荒谬行动踏出可哀可叹第一步[1]的前一刻，我又受到两面夹击：一方面是令尊在我的俱乐部里留了一张名片攻讦我，另一方面是你用一些恶心程度不遑多让的信挞伐我。在我任你把我拉到初级法庭申请那纸荒唐拘捕令那天早上，你又出

---

[1] 指对波西父亲提告的事情。他不只没有打赢官司，反给自己惹上官司，从原告变为被告，终致坐牢。

于最可耻的理由给我写了一封最恶毒的信。夹在你们父子中间让我晕头转向。我的判断能力舍我而去，取而代之的是恐惧。容我坦白说，在你们的夹击下，我看不到有路可逃。我像脚步蹒跚的牛那样，盲目地走进屠宰场。会走到这一步，是因为我犯了一个心理学的大错。我一直以为，在小事情上事事迁就你无伤大雅，因为一旦遇到大事情，我的意志力自然会重新振作，发挥出原有的威力。事实却不是如此。在前面所说的那个重大时刻，我的意志力完全不见踪影。人生其实无所谓大事小事之分，每件事都是同等的价值和同等的规模。我养成了事事迁就你的习惯（起初只是因为懒得计较），而这习惯在不知不觉中成了我本性的一部分。在我不自知的情况下，它已经把我的性情定型为一种永久和致命的心态。这就是何以佩特[1]会在其散文集的跋里说："失败源于形成习惯。"牛津那些笨蛋还以为他说这话是故意跟亚里士多德的《伦理学》唱反调，不晓得其中潜藏着一个莫大和可怕的真理。我无知地任你榨干我的人格力量，而"形成习惯"所带给我的还不只是失败，更是毁灭。你在精神层面对我的杀伤力甚于艺术层面。

拘捕令下来之后，一切当然便完全落入你意志的主

1　佩特：十九世纪英国散文家、文学和艺术批评家、唯美主义理论家，是王尔德最常引用的作者之一。

导。当时，我本应留在伦敦听取律师的意见，冷静思考一下我是如何掉入自己布下的蠢陷阱（令尊至今还这样称呼它）的，但你硬要我带你到蒙特卡洛去玩。在那个天底下最让人反感的地方，你没日没夜地赌，赌场开到多晚便赌到多晚。因为我对百家乐缺乏兴趣，只有在一旁枯坐的份。你甚至不愿意抽五分钟空和我谈谈你和令尊所带给我的困境。我唯一的作用是为你支付饭店开销和为你补给赌资。只要我稍稍提到我即将面临的磨难，你便满脸不耐烦的表情。侍者推荐的一种新品牌香槟更让你感兴趣。

回到伦敦之后，那些真正为我着想的朋友都劝我走避国外，不要去面对一桩不可能打赢的官司。你却说他们是居心不良，又说我若是听从他们便会变成懦夫。你逼我留下来，逼我在证人席上用荒谬和愚蠢的伪证顶住一切诘问。到头来，我当然成了阶下囚，而令尊则成了当时得胜的英雄——还不只是英雄，更是不朽者。就像历史曾经出于什么滑稽原因而让克利俄（Clio）成为众缪斯女神中最不正经的一位，令尊也将以好父亲的形象永存于主日学校的读物里，而你亦会被媲美为婴儿撒母耳[1]。至于我，则会

---

[1] 撒母耳：《圣经》中的知名先知，据记载，他刚断奶便被母亲献给上帝，要让他终身侍奉上帝。王尔德这里是说世人会把波西看得像婴儿撒母耳一样圣洁无邪。

是被打入十八层地狱，与吉尔斯·德·莱斯和萨德侯爵[1]一类的人渣排排坐。

我当然早该摆脱你。我早该像人们抖掉衣服上的虱子那样，把你从我的生活中抖掉。埃斯库罗斯[2]最精彩的一出戏里有这么一段：一个大领主把一头小狮带回家养。小东西每逢大领主喊它都会眼睛一亮，又会摇头摆尾讨食物吃，让主人疼爱有加，不料这小狮长大后兽性复萌，把大领主本人、他的房子和财产全给毁了。我觉得我也是养狮为患。但我的错不在没有离开你，而在离开过你太多次。若是没记错，我固定地每三个月会结束你我的友谊一次，而每次你总是用哀求、电报、书信求我原谅，不然就是找你或我的朋友代为说项。就我所记得的，最早一次发生在一八九三年三月底，当时我们待在戈灵。那一天，当你负气走出我租赁的房子之后，我决计不再跟你说话，也决计无论如何不让你跟我在一起，因为前一晚你大吵大闹一通，让我反感之极。但你从布里斯托尔（Bristol）写信

---

1 吉尔斯·德·莱斯：法国元帅，圣女贞德的战友，以生活放荡和信奉撒旦教而恶名昭著，最后因谋杀小孩罪被处决。萨德侯爵：法国作家，著有《瑞斯丁娜》（*Justine*）和《闺房哲学》（*Philosophy in the Bedroom*）等。Sadism（虐待狂）一词就是源自他的名字，因为他的作品充斥性暴力描写。他曾因多项罪名被判死刑，但从未执行，最后死于精神病院。

2 埃斯库罗斯：古希腊剧作家。王尔德所提的情节出现在《阿伽门农》（*Agamemnon*）。

和发电报来求我原谅。然后你的导师[1]（他还没离开我家）又出面求情，说你有些时候真的控制不了自己，不是故意的；又说莫德林学院大部分人也持相同看法。于是我答应再见你一面，而我当然也原谅了你。回城的路上，你央求我把你带到萨沃伊饭店去玩。这对我而言确实是个致命让步。

三个月后（即六月，当时我们还待在戈灵），有个周末，你一些牛津的朋友来访，从周六待到周一。他们临走那个早上，你又当众对我发了一顿可怕至极的脾气，逼得我必须再次提出分手。那时的情景还历历在目：我们站在平坦的槌球场里，四周是漂亮的草坪，而我向你指出，我们在一起对双方都没有好处，因为再这样下去，你绝对会毁了我，而我也显然并未能把快乐带给你。只有彻底分手才是合乎哲学的明智之道。你吃过午饭后臭着脸离开，事前交给管家一封恶毒的信件，要他等你走后再交给我。但不到三天，你又发来电报求我原谅，求我让你回来。我租那屋子原是为了取悦你，我雇你的仆人为仆原是应你之请，我也总是为你的可怕脾气感到深深遗憾，认为你只是不由自主并深受其害。更何况我还对你充满情意。所以我

1　指波西的大学导师坎贝尔·道奇森（Campbell Dodgson）。

答应让你回来，并原谅了你。再三个月后的九月，你又开始新一轮的大吵大闹。这一次的起因是我指出你在把《莎乐美》翻译为英文的时候，犯了一些小学生才会犯的错误。如今你的法文想必已大有长进，应该看得出来那译文既配不上原作，也配不上牛津人的身份。但当时你还没有这种见识，而在一封措辞激烈的信中，你表示你对我"毫无知性方面的亏欠"。我记得，读到这话时，我感到那是你我交往期间你说过的唯一一句至理名言。我由此明白，当个没有文化修养的人会更适合你。我这么说并不是要怪你，而只是想指出一个有关人与人相处的事实。一切人际纽带（不管是婚姻还是友谊）说到底都是一场交谈，而交谈必须有共同基础，在文化修养程度极不对等的两个人之间，唯一可能的基础就是最低层次的一种。鸡毛蒜皮的思想和行为一样可以很可爱。我曾用它们作为一种非常杰出的哲学的基石，以戏剧和吊诡语言的形式表达出来。但你我生活中的蠢话蠢事让我厌倦异常：你唯一的话题是烂泥巴[1]。你开口闭口净谈这些，它们无疑极度引人入胜，但听多了还是让我感觉无比单调，倒尽胃口。它们常常让我无聊得要命，但我仍然接受，就像接受你对杂耍剧场的

---

1 "烂泥巴"指同性恋话题。

狂热，接受你在吃喝上躁郁症似的铺张无度。换言之，我只是在强忍，以此作为多理解你一点的代价。离开戈灵之后，我去了迪纳尔[1]半个月。你因为我不带你去而大发雷霆，在我们还住在阿尔伯马尔饭店（Albemarle Hotel）时便闹了几次，接着又连续发电报到我暂住几天的乡村别墅骂我。我先前解释过何以不让你随行：你有责任多陪陪家人，因为你一整个夏天都在别处过。我话是这样说，但实际的理由是，任何情况下我都不可能容许你与我同行。你我黏在一起已快十二周。我需要休息，需要从与你共处的可怕压力中解放出来。我必须有一点点时间独处，那是知性的一种必需。所以我得承认，从你的信中（上面引用过的那封），我看出一个可以结束我们致命友谊的大好机会，于是就像三个月前在戈灵一个晴朗六月天的早上那样，向你提出分手。然而，这时又有人出面为你说话（不瞒你说，这人是我的朋友，他曾在你有困难时帮助过你）。他说，如果我像退回小学生作业那样把你的译文退回给你，对你的伤害未免太大，又说我在知性上对你要求太过严苛，而且，不管你对我说过什么或做过什么，你对我都是一片挚诚。这番劝说让我怦然心动。首先，我想到你在文

1　迪纳尔：位于法国。

学上刚起步，我不应该成为第一个泼你冷水或让你泄气的人，何况我也清楚地知道，除非由一个诗人来翻译《莎乐美》，否则绝不可能在任何程度上传达出它的节奏和色彩。另外，"一片挚诚"在我看来（当时如此，至今还是如此）是一种美好事物，不应轻言舍弃。所以我就答应接受那译文，也接受你回来。然后，刚好又是三个月之后，你又当众闹了几场。最让人厌恶的一次发生在周一傍晚，当时你把两个朋友带到我住的套房去。第二天，为了躲你，我随便给家人编了个必须马上出远门的可笑理由，又留给仆人一个假地址，以防你会搭下一班火车追踪而至。记得那天下午，坐在火车车厢里向巴黎疾驰时，我只觉得自己的处境荒谬至极：我堂堂一个世界知名人物，竟为了切断一段对知性和精神两方面都有害的友谊，逃出英国；那个逼得我夹着尾巴逃走的不是什么从下水道或泥潭跃入现代生活的可怕怪物，而是阁下——一个与我同一社会阶层的人，曾经像我一样上过牛津大学，还是我家一个固定的座上宾。就像往常一样，你那些恳求原谅和表示知错的电报随后便到，但我没有理会。最后你威胁说，除非我答应见你一面，否则无论如何都不答应到埃及去。是我央求令堂把你送到埃及的（我事前询问过你，提出的时候你也在场），因为继续待在伦敦只会毁掉你自己的人生。我知道，如果你不去埃及，令堂将会失望透顶。为她着想的缘故，我答应了见你，而在强烈情感的驱使下，我也原谅了你过去的一切——但没有对未来做出承诺。

回到伦敦的第二天，我坐在房间里，悲伤而认真地思考这个问题：你到底是不是真如我所想的那样，浑身充满可怕的缺点，对自己和别人来说都是彻底的祸害，不远离你的话将带来致命后果。我思考了整整一周，不断琢磨我对你的判断会不会不公平、有冤枉你之处。最后，我收到令堂的来信。这信彻底印证了我对你的每一个印象。她谈到你那盲目夸张的虚荣心，说这虚荣心让你鄙夷自己家人，让你把你那位老实人哥哥视为"庸俗之辈"。她提到你的脾气是那么的大，让她不敢过问你的交友状况；她谈到你对金钱的态度最让她心忧。她当然也看出可怕的家族遗传让你背上多大的重担。她坦然承认这一点，语气充满忧惧："他是我几个孩子中继承了道格拉斯家族致命性情气质的那一个。"信的最后，她说她觉得有责任坦言，依她之见，你与我的友谊大大助长了你的虚荣心（虚荣心是你所有缺点的根源），又恳切求我不要在国外与你会面。我马上回信，说我完全同意她的每一句话。我还补充了更多，把能说的都说了。我告诉她，你我是在你就读于牛津的时候认识的，那时你惹上性质非常特殊的大麻烦，前来求助于我。我告诉她，你后来的生活如是，继续受同一性质的麻烦所困扰。因为你把错推到去比利时的同伴头上，而令堂在信中责怪我把你介绍给那个找你一道去比利时的同伴（你说是他出的主意），我便告诉她真正出主意的是谁：阁下。我在信末保证，我没有一丝要与你在国外会面的念头，又求她设法把你留在国外——可能的话帮你弄个荣誉参赞当当，不行的话也让你借这机会学习几种外语。总之是用她想得到的任何理由把你留在埃及至少两三年。此举既是为了你好，也是为了我好。

　　这期间你从埃及不断写信给我，每个邮班都少不了你的信。我全然不当一回事，每封信都是读过便撕掉。我铁了心不再与你有任何瓜葛。吾意已决，也很高兴可以重拾被你打断的艺术创作进程。没想到，三个月后，令堂却出于她一贯的软弱（这软弱对我人生悲剧的贡献并不亚于令尊的蛮横个性），写信来帮你说话。她告诉我（我毫不怀疑是你授意的），你因为我不回信而食不下咽、睡不安稳，而为了让我不至于找借口不写信，还把你在雅典的地址告诉我（雅典当然是一个我熟悉得不能再熟悉的城市）。她的信无疑让我讶异万分。我无法明白，鉴于她在十二月写给过我的那封信和我的回信，她此时又怎么会设法修复或更新你我那份不幸的友谊。我当然回信，信中再次呼吁她设法帮你在某间驻外大使馆谋一职位，以防止你回国。但我并没写信给你，也没理会你发来的电报。没想到，最后你居然写信给我太太，求她运用影响力促使我给你写信。你我的友谊一直是她的烦恼之源：不只是因为她不喜欢你的为人，还因为看出我已被你我的友谊所改变，而且不是往好的方向改变。但就像她一向以最雅量好客的方式对待你，她这一次也无法忍受我对我的任何朋友无礼。她认为（应该说知道）这不是我一贯的为人。出于她的请求，我发了电报给你。我还清楚记得这电报的措辞。我说，时间可以治愈每个伤口，但接下来许多个月，我将不会写信给你，也不会见你。没想到，你一收到电报便毫不迟疑地启程，动身去巴黎，路上又不断发来热情洋溢的电报，求我无论如何至少再见你一面。你在一个周日的深夜抵达巴黎，但我在你预订入住的饭店留了一封短柬，表示我将不会见你。第二天早上，我在泰特街收到一封十至十二页的电报。你在电报中表示，不管你对我做过什么，你都不能相信我会永不再见你。你提醒我，为了见我一面，你六日六夜兼程横跨欧洲，中途完全没有停歇。我必须承认，你的电文表现出最苦情的哀求，结尾处又隐隐以自杀相威胁，让人读了于心不忍。你以前常常谈到家族中有多少人是双手沾满自己的鲜血：你叔叔确实是自杀而死，你祖父可能是死于自杀，还有许多人后来发了疯[1]。基于同情，基于难忘的旧情，基于想到你的死会对令堂构成几乎不可承受的打击，基于想到你如此年轻的生命就此断送实在可怕（必须承认，这生命虽然包含各种丑陋瑕疵，但仍然包含着未萌芽的美），我答应再见你最后一次（若还有必要找什么借口的话，光是基于人性考虑我便有义务这么做）。我去了巴黎，而一整个晚上，不管是在瓦赞（Voisin）餐厅吃晚饭还是在帕亚尔（Paillard）餐厅吃消夜，你都泪如雨下，没有停过。你看到我时流露的真心和欢快，你一有机会就抓住我手的举动，都像一个柔顺和悔过的小孩。你的悔悟之意在当时是那么单纯而真诚，让我同意恢复你我的友谊。回到伦敦的两天后，我们在皇家咖啡厅吃午餐，被令尊撞见，他走过来坐下，喝了我的葡萄酒，然后，当天下午，他写了一封信给你，信中对我展开了第一轮攻讦。

说来也许奇怪，但与你分手的责任（这一次我不会说是"机会"）后来再一次落在我身上。不用我提醒了吧，这次的起因是一八九四年十月十日到十三日那几天，你在布赖顿对我的刻薄态度。那是三年前的旧事了。对你来说，三年前发生的事当然是远之又远，但对我们这种在牢里度日的人

---

[1] 道格拉斯的父系一脉有不少人是凶死。他祖父死于枪支走火，他叔叔死于割喉自杀。

来说（这种人的生活除了悲苦没有别的事），时间是以痛苦的搏动来计算的，是以咀嚼苦涩的往事来记录的。我们没有其他事好想。你听起来可能奇怪，但痛苦是我们赖以存在的方法，是唯一可以让我们意识到自己还存在的方法。回忆旧痛可以提供证据，证明我们和旧时的那个我具有连续性。一如现在的我和现实中的快乐隔着一道深渊，我和记忆中的快乐也隔着深渊。如果你我共同生活的那段日子果真如外界所想象的那样快乐无忧和充满笑声，那我将会无法记得其中任何一个段落。相对应地，正因为它充满苦味、不祥之兆、可怕枯燥的争吵和不得体的暴力，我如今才可以看见或听见每起事件的每个细节。确实，除了这些，我如今很少能看见或听见别的。监狱生活是那么的痛苦，以至于每次我被迫去回忆你我往日的交往情况时，总觉得那是一首序曲，是我每天都得承受的各种煎熬的前奏。事实上，站在现在回顾往事，我的人生根本就是一首悲伤交响曲，一乐章一乐章地推向某个结局，其中每个环节都有其必然性，一如艺术上处理每个重大题材的一贯手法。

　　我谈到三年前你有三天对我很刻薄，对不对？那时我一个人待在沃辛，想把一个剧本完成。中间你来了两次。后来你又突然出现，还带着一个同伴，要求我让他住一晚。我断然拒绝了（你现在应该看得出来，这要求有多么不恰当）。我当然还是招待了你们，因为我别无选择——但我是在别处招待你们，不是在家里。第二天周一，你朋友回去工作，而你留了下来，住在我那里。但你已经在沃辛待腻了，坚持要我带你到布赖顿的格兰德饭店散心（我毫不怀疑，你这样要求还是因为不满我把全部心思放在写作上）。到达布赖顿那个晚上，你病倒了，微微发烧，得的是那种被人愚蠢地称为流感的病。如果这不是我认识你之后你第三次身患此症，便是第二次。我对你无微不至，不只提供给你各种金钱买得到的慰藉（昂贵的水果、鲜花、礼物和书本），还提供给你金钱买不到的殷勤照顾、柔情蜜意和爱。其间，除了早上散步一小时和下午坐马车一小时去买东西，我不曾离开过饭店。因为你不爱吃饭店提供的水果，我便跑到伦敦买来上好的葡萄。我还编些故事说给你听，使你解颐，要睡也是睡你旁边或隔壁房间。每个晚上我都坐在旁边陪你哄你，让你安心。

你在四五天之后康复，而为了把剧本写完，我搬出饭店赁屋而居。你当然跟了过来。安顿下来的第二天早上，我感到身体极其不适。你当时有事非得到伦敦一趟，但答应下午便会回来。你在伦敦见了一个朋友，可直到第二天很晚才回到布赖顿。当时我已发着高烧，而据医生诊断，我是从你那里感染了流感。我发现，对生病的人来说，没有比住在出租屋更不方便的了。起居室在二楼，我的卧室却在四楼。我没有仆人伺候，甚至没有人可以帮我送信或购买医生吩咐的东西。但因为有你在，我并不惊慌。然而，接下来两天，你却把我一个人晾在一边，让我既缺人照料，也要不到任何想要之物。我不是指要不到葡萄、鲜花或精致的礼物，只是指要不到必需品。我连医生吩咐我喝的牛奶都喝不到，想喝柠檬水更是不可能的事。我求你到书店帮我买本书，说是如果找不到我指定的那一本，就随便挑一本。你却懒得跑一趟，害我一整天无书可看。好不容易等到你回来之后，你若无其事地告诉我，错不在你，因为你已买了书，也吩咐书店送过来，却不知怎么搞的没有送来（事后我无意中得知，你这番话完全是鬼话）。毋庸说，你这期间的开销（包括马车费和在格兰德饭店的晚餐费）完全由我供应，而且你也只有在要钱时才会出现在我的床头。周六那天晚上，鉴于你从早上起便放着我不管，我要求你吃过晚餐之后回来，陪我一下。你带着恼怒的口气和不优雅的手势答应了。我等你等到十一点，始终不见人影。于是，我在你房间里留下一张便条，提醒你你答应过我却又食言。到半夜三点，我因为睡不着又渴得要命，便强撑起身体，下楼去起居室，希望可以找到水喝。没想到我却看见了你。你马上兜头盖脸对我破口大骂，措辞之粗俗只有毫无节制和毫无教养的人才说得出口。通过"自我中心"这种可怕的炼金术，你把你的理亏转化成了暴怒。你指控我，说我指望你在我生病时陪我是一种自私心态，指控我不应在你和你的娱乐之间作梗，指控我设法剥夺你的快乐。你说（我知道这话不假）你会在午夜回来，只是为了换套衣服，好再到别处去寻欢作乐，却不意看见我留的信，这让你大为扫兴，害你重新作乐的能力大减。我回到楼上，整晚都睡不着，直到破晓之后许久才弄到东西止息我那因发烧而引起的口渴。你在十一点走进我房间。你前一晚的吵闹让我意识到，我的信到底对你的放纵起了一些抑制作用。到了早上，你看似已经恢复常态。我自然会等着听你以什么借口解释你的行为，用什么方式请求我原谅——因为你绝对相信，不管你干了些什么，总是会得到我的原谅（说真的，这是我最喜欢你的地方，或许也是你身上最美好的部分）。不过，我猜错了。你非但没有道歉，求我原谅，反而把昨晚的不满又宣泄了一遍，唯一不同的是这次更激烈和更凶猛。我最后只好叫你出去。你假装照办，当我把埋在枕头里的头抬起，却看见你站在原地，随后你又突然含着狞笑和歇斯底里的怒气朝我走过来。我心里一惊（是什么原因我也说不清），马上从床上跃起，赤脚走了两层楼梯，逃到起居室，一直待到房东（是我摇铃找他过来的）保证你已经离开我卧室为止。他又保证会留在附近，以防万一。一小时之后（其间医生来过，发现我处于一种神经高度紧张的虚脱状态，烧得也更厉害了），你默默走进卧室。你是为钱而来。在梳妆台和壁炉架搜刮过一遍之后，你便带着行李离开了。需要我来告诉你，在接下来卧病孤苦的两天，我是怎样看你的吗？需要我来提醒你，即便只是泛泛之交，你对病中人表现出的这样的行为也是可耻的吗？我由此意识到，最终时刻已经来临，并由此感到大大地松一口气。我知道，从今以后，我的艺术和人生将会在各个可能的方面都变得更自由、更美好和更美丽。我人在卧病，心里却很轻松。一想到这分手将是不可挽回的，我便感到心灵平静。我在周二退了烧，几天来第一次可以下楼用餐。周三是我的生日，桌上放着一堆贺电和信件，其中一封是你的亲笔信。要展信披读的那一刻，我满怀惆怅，因为我知道，这一次我不会再因为你的一句柔情之言或忧伤之语而原谅你。但我完全被骗了，我低估你了。你会在我生日写信来，只是为了把前两次的谩骂写成白纸黑字，用更精心和更慎重的方式把它们重现一遍！你用你那些不入流的俏皮话挖苦我。你说，整件事情让你最得意的是你回伦敦前先去了格兰德饭店，把吃午餐的账记到我头上。你恭喜我还算聪明，懂得赶忙从病床上爬起来，飞奔下楼逃命。你还强调："那是你的凶险时刻——比你猜想的还要凶险。"唉，不用你说我也能感觉得到！我不知道的只是你当时是想把为吓唬令尊而买的那把枪掏出来（你曾经在一家餐厅里发射过它一次：当时你以为枪膛里没有子弹），还是想抓起那把放在桌子上你我中间的餐刀，还是想要（因为盛怒使你忘了自己身材比我瘦小）对我来一番拳打脚踢。我至今还不知道答案。我唯一知道的是我当时被一股彻底的惊恐攫住，晓得若是不赶快逃出卧室，你就会做出或是尝试做出某种会让你愧疚一辈子的行为。那之前，我只从另一个人那里体验过一次这种大惊恐。当时我人在泰特街的书房里，面前站着令尊，处于我们中间的是霸凌（换言之是他的好朋友）。令尊挥舞着癫痫发作似的小手，满嘴只有他的污秽脑袋才想得出的污言秽语，一再叫嚣着威胁我（他后来说到做到）。那一次，先走出房间的人是他，是我赶他走的。但与你的那一次，先走出房间的人是我。这不是我第一次被逼着救你，免得你做出蠢事。

你的信这样作结："你只要不是站在基座上便会没啥意思。下次你生病我会马上闪人！"[1] 唉，这种话透露出的

1　指生病让王尔德变回凡人，不再像是站在基座上的神像，让人仰之弥高。

是多么粗鄙的嘴脸，多么匮乏的想象力！透露的是多么的麻木不仁，多么平庸的性情气质！待在不同监狱期间，这几句话在我的脑子里响起过不知多少遍。我对自己把它们说了一遍又一遍，端详它们，希望从中看出（但愿不是不公允的）你奇怪沉默的端倪。既然我是因为照顾你而被你传染致病，你写出那样的话当然是既粗鄙又残忍，但即便不是如此，世界上任何一个人写那样的话给另外一个人，都是一种无可原谅之罪（假定世界上有无可原谅的罪）。

坦白说，读罢你的信，我有一种近乎被污染的感觉，就像因为曾与你这种人为伍，我的人生已无可挽回地变脏和变下贱。我的确是已经变脏和变下贱，但要到六个月后，我才完全明白自己有多脏和多下贱。我计划周五回伦敦，又打定主意要去见乔治·刘易斯勋爵[1]，请他代我写一封信给令尊，声明我已决定在任何情况下都不允许你进我的屋子，与我同桌吃饭、交谈或一起散步，总之是不管何时何地都不容许你在我身旁。等这事办好，我会再写信通知你我采取了什么行动，但不会解释理由，因为理由你无疑已了然于胸。我是周四晚上打定这些主意的。然而，到了周五早上，当我坐下来要吃早餐时，事情却有了戏剧性

1　乔治·刘易斯勋爵：王尔德的律师朋友。

的变化。我打开报纸，看见上面刊登了一封电文，说令兄（也就是那位真正的一家之主、爵位的继承人和家中的栋梁）被发现死在一条沟渠中，身边搁着他发射过的手枪。我们现在当然知道那是意外，但当时以为那是更黑暗的原因造成的。令兄为任何认识他的人所喜爱，却这样突然死掉，而且几乎就是死在成婚的前夕，当然会叫人万分悲痛。一想到你会多么哀伤，一想到令堂会因这丧子之痛而有多么锥心刺骨（特别是因为这儿子一直是她的安慰和喜乐之所系：她曾告诉我，令兄从诞生之日起便从未让她操过心和掉过泪），我便对你和你家人产生无限哀怜。当时你另外两位兄长都不在欧洲，所以令堂和令妹唯一能依赖的便只有你：不只要依赖你的陪伴以缓解痛苦，还要依赖你处理各种劳神费心的后事。想到这些，连带想到人世间的种种哀愁，我便心潮起伏、五内翻腾，也顿时忘却对你的愤懑和怨恨。你固然在我病中对我不仁，但我不容许自己在你处于丧兄之痛中对你不义。我当即给你发去一通电报，致上我最深切的同情，随即又写了一封信，邀你方便时到我家来。因为，我觉得在这个节骨眼丢下你（而且是通过律师来传达），对你会是太过可怕的一件事。

从悲剧发生现场一回到城里，你便马上到我这里来。你穿着丧服，眼睛还沾着泪水，样子非常甜美、非常单纯。你像无依无靠的小孩似的向我寻求慰藉和帮助。我为你打开我的门、我的家、我的心。我把你的悲苦当成我自己的，好让你能够承受。我绝口不提你在我病中的刻薄态度、你那些不堪入耳的谩骂和你那封不堪入目的信。你发自心坎的悲伤似乎带着你前所未有地靠近我。你从我家带去鲜花，供在令兄坟上。这些花象征的不只是他的生命有多美，还象征着所有正在冬眠和有朝一日会被带入光中的生命有多美。

诸神生性古怪，他们不只会假借我们的陋习恶癖来加害我们[1]，还会利用我们的温良恭俭来惩罚我们：要不是我曾对你和你家人带着怜悯和感情，如今就不用在这个可怕的鬼地方痛哭流涕了。

当然，在你我所有的相处关系中，我除看见了命运女神之外，还看见了劫数女神：她的步履总是飞快，因为她要前往的是流血之地。你继承了令尊的血统。那是一个可怕的血统，凡与它通婚的人都会倒大霉，凡与它交朋友的人都会厄运连连，会让拥有它的人不是置自己便是置别人于死地。在让你我人生道路交会的每个机缘（不管你是找我享乐还是向我求助），发生过大大小小的事，但即便看

1　语出莎士比亚剧作《李尔王》第五幕第三场，原话为："公正的诸神用我们的风流罪作作为惩罚我们的工具。"

似最微不足道的事，其含义之重大并不下于从屋梁纷纷飘下的尘埃或是树木落叶。因为在每件大小事情之后，劫数女神皆会尾随而至，一如哀叫所引起的回声或猛兽扑食时投下的影子，从你我友谊的一开始便是如此。这友谊源于你写给我的一封信——一封无比凄切又魅力十足的信。你在信中求我帮你脱离一个对任何人来说都极可怕的处境（对一个就读于牛津的年轻人来说更是可怕）。我伸出了援手，借助乔治·刘易斯勋爵之力帮你解了围。然而，后来因为你在他面前以我的朋友自居，最终使得我失去他的尊敬和友谊（一份长达十五年的友谊）。当我无法再得到他的忠告、帮助和关心时，我的人生便失去了最重要的一位救生员。

又例如，你寄过一首很美的诗给我（为大学诗社写的），想要得到我的青睐。我在回信中极尽文学想象力之能事，把你比作许拉斯、雅辛托斯、琼奎伊尔和纳西瑟斯[1]，或是比作某个受大诗神以爱眷顾和彰显过的人。这信犹似取自莎翁十四行诗的其中一段，再改以小调演绎，只有读过柏拉图《会饮篇》（*Symposium*）或领略得了古希腊大理石像神韵的人方可理解它的宗旨。坦白说吧，不管两

---

[1] 许拉斯、雅辛托斯、琼奎伊尔和纳西瑟斯，这四位都是以年轻俊美著称的古希腊神话人物。

所大学哪个优雅年轻人寄给我他写的诗，遇着我心情快活和率性的时候，我都一定会回他一封相似的信，因为我知道他必然具备充分的智慧或学养，能够正确诠释信中那些想象力翩翩的意象。但看看我写给你的那封信落得什么下场！它先是从你那里流入你一个可憎的同伴的手中，然后又从他那里流入一帮敲诈者手中：它的一些抄本被寄给我住在伦敦的朋友，寄给正在上演我作品的剧院的经理。人们对它的意旨有种种猜测，但就是没有人猜对。整个社会被一个最荒诞不经的流言弄得沸沸扬扬：这流言说我为了赎回一封写给你的不雅信件而付了一笔巨款。这谣言构成了令尊对我最恶劣攻讦的基础。我向法庭出示原信以展示它的真面目，却被令尊的律师说成一封下流信件，用意是暗暗败坏一个纯洁心灵。这信最终构成了对我刑事起诉的部分罪状。法院接受了这证据，学养太少却以道德挂帅的法官又有他自己解读那信的方式。于是我被送进牢房。这就是我给你写一封优美的信的下场。

　　当我在索尔兹伯里（Salisbury）和你待在一起那一次，你收到一个从前同伴的恐吓信。你求我去见那个写信人，帮你解围。我去了，结果我被迫把你干过的一切一肩扛，并为此负责。然后，当你无法拿到学位，不得不从牛津退学时，你发电报到伦敦给我，求我去找你。我马上照办。你说你在目前的情况下不想回家，想要到戈灵散散心。我带你去了。你在戈灵看上一栋房子，我为你租了下来——此举从各方面来看都是我毁灭的开始。另外，有一天你来找我，让我帮一本即将创刊的牛津大学生杂志供稿。杂志创办人是你一个朋友，其名字我从未听过，他的底细我也一无所知。为了取悦你（我何时不是千方百计取悦你？），我把原为《周六评论》撰写的一页吊诡语寄给他[1]。当时我万万没想到，几个月后我就因为该杂志的性质而站在了中央刑事法庭的被告席上，它构成了政府起诉我的罪名的一部分。我被传去为你朋友写的文章和你写的诗辩护。对前者，我无从辩解；至于后者，出于我对你年轻生命和年轻文学的绝对忠诚，我强力辩护到底，绝不容许有人中伤你为不雅诗人。但我照样因为你朋友的杂志和你那句诗（"那种无人敢称其名的爱"）坐了牢。我在圣诞节送过你一件"非常漂亮的礼物"（这是你在道谢函中的形

---

1 一八九四年十二月，王尔德写的警句（共二十五句）发表于一群牛津大学生创办的杂志《变色龙》（*Chameleon*）。同一期还刊登了道格拉斯的诗《两种爱》（*Two Loves*），其中包含那句声名狼藉的诗句："那种无人敢称其名的爱。"后来，这两篇在法庭上都被用作不利于王尔德的证据。《周六评论》（*Saturday Review*）是一本维多利亚风格杂志，王尔德曾以匿名方式在其上发表过警句（包含上述二十五句，外加十九句），题为《供受教育过度发达者学习的格言》（*A Few Maxims for the Instruction of the Over-Education*）。

容），记得吗？我早知道你看上了眼，所以买来送你，价钱是四十英镑，顶多五十英镑。后来财产查封官查抄我的藏书拿去拍卖，为的就是偿付这件"非常漂亮的礼物"。查封执行令就是因为这东西才会来到我家。另外，在那个可怕的最后关头，也就是那个致命的周五[1]，当你在汉弗莱斯[2]的律师事务所催我下定决心申请拘捕令和向令尊提告时，唯一能让我逃过劫数的借口（大可说是我能抓住的最后稻草）便是我付不起高昂得可怕的诉讼费用。我当着你的面告诉律师，我手头没有足够的钱支付这庞大费用。你晓得我这话一点不假。我真的是没钱，否则当天根本用不着在律师事务所里有气无力地同意自毁前程，而是早去了法国，自由而快乐，远离你和令尊，不用再管他的下流名片和你的可恶信件。问题是埃文代尔饭店（Avondale Hotel）的人坚持不让我离开。你和我在饭店里一共住了十天，而且让我大为生气的是，你还找了一个同伴来与我们同住。那十天的开支接近一百四十英镑。饭店老板坚持要我结清费用，否则坚决不让我把行李带走。这就把我困在伦敦了。要不是这笔账，我在周四早上便去了巴黎。

---

1 "那个致命的周五"指一八九五年三月一日。当天，王尔德对昆士伯里侯爵（波西的父亲）正式提告。
2 汉弗莱斯是王尔德三次官司中的律师。

当我告诉律师，我没有钱负担巨额诉讼费时，你马上插嘴。你说你家人将会完全乐意支付所有必要开支，因为令尊对家里每个人都是个大梦魇；你说你们常常讨论是不是有什么方法可以把令尊送入精神病院，好除去一个祸害；你说令尊每天都会让令堂和家里每个人不好过，所以如果我能出面把他关到牢里，你全家将会奉我为英雄和恩人，而令堂的富有亲戚也一定会乐于为我支付打官司的一切花费。听了这个，律师当即拍板定案，而我也匆匆前往法院提告。我再没有不去的借口。我被迫卷进了浑水。事实上，你家人后来并没有代我偿付诉讼费用，而我之所以会宣布破产，完全是令尊干的好事，是因为我欠他区区七百英镑。这期间，我太太又就留给我的生活费应是每周三英镑还是三英镑十先令的争执与我反目，着手安排离婚诉讼。这样一来，我当然又会受到新的指证和吃上新官司，随之而来的可能是罪名更加严重的起诉。我当然完全不知道我太太的律师会怎样打这场官司，但知道他深为倚重的证人的名字。你晓得那证人是谁吗？就是你在牛津念书时伺候你的仆人，后来应你之请，那年夏天我们住在戈灵时我又雇了他当仆人。

　　至此，我不用再多举例子，以证明在大大小小的事情上，你都把我带到了在劫难逃的境地。有时候我会觉得，你只是个傀儡，受一只神秘而看不见的手操纵，用以制造各种可怕的事件，以导向一个可怕的结局。但傀儡也有自己的七情六欲，他们会在他们的表演里添油加醋，为一出讲述盛衰的戏码加入转折，以满足他们一时兴起的怪念头和胃口。人类生命的永恒吊诡在于，我们总是完全自由又总是完全受法则宰制。我常常想，如果你那谜样的个性有任何原因解释得了的话，这就是唯一的解释——哪怕它会让原来的谜玄之又玄。

你当然有你的错觉，不只有，还生活在其中。你总是透过游移不定的薄雾和有色的薄纱看世界，以致把一切全看走了样。例如，我清楚记得，你以为完全把家人和家庭生活置之脑后，便足以证明你多么能够欣赏我的价值，以及足以证明你对我一片挚诚。在你眼中无疑是如此。但请不要忘了，与我在一起，你可以享受到高档的生活、无限的欢愉和数不尽的金钱。与家人同住让你百无聊赖。借你自己写过的一句话来说，"索尔兹伯里的廉价葡萄酒"让你不是滋味，与我在一起却不然。除了我的知性吸引力，你还可以享受到各种声色犬马的生活带来的欢愉。当你找不到我做伴时，你退而求其次找来代替我的人可真令人不敢恭维。

另外，你以为给令尊写一封律师信，说你宁愿放弃他每年给你的二百五十英镑生活津贴（我猜这数字是令尊扣掉他帮你还掉那笔牛津债款之后得出的），也不愿切断你我的永恒友谊，便是表现了一种捍卫友谊的侠义精神，表现了一种最高贵的自我牺牲精神。但放弃那笔小小年金，完全不代表你打算放弃任何一项最肤浅的奢侈享乐和最不必要的铺张浪费。正好相反。你对奢侈享受的胃口变得前所未有地强烈。我和你（连同你那意大利仆人）在巴黎八天的花费接近一百五十英镑：光是在帕亚尔餐厅吃饭便花掉八十五英镑。照你的这种开销法，即便你只是一个人吃饭，在消遣玩乐方面也挑选比较便宜的，你一整年的进项照样维持不了三周的生活。另一方面，你放弃年金之举虽然只是一种门面之勇，但它至少让你有一个名正言顺的理由来靠我供养。事实上，这也是你在很多场合动用的理由，你还把它的功能发挥得淋漓尽致。没有什么比这种持续不断的榨取（主要是榨取我，但我知道令堂也被榨取一些）更让人心烦，因为你在榨取时（至少在我这边是如此）从不会有一个"谢"字，也毫无一点节制的意识。

你的另一个错觉是，以为用一些满纸污言秽语的信件、电报或明信片攻击令尊，就是为令堂出了气，就是为她在婚姻中遭受的许多委屈报了仇。这是你一个相当大的错觉，无疑也是最糟糕的一个。事实上，如果你真想为令堂报复令尊，如果你认为这是身为人子的一部分责任，那真正应该做的是当个乖巧的儿子，是不让她害怕跟你谈些严肃的事，是不去签些要她擦屁股的账单，是温柔对待令堂，不再在她的日子里增添愁烦。令兄弗朗西斯就是这样：虽然如花般凋谢，但他在短短的人生里用体贴和善良大大减少了令堂的辛酸。你本应以他为榜样的。你的一个更大的错觉，是以为如果可以成功唆使我让令尊吃牢饭，令堂就会无比高兴和快乐。我可以肯定你想错了。想知道一个女人看到丈夫（或说看到她子女的父亲）穿着囚衣被关在牢里是什么感觉，写信问问我太太吧，她会告诉你的。

我一样有错觉。我原以为，人生是一出妙趣横生的喜剧，而你是剧中的许多优雅人物之一。到头来却发现它是一出叫人恶心想吐的悲剧。我的人生是一场大灾难，而其险恶罪魁（这罪魁之所以险恶在于其苦心孤诣、志在必得）就是脱下欢乐面具之后的阁下本人。那面具不但欺骗了我，也欺骗了你自己，让你我都误入歧途。

我正在承受多大的痛苦，你现在应该明白一二了吧？有份报纸（没记错的话是《佩尔·摩尔公报》）报道我一出新戏的彩排情况时，形容你像个影子那样尾随我。事实上，在监狱里，对你我那段友谊的回忆，也像影子般盘桓在我左右。它看似从不曾离开我。它会在夜里唤醒我，一遍又一遍述说同一个故事，把我折腾得睡意全消，彻夜不能成眠。到了破晓，同样的事情又会重演一遍。它会尾随我到监狱中庭，让我一面拖着沉重的脚步绕圈走，一面喃喃自语。我被迫去回忆你我相处的每个痛苦时刻的每个细节。每件在那些惨淡年头发生过的事情，无一不在我那个专留给悲苦和绝望使用的脑袋里再次上演。你声音里的每个扭曲、你每一个神经兮兮的手势、你的每一句恶言恶语，无一不在我眼前历历如绘。我会回忆起那些我们散步走过的街道或桥梁，回忆起曾围绕我们的每一片墙壁或树林，回忆起大钟指针指着某个数字，回忆起风吹的方向，还有月亮的形状和颜色。

我知道对我所说的这一切，你会怎样回答。我知道你会说你爱我，说在命运之神用丝线把我俩互不相干的人生编织成一个猩红色图案的那两年半之间，你确实爱着我。对，我知道是这样没错。因为不管你对我多坏，我总是感受得到你心底确实爱着我。我当然也清楚地知道，让你爱我的原因还包括我在艺术界的地位、我引人兴奋的人格特质、我的金钱和我奢华的生活。千百个条件加起来让我卓尔不群、魅力无穷，而这些条件的每一项都足以让你心醉神迷，让你对我缠着不放。然而，除此以外，我还有其他特质吸引着你。基于我对你的某种奇怪吸引力，你爱我远胜于爱其他人。但你就像我一样，生命里包含着一场可怕悲剧，不同只在于你我的悲剧在性质上完全相反。想知道你的悲剧是什么吗？那就是：在你心中，恨的感情总是强于爱。你对令尊的恨是如此之甚，以致完全超过、压倒和遮蔽了你对我的爱。这两种力量在你内心完全没有交战可言，有的话亦是极小规模：你的恨太巨大了，生长速度也恐怖得吓人，让你的爱完全没有招架之力。你不明白，一个灵魂的空间无法同时容纳大恨和大爱。它们无法在一间雕琢精美的屋子里并存。爱由想象力滋养，可以让我们变得更有智慧、更善良和更高尚。透过爱，我们得以把生命看成一个整体；透过爱，也只有透过爱，我们得以除欣赏别人的理想状态外还欣赏他们的现实状态。只有美好的事物和构思美好的事物可以滋养爱。相反，任何事物都可以滋养恨。这些年来你喝过的每一杯香槟、吃过的每一盘甘肥料理，无一不曾滋养你的恨，让它愈来愈臃肿。为了迎合你的仇恨，你拿我的人生当赌注，一如你用我的金钱来赌博：两者都是漫不经心、义无反顾和不计后果的。你认为，如果赌输了，输的人不会是你，但如果赌赢了，你会同时获得赢家的快感和实利。

恨会蒙蔽眼目。这是你没意识到的。爱可以让人读出最遥远星星的信息，但恨对你的蒙蔽是如此之甚，让你的视线范围从不超出你那些最平凡的欲念，让你就像被困在一个狭窄和四面是墙的花园里，而花园里的花草早已因过度的欲念而枯萎。你个性里有一个真正致命的缺陷：严重缺乏想象力。这缺陷完全是你心里住满恨所造成的。一如青苔会啃咬某些植物的根部，使之变得枯黄，你的恨也不动声色地啃噬你的人性。到最后，你眼里会只剩下最琐碎的利益和最卑下的目标。你那本来可以通过爱来扶植的才智，如今已为恨所毒化和瘫痪。令尊第一次攻讦我，是在一封写给你的私人信件里把我当成普通人来攻讦。一读到那信，看到他那下流的威胁口吻和粗鄙言辞，我马上明白，我不平静日子的地平线上正酝酿着一场可怕的风暴。我当时告诉你，我可不要当你们父子厮杀的棋子。我还说，对令尊而言，扳倒我会比扳倒德国的外交大臣更值得高兴；把我卷进你俩的战争（哪怕只是一下子）对我是不公道的；我的人生还有重要得多的工作要做，不值得花时间去跟一个老是醉醺醺、不体面和脑筋有缺陷的人吵架。但你就是无法明白，恨蒙蔽了你的眼目。你坚称你们父子间的争吵与我无关，也不容许令尊干涉你的交友状况，说把我卷进去对我是最不公道的。我当时不知道，在给我看信以前，你已给令尊发去一封愚蠢粗野的电报，作为反击。这行动当然又会引起另一个愚蠢粗野的回应。人生的致命错误不在不理智（有时不理智的时刻反而是人生的优美时刻），而在太讲逻辑。两者迥然不同。那封电报制约了你与令尊此后的全部关系，结果则是制约了我的整个人生。它的不可思议之处在于其内容连最普通的街头顽童读了都会脸红。从发出无礼电报到寄出一封趾高气扬的律师信只是一种逻辑的必然进程，而你给令尊发律师信的结果当然是刺激得他变本加厉。你让他别无选择，只能进行到底。你逼得他非为他的名誉而战不可——更精确的说法是为他的不名誉而战，因为你的电报更能让他感到自己的不名誉。所以，他下次攻讦我，便不是在一封私人信件里把我当成普通人来攻讦，而是在一个公众场合把我当作公众人物攻讦。他来我家吵，我不得不把他撵出去。然后他又一家家餐厅找我，企图要当着全世界的面羞辱我，好让我不管反击或不反击都一样臭名远扬。那节骨眼显然是你应该出面的时候。你应该去对他说，为了不让我陷入那么丑陋的攻讦中、那么羞辱性的迫害中，你愿意马上中断你我的友谊。不是吗？我猜你现在已经意识到这是你本该做的事。但在当时，你连这样做的念头都没闪过。恨蒙蔽了你的眼目。你当时唯一能想到的（除了继续给令尊写些羞辱性的信和电报）是买一把手枪，后来你在巴克莱餐厅放了一枪，让自己出尽洋相[1]。在你看来，你对于自己可以引起令尊与我这种身份地位的人发生可怕争吵，感到很愉快。我想这是自然不过的，因为它满足了你的虚荣心，奉承了你的自负感。假若整件事情是以令尊得到你的身体（那是我不感兴趣的）而我得到你的灵魂（那是他不感兴趣的）落幕，你一定会非常难过。你嗅到一个让令尊大大出丑的机会，就赶紧扑过去。想到有场大战将要开打而你不会被波及，你快活得不得了。那一季度的其他时间我不曾看你如此开心过。你唯一的失望是看到什么都没发生，因为我和令尊没有再碰面，吵架没有再升级。为了自我安慰，你再次给他发送一些不堪入目的电报，最终弄得那个可怜虫不得不写信告诉你，他已吩咐仆人不管任何情况都不准把你的电报呈上。你并不气馁，你看出明信片的大用，便把它的功用发挥得淋漓尽致。通过明信片，你对令尊的穷追猛打更甚于往昔。我并不认为他真的会善罢甘休。他遗传了家族基因中强悍的攻击本能，而他恨你之深不下于你恨他。我则成为你俩的马前卒，同时是你俩的攻击性武器和防御性武器。令尊会渴望惹事扬名不只是出于个人禀性，还是出于家族禀性。

---

[1] 波西以为枪里没有子弹，出于贪玩开了一枪。

即便他的兴头有过低落的时候，你的信和明信片一样可以马上煽起他心底那股历史悠久的求名之火。事实也证明果真如此。所以他自然会愈来愈过分。既然已经在私下将我视为普通人中伤过，又在公众场合将我作为公众人物中伤过，他决定要对我发起最后和最大的一次攻击：在我的艺术作品上演之处攻击作为艺术家的我。在我一出戏的首演之夜（按：《不可儿戏》），他冒名买了一个座位，阴谋要打断演出，当着观众的面中伤我和污蔑我的演员，或是等到我谢幕时谩骂我和用东西扔我，总之是要用丑陋的方式借我的作品毁了我。纯粹是出于偶然，他没有得逞：因为心情像是喝醉酒那样飘飘然，他向旁边的人透露自己的意图，并为之得意扬扬。警察闻讯而来，把他驱逐出剧院。那时你的机会来了。那正是你的机会。难道你现在还看不出来吗？你本该站出来，表示你无论如何不愿意我的艺术因为你而毁于一旦。你知道我的艺术对我有什么意义：它是我诞生为人的首要使命。我在自己悟得这个使命之后又向世人揭示它。艺术是我人生的真正激情所在，与之相比，我对其他东西的爱不啻泥浆水之于红酒，沼泽地萤火虫之于月亮。难道你至今还不明白，缺乏想象力是你个性里真正致命的缺陷？你当时该怎样做是明明白白的，这些事也并不难做，但恨蒙蔽了你的眼目，使你什么都看不见。我不可能向令尊道歉，因为他有近九个月一再用最不堪的方式侮辱和迫害我。我也无法把你从我的人生里甩掉。我试了又试，甚至不惜离开英国，前往海外，指望可以逃离你，但一切努力皆属徒劳。你是当时唯一可以做点什么的人。整件事情的关键全系于你。那原是一个大好机会，让你可以对我向你表现过关爱、仁慈和慷慨做出少许回报。哪怕你只懂欣赏我作为艺术家的十分之一的价值，你都会那样做。但恨蒙蔽了你的眼目。我说过："透过爱，也只有透过爱，我们得以除欣赏别人的理想状态外还欣赏他们的现实状态。"但爱的能力已在你内心死掉。你念兹在兹的只是怎样把令尊关入牢里。用你的话来说，看见他"站在被告席"是你的唯一心愿。这句话你天天挂在嘴边，成为我们日常谈话中的许多陈词滥调之一，你每顿饭都要提它一提。好吧，你的渴望得到满足了。不管你渴望什么，"恨"总是会一一满足你。它是个极尽纵溺能事的主子，对每个伺候它的仆人莫不如此。所以，有两天时间，你与法警一样高坐堂上，得以饱览令尊站在中央刑事法庭被告席出丑的样子。但到了第三天，站在被告席的人变成了我。发生了什么事？在恨的丑陋赌局中，你们两个都以我为骰子，而你不巧输了。就是这么回事。

我不得不把你做过的事写出来，因为那是你非得去悟明的。迄今为止，你我已经认识了超过四年。其中有一半时间我们待在一起，另一半时间则是我因你我的友谊蹲在牢里。如果这信真能到你手上，我说不准你会是在哪里收到。但你现在八成在罗马、那不勒斯、巴黎或威尼斯，总之是个滨海或滨河的漂亮城市。现在围绕着你的即便不是与我在一起时那些无用的奢华排场，也必然是一些娱心意、悦耳目的物事。生活对你而言真的很美好。然而，如果你够聪明，如果你希望人生变得更可爱，就应该将我这封可怕的信（我知道它可怕）作为你人生的一个危机和转折点，因为写它对我来说就是如此。你白嫩的脸蛋总是只要喝了点酒或高兴便绯红起来。假若读着这信时你会不时因为愧疚而满脸通红，就像是被熔炉烤炙似的，那对你会更有益处。最要不得的缺点莫过于浮浅。凡经过悟明的都会归正。

接下来我应该谈拘留所了，对不对？在警察局牢房关了一晚之后，我被用有篷货车送到拘留所。当时你殷勤备至，每天下午（至少是"几乎"每天下午）都不嫌麻烦，坐马车到霍洛韦[1]来看我。你也会写来一些甜美的信。可你不曾有一刻想到过，害我坐牢的那个人其实不是令尊。从头到尾，该负责的人都是你。就连看见我被关在一个木

---

1 霍洛韦：王尔德第一次受审期间（一八九五年四月六日到二十六日间）所待的监狱。

笼子里，你那已死和毫无想象力的心性一样无法被唤醒。你固然有一点伤心难过，但那只像看了一出颇为悲伤的戏剧之后的伤心难过。你从未悟到你就是这出丑陋悲剧的真正作者。我看出你完全不了解自己干了什么。我没有向你指出这个，因为那本应由你的心来告诉你，我不想越俎代庖。真正的悟明只能来自一个人的内心，但恨把你的心变硬，让它变得无知无觉。一个人自己无法感受到和了解的事情，你跟他说了也没用。那我现在为什么又要在信中指出来呢？是因为你在我坐牢这段漫长时间里所表现的态度和沉默让此举变得必要。另外，事态的最后发展显示，打击全落在我一人身上。这倒是我乐于见到的。我有许多理由甘心受苦，然而，看到你那副完全盲目和任由自己盲目的样子，我还是充满了鄙夷。我记得你那时为我的事投稿给一份小报，文章被刊登出来，你为此得意得不得了。老实说，你那篇文章拘谨节制，不痛不痒，只能算平庸之作。你在文章中呼吁应该唤起"英国大众重视公平比赛的意识"，应该还"一个被打倒的人"以公道，还有其他诸如此类无聊的话头。像这种信，即便是某个你不算太熟但值得尊敬的人受到不公指控，你也是会写的。但你认为你写了一封了不起的信，认为它几乎可以证明你具有堂吉诃德般的侠义精神。我晓得你也给其他报纸投过稿，只是未被采用。但这些文章无非是要告诉别人，你恨着令尊。没有人会在乎你恨不恨他。你还有待学会的一点是，恨是一种不断否定知性的表现，是一种情感萎缩症的表现，它除了会杀死当事人自身，什么都杀不死。投稿给报纸公然宣称你恨着某个人，等于披露你得了某种不可告人和值得丢脸的疾病。你恨的对象是令尊，或你们父子彼此相恨的事实，并没有使你的恨变得更高贵或优美——它若有显示什么，那就是，你得的是遗传性疾病。

关于你的盲目，我又想起另外一件事情。当一项法院判决在我家执行，当我的藏书和家具被查封而我破产在即之际，我自然而然会写信告诉你这事。我在信中没提，财产查封官之所以会进入你以前常常在这里进餐的我家，是因为我为了买礼物送你而欠下了一些货款。我心想（不管是对是错），这也许会让你有点难过。所以我就略过不谈，只告诉你查封财产的事和有哪些财产被查封。我认为那是理应让你知道的。没想到你从布洛涅[1]写来的回信竟是一派近乎喜悦的口气。你说你知道令尊"目前手头紧"，他为支付打官司的费用被迫筹措了一千五百英镑，而我的破产可以让他"大大失分"——因为如此一

1　布洛涅位于法国北部。

来，他将无法从我这里获得任何赔偿！你现在明白恨可以把人蒙蔽至何种地步了吗？明白我说恨是一种只能杀死当事人的萎缩症时，不过是在科学地陈述一个心理学事实了吗？因为破产，我拥有的所有宝贝都得拍卖掉，包括：伯恩-琼斯（Burne-Jones）、惠斯勒（Whistler）、蒙蒂塞利（Monticelli）、西门·所罗门斯（Simeon Solomons）的画；我珍藏的瓷器；我珍藏的许多诗集（几乎涵盖这时代每一位诗人：从雨果到惠特曼，从斯温伯恩到马拉美，从莫里斯到魏尔兰）；我父母装订精美的著作的各种版本；中学和大学的奖状；各种豪华版书籍；等等。我失去了一切，但你全然不当一回事。你说我给你列举这些拍卖项目让你读得无聊透顶。你唯一想到的是令尊最终可能要破财几百英镑，并为他这微不足道的损失乐不可支。有关他的诉讼开支，我想有件事情你也许会有兴趣知道：令尊曾在奥尔良俱乐部公开说过，即使官司要花他两万英镑他也是甘之如饴，因为官司带给他太多的快乐和太美妙的胜利滋味了——光是我得坐两年牢便让他称心如意，而可以成功把我弄得公开宣布破产更使他始料未及，额外津津有味。这是我受辱的最高点，也是令尊大获全胜的最高点。我心里明白，要不是因为令尊曾经向我索赔，你至少会对我失去所有藏书表示最大的同情。因为这损失对一个文人来说是无可弥补的，是所有物质损失中最让我心痛的项目。如果你还记得我是怎样在你身上大把花钱，这些年来是怎样供养你的，你也许会愿意费些事，把我的一些藏书买回来。最贵一批的拍卖价还不到一百五十英镑，只大约相当于我平常为你而花的一周的开销。可是你因为想到我的破产可让令尊损失几毛钱而乐昏了头，以至于忘记应该帮我把一部分藏书买回来，作为对我的一点点报答——这报答简单、轻易、不昂贵、理所当然，又让我大为受用。所以，"恨会蒙蔽眼目"之说一点都不错吧？你看出来了吗？如果还没有，就再试一次吧。

毋庸说，当时和现在，我都对你被恨所蒙蔽这一点看得清清楚楚。但我提醒自己："我必须不惜任何代价把爱保存在心里。如果坐牢期间我不再有爱，我的灵魂将会落得什么可怕模样？"被关在霍洛韦期间我会努力继续写信给你，为的就是把爱保持为我心性的主音调。我本可在信里把你臭骂一顿，把你羞辱得体无完肤。我本可向你举起一面镜子，让你看看一副自己都认不出来的嘴脸，直至看见它流露出像你一样的惊恐表情才惊觉镜中人是谁，自此永远恨他和恨你自己。我不仅不愿意恨某人，甚至还愿意为某人顶罪受过。若要自保，我大可在两次受审期间将事情和盘托出——此举虽然无法让我免于不光彩，但至少可

以让我免去牢狱之灾。若要自保，我大可指出控方证人
（最重要的那三个）是经过令尊及其律师教唆的，证词是
精心编造且经过彩排的，对我的指控是绝对的移花接木，
是把另一个人的所作所为安到我头上[1]。我本可使法官把他
们一个个赶下证人席，滚蛋得比那个做伪证的阿特金斯[2]
还快。那样，我便可以吹吹口哨，双手插在口袋里，无罪
一身轻地走出法庭。有最大的压力逼着我这么做。那些
真正关心我福祉或我家人福祉的人都这么劝我、求我这么
做，甚至是苦苦哀求。但我拒绝了，没有选择这步棋。我
不屑为之。我后来不曾有片刻为这个决定后悔，哪怕是在
牢狱生涯最煎熬的日子里仍是如此。肉体的罪算不了什
么——如果说它们是该治的病，那便该留给医生来治。只
有灵魂的罪真正可耻。如果是通过上述手段获得开脱，我
将一辈子良心不安。但你真认为你配得上我对你表现的
爱，或真认为我有过哪一刻觉得你配吗？你真认为，在你
我交往期间，你配得上我对你表现的爱，或真认为我有
过哪一刻觉得你配吗？我知道你不配。但爱不是市场里
的买卖品，不能用小贩的秤来论斤算两。就像知性之乐

---

1 王尔德这里暗示真正的指证他与三个男妓有染的人是波西。
2 阿特金斯：王尔德第一次受审时的控方证人，法庭裁定他做伪证，王尔德
也因此无罪获释。

一样，爱会因为感受到自身的存在而喜乐。爱的目的——不多也不少——就是付出爱。你是我的敌人，与我不共戴天。我把整个人生奉献给你，以满足你各种最卑下的人类激情（包括仇恨、虚荣心和贪婪），你却弃如敝屣。不到三年时间，你就把我给毁了——从任何角度看都是彻底地毁了。但为我自己着想，我别无选择，只能继续爱你。我知道，若是我放任自己恨你，那么，在那片我曾不得不走过的人生荒漠里，每块岩石都会失去它的凉荫，每棵棕榈都会枯萎，每口水井都会变为毒井。你开始有一点了解了吗？你的想象力是否已从漫长的昏睡中苏醒过来了？我已经让你知道了恨是何物，现在，你是不是也开始有点明白爱是何物，它的本质何在。你现在学会仍不嫌晚，哪怕为了教会你这个，我得付出坐牢的代价。

可怕的判决下来之后，当囚衣已经加诸我身而牢房门也关上，我颓然坐在我奇妙人生所剩下的废墟之中。痛苦使我窒息，恐惧使我发昏，辛酸使我茫然。但我仍然不愿意恨你。我每天提醒自己："今天我必须把爱保存在心里，否则我将无从挨过这一天。"我提醒自己，不管怎样，你对我都没有不安好心。我要自己这样想：你的过错只在于胡乱张弓，不巧把箭射进了国王铠甲的接缝处。我觉得，我连最小的一个忧伤、最轻微的一个损失都拿出来跟你计较，对你并不公道。我决计要把你当成像我一样的受苦者。我逼自己相信，长久遮蔽着你眼睛的阴翳终必脱落。我喜欢心痛地想象，当你谛视自己一手造成的可怕杰作时，会是多么惊惧惶恐。有些时候（包括我一生中最黑暗的那段日子在内），我甚至渴望可以去安慰你。我确信你一定已经悟明自己做了什么。

那时我万万没有想到你身上会有那个最要不得的缺点：浮浅。当我知道狱方规定我一开始只许写信给家人谈家务事时，我真的非常难过。但我的小舅子先前来信告诉我，我太太表示，只要我愿意写一封信给她，她就会为了我和两个孩子着想，不提出离婚诉讼。我也感到自己有责任写那信。其他理由不说，一想到要与西里尔分离我便受不了。他是那么的漂亮、贴心和可爱，以至光是他小脑袋瓜上的一根金发，对我来说都比（我不会拿你来比）普天下的宝石加起来还要珍贵。我一直都这样认为，只是从前察觉不到，等察觉到已为时太晚。

你申请出国两周之后，我从罗伯特·谢拉德（Robert Sherard）那里得到关于你的消息。这位天底下最勇敢、最侠义的好人前来探监，除了说别的事情还告诉我，你将在扭怩作态和堪称文学腐败渊薮的《法兰西信使报》（*Mercure de France*）发表一篇谈我的文章，还会随文刊登我的几封书信。他问我这事是不是经过我授意。我听了又惊又恼，马上下达制止令。你一向把我的信乱放，结果不是被你那些爱勒索人的同伴偷去，就是被饭店侍者或家里女佣顺手牵羊拿去卖。对于这个，我可以谅解：你只是因为不懂得欣赏那些信才会漫不经心。但这一次你是刻意要从剩下的书信里挑出一部分来发表，这让我几乎不敢相信。你挑了哪些信呢？我无从得知。这是我得到有关你的第一则消息。它让我不快。

第二则消息紧随其后。先是令尊的律师来了监狱，当面递交给我一份破产通知：令尊因为要不到向我索偿的诉讼费（只是区区七百英镑），向法院申请宣布我破产。我必须出庭。不管当时还是现在，我强烈认为这笔费用应该由你的家人支付（我稍后还会再谈这个话题），是你亲口保证过你家人会支付的。就因为你这么说，我的律师才会接这案子，你绝对应该负责。即便你没有代表家人做出承诺，你也理应觉得，既然我的身败名裂是你一手造成的，那你至少应该帮我免去破产的额外耻辱。何况那只是不足挂齿的一丁点钱，还不到我在戈灵短短三个月内为你花掉的数目。这个暂且按下不表。但就因为这件事，我得到过你的口信。话说律师事务所职员来拿我的证言和声明那天，办好正事之后，他从口袋掏出一张字条，看了看之后低声对我说（当时我们隔着桌子对坐，旁边站着一个狱卒）："百合花王子请你记住他。"我瞪着他看。他把同样的话重说了一遍，我百思不得其解。他神秘兮兮地补充一句："那位先生目前在国外。"我恍然大悟，跟着笑了起来。这是我整个牢狱生涯第一次笑，也是最后一次笑。万千的鄙夷尽在这一笑中。百合花王子！我笑，是因为明白了没有任何事情可以让你开窍（后来发生的事情也证明了这一点）。你仍然自视为一出无聊喜剧中的优雅王子，而不是悲剧里的伤心角色。对你而言，曾经发生过的一切不过是帽子上的一根羽饰，不过是别在马甲上的一朵花。帽子下面是一个狭窄的脑袋，马甲后面藏着一颗仇恨的心（这颗心只有恨可以温暖，碰到爱就会冰冷）。百合花王子！对，你完全有理由用一个化名与我联络，因为我已经成了一个无名无姓之人。被监禁在一座偌大的监狱里，我不过是长廊里一间单人牢房门上的数字和字母罢了。我只是一千个无生命的数字之一，只是一千个无气息的生命之一。不过，让我纳闷的是，要取化名的话，不是有很多历史人物的名字更适合你，而且是可以让我一下子便领悟的吗？我一开始并没能隔着那个只适合用在化装舞会的亮晶晶面具认出你。唉，要是你的灵魂曾因忧伤而受伤，曾因愧疚而谦卑，就断不会选用那么俗丽的伪装来潜入痛苦山庄[1]！生活中的大事就如它们本身显现的样子，又正因如此而往往难于诠释，但生活中的小事是象征，最容易让我们得到惨痛教训的正是那些小事。你选择那样的化名固然只是一时兴起，但它仍然具有象征性。它把你揭穿了。

六周后又来了第三则有关你的消息。那时我生了重病，卧床在监狱医院，但有一天，我被叫出去，听典狱长转达你的口信。他读了一封你写给他的信，信中说你打算发表一篇"有关王尔德先生案子"的文章，将刊登在《法兰西信使报》（出于让人费解的原因，你特别注明该报"相当于我们英国的《双周评论》"），而你急于取得我的同意，让你引用我的信。哪些信？我从霍洛韦监狱写给你的那些！它们本应是你在这世上弥足珍贵和最私密的东西，没想到你却打算拿来发表，让病恹恹的颓废派（décadent）有奇可称，让八卦专栏作家有文章可造，让拉丁区[2]的文化小名流有茶余饭后的谈资！即使你的良知没有发出反对你这种下流举动的呼号，你至少应该记得我在一首十四行诗里抒发过我对济慈书信拍卖会的观感，并最终了解这几句诗的深意：

1　"痛苦山庄"指监狱。
2　拉丁区：巴黎的文教区。

我看他们爱的不是艺术

这些人打碎诗人的水晶心脏

一双双猥琐的小眼睛虎视眈眈[1]

　　你想用你那篇文章来显示些什么呢？显示我对你有多么深情吗？巴黎的浪子族（gamin）对此都知之甚详：他们全都读报，而且大部分都会给报纸写稿。是想显示我是个天才吗？法国人早知道我是天才，而且对我才华的独特之处了解得比你已认识或可望认识的还要清楚。是要显示天才人物常常会有一些古怪乖僻的激情吗？这是了不起的见解，但应该留给隆布罗索[2]来分析。那是他的强项，不是你的。何况心理病态现象也非天才独有，普通人中间一样看得见。你的文章是要显示，在你和令尊的仇恨战争中，我同时是你们的剑和盾吗？甚至是显示，要不是你在我脚边撒了网，他根本逮不着我吗？这倒是事实。不过我听说，亨利·博埃[3]已经提出过同一论点。即便说你是想

1　出自王尔德的诗《济慈情书被拍卖有感》（On the Sale by Auction of Keat's Love Letter）。

2　隆布罗索（Lombroso，1836—1909）：意大利医生、犯罪学家，其著作《罪犯》（The Criminal）和《女犯》（Female Offender）在欧洲各国都大有影响力。

3　亨利·博埃：法国人，大有影响力的文学与戏剧评论家。他曾在王尔德被判刑之后为文声援。

要帮他的腔，也用不着发表我的信——至少是用不着发表我在霍洛韦监狱写的那些。

对我的质疑，你也许会回答说："你不是在写自霍洛韦监狱的一封信中请求过我，请我就能做到的范围内，在一小部分世人面前还你以一点公道吗？"不错，我是请求过你。但请想想看，我如何会落得现在的田地。你以为是因为我与那些控方证人的关系[1]吗？我与那些人的关系不管是真是假，都不会让政府或社会感兴趣。他们对这方面本来一无所知，也懒得理会。我会蹲牢房，是因为想把令尊扳倒，把他送进监狱。我的行动当然是失败了。我的辩护律师举手认输。令尊扭转了形势，反过来把我送进监狱，让我至今还待在牢里。这就是何以世人会瞧不起我。这就是何以我非得一天天、一小时、一分钟地把这可怕的徒刑服完。这就是何以我要求提前释放的申请会遭到拒绝。

你本是唯一可以对整件事情起澄清作用的人。你本来用不着冒什么被取笑或被责备的风险，便可以在某种程度上还原真相。我当然不指望或期望你会和盘托出当初你在牛津惹上麻烦而求我帮助时，抱的是什么目的；或你之所以有近三年时间几乎从未离开我身边，抱的是什么目

---

1 指同性恋关系。王尔德这里是要指出，他会被定罪，根本原因不在同性恋行为。

的（假设有目的的话）。我也不指望你会把我多次想要离开你的经过像写流水账那样交代出来（我曾无数次想斩断你我的友谊，因为它不管对我作为一个艺术家、作为一个有地位的人，甚至只是作为社会一员，都有着莫大的杀伤力）。我也不会要你把三天两头必闹一次脾气的场面描述一遍，要你把你那些妙不可言的电报内容（谈情说钱共冶一炉）公布出来，或是要你（像我不得不做的那样）引用你那些不堪入目和无情无义的书信段落。尽管如此，我还是认为，如果你能够对令尊就你我友谊所讲述的那个故事版本做出抗议，对你对我都会有好处（他的故事版本既古怪又恶毒：有关你的部分荒诞不经，有关我的部分含血喷人）。现在，他的故事版本已经俨如正史了：被人引用，被人相信，被人拿来发挥。布道家把它写入讲道词，道德家把它引为鉴戒。我这个曾受男女老少仰慕的人，却得接受一个粗人兼小丑的判决。正如我在稍前不无怨尤地说过的那样，整件事情最讽刺的是令尊将摇身变成主日学校教材里的英雄，你将会与婴儿撒母耳同列，而我将会与吉尔斯·德·莱斯和萨德侯爵排排坐。我敢说这是最好不过的结果。我一点都不想抱怨。人在狱中会学到的许多道理之一，便是事有必至，理有固然。我也毫不怀疑，与我更相称的同侪是那个体现中世纪野蛮精神的人渣和《瑞斯丁娜》的作者[1]，而非桑福德与默顿[2]。

不过，在写那封信时，我真的是觉得，不管为你好还是为我好，推翻令尊为熏陶庸俗大众而通过他律师宣扬的那个故事版本，都是一件该做的事。我也是因此才会建议你思考和写出一些可以稍正视听的东西。这起码比你乱涂鸦，给法国报纸和盘托出你父母的婚姻生活有意义。法国人会管你父母的婚姻是幸福还是不幸福吗？难以想象还有什么比这个更让他们不感兴趣的了。他们会感兴趣的问题是：以我这么不凡的一个艺术家（他曾经通过他所代表的学派和运动对法国思想发挥显著影响），何以会过上那样的生活，而后来又怎么会去挑起那么愚蠢的一桩官司？我给你写过许多信（恐怕多到数不清），谈到你是怎样把我的人生拖向毁灭，谈到你是如何放纵自己的喜怒无常，也谈到我有意——不，是"下定决心"才对——要同你一刀两断。假如你的文章是要引用我的这些信，我倒是可以体谅（哪怕照样不会同意让你引用）。记得令尊的律师在法庭上为了

1　"体现中世纪野蛮精神的人渣"和《瑞斯丁娜》的作者"分别指吉尔斯·德·莱斯和萨德侯爵。

2　桑福德与默顿（Sandford and Merton）：少年小说《桑福德与默顿的故事》（*The History of Sandford and Merton*）中的两位主角，个性阳光善良。该小说由托马斯·戴（Thomas Day）写成于十八世纪，但至十九世纪仍相当流行。

让我自取其辱，出示了一封我写的信。那是我在一八九三年三月写给你的，信中说我与其忍受你那些似乎让你乐在其中的无休止的大吵大闹，倒不如"被每一个伦敦房东勒索敲诈"。看见你我友谊的这一面竟然就这样公之于众，我真是伤心极了。而你对那么珍贵、精致和美的东西如此不痛不痒、迟迟不懂得欣赏，乃至要拿来发表。你可知道，我会写那批信，是为了设法用它们来保存住"爱"的精神与魂魄，好让我的身体哪怕受尽屈辱，"爱"仍然可以活在这身体里。你的所作所为带给我最深的痛苦，最揪心的绝望——当时如此，至今仍是如此。至于你为什么会那样做，我只怕是再了解不过了。如果说"恨"蒙蔽了你眼目，那"虚荣心"则更是用铁丝线把你的眼皮完全缝起来。我说过："透过爱，也只有透过爱，我们得以除欣赏别人的理想状态外还欣赏他们的现实状态。"但"爱"的能力被你以自我为中心的心态给磨钝了，复因为被荒废太久而不堪使用。你的想象力和我的身体一样，都是身在囹圄之中。"虚荣心"是这囹圄的窗口铁栏杆，而狱卒的名字叫"恨"。

这一切发生在前年的十一月初。在这么久远的日期和现在的你之间，想必横隔着一条大河。你大概极少会望向河对岸，有的话也大概极少看得清楚。但对我而言，一切仿佛发生在昨天——不，应该说是发生在今天稍早的时候。痛苦是一个长长的瞬间，它不知道何谓季节，它只由种种心绪构成，而这些心绪总是回环往复。在我们这种人身上，时间是不会向前前进的。它只会旋转，绕着一个痛苦中心打转。监狱生活是一种停滞的生活，事无大小都受到一成不变的模式规范，所以我们不管是吃是喝、是坐是卧、是祷告还是下跪（至少是为祷告而下跪），都得遵循一些铁律。这种让人麻木的凝滞让每天的每个细节都无比相似，而这种凝滞又会让人不停想念外面那个以不停变化为本质的世界。我们想念播种时节，想念收割时节，想念农人在田里插秧的情景，想念葡萄工采收葡萄的情景，想念果园被落花染白或果子撒了一地的情景。但我们对外面正在发生什么一无所知，也无从得知。我们这种人的季节只有一个：悲伤之季。太阳和月亮看似已从我们头上挪走。哪怕外头艳阳高照和万里晴空，但能够从小小铁窗厚重玻璃漏进来的光线总是灰蒙蒙和只有一点点。一如我们的心总是处于午夜时分，牢房里总是晨昏不辨。我们的脑袋就像我们的时间一样，停止了运转。很多事情你大概已忘到九霄云外，我却身历其境，而到了明天还会再经历一次。记住这个，你就会有点明白我何以要写信给你，而且是用这种写法。

我在一周之后转监到这里。家母在三个月后辞世。你比谁都清楚我爱她有多深，敬她有多高。她的死是那么可怕的噩耗，以至于我虽曾是语言文字的大师，也无法道尽内心的哀伤和愧疚。其实，即便在我作为艺术家的巅峰时期，一样不可能找到足够的词语可载动如许沉重的大恸。家母和家父传给了我一个响亮和尊贵的姓氏（它不只在文学、艺术、考古学和科学上放过光芒，还在我祖国的历史和我民族的演化史中放过光芒），但我已让这姓氏永远蒙羞。我任它沦为下贱人中间的下贱笑柄，我把它拖入泥淖，我把它丢给蠢材当蠢材的同义词。我的深创剧痛非笔墨所能形容。我太太当时对我还很仁慈体贴，为了不让我从闲杂人或不相干的人口中先听到这消息，她虽身在病中，仍不辞千里迢迢，从热那亚回到伦敦，亲自告诉我这个无可补救的消息、无可补赎的失丧。仍然顾念着我的朋友纷纷向我致以哀悼。就连一些与我素未谋面的人在得知我的残破人生又添新愁之后，一样会写信请狱方向我传达慰问之意。唯独你当成事不关己，站得远远的，没捎来一句话，没寄来一封信。对你的所作所为，最适当的态度是弗吉尔教但丁怎样对待那些动机肤浅和缺乏高贵情感的人所说的那样："别谈他们，只管看着他们，从旁走过便好。"[1]

1　出自但丁《神曲·地狱篇》第三首诗。

然后又过去了三个月。挂在牢房门外边的行事历告诉我：五月到了。朋友们又来看我，我照样问起你的情况。我听说，你住在那不勒斯的别墅里，正准备出版一部诗集。会面快结束时，他们不经意地提起，你要把这诗集题献给我。这消息让我有想吐的感觉。我什么都没说，默默回到牢房，但内心充满鄙夷和冷笑。我心里想：你怎么敢未征得我同意，便把诗集题献给我？你怎么有这种胆子！你也许会说："在你盛名如日中天那时候，不是同意过我把早期作品题献给你吗？"没错，我是答应过。事实上，我愿意接受任何刚踏上艰难而美丽的艺术之路的年轻人向我致敬。对一个艺术家来说，来自任何人的致敬都是甜蜜的，但又以来自年轻人的致敬最为甜蜜。月桂树的花叶一被苍老的手摘下便会枯萎，只有年轻人有权为一位艺术家戴上桂冠，那是年轻生命的特权——但愿他们明白这个道理。我是答应过你，但彼一时也，此一时也。彼时我名扬四海，此时却贱若尘泥。你要晓得，"兴旺""欢乐"和"成功"这些东西有时会很粗糙，但"悲伤"是所有受造物中神经最敏感的一种。在整个思想或运动空间之中，没有任何动静不会引起"悲伤"以精准而猛烈的节奏与之共振。与之相比，那种用来测定电力流向的金箔片要粗糙多了。悲伤是一个伤口，除了爱之手，别的手一碰就会流血——

它被爱之手碰过之后还是会流血，但不是因为痛。

既然上次你可以通过旺兹沃思监狱的典狱长，征求我同意让你把我的信发表在"相当于我们英国的《双周评论》"的《法兰西信使报》上，这次为什么就不能通过雷丁监狱的典狱长，征求我同意让你把诗集题献给我呢？是不是因为我在前一次断然拒绝而你也拿我没辙（你清楚知道信的著作权不管过去或现在都完全属于我），这一次你却可以自行其是，等我得知和想要干涉时已为时太晚？我现在是个身败名裂的囚徒，单凭这一点，你若是想要在诗集扉页写上我的名字，就应该求我行个方便，赐你这份荣耀与特权。这才是对待蒙羞受苦之人的应有态度。

哪里有悲伤，哪里就有圣所。你总有一天会明白这个道理。在明白它之前，你对人生一无所知。罗比和与他相同品性的人都懂得这道理。我记得，我被两个警察从监狱带到破产法庭那天，罗比等在那条长长和阴森的走廊里。当我戴着手铐低着头从他身边走过时，他当着一大群人的面掀起帽子向我致意。这个贴心的小举动让本来闹哄哄的走廊顿时鸦雀无声。其实，比这更小的善良举动便足以让人进天国了。正是本着这种精神、这种爱心，圣徒才会跪下为穷人洗脚，或是俯身亲吻麻风病人脸颊。我后来没有向罗比重提这事，所以直到现在还不知道，他有没有意识到我曾把他掀帽致意的动作看进眼里。我当然感谢他，但这种感谢是无法用语言道尽的。所以我就把它珍藏在心里，当成暗暗欠下的一笔债务，对此我高兴地想，那是一笔我不可能还清的债务。我把它存在心里，以我的许多泪水作为没药与肉桂，让它永不腐朽和永葆芬芳。当"智慧"已经于我无益，当"哲学"已经于我无助，当别人试着用来安慰我的名言警句在我嘴巴里尝起来犹如粪土之时，罗比毫不起眼的小小举动却为我开启了所有怜悯的水井。它让沙漠得以盛开玫瑰，让我可以走出被孤单放逐的苦涩，得以与世界那颗受伤和破碎的大心和谐一致。哪一天，当你不单单能明白罗比的举动有多美，还明白了它对我有多么重大的意义时，你兴许就能悟明你原应本着何种精神和态度来央求我同意你把诗集题献给我。

不过你猜得没错：我无论如何不会同意接受你的题献。如果你来征询我，我固然会感到高兴，但为了你着想，我还是会不顾你的感受，拒绝所请。因为，一个年轻人的第一本诗集应该像是春天初绽的花朵，一如莫德林学院草坪上的山楂树花或卡姆纳野地里的樱草，不应该让它背上一出可怕悲剧和可怕丑闻的沉重包袱。如果我答应让我的名字出现在诗集的最前面，那将是艺术上的一大败笔。它会让整部作品散发出一种不对劲的气氛，而对现代艺术而言，

"气氛"关系重大。现代生活复杂而具有相对性，这是它的两大特征。要表现第一个特征，我们需要创造一种讲究幽微对比、富有暗示性和视角独特的氛围；要表现第二个特征，我们需要创造一个背景。这就是何以雕塑不再是一种表现派艺术（representative art），而音乐则成了表现派艺术。这也是何以文学从过去直至永远都会是最高的表现派艺术。

你应该让你的小诗集散发出西西里和阿卡迪亚的田园风味，而不是弥漫着被告席和牢房的混浊恶臭。你的题献之举还不只是一种艺术品位的败笔，从其他角度看它一样完全不恰当。它会显得你是在延续你在我被捕前后的行为举止。它会予人一种印象，让人觉得你是在假装勇敢，是你在羞耻街巷[1]贱买贱卖那种勇气的一个示例。就你我的友谊而言，复仇女神已经把你我像拍苍蝇那样拍得稀巴烂。在我身陷囹圄时把诗集题献给我，实在像是一种自作聪明的耍嘴皮子。耍嘴皮子是你从前写那些可怕书信时的一种绝活，你乐在其中又引以为傲——我由衷希望，你已经改掉这种坏习惯。你把诗集题献给我将不会产生你希望的那种严肃而美好的效果（我确信这就是你的动机）。要是你曾询问过我，我一定会劝你把出版诗集的计划延后一

---

1 "羞耻街巷"指花街柳巷。

点实行；又如果你不愿接受这劝阻，我就会建议你先是以匿名方式出版，等到赢得一些知音的赏识（知音的反应是唯一值得我们在乎的），才转过身来对世界说："你们赞叹的花朵就是我栽种的。现在，我要把它们题献给一个被你们视为贱民和弃儿的人，以表达我的爱、尊敬和钦佩。"但你选了错误的方法和错误的时机。爱是讲策略的，文学是讲策略的，而你对两者都不敏感。

　　我这么长篇大论，无非是想让你充分明白，何以我在得知你的计划后，会马上写信给罗比奚落你，又请他抄录一份转寄给你，务求终止你的计划。我会那样做，是因为觉得最后关头已经到了，再不做些什么让你对自己干过的事有所悟明，恐怕就来不及了。盲目如果过甚会让人变得丑陋古怪，而没有想象力的心性如果迟迟得不到唤醒、没做些什么补救的话，也会完全变成化石，变得彻底无感无知。这样的人也许还能吃、还能喝、还能寻欢作乐，但灵魂会彻底死掉——就像但丁笔下的布兰卡·德奥里亚[1]那样。我的信似乎适时转寄到你的手上。就我判断，它带给你的震撼有如五雷轰顶，因为你在给罗比的回信中说我的信让你"丧失了所有思考和表达能力"。显然真的是那样，

1　布兰卡·德奥里亚是《神曲·地狱篇》里的角色。

不然你不会只想到写信向令堂告状。不用说，令堂出于她一贯的盲目（她从不知道什么才叫真正对你好，也从而铸成了她自己和你的不幸），当然又是百般安慰你，把你哄回到原来的自我感觉良好状态。在我这方面，她则是告诉我的一些朋友，我信中那些严厉措辞让她"非常恼怒"。事实上，她不只对我的朋友说过这种话，还对不是我朋友的人说过（毋庸说，这类人的人数要多得多）。我还听说（消息来源是一些和你与你家非常友好的人），有不少人本来对我这么杰出的天才落得这么不堪的处境寄予同情，但经令堂那么一说，这些同情已烟消云散。他们说："啊，他早先想把人家的慈父弄进监牢里不成，现在又转过来把这失败归咎于人家那无辜的儿子。真是活该受人贱视！"依我之见，当令堂听别人提到我时，即便她不愿出于让我家破人散（不小的一份责任）表示难过或后悔，更好的做法也毋宁是保持沉默。至于你嘛，难道你现在不认为，你更好的做法不是写信向她告状，而是直接写信给我，鼓起勇气说出任何你想说的话？我写那封信已经是快一年前的事了，你不可能一整年都"丧失了所有思考和表达能力"吧？那你为什么没写信给我呢？你从我的信里看得出来，你的举止态度伤我有多深，让我有多生气。还不只是这样。从前，我常常告诉你，你总有一天会把我毁了。你听了只是笑。在你我交往之初，埃德温·利维[1]看见我老是被你拿来当挡箭牌、老是得为你的"牛津灾厄"（姑妄这样称之）出力甚至出钱，不惜花了整整一小时劝我不要与你来往（当时我为你的事找他商量和帮忙）。后来，我在布拉克内尔把那次长谈的内容给你说了，你的反应又是笑。更后来，当我告诉你，就连那个落得在被告席站我旁边的不幸年轻人[2]也曾不止一次提醒我，你比我认识的任何普通阶层的毛头小子还要致命，你的反应还是笑（差别只是笑得没那么开怀）。当我一些较审慎或交情不够深厚的朋友因你我的事而规劝我或离开我时，你知道之后是不屑地笑。当令尊第一次写信给你攻讦我，而我说我不想当你俩互斗的马前卒并且被祸及时，你也是笑——这一次是狂笑。然而，我预言过的每件事后来都成真了。所以你没借口说不知道事情会是那样演变。你为什么不给我写信呢？是因为胆怯吗？是因为麻木不仁吗？到底是什么原因？我是生气，也在信中对你大发脾气，但这只让你更有理由回信。因为，如果你认为我的信公道，固然应该回信；而如果你认为我的信有一丁点

1　根据埃德温·利维写给王尔德的两封信（现藏洛杉矶加州大学克拉克图书馆），我们有理由猜测利维是个放债人。

2　指艾尔弗雷德·泰勒（Alfred Taylor），他在王尔德的两次受审中同列被告，最后也是以有伤风化罪被判刑两年。据说他为王尔德介绍过若干年轻人。

不公道，也应该回信反驳。我等着一封信。即便你不顾念我的往日浓情、不顾念我那不畏千夫所指的爱、不顾念我上千个未获亲善回应的亲善举动和上千笔你未还的恩惠人情，那么，至少是基于道义（这是所有人类纽带中情感最贫瘠的一种），你也应该写信。你不要推说，不写信是因为你以为狱方只允许我收家人写来谈正事的信。你再清楚不过，罗比每三个月便会写来一封信，告诉我一点文学界的动态。没有什么要比他的信更具魅力：这些信机智、一针见血、轻松幽默，是货真价实的信。它们就像是一个人面对另一个人说话，不啻法国人所说的 causerie intime（亲密交谈）。信的内容以各种旁敲侧击的方式表现出罗比对我的拳拳服膺：一会儿衬托出我的判断力，一会儿衬托出我的幽默感，一会儿衬托出我的审美眼光，一会儿衬托出我的文化素养。他的信以一百种含蓄的方式提醒我，我一度在许多人眼中是艺术风格的仲裁者之一，在有些人眼中甚至是最高仲裁者。罗比显示了他既懂爱的策略，又懂文学的策略。他的信是我和那个美丽而不真实的艺术世界的小小信使——我一度是那世界的霸主，而要不是我被诱入一个不完整的生命（这生命感情粗糙残缺，有着不会辨味的嗜好、无底的欲望和不知方向的贪婪），本来也会继续是那世界的霸主。不过，不管我有多喜欢知道文艺界的消息，你想必猜得到，我会更想知道（哪怕只是出于最普通的好奇心）你的事而不是知道艾尔弗雷德·奥斯汀[1]准备出一部诗集，或是斯特里特开始为《每日纪事报》（*Daily Chronicle*）写剧评，或是那个连念篇颂词都会结结巴巴的梅内尔太太被推荐为新一任的诗风定向人[2]。

唉，若换成你正在坐牢（我不会假设是我害你坐牢的，因为那样太可怕了，我承受不了。我假设你是因为自己的过失而坐牢，例如误交损友、在情欲的泥淖中滑倒、信错人、爱错人，诸如此类），在这种情况下，你认为我会弃你于不顾，任由你在黑暗孤单中度日，不去想想办法（不管多微不足道的办法）减轻你的痛苦重担？难道你认为我不会设法让你知道，你受苦便是我受苦，你哭泣我便也会流泪？如果你成为阶下囚，受到所有人鄙夷，我便会用我的凄苦筑屋等你回来居住，并在里面贮存起人们拒绝给予你的一切（还百倍添加），以供你疗愈之用。要是什么原因让我没法接近你，被剥夺去与你相见的快乐，连透过铁窗看

1　艾尔弗雷德·奥斯汀（Alfred Austin）：一八九六年崛起的英国桂冠诗人。王尔德曾公开批评他的作品。

2　梅内尔太太（Mrs. Meynell）即爱丽斯·梅内尔，女诗人和小品文作家。一八九五年，帕特穆尔（Patmore）投书《周六评论》，推荐她出任新一任的桂冠诗人。帕特穆尔的诗集系列《家中天使》（*The Angel in the House*）歌颂爱情与婚姻，极为畅销。

看你的可怜样子都不行，我就会一年四季写信给你，盼着其中的只言片语可以把我百万分之一的爱意转达到你耳朵里。即便你拒绝收信，我照样不会少写，好让你知道，总是有些信等着你看。很多人都是这样待我的。他们每三个月便会写封信给我，或要求狱方批准他们写信。这些信都由狱方保管，等我出狱才会交到我手中。我知道有这些信存在，我知道写这些信的人是谁，我知道这些信里充满同情、怜惜和关爱，这就够了。我无须知道更多。但你的缄默让我心寒。你的缄默不是以"周"或"月"为单位，而是以"年"为单位。快两年了，即便像你这样快乐无忧、日子过得飞快、追逐欢乐追逐得直喘气的人，两年亦不会是一段很短的时间。你的缄默是站不住脚的，是无可辩解的。我知道你有一双泥足[1]。谁比我更清楚呢？我写过这么一句警句：正是泥足让一座金身珍贵。写它的时候，我心里想着的就是你。但你为自己塑造的形象并不是有泥足的金身。使用大路上被两角四蹄畜生踩过的烂泥，你为自己塑出一个与本尊像得十足的形象，以至不管我曾对你有过什么秘密向往，如今都不可能有鄙夷和不齿之外的感受。别的事就不提了，光是你的无动于衷、你的明哲保身、你的麻木

---

1 "泥足"（feet of clay）在英语俚语中指"隐藏着的缺点"。

不仁、你的谨小慎微都让我在落难当时和之后加倍神伤。

其他被扔到牢里的苦命人虽也被夺去世间种种美好事物，但他们至少是安全的，用不着再担心各种最要命的明枪暗箭。他们可以躲在牢房的阴暗角落里，以他们自身的耻辱作为避难所，得以不受打扰地受苦。但我的情形不同。一波接一波的悲苦不断敲击牢房的门，要把我够着。监狱把大门敞开，任由它们进来。我的朋友没几个获准见我，我的仇敌却通行无阻。我两次被带到破产法庭公开亮相，又两次在众目睽睽之下转移监狱，忍受着嘲笑目光难以言传的羞辱。后来，死亡信使又给我捎来消息。他走了之后，我陷入完全的孤单，在无人安慰的情况下独自承受不可承受的丧母之痛，被悲恸和愧疚吞噬（至今一想到家母还是如此）。然后，未等这悲痛稍减，我又收到太太一封措辞严厉、刻薄和激烈的律师信。它让我备受贫穷的取笑和威胁。我受得了贫穷，也受得了更惨的情况，唯独受不了法律把我两个孩子判走[1]。这是我无限沮丧、无限痛苦、无限悲伤的一个源泉，而且也永将如此。法律竟敢那样判决，竟能那样地自作主张，认定我不适合与自己的子女在一起，这真是令人发指。与这个判决相比，坐牢的耻

---

[1] 王尔德的太太在一八九七年取得两个孩子的监护权。

辱根本不算什么。我嫉妒其他和我一起在监狱院子放风的囚犯。他们的子女肯定在等着他们出狱、盼着他们回家，决计要好好孝顺父亲。

穷人要比我们更有智慧、更仁慈和更能将心比心。在他们眼中，坐牢是一出悲剧、一种不幸、一场灾祸，应该寄予同情。谈到谁坐牢的时候，他们只会说那人"正在倒霉"。这是一句满含爱之智慧的话语。但对我们这个阶层的人来说，事情是别的样子。我们认为牢狱会把一个人变为贱民，我或像我这样的人会被认为几乎没有权利享受空气和阳光，我们的出现会污染别人的快乐，我们重出社会之后会变成不受欢迎的人物。重新出现在月光之下[1]不是我们的权利。就连我们的子女也会被带走，使我们与人类最可爱的联结被斩断。哪怕我们的儿子还活着，我们仍注定孤独终老。亲情本是唯一可以疗愈和帮助我们，唯一可以给我们受伤的心止痛和为我们痛苦灵魂带来平安的事物，我们却被拒绝获得它。

让一切雪上加霜的是一件不起眼却铁一般的小事：你

---

[1] 在《哈姆雷特》第一幕第四场，哈姆雷特看见父亲的鬼魂之后，问道："为什么你长眠的骸骨不安于坟茔，为什么安葬着你遗体的坟墓张开它的大理石两颚，把你吐出来？为什么你这已死的尸体要全副甲胄，重新出现在月光之下，使黑夜变得这样阴森，使我们这些为造化所玩弄的愚人感到不可思议的恐怖，心惊胆战？"

的行径和你的缄默。通过你做过和你应做而没做的，你让我漫长牢狱生涯的每一天更加难熬。就连狱中的伙食也因你的态度而更难下咽了。你让我的饭变苦，让我的水变臭。你让本该帮我分担的悲苦倍增，把本该帮我减轻的痛苦刺激为巨大创痛。我毫不怀疑你不是故意的。我知道你不是故意的。你会那样，纯粹是因为"你个性里真正致命的缺陷：完全缺乏想象力"。

但说到底，我还是必须原谅你。我不得不如此。我写这信的目的，不是把怨尤注入你的心里，而是从我心中摘除怨尤。为我自己着想，我必须原谅你。一个人不能永远在胸口养着一条小毒蛇，不能每夜都醒来往自己的灵魂里栽种荆棘。只要你帮我一点点忙，我要原谅你就一点也不难。从前，不管你对我做了什么，我总是原谅你。那对你一点好处都没有。只有没有任何瑕疵成分的人才原谅得了别人的罪。但现在因为我身处耻辱和不光彩的境地，情形便不同了，我的原谅对你会变得意义重大。你总有一天会悟明的。但不管你是早悟明或晚悟明，是很快悟明或永不悟明，摆在我前面的道路都是清楚的。我不能容许你因为毁了像我这样一个人而一辈子背负着良心的包袱。这包袱有可能会让你变成行尸走肉，或是让你惨痛不堪。我必须把它从你那儿挪走，往自己肩上扛。

Suffering

is

permanent

obscure

痛 苦 是 一 个 长 长 的 瞬 间 ， 它 不 知 道 何 谓 季

and

dark

And

has

the

nature

of

Infinity

我必须告诉自己，即便你或令尊现在强大一千倍，也不可能毁得了我这样一号人物；毁了我的是我自己；除了我自己，没有人（不管大人物还是小人物）毁得了我。我很愿意这样告诉自己。我正在努力如此，哪怕你目前可能看不出来。但请想想看，既然我能这么毫不留情地指控你，那我对自己的指控又会是何等的毫不留情。你对我的加害固然可怕，但远远及不上我对自己的加害。

我曾是这时代的艺术文化象征。我刚成年便意识到这一点，后来又使我的时代意识到这一点。很少人能在有生之年便能企及如此高的地位，并受到如此广泛的公认。一个不凡人物的不凡即使被人看出，也通常由后来世代的历史学家或评论家看出，其时，那人及其时代早已远去。我却不同，我体会到自己的不凡，后来又叫别人体会到。

拜伦也是其时代的象征人物，但他象征的是该时代的激情和这种激情的委顿。我象征的事情要更为崇高、更为恒久、更为事关重大，范围也更为广阔。

诸神几乎赐给了我一切。我拥有天赋、显赫家世、崇高地位、卓越智慧和知性冒险精神。我让艺术变成一门哲学，让哲学变成一门艺术。我改变了人们的心灵和事物的颜色。我的所言所行无不使人称奇：在我手中，最客观的一门艺术形式，即戏剧，被改造成像是抒情诗或十四行诗那样的个人表达形式，而且题材变得更为开阔、人物变得更为丰富；不管是戏剧、小说、有韵诗、散文诗、含蓄的对话录或奇想的对话录，无不绽放崭新形态的"美"。在"真"这个方面，我指出"假"也是一种"真"，点出"真"与"假"不过是知性表现的不同形式。我把艺术奉为最高真实，把人生视为只是虚构的一种。我唤起这个世纪的想象力，让它环绕着我创造出神话和传奇。我凭一句妙语便可概括所有思想体系，凭一句警句便可涵盖天地万有。

但除这些以外，我又干了一些迥然不同的事。我任自己受到诱惑，长时间掉入糊里糊涂和声色犬马的魔咒。我以当一个漫游者（flâneur）、一个花花公子、一个时尚人物为乐。我任自己被一些小格局和目光如豆的人围绕。我成了自己才华的挥霍者，我虚掷无价的青春，图的只是一种古怪的快感。因为厌倦了老是站在高峰，我蓄意跳入深渊，寻找新的刺激。就像我在思想领域好作吊诡之语，我在行为领域也好作乖张之举。但说到底，欲望是一种残疾或疯狂，又或两者兼是。我变得不顾别人的感受，只图自己快活，快活完便拍拍屁股走开。我忘记了，日常生活最小的一个行为都足以培养或瓦解我们的品格。所以，不管我们在暗室里干过什么勾当，都总会有一天由自己站在屋顶上大声说出去，弄得尽人皆知。我不再是自己的主人，我不再是自己灵魂的船长，也不再认识它了。我任由你支配我，任由令尊吓唬我，最终让自己颜面丢尽。如今，我一无所有，唯一剩下的只有彻底的谦卑。在你那里，也同样只剩下一样东西：彻底的谦卑。所以，你最好还是从云端下来，与我在尘泥中一道学习这功课。

我被关在牢里快两年了。出于热爱自由的天性，铁窗生涯让我陷入狂乱的绝望，让我被惨不忍睹的悲苦淹没，让我狂怒又无计可施，让我怨天怨地，让我痛苦得大哭，但有时又会忧伤到发不出声音。因为尝遍了人间每种可能的苦涩情绪，我比华兹华斯本人对他这两句诗还要体会更深：

> 这痛苦恒久、模糊而暗黑
>
> 直像无边无际[1]

我固然有时会觉得受这无边痛苦是活该，并为此觉得痛快，却无法忍受它们毫无意义。然后，我慢慢发现我心性里藏着某种东西，并由此得知，普天下没有无意义的事情——更不用说是痛苦。那东西就像野地里的一个宝藏，深藏在我的本性里。它就是谦卑。

1　出自华兹华斯的唯一一出戏剧《边界人》（*The Borderers*）第三幕。

这是我唯一还剩下的财产，也是最美好的一项财产：它既是我已得到的终极发现，又是一个崭新发展的开端。因为它直接来自我自己，所以我知道它来到的时间恰恰好。它不可能早早到来，或是晚点才来。如果它是由别人告诉我的，我会拒绝接受。但既然它由我自己找到，我就想保有它。我必须如此。这东西包含着生命的要素，可以带给我新生[1]（Vita Nuova）。天地万有就数它最为奇特。它既是你给不了别人的，也是别人无法从你那儿拿走的。想要得到它，唯一的办法是把你拥有的一切通通割舍。失去一切之后，你自会知道自己拥有它。

既然悟明了我内心有谦卑，我便清楚知道自己有什么该做——应该说是必须做。对，我是说"必须"。用这个词语的时候，我不是暗示有什么外来的制约或命令，要我非那样做不可。任何外来的制约或命令我概不接受。现在的我比以往任何时候更加是名个人主义者。除非得自于我的内心，否则没有任何东西在我眼中有价值。出于天性的驱使，我要寻找一种崭新的自我实现方式。这是我唯一关心的。而为了自我实现，我非做不可的第一件事便是摆脱对你的任何怨念。

---

1 "新生"是但丁一本诗集的名字。

我已经一文不名，彻底无家可归。可世界上还有更惨的事呢！老实说，比起继续对你或对世界心怀怨恨，我宁可出狱后开开心心沿街乞讨。即便我无法从富有人家乞讨到什么，也总会从贫穷人家要到一点东西。身家殷实的人往往贪婪吝啬，反观财富不丰厚的人总是乐于分享。只要心中保存着爱，我就毫不介意夏天睡在凉爽的草地上，冬天睡在温暖的干草堆或大谷仓里的阁楼里。身外之物对我已毫无意义。由此你足以看出，我已达到的是多么浓烈的一种个人主义。又也许我尚未达到，只是身在途中——因为那毕竟是一条漫漫长路，况且"凡我走过之处皆荆棘丛生"[1]。

　　我当然知道自己不会落得要在大路上行乞，而如果我会于夜晚躺在凉爽的草地上，也只是为了给月亮写十四行诗。我出狱那天，罗比将会在监狱大门外等着我，而他代表的不只有他自己，还有许多其他人的关爱。我相信，在他们的资助下，我至少可以过上一年半的闲暇生活。那样的话，我即便写不出一些好书，也起码可以读些好书。还有比这更大的人生乐事吗？之后，我希望可以重振我的创作力。但假若事情完全是另一个样子（即假若我在世间不剩一个朋友，假若没有一户人家只是出于同情而收留我，

────────────

1　语出王尔德自己的剧作《无足轻重的女人》。

假如我不得不穿着破斗篷沿门托钵），我仍然会不以为意。因为只要我心里没有怨恨、芥蒂和鄙夷，我便比任何身穿锦缎和被恨心弄得病恹恹的人更能平静而自信地面对人生。届时我亦将毫无困难地原谅你。不过，要让我有这份荣幸，你必须先切感到自己想要得到原谅。当你真的想要它之时，自会发现它正等着你。

毋庸说我的任务不止于此，真是只有这个任务的话反而好办多了。我必须做的事还有很多。有更陡的山等着我爬，有更幽暗的谷地等着我穿过。这一切我必须独力完成，无论是"宗教""道德"还是"理性"都帮不上忙。

"道德"帮不了我。我生来便是个反律法主义者（antinomian）。我是为了打破成规而生，不是为了循规蹈矩。另一方面，虽然我不认为任何行为有对错可言，却认为一个人让自己变成什么样子有对错之分。学会这道理可让你受益匪浅。

"宗教"帮不了我。别人都信仰些看不见的东西，但我只信仰摸得着和能看见的。我的诸神是住在用手建成的殿堂中，而我的教义是在实际经验范围内打造完整。但这教义也许太完整了：因为就像许多把他们的天国建造在地上的人一样，我除了看见天国的美，还看见地狱的恐怖。我难得想起宗教，但每逢想起，我都觉得自己会乐于建立一个由无法信仰宗教者所组成的教团——你大可以称之为"无天父者兄弟会"。这兄弟会也有祭坛，但祭坛上不点蜡烛；也有教士，但"平安"在他心里没有位置；也有圣餐礼，但用的是没祝圣过的饼和空葡萄酒杯。一切为"真"的东西都必须自成一个宗教。所以，不可知论者[1]就像信徒一样，需要敬拜仪式。它会栽种自己的殉教者，收割自己的圣徒，天天为上帝的藏头露尾之举献上赞美。但不管是信仰还是不可知论，都必须发自内心，它的各种象征符号必须由我们自创。只有具有灵性之物才创造得出自己的形式。如果我无法从内心找到它的奥秘，便将永远找不着它。凡不是我们本已具有的将永远不会来找我们。

"理性"帮不了我。它告诉我，判我有罪的法律是错误和不公不义的，让我受苦的监狱制度是错误和不公不义的。然而，出于某种理由，我必须把这两者看成正确和公义的。就像艺术只关心某一物在某一时刻与自身的关系，品格的精神演化亦复如是。我必须让发生在我身上的一切变得有益。硬板床、难吃的伙食、扯棉絮的硬绳子（它会把人的手指磨得又痛又麻）、从早到晚像奴隶般的劳动、就像出于必要似的各种规章和叱喝、丑怪得不堪入目的囚

---

1 "不可知论者"指那些认定人无法断定上帝存在与否的人，有别于无神论者。

衣，还有孤单和屈辱——我必须把这一切转化为一种灵性的体验。身体受过的每一项苦无一不是我必须拿来用作提升灵魂的灵性之资。

我希望有朝一日能做到这个：不带一丝忸怩造作地告诉别人，我人生有两大转折点，一是家父把我送到牛津念书，一是社会把我扔进监狱。我不会说它们是能够发生在我身上的最大美事，因为那听起来太苦涩了。我宁愿这样说（或者听到别人这样说我）：在"性偏离"这事情上，我只是我所处时代的典型产儿，而因为性偏离，我把我生命中的美事变成了恶事，又把生命中的恶事变成了美事。不过，其实我怎样说自己或别人怎样说我都无关紧要。要紧的是，为了让我剩余无多的人生不致残缺和不完整，我有一个非执行不可的任务：把加诸我身的一切吸收到自己内心，不带抱怨、恐惧和勉强地加以接纳，使它们成为我的一部分。最要不得的缺点莫过于浮浅。凡经过悟明的都会归正。

刚被关进监牢的时候，有些人劝我设法忘了自己是谁。真听他们的我就完了。我后来之所以找到些许安慰，就是因为我悟明了自己是谁。可现在又有另一些人劝我，待我出狱后，我应该设法忘记自己坐过牢。我知道这种忠告同样要命。因为如果我真的照他们说的去做，那将意味着我会被一种不可忍受的耻辱感永远萦绕，意味着那些对我和任何人来说都意义重大的事物——太阳和月亮之美、四季的风姿、黎明的乐音、深夜的岑静、穿过叶隙的雨水、悄悄爬上草地使之泛出一片银光的露珠——将会在我眼前蒙上污垢，失去它们的疗愈力量、失去它们传达喜乐的力量。抵赖过去就是在阻遏自己成长，否认过去就是逼自己的生命说谎。那不啻灵魂的自我否定。因为就像我们的肉体什么都吸收（既吸收神父或圣灵净化过的东西，也吸收世俗和不洁的东西，然后把它们通通转化为力与美，转化为矫健的肌肉和漂亮的皮肤，转化为头发、嘴唇和眼睛的线条和色泽），灵魂也是如此。灵魂一样有摄取营养的功能，可以把本来卑贱、残忍、下作的东西转化为高尚的思想和高雅的情怀。犹有进者，灵魂还经常透过原为亵渎和摧毁而设的事物，把自己最完美的样子显现出来。

我必须坦然接纳我是一座普通监狱里的一名普通囚犯的事实。你听起来可能会奇怪，但我必须教会自己的一点是：不要以坐牢为耻。我必须把坐牢视作惩罚而加以接纳，因为一个人若是耻于接纳惩罚，他的罚就是白受了。在我的那些罪名中，当然有许多是我没做过的，但其中也有很多是我做过的。况且，我人生还做过更多该被定罪而未被定罪的事。我在前面说过，诸神生性古怪，除了会用我们的陋习恶癖来加害我们，还会利用我们的温良恭俭来惩罚我们。基于此，我必须接纳一个事实：人不只会因行恶受罚，还会因行善受罚。我毫不怀疑人因行善受罚是合理的，因为它可以帮助人悟明自己所做过的事，让人不致太自负。如果我能不以受惩罚为耻（这是我希望做到的），那我就能自由地思考、行走和生活了。

许多人出狱后会把他们的牢房带到外面的世界，把它当成一个秘密的耻辱藏在心底，最后落得像是中毒的动物般，爬到某个洞里死在里面。他们会那样做真是可悲，而社会把他们逼成那样真是大错特错。社会自认为有权对个人施加可怕的惩罚，可身上偏偏又具备那个最要不得的缺点（对，就是浮浅），以至于不能悟明自己干了些什么。所以，每当它惩罚过一个人之后，就撒下他不管，不知道它这是在对该人负有最高责任那一刻遗弃了他。这种回避真是丢脸啊，就像是还不起债的人避见债主，或是对别人造成无可补救的伤害后一走了之。要是我能悟明我何以会被惩罚，而社会也悟明它何以要施加惩罚，那双方就会互不相欠，不再有怨或恨。

我当然知道，在某种意义上，我要做到这个比别人困难得多。与我被关在同一座监狱的盗贼和社会弃儿很多都是苦命人，但他们在很多方面都比我幸运。不管当初他们是在灰色的城市还是在绿色的乡村犯案，都只算是小地方。所以，他们出狱后若想找个无人知道他们底细的地方住下，要走的路程顶多是一只鸟从黎明飞到黄昏的距离。但对我而言，"世界缩小到只有巴掌大"[1]，不管去哪里都会看到刻有我名字的石头。因为我不是从寂寂无闻跌入一时的恶名，而是从一种永恒的荣耀跌进一种永恒的耻辱中。有时我会觉得，老天爷是要借我显示一个道理（假如还有必要显示的话）：从名满天下到臭名远播只是一步之遥——甚至不到一步。

不错，处处都会有人认出我，对我的底细了如指掌。但这对我不无好处。因为那将迫使我必须重振我作为艺术家的雄风，而且是愈快愈好。只要我能够再次创作出美妙的作品（哪怕只是一部），就可以挡掉恶毒鬼的明骂、胆小鬼的暗讽，把冷言冷语者的舌头连根拔出。如果世界要为难我（这是一定的），那我也要为难世界。人们必须调整他们对我的态度，必须在论断我的同时也论断他们自己。毋庸说，我说的"人们"不是泛指所有人。我现在唯一在乎的是艺术家和受过苦的人，也就是那些知道何谓"美"和知道何谓"悲伤"的人。我也不会对世界索要些什么。我唯一关心的是我自己对人生的心态，而我感觉，不

---

1 出自《无足轻重的女人》第四幕。

以自己受过惩罚为耻是我必须首先做到的一件事。这是为我的完美着想，也是因为我太不完美了。

那之后，我必须学习怎样过得快乐。我一度凭本能知道"快乐"为何物，或自以为知道。从前，我心中总是春意盎然。我的性情气质与快乐同声相应。我让欢愉在我的生活中排满，就像是把葡萄酒斟满到杯沿。但如今，我从一个全新的立足点看待人生，甚至连想象快乐也变得极端困难。记得在牛津念书的第一学期，我读了佩特的《文艺复兴》（这书一直对我的人生发挥着奇特的影响力），得知但丁在他的《神曲》里把那些动辄愁眉苦脸的人安排在地狱最底层。接着我跑到学院图书馆，找出《神曲》同一段落，读到这些总是愁眉苦脸的人唉声叹气地说：

> 从前，在阳光灿烂
>
> 喜气洋洋的甜美空气中
>
> 我们总是愁颜不展[1]

我知道教会谴责懒散忧郁（accidia），但这种主张让我觉得匪夷所思，怀疑它是不是就像"罪"的观念一样，

1　出自但丁《神曲·地狱篇》第七首诗。

是某个对真实生活一无所知的教士凭空杜撰的。我也不明白，既然但丁曾说过"悲伤让我们得与上帝重新婚配"[1]这话，又怎么会对那些溺于忧郁的人如此严厉。但当时我并未料到，忧郁将会成为我人生的最大诱惑之一。

关在旺兹沃思监狱那段日子，我真想死掉。那是我唯一的渴望。然后，等我在监狱医院躺了两个月，再被送至现在这所监狱之后，我发现自己身体愈来愈好。这使我怒不可遏，我决计要在出监的同一天自杀。但过了一段时间，随着这种坏情绪逐渐消退，我决定活下去，但要活得像个穿紫袍的国王那样，整天把郁郁不乐穿戴在身上。我决心不再微笑，决心不管走进哪栋屋子都要像是走进一户正在治丧的人家，不管与哪个朋友走在一起都要用沉重的步履显示心情的沉重。我要让他们知道忧愁才是人生的真谛，要用我的痛苦去让他们变得残缺。可现在我已经有了很不同的想法。对来探监的朋友拉长一张脸既缺风度又不厚道，因为这会逼得他们为了表示心有戚戚，把自己的脸拉得更长。我不应该在他们一坐下，便拿出苦药草和火葬场烤出的肉块招待他们。我必须学会欢愉和快乐之道。

上两次获准见客时，我努力在朋友面前表现得愉快，

1　出自但丁《神曲·炼狱篇》第二十三首诗。

以此作为对他们大老远从伦敦跑来看我的报答。我知道这只是一种小小的报答，但又肯定是最能让他们受用的报答。上周六，我和罗比会面了一小时，过程中我努力把真实感受到的高兴心情表现出来。有一件事情可以证明我这么做是对的：入狱以来第一次，我真正渴望活下去。

摆在面前的任务是那么多，我无论如何非得完成一小部分，若是那之前便死掉，可真是天大的悲剧。我已经明白艺术和人生应该往哪个方向发展，以及要如何才能达到完美。我渴望活下去，以便可以探索一个对我而言简直是全新的世界。你想要知道这个新世界是什么样子的吗？我想你猜得到它的样子，它便是这一两年来我生活在其中的那个世界。

换言之，悲伤和它曾教给我的一切便是我的新世界。我过去全是为了享受快乐而活。我回避悲伤和各种痛苦，我厌恶它们。我决计尽可能不理睬它们，视它们为一种不完美。它们在我的人生蓝图里毫无位置，在我的哲学里毫无地位。但家母一向把人生视为一个整体，过去常常向我引用歌德的几句诗（这诗是卡莱尔抄在他多年前送给家母的一本书上，译文大概也是出自他手笔）：

谁若不曾将悲伤和饭吞

谁若不曾中宵以泪洗面

无眠直至天明

谁便不会认识汝等：汝等上界之奇妙力量[1]

　　这也是高贵的普鲁士王后[2]受到拿破仑粗暴对待，遭放逐期间爱引用的诗句。家母在她烦恼重重的晚年常常引用这些诗句，但我拒绝承认或接受它们潜藏着的巨大真理。我不能理解这真理。我清楚记得，听到家母给我念这几句诗，我常常抗议说："我不想吃饭时和着悲伤吞下，不想以泪洗面度过一整夜、无眠等待更凄苦的天明。"我当时不知道这正是命运之神为我安排的命运，不知道我未来将会有一整年时间除以泪洗面外，几乎不能做别的。最近几个月，经过可怕的挣扎和困惑之后，我终于能够领悟到一些潜藏在痛苦核心里的道理。神职人员和只知照本宣科的人有时会把"痛苦"说成一种奥秘。但"痛苦"的确是一种神启。它会让你看见从前所未看见的。因为它，你会得到一个看待过去的全新的立足点。也因为它，你对艺术之为何物会产生知性和情感两方面的悟明，得到最清晰分

1　出自歌德的小说《威廉·麦斯特的学习时代》（*Wilhelm Meister's Apprenticeship*）第二卷第十三章。

2　指路易莎王后（1776—1810）。普鲁士在耶拿之战（1806年）败给拿破仑之后，她和丈夫威廉三世遭到放逐。

明的观照和最刻骨铭心的体会，不再像从前那样，只是凭直觉隐隐约约感受到。

我现已明白，悲伤既是人类所能企及的最高的情感境界，也是所有伟大艺术的本质和试金石。艺术家一直努力追求的，都是这样一种存在方式：在其中，灵魂与肉体浑然一体，不可分割；在其中，外在乃内在的表达；在其中，形式可以带来悟明。这种"存在方式"为数不少：有一阵子，青春和关注青春的艺术可以作为其一个典范；又有另一阵子，我们会觉得现代风景画[1]（以其对印象的敏感和观察入微，以其暗示外界事物寄寓着精神，以其心绪、调子和色泽的别具寓意）用图画方式体现出古希腊人那些完美雕像所展现的精神。音乐是这种"存在方式"中一个复杂的例子，而一朵花或一个小孩则是它的一个简单例子。但不管是人生还是艺术，悲伤都是其终极的本质。

欢乐与笑声的背后可能潜藏着急躁、粗俗、刻薄和麻木不仁，但悲伤的背后总是只有悲伤。与快乐不同，痛苦是从不戴面具的。艺术真理不系于本质观念（essential idea）与偶然存在（accidental existence）之间的符合：它不是影与形的相似，不是空谷回声，更不是水中月之于月亮

---

1 "现代风景画"应该是指印象派绘画。

本身，或水中纳西瑟斯[1]的倒影之于纳西瑟斯本人。艺术真理系于事物与自身的统一：系于以外在表达内在，系于灵魂的肉身化，系于精神充满于肉体。基于这个理由，没有任何真理要比悲伤更真。有时候我甚至觉得，悲伤是唯一的真理。其他事物有时只是眼睛或口腹的幻觉，唯一作用只在蒙蔽前者和撑坏后者。但悲伤是天地万象的建材：不管是一个小孩还是一颗星星的诞生，总是有痛楚伴随。

悲伤的奇特之处还不止于此，它还是一种高浓度和非同寻常的实在。我说过，我一度是这个时代的艺术与文化之象征，但与我一起待在这鬼地方的所有苦命人莫不是生命奥秘之象征。因为生命之奥秘就是"痛苦"，它潜藏在万事万物的背后。有生之初，我们总是把"乐"放得很大，也把"苦"放得很大，所以必然会把所有憧憬导向快乐，追求的不只是"一两个月光吃蜂蜜过活"[2]，还是一辈子都不吃别的，光吃蜂蜜。殊不知，我们这样做其实是让自己的灵魂挨饥受饿。

记得有一次我曾和一位心性最美好的人谈过这话题。这位女士[3]在我入狱前后所表现出的同情和高贵关爱都非

---

1 纳西瑟斯：古希腊神话中的美少年，喜欢对着湖水顾影自怜，后溺死在湖中，化为水仙花。

2 英国诗人斯温伯恩（Swinburne）的诗句。

3 "这位女士"指阿德琳·舒斯特（Adeline Shuster），她是一位德国银行家的千金，以为人慷慨和有慧眼著称。

笔墨所能形容。虽然她自己不知道，但在让我较能忍受自己不堪的处境一事上，她比世上任何人都更有帮助。这帮助不在于她做了什么，而只在她这个人本身。通过她之为她，你会知道何为人生的理想境界，而且会受感召走向那境界。她的灵魂足以让普通的空气变得芬芳，她流露的灵性和自然简单得就像阳光和海水。她了解"美"与"悲伤"是携手同行的，携带的也是相同的信息。我清楚记得，在一次谈话中，我对她说："光是伦敦一条小巷里的'痛苦'便多得足以证明上帝不爱世人；另外，只要什么地方有人悲伤（哪怕只是某个小孩因犯错被罚而哭），便足以让造化的整张脸被毁容。"没想到那位女士却说："你完全想错了。"但我不相信。当时我还没有达到她的境界，无法产生她持有的信念。但如今，我看出来了，这世界之所以会那么苦难深重，唯一的解释就是有某种"爱"的存在。我想不出其他可能的解释。那是我深信不疑的真理，因为如果真是如我说过的那样，"悲伤"是天地万象的基本建材，那打造天地万象的便只能是一双"爱"之手，因为除"悲伤"外没有别的途径能让人的灵魂（天地万象为之而设）达到至善至美的境界。快乐是给美丽以身体，但痛苦是给美丽以灵魂。当我说我"深信不疑"这真理时，口气未免太狂妄了。就像看见一颗完美的珍珠那样，我们从远处看见了上帝之城。它太神奇了，以至看起来像是一个小孩在夏日花一天时间便可到达。小孩是有可能，对我这种人和以我现在的处境来说却要另当别论。人可以在一瞬间悟明，但又常会在随后沉甸甸的十几小时里把它忘得一干二净。想要停留在"灵魂所能登上的高峰"[1]何其难哉。人可以谛思"永恒"，却只能在"时间"里缓慢移动——至于狱中的时间过得有多慢更是毋庸说了。更何况，在我的牢房里，或说在我心中的牢房里，疲惫和绝望总是会慢慢爬回来，它们是那么的倔强，以至你唯一能做的只是洒扫房屋迎接它们，就像是迎接一个不速之客或刻薄的主子。如果说它们像奴隶，那我就是奴隶的奴隶，而我们会落到这步田地则是出于阴差阳错或咎由自取。有一件事你目前可能难以相信，但它千真万确：比起我这个得以跪在牢房里刷洗地板展开一天的人，自由自在又无所事事的你会更容易学会谦卑。这是因为，牢狱生活（它包含数不清的剥夺和规章）会让人产生反抗心理。换言之，牢狱生活的最可怕之处不在于它会使人心碎（心本就是为破碎而设），而在于它会使心变成石头。有时我会觉得，如果我不拉长一张脸或不翘起嘴角表达我的不屑，就会挨不到天黑。然而，

1　出自华兹华斯的《远游》（ *The Excursion* ）一诗。

反抗心理会让人——借教会爱用的一句话来说——无法领受上帝的恩典。教会爱说这话良有以也，因为反抗心理会堵塞住灵魂的通风口，把天国的空气隔绝在外。尽管有这些难处，我还是必须在监狱里学会这功课，因为只要我的脚是走在正道上，只要我的脸是对准"那扇称为'美门'[1]的门"，我的心自然充满喜乐，用不着害怕常常在泥淖中摔倒，常常在迷雾中不辨东西。

这新生[2]（我是因为热爱但丁才这么称呼它）当然一点都不新。它不过是我从前的人生通过发展和演化所构成的延续。记得快要拿到学位的六月的某天早上，我和一位朋友沿着莫德林学院鸟声处处的小径散步时，我对他说："我要尝遍世界这个大花园里每一种树木的果实，要带着灵魂里的全部激情投入世界。"我真的这样做了，但我犯了一个错误：只让自己的活动范围局限在花园向阳的一边，而回避幽暗的一边。我回避"失败""不名誉""贫穷""悲伤""无望""痛苦"甚至"眼泪"，我回避从痛苦嘴唇说出的破碎言辞，回避会让人如走在荆棘丛里的"悔恨"，回避会让人自我谴责的"良知"，回避会惩罚人的"自轻自贱"，回避会让人选择麻布为衣和苦胆汁为饮的

1　语出《圣经·使徒行传》三章二节。原文为"那门名叫美门"。

2　参见第 87 页注释。

"大怵"——这一切都是我害怕的。但正因为决心不去认识它们，我最终被逼把它们逐一尝遍——确实，有几个月时间，除了这些饲料，我没有别的饲料。我一点不后悔曾经为享乐而活，我把享乐生活过到了极致，因为人做什么都应该追求极致。没有哪种形式的欢愉是我未体验过的。我甘于把我灵魂的珍珠投到一杯葡萄酒里；我循着笛声在开满樱草花的路上 [1] 行进；我过着畅饮蜂蜜的日子。但无止境地这样生活下去是不对的，因为那是画地自限，我必须跨越。花园的另一边同样有秘密等着我去发现。

当然，所有这些悟明在我的作品里早有预兆，早有伏笔。它们有些出现在《快乐王子》中，有些出现在《年轻的国王》中（特别是书中主教对那个跪地小孩所说的话："难道创造苦难的他不是比你更有智慧吗？"但写这话的当时，我只把它当漂亮话头）。《道林·格雷的画像》如果说是一件金衣裳，那"乐极生悲"这题旨就是缝起整件衣裳的紫丝线。它在《作为艺术家的批评家》（*The Critic as Artist*）一文里以许多不同的色调呈现，但在《人的灵魂》（*The Soul of Man*）里则表现得直截了当，一目了然。它是《莎乐美》里反复响起的主题基调之一，让此剧显得就像一出音乐作品。在我那

---

1 "开满樱草花的路上"指"寻欢作乐的生活"。

首散文诗里，它体现在那个从"过眼云烟快乐"铜像走出来的男人必须为自己铸一座"天长地久悲伤"的铜像。事情不可能是别的样子。在人生的每个瞬间，我们是谁这问题除取决于我们既有的那个"我"，还取决于我们将要成为的那个"我"。艺术是一种象征，因为人本身就是一种象征。

倘若我能彻底到达此境界，那就会是艺术家生命的终极体现。因为艺术家生命不过是自我的发展。在艺术家眼中，"谦卑"意谓他愿意坦诚接纳所有经验，一如"爱"不过是意谓他乐于向世人揭示灵与欲之美。佩特在《伊壁鸠鲁信徒马里乌斯》(*Marius the Epicurean*) 中企图调和艺术家生命和最深刻、最甜美及最严肃意义下的宗教性生命。但马里乌斯毕竟只是个旁观者：他固然是个理想的旁观者，因为他懂得用"相恰的感情谛视生命的风景"[1]（华兹华斯认为这就是诗人的真正目标），然而，由于只是个旁观者，马里乌斯太过关心神殿里的器皿是否好看，以至于看不见这神殿是一座悲伤之殿。

与之相比，基督的生命和艺术家生命的关系要密切和直接得多。我愉快地回忆起，在悲伤女神还没占去我的日日夜夜和把我绑在她车驾后面之前，我曾在《人的灵魂》一书

1　出自佩特的《鉴赏集》(*Appreciations*)。

中指出，谁要是想有个像基督般的人生，就必须完全和绝对地当他自己，而被我引为这类人的榜样的，除了山坡上的牧羊人和监牢里的囚犯，还有画家（对他们来说世界是一场盛会）和诗人（对他们来说世界是一首歌）。记得有一次我在巴黎某家咖啡馆对安德烈·纪德（André Gide）说过，虽然我对形而上学只有一丁点兴趣又对道德哲学兴趣全无，但柏拉图或基督说过的话都无一不可直接移植到艺术的领域，并借此得到最圆满的体现。我说的这条通则既新颖，又深刻。

在基督身上，我们除了看到个性与完美的紧密结合（这是古典主义与浪漫主义的真正分野，也使基督成为浪漫主义运动的真正先驱），也看到基督天性的基础与艺术家毫无二致，换言之，他的天性是以一种浓烈、火焰般的想象力为基础。基督在整个人类关系领域所悟出的那种"充满想象力的同理心"（imaginative sympathy），也是艺术家创造力的唯一诀窍。靠着这种同理心，基督体会得到麻风病人的疼痛、盲人的黑暗、只知追求享乐者的大不幸和富人的"贫穷"。你看出来了吗？当你在我病中写道"你只要不是站在基座上便会没啥意思。下次你生病我会马上闪人！"时，你和艺术家的真正气质或马修·阿诺德[1]所说的"耶稣之秘密"

1　马修·阿诺德：十九世纪英国诗人。

都天差地远。无论是艺术家气质还是耶稣之秘密，都会教你应该对别人的遭遇感同身受。如果你需要一句座右铭好晨昏温习，好叫自己愉快或痛苦，那就把以下两句话写在你家墙壁上，让太阳为它镀金，让月亮为它镀银吧："人饥己饥，人溺己溺。"要是别人问你这座右铭是什么意思，你就回答说，它意谓"基督的心灵与莎士比亚的脑袋"。

基督确实属诗人之畴。他的整个人性观都从想象力涌现，也只有透过想象力才能悟得。基督之于世人的意义，一如上帝之于泛神论者。他是第一个把不同种族视为一体的人。在他之前，神是诸神，人是诸人。唯有他看出，生命的山岳上只有"上帝"和"人"，而通过把同理心神秘主义化，他让自己成为两者的肉身，所以既自称"神子"，又自称"人子"。他比历史上任何人都更大地唤醒我们的惊奇意识（这是浪漫主义总是追求的）。他还有一个让我觉得近乎不可思议之处。明明只是个加利利乡下人，他却想象自己可以一肩挑起全世界的重担，即扛得起一切已发生和未发生的罪孽与苦痛：包括了尼禄、恺撒·博尔吉亚（Caesar Borgia）、教皇亚历山大六世和那个身兼太阳祭司的罗马皇帝[1]的罪孽，包括了那些名字为"群"（Legion）

---

1 这里列举的几个人都是历史上恶贯满盈的人物，最后一人是指罗马皇帝埃拉伽巴路斯（Elagabalus）。

并住在墓穴里的人[1]的痛苦，还包括那些被压迫的民族、工厂童工、窃贼、囚犯、社会弃儿的痛苦——他们被压迫得发不出声音，喑哑的呼求只有上帝听得到。但基督不只想象自己有能力一肩挑起全世界的重担，还真的做到了。现在，凡是能够与基督人格发生感通的人（哪怕他们不会向他的圣坛鞠躬或向他的祭司下跪），一样会神奇地发现，他们的罪不再丑陋，他们的悲伤中有美存焉。

我说过，基督属诗人之畴。这是真的，雪莱和索福克勒斯[2]都是他的同侪。但他的整个人生还是一首最神奇的诗：若论引起"悲悯与惊骇"[3]的效果，则全体希腊悲剧都难以望其项背。出于诗中主角的绝对纯洁无咎，整首诗的格局提高到了一个浪漫主义艺术的高度（"底比斯后人"固然也是遭遇悲惨，却是自作自受，所以他们的悲剧故事达不到这种高度[4]），也显示出亚里士多德在其论戏剧的著作中，认为观众不会忍受得了一个毫无过失的人罹祸之说是大错特错。不管是在埃斯库罗斯还是但丁笔下（两人都

---

1 "那些名字为'群'并住在墓穴里的人"指鬼，这里用了《圣经》的典故。

2 索福克勒斯：古希腊三大悲剧家之一。

3 王尔德这里是指涉亚里士多德在《诗学》提出的理论：悲剧可以引起观众的悲悯与惊骇之情，带来情绪上的净化。

4 指埃斯库罗斯的悲剧《七将攻打底比斯》达不到浪漫主义艺术的高度。《七将攻打底比斯》讲述底比斯国王俄狄浦斯两个儿子为了争夺王位，自相残杀而两败俱伤。

是善于触动恻隐之心的大师），是在莎士比亚（所有伟大艺术家中最有菩萨心肠的一位）笔下还是在凯尔特人的全部神话和传说中（它们总是透过泪眼显示世界的美好，总是把人生看作一朵花），我们都找不到什么在结合悲情的直接性和悲剧效果的崇高性一事上，可与"基督受难"的最后一幕勉强接近，遑论旗鼓相当。这一幕所包含的一切——基督与门徒共进最后的晚餐（座中已经有人悄悄把他出卖）；月夜在橄榄园的内心挣扎；那个假朋友走上前，用一个吻把他的身份泄露；那个他倚重为磐石的门徒在日出鸡啼前三次不承认认识他；他的绝对孤独、他的顺服、他的接纳一切；大祭司怒撕他的衣服；总督要水洗手，徒劳地想洗净沾满无辜者鲜血的双手和千古骂名；那悲怆的加冕典礼[1]（真是有史以来最震撼人心的其中一幕）；这个无辜之人当着他心爱母亲与门徒的面被钉上十字架；兵丁为分他的衣服而拈阄；他那留给世界最永恒象征的死亡；最后他被葬在一个富人的墓穴里，宛如王子般被抹上珍贵的香料和裹上埃及亚麻布——这一切，光从艺术的角度看便不能不让人心怀感激。每当想到早已失传的古希腊合唱曲，我的喜乐和敬畏之情便会油然而生。

---

1 《圣经·马太福音》记载，兵丁为戏弄耶稣，给他戴上一顶荆棘编的冠冕，又在他右手放一根芦苇，跪在他面前说："恭喜，犹太人的王啊！"

然而，基督的整个人生（哪怕圣殿里的幔子因他的死裂为两半，黑暗笼罩大地，石头滚落到墓穴前[1]）说到底还是一首田园牧歌，因为这人生把"悲伤"和"美"在意义和显相（manifestation）两方面都完全合为一体。想到基督，我们会觉得他像个与同伴在一起嬉笑的年轻新郎（他对自己用过这比喻），或者像个领着羊群穿过山谷寻找青草地或清溪的牧羊人，或者像个想用音乐为上帝之城筑城墙的歌者，或者像个爱心多到全世界都装不下的人。在我看来，他行的神迹就像春天降临一样怡人，也一样自然而然。我一点都不难相信这些神迹的真实性，一点都不难相信它们是他的人格魅力所造就的：光是他的出现便足以把平安带给受痛苦煎熬的灵魂；光摸一下他的衣服或手便可使人忘掉痛楚；他可以让一辈子都看不见生命奥妙的人眼睛明亮起来，宛如盲人复明，又可以让一辈子只听见靡靡之音的人第一次听见"爱"的声音（并感觉这声音"悠扬如阿波罗之琴音"[2]），宛如聋而复聪；他走来，邪恶的情欲便会遁走，让那些一辈子活在贫乏想象力里的人觉得自己就像死

---

1 《圣经·马太福音》记载，耶稣在十字架上断气之后："忽然，殿里的幔子从上到下裂为两半，地也震动，磐石也崩裂，坟墓也开了，已睡圣徒的身体，多有起来的。"

2 出自约翰·弥尔顿的《酒神之假面舞会》（Comus）。

而复生[1]；在山上，听他讲道的几千人因为太入神，全然忘了饥饿口渴和种种世间挂虑；酒宴上[2]，他说的话太过美妙动听，以至粗糙的菜肴尝起来犹如人间美味，清水尝起来犹如美酒[3]，而整个屋子也仿佛弥漫着甘松油的芬芳。

勒南（Renan）写的《耶稣传》堪称"第五福音书"，所以称之为《多马福音》[4]亦无妨。在这书里，他指出，基督的了不起之处是他死后受到的爱戴不下于生前。若说基督属诗人之畴，那他就是所有有爱心者的领队。他看出爱就是世界失落已久的钥匙（历代智者莫不致力于寻找这钥匙），也只有通过爱，人才到得了麻风病人的心里和上帝的跟前。

更重要的是，基督是最无可超越的个人主义者。就像"接纳一切经验"的艺术家的态度那样，谦卑只是一种显相。基督着眼的总是人的灵魂：他称之为"上帝的国"，又说它存在于每个人心里。他把它比作小东西：一粒种子、一撮酵母或一颗珍珠。这是因为，一个人只有抛下一切、舍弃所有习得的文化和非己之物，方能把自己的灵魂给活出来。

---

1 以上是在"解释"耶稣何以能使盲人看见、使聋人听见和使死人复活。

2 此处指涉耶稣以五饼二鱼喂饱五千人的神迹。

3 此处指涉耶稣在一个婚宴上把清水变为美酒的神迹。

4 《新约全书》只包含四部福音书，但相传耶稣另一个门徒多马也写了一部福音书。

出于意志上的倔强和个性上的桀骜不驯，在直到失去西里尔之前，我不管碰到再大的打击，都可以咬牙挺住。我失去了名声、地位、幸福、自由和财富，成了阶下囚和穷光蛋。但我仍有一件美好的东西，那就是我的长子。然而，法律突然把他从我这里夺了去。这打击让我魂飞魄散，不知所措。我跪倒在地，低着头，哭着说："一个孩子的身体就像主的身体——两者都不是我所配得的。"这一刻似乎拯救了我。我当下明白，我唯一能做的只是接纳一切。自此以后，我的心情（你听来无疑会觉得奇怪）变得比原来开朗得多。

理由当然是我已触及了我灵魂的终极本质。我曾多方面与它为敌，到头来它却像个朋友那样等着我。凡与自己灵魂发生接触的人都会变得像小孩一般单纯（基督也说过我们应该变得如此）[1]。可悲的是，能在死前"拥有自己的灵魂"[2]的人寥寥无几。正如爱默生说过："在任何人身上，最罕见的莫过于不从众的行为。"大部分人活得不像自己，他们的意见全来自别人，他们的生活是一种模仿，他们的激情是一种拾人牙慧。基督不只是无可超越的个人主义

---

[1] 《圣经·马太福音》记载，耶稣说过："我实在告诉你们，你们若不回转，变成小孩子的样式，断不得进天国。"

[2] "拥有自己的灵魂"语出阿诺德的《一个南方夜晚》（*A Southern Night*）一诗。

者，还是历史上第一位个人主义者。有些人把他说成普通的慈善家，就好像他只是十九世纪那些伪善的慈善家之一；另一些人把他说成利他主义者，就好像他不懂科学[1]，只知感情用事。但他既非慈善家，亦非利他主义者。他当然同情穷人、囚犯、下等人和处境悲惨的人，但他更同情的是有钱人、心硬的享乐主义者、挥霍自由而被物奴役的人和衣美服住华宅的人。在他看来，比起贫穷和悲伤，财富和快乐是更大的悲剧。至于说他是利他主义者这一点，又有谁比他更清楚，左右我们的是神召而非主观意愿，知道荆棘丛中不可能采得葡萄、蓟丛中不可能采得无花果。

他的信条不是要我们明确地把为别人而活定为人生目的，这不是其信条的基础。当他说"当宽恕仇敌"时，他不是要我们为仇敌着想，而是要我们为自己着想，另外也是因为爱比恨美。当他要求那个他喜爱的年轻官吏"变卖一切财产分给穷人"时，他也不是要对方为穷人着想，而是要对方为自己的灵魂着想（这灵魂已被万贯家财斫伤）。他的人生观与艺术家并无二致：凡艺术家都知道，出于自我完善的必要，诗人必须歌唱，雕塑家必须用青铜思考，画家必须以世界作为自己心绪的镜子。这法则确定不移，

1　十八、十九世纪的社会"科学"认为人人自利可以为整个社会带来最大利益。

一如山楂树必然于春天开花，麦子必然在秋收时节转为金黄，月亮必然盈亏往复。

另一方面，尽管基督未要求世人"为别人而活"，他却指出别人的生命与我们自己的生命毫无差异。就这样，他给了人一个向外延伸和硕大无朋的生命。自他以后，每个独立个人的历史都是世界历史[1]，或是可以被打造为世界历史。"文化"当然也强化了人的个性。艺术让我们的心灵变得具有多重性。那些具有艺术气质的人会与但丁一道被流放，由此认识到生命是杯苦酒和面前的阶梯何其陡峭[2]。他们有时固然得享片刻歌德所谓的那种宁静与从容，但又太清楚波德莱尔何以要对上帝这样呼求：

> 主啊，请赐我以力量和勇气
> 让我可以直视我的肉体与内心，不以为耻[3]

另外，他们从莎士比亚的十四行诗里抽绎出爱的真谛，并把它据为己有（这也许只是自找罪受）。复因为听过肖邦的某首夜曲、把玩过某些古希腊艺术品，或读过那

1　这里和以下大半段话王尔德都是在自况。
2　"面前的阶梯何其陡峭"一语出自但丁《神曲·天堂篇》第十七首诗。
3　出自波德莱尔《恶之花》（*Les Fleurs du Mal*）。

篇有关某个男性死者与某个女性死者爱得死去活来的故事，他们学会用一双新的眼睛望向现代生活。但不管他们想表现什么，作为艺术气质的同理心都必不可少。所以，不管是出之以文字还是色彩、出之以音乐还是大理石、出之以埃斯库罗斯戏剧里的彩绘面具还是某个西西里牧羊人的芦笛，基督和他的信息必然已被揭示过。

对艺术家来说，表达是他们能思考世界的唯一方式。对他们来说，哑的东西等于死物。基督却不是这个样子。挟着一种宽度和神奇程度让人惊畏的想象力，他把整个痛苦的无声世界纳为他的王国，使自己成为它的永恒喉舌。他在那些"被压迫得发不出声音"的人中间挑选门徒；他致力于成为盲人之眼、聋人之耳，要在那些舌头被绑住的人唇上发出呐喊；他的愿望是充当千千万万无处可求告的人的号角，好让他们的声音可以达于上天。出于他的艺术家天分，他知道"悲伤"和"痛苦"是体现"美"的不二法门，但又知道一个理念若是没有"肉身"便毫无价值，于是便把自己塑造为悲伤之人[1]的形象。这个形象后来让"艺术"为之倾倒，为之疯狂——从不曾有哪个希腊神祇能有此等成就。

因为尽管希腊诸神皮肤白皙粉嫩、四肢健壮矫捷，

1　旧约先知以赛亚曾预言上帝派来人间的弥赛亚将是一个"悲伤之人"（Man of Sorrows），即吃尽苦头的人。

内心却不怎么堂皇。阿波罗弧形的前额宛如初升于山顶的半轮旭日，双脚犹如银河彩凤，他却对玛耳绪阿斯（Marsyas）心狠手辣，又杀死尼俄柏（Niobe）[1]所有子女。别名帕拉斯（Pallas）的雅典娜虽有着一双钢盾似的眼睛，却对阿剌克涅（Arachne）毫不怜悯。天后赫拉唯一可傲人之处是她的排场和孔雀。至于众神之父本身，则太过垂涎凡间女子。古希腊神话中最有启发性的角色有两位（启发性分别在宗教和艺术方面）：一位是得墨忒耳（Demeter），但她是大地女神，不是奥林匹亚诸神之一；另一位是狄俄尼索斯（Dionysus），但他妈妈是会死的凡人，而且就是死在儿子诞生的那一刻。

然而，现实世界从它最卑微的底层产生一个远比普洛塞庇娜（Proserpina）之母或塞墨勒（Semele）之子[2]更神奇的人物。出身于拿撒勒的一家木匠行，这个人比任何神话或传说所创造过的人物都要伟大无数倍，命中注定要向世人揭示葡萄酒[3]的奥秘和百合花[4]的真美所在，而这不管

---

1 尼俄柏：希腊神话中底比斯王后。
2 "普洛塞庇娜之母"和"塞墨勒之子"分别指得墨忒耳和狄俄尼索斯。
3 耶稣在最后晚餐时曾举起杯说："这杯（葡萄酒）是用我的血所立的新约，你们每逢喝的时候，要如此行，为的是记念我。"
4 耶稣曾以百合花为喻，劝诫人们不要去吃喝穿戴忧虑："何必为衣裳忧虑呢？你想野地里的百合花怎么长起来；它也不劳苦，也不纺线；然而我告诉你们，就是所罗门极荣华的时候，他所穿戴的还不如这花一朵呢！"

是得墨忒耳还是狄俄尼索斯都办不到。

　　基督把先知以赛亚的预言（"他被藐视，被人厌弃；多受痛苦，常经忧患。他被藐视，好像被人掩面不看的一样"[1]）视为预示他的来临，又以自己的人生应验了这预言。"预言应验"这种事没什么好大惊小怪的。每件艺术作品都是一个预言的应验，因为每件艺术作品都是一个理念的形象化。每个人都应该让自己成为一个预言的应验，因为每个人都应该去实现某个存在于上帝或人类心中的理想。基督找到了他属意的预言，并成就了那预言，让那位弗吉尔派诗人[2]得以圆梦（以赛亚不管住在耶路撒冷还是巴比伦时都是这样梦想的[3]），让世界企盼了许多个世纪的那个人得以在他身上体现。以赛亚形容，这个理想人物有一个显著特征："他的面貌比别人憔悴，他的形容比世人枯槁。"[4] 一旦艺术明白了这道理，它便如花盛放，因为在基督身上，艺术的真谛被前所未有地彰显出来。因为不就像我说过的，艺术真理是"系于以外在表达内在，系于灵魂的肉身化，系于精神充满于肉体"吗？

1　《圣经·以赛亚书》五十三章三节。

2　弗吉尔派诗人：指以赛亚。有些人认为古罗马大诗人弗吉尔在诗中曾预言过基督的来临，故云。

3　犹太人一度亡国，全部精英（包括以赛亚）被掳至巴比伦。

4　《圣经·以赛亚书》五十二章十四节。

在我看来，历史发展的许多憾事之一，是基督带来的文艺复兴固然造就了沙特尔（Chartres）大教堂、"亚瑟王传奇"、圣方济各的人生、乔托的画和但丁的《神曲》，却未能贯彻到底，横遭无聊乏味的古典主义文艺复兴所打断，所以我们才又会有了彼特拉克的十四行诗、拉斐尔的壁画、帕拉第奥式建筑风格、形式化的法国悲剧、圣保罗大教堂和蒲柏的诗——总之是各种根据死规则堆砌出来而不是发自内心、有灵性贯穿的作品。但不管何时何地，只要哪里有浪漫主义冒出头来，哪里就会有基督的身影，就会有基督之魂存焉。他显现在《罗密欧与朱丽叶》里，显现在《冬天的故事》中，显现在普罗旺斯诗歌里，显现在《古舟子咏》中，显现在《无情妖女》中[1]，显现在查特顿（Chatterton）的《仁爱之歌》（*Ballad of Charity*）中。

拜他所赐，艺术世界才会如此异彩纷呈：雨果的《悲惨世界》，波德莱尔的《恶之花》，悲天悯人的俄国小说，伯恩－琼斯和莫里斯的染色玻璃、挂毯和工艺，魏尔伦的人生和诗，乔托的塔，兰斯洛特和桂妮薇儿[2]，汤豪塞

---

1 《古舟子咏》（*The Rime of the Ancient Mariner*）是柯勒律治的诗，《无情妖女》（*La Belle Dame sans Merci*）是济慈的诗。

2 "兰斯洛特和桂妮薇儿"指"亚瑟王传奇"。桂妮薇儿是亚瑟王的王后，兰斯洛特为圆桌武士之一，后来与王后发生不伦恋情。

（Tannhäuser），米开朗琪罗那些浪漫而让人心里不宁静的大理石雕像，尖顶建筑，以及对花朵和孩童的钟爱——确实，古典艺术并没有留多少空间供花朵成长或供孩童玩耍。但自十二世纪至今，花朵和孩童以不同的方式在不同时期不断出现于艺术里，来去无定且不按常理出牌，完全符合了花朵和孩童的风格。

基督之所以能够成为浪漫主义运动生气勃勃的中心，是因为他天性富于想象力。诗剧和歌谣里的古怪角色都是别人想象出来的，但拿撒勒人耶稣完全是凭自己的想象力创造自己。若说以赛亚的预言和基督的出现有什么关系，那这关系也不多于夜莺歌声与月亮升起的关系。基督既是对以赛亚预言的确证，又是对这预言的否定。因为他每实现以赛亚的一个预言，就会摧毁另一个。培根说过，所有的美都存在着"某种比例上的独特之处"[1]。而基督也说过，凡是由"灵"所生的人（换言之是喜欢让自己成为具有活力的人）都像风，"随着意思吹，你听见风的响声，却不晓得从哪里来，往哪里去"[2]。这就是何以艺术家会对基督如此着迷。他具备了生命的所有色调：神秘、怪异、悲情、富暗示性、狂喜和爱。他激起人的惊叹之心，并创造

---

1 语出培根的《论美》（*Of Beauty*）。

2 《圣经·约翰福音》三章八节。

出一种唯有他一个人明白的心境。

　　说到这里，我很高兴地想到，如果说基督是"想象力的佼佼者"[1]，那世界本身也应该由同一质料所构成。我在《道林·格雷的画像》里说过：世界最大的罪固然都在头脑里犯下，但世上的一切原就是发生在头脑里。通过科学，我们如今已经知道，我们并未看见我们眼睛所看见的，也未听见我们耳朵所听见的。眼睛耳朵不过是传输感官印象的管道（有时传递得充分些，有时不那么充分），而让我们看见罂粟花之红、闻到苹果之香和听到云雀之歌的，是头脑。

　　最近我花了点功夫钻研基督的四部散文诗。圣诞节的时候，我设法弄来了一部希腊文原文的《新约全书》，每天早上打扫过牢房和刷好盆罐之后，就会读一点福音书——随手翻读十来节经文。那是展开一天的愉快方式。对过着纷纷扰扰和毫无节制生活的你来说，若是每天也读点福音书，那将会有莫大神益。它会带给你说不完的好处，而且福音书的希腊文都相当简单。我们以前固然听过福音书的经文无数遍（一年到头都听得到），但正因为那样，我们的听觉反而受到污染，以致无法领略福音书的朴素、清新和明了的浪漫神韵。我们听别人念过太多遍，念

1　出自莎士比亚剧作《仲夏夜之梦》第五幕第一场。原文为："疯子、情人和诗人都是想象力的佼佼者。"

得又差，而所有重复都是反灵性的。回头读希腊原文，感觉就像走出一间狭窄幽暗的屋子，走进一片百合花园。

后来，想到我读到的有可能就是基督的原话（ipsissima verba），我的愉悦之情又增加了一倍。人们一直认为基督说的是亚兰语，就连勒南也这样主张。但我们现在已知道，那位加利利乡下人就像今日的爱尔兰乡下人一样，是操双语的，而希腊语是当时整个巴勒斯坦（甚至整个罗马帝国东部）的日常语言。我向来不满意于只能凭着翻译的翻译[1]知道基督说过什么。令我高兴的是，读希腊文《圣经》会让我有一种感觉：查米德斯[2]听过基督讲道、苏格拉底与基督讨论过问题，而柏拉图了解基督的微言大义。我喜欢想，他真的是说过 ἐγώ εἰμί ὁ καλός（我是个好牧羊人）这句希腊文；在他指出野地里的百合花不劳苦也不纺线时，原话真的是 καταμα θετε τὰ κείνα τοῦ ἀγροῦ πῶς αναξάνει οὐ κοπιᾶ οὐδὲ νήθει，而他死前也真的只是说了 τετέλεσται（"成了"）一个单词，以表示"我的生命完成了，成就了，圆满了"。

读福音书时，又特别是读《约翰福音》时（有人认为

1　翻译的翻译指从希腊文《圣经》翻译过来的《圣经》的英译本。
2　查米德斯是柏拉图一部对话录的中心角色，年轻俊美，个性中体现出"节制"的美德（"节制"是该对话录的主题）。王尔德写过一首叫《查米德斯》的诗。

这福音不是圣约翰本人所写而是早期诺斯替教派教徒所假托），我除了注意到基督不间断的想象力是所有灵性生活和物质生活的基础，还注意到，对基督来说，想象力不过是"爱"（Love）的一种形式，而"爱"又是他用"主"（Lord）这个字的时候的全部意义所在。大概六周以前，因为医生的意见，我获准吃白面包（监狱的日常伙食是粗糙的黑面包或半黑面包）。一吃之下，我觉得美味极了。你听了这个一定会奇怪，纳闷这世界怎么会有人觉得干巴巴的面包可口。但我可以向你保证这是真的。白面包是那么美味，以至每一顿饭结束时，我都会把盘子里残留或掉落在桌布上的面包屑仔细拾起来，吃得一粒不剩。我这样做不是因为还不饱（我现在的伙食分量非常充足），而纯粹是因为不想浪费上天的赐予。

就像所有个性迷人的人一样，基督不只可以说出些美妙动人的道理，还可以叫别人说出。我爱极了圣马可记载的一件事。基督为了考验一个希腊妇人的信念，拒绝答应为她女儿驱鬼，说是不好把儿女的饼丢给狗吃，没想到那妇人回答说："狗在桌子底下也吃孩子们的碎渣儿（'狗'的希腊文原文作κυνάρια，应该翻译为'小狗'才对）。"[1]大

1　事见《圣经·马可福音》七章二十六节至三十节。

部分人都是为得到爱与赞美而活，但我们更应该做的是凭借爱与赞美而活。如果我们得到了任何爱，那不管这爱有多么少，我们都应该要晓得那不是我们所配得的。没有人配得到爱，但上帝爱世人，而这显示，"永不配得到爱的人照样会得到永恒的爱"已经被写成神圣的大经大法。如果你觉得这话不中听，我会换个说法：每个人都配得到爱——只有自以为配得到爱的人除外。爱是我们应该跪下来领受的圣体[1]，而且领受时应该在嘴里和心里默念："Domine, non sum dignus.（主啊，我不配！）"但愿你有时会思索这道理。你很需要它。

　　假如有一天我会重新提笔（指的是创作艺术作品），那只有两个主题是我想要表达和通过它们来表达自己的：一是"基督是生命中浪漫主义运动的先驱"，另一是"艺术家生命与为人处世的关系"。第一个主题当然是极为吸引人的，因为我在基督身上不只看到浪漫主义最高典范的各种要素，还看到浪漫主义气质的各种偶然成分，甚至率性成分。他是第一个指出人应该过"花朵般"[2]生活的人。他把这要求体现出来。他也指明"小孩"是我们应该设法变成的那种人。他把儿童树立为他们长辈的楷模，而我一向

1　指基督教圣餐礼中的圣饼，被认为是耶稣身体的象征，故又称圣体。
2　"花朵般"即应该像百合花那般生活，不为吃喝穿戴忧虑。

都认为这是儿童的首要用途（虽然完美事物通常都不具备用途）。但丁形容，从上帝手中造出来的时候，人的灵魂"会像个小孩那样又哭又笑"，而基督也认定，每个人的灵魂都应该像个小孩那样又哭又笑。他知道生命是变化的、流动的、活跃的，任由它僵化为任何固定形式等于让它死亡。他说过人不应该太过重视物质，说过不切实际是一种了不起的态度。他说得真棒："鸟都不用操心，何况人呢？不要为明天忧虑。生命不胜于饮食吗？身体不胜于衣裳吗？"古希腊人也说得出最后一句话，那是一种地道的希腊情绪气质。但只有基督可以同时说出最后两句话，把生命的精义以最完美的方式概括起来。

他的道德观可以用"同理心"三字道尽，而道德观本应如此。即便他一生只说过这句话"她许多的罪都赦免了，因为她的爱多"，他已今生无憾。他秉持的正义观是诗性正义 [1]（poetical justice），而正义观本应如此。基于这种正义观，乞丐会因为今生所受的苦而得以进天国。我再也想不出更好的理由，来解释为什么乞丐可以进天国。根据这种正义观，那些傍晚凉爽时分在葡萄园干活一小时的人，和那些在大太阳底下工作一整天的人应该得到一样的

---

1 "诗性正义"原是指"善有善报，恶有恶报"的观念，但从下文观之，王尔德把它的内涵加以扩大。

报酬。为什么不应该是这样呢？其实，大概我们谁都不配得到什么报酬。基督才懒得管那些呆板和了无生气的机械化思想系统（它们把人当成物），所以就把每个人看成一样的，也因此把他们做的事都看成一样的。在他眼里，通则并不存在，有的只是例外。

在他看来，浪漫主义艺术的主音调才是现实生活的恰当基础，除此不可能有别的基础。有一次，有个女人触犯了律法，一些不安好心的人把她带到基督面前指给他看律法上写明她该得的刑罚，又问基督该如何处置。但他就像没听见似的，只管蹲在地上用手指写字。经过再三催问，他才抬起头说："你们中间谁是没有罪的，谁就可以先拿石头打她。"任谁说出这话，一生便是没有白活。

就像所有具有诗性气质的人一样，基督偏爱无知的人。他偏爱无知的人，是因为知道这些人的灵魂总是有足够的空间容纳伟大的理念。但他受不了愚蠢的人，特别是那些被教育弄愚蠢的人。这种人意见多多，却什么都不懂。用基督的话来说，这种人手里拿着知识的钥匙却不用它，又不准别人用它，哪怕这钥匙也许可以开启"上帝之国"的大门。基督的首要敌人是庸俗之辈非利士人（Philistines），而每个世代的光之子（child of light）都会遇上这种人，并不得不与之战斗。庸俗之辈是基督生活的那个时代和社会的主流。这种人无知透顶、装腔作势、抱残守缺、崇拜功名利禄，却又可笑地自矜自大——就此而言，基督时代耶路撒冷的犹太人和我们时代的英国庸俗之辈堪称难兄难弟。基督把这些人的装腔作势嘲笑为"粉饰的坟墓"。他把功名利禄视为绝对可鄙之物；他不愿看见任何人成为任何思想体系或道德体系的牺牲品；他指出，形式和礼仪是为人的益处而设计，不应削足适履地要人去迁就形式和礼仪；他认为守安息日的规定可以不用理会。冷冰冰的慈善捐献、招摇过市的当众施舍和中产阶级的繁文缛节都被他嗤之以鼻，大加痛斥。对于我们这种人，所谓"正统"只是一种图方便和不聪明的默认，可到了庸俗之辈手中，"正统"就变成了可怕和致人瘫痪的暴君。基督打翻这一切，指出唯有"灵"有价值。他乐得向那些庸俗之辈指出，他们自以为熟读《律法书》和《先知书》，其实对它们的真意并无丝毫理解。这些人以为只要抽一小部分时间（就像奉献每天的十分之一那样）把规定的责任尽好就没他们的事，但基督一再强调完全活在当下的重要性。

被他从罪中拯救的那些人之所以得救，全然是因为他们生命中表现出一些美好时刻。例如，当抹大拉的马利亚见着基督之后，便毫不心疼地打破一个情人（她共有七个情人）送她的一瓶丰腴香膏，抹在基督因赶路而疲倦和沾满尘土的脚上。就因为这一刻，她得以与路得和贝雅特丽齐[1]同坐在天国的白玫瑰丛中。在某种意义上，基督所说的一切都不过是在提醒我们，我们的灵魂应该时时刻刻保持美好，总是随时准备好迎接"新郎"[2]，总是随时等着听见"情郎"的声音。就像庸俗之辈代表的是未被想象力照亮的人性，基督把生命中的一切美好都视为"光"的一种表现。事实上，想象力就是世界的光：世界由它所造，可世人不明白它。又因为想象力不过是"爱"的一种显相，世人便因为爱心大小的不同而区分为不同几类。

然而，基督最具浪漫主义色彩的时刻是他与罪人打交道的时刻。在某种意义上，这也是他最具写实主义色彩的时刻。世人一直那么爱这位圣人，是因为他是通向上帝至善至美的最短途径，然而，出于某种超凡入圣的本能，基督自己总是深爱着罪人，认为罪人是通向人类至善至美的最短途径。基督的主要渴望不是改造罪人，一如他的主要渴望不是减轻世间的痛苦。把一个有意思的盗贼改变为乏味的老实人不是他的目的。"囚犯援助会"和其他类似的现代社会运动在他眼里不会有多少分量。把一个税吏改变

---

1 路得是《圣经·路得记》中的贤德妇人。贝雅特丽齐是但丁钟爱过的女子，也是他撰写《神曲》的主要灵感源泉。

2 耶稣有时把上帝或天国比喻为人类的"新郎"或"情郎"。

为一个法利赛人，在他看来根本就不是什么大成就。他真正了不起之处在于，以一种世人还不能理解的方式，他把罪孽和苦难提升为一种美而神圣的东西，一种完美的表现。这信条听起来相当危险。它也确实危险（一切了不起的信条都是危险的）。但那毫无疑问就是基督的信条，而我本人也毫不怀疑这信条为真。

罪人当然必须忏悔，但为何必须？理由很简单：非如此，他便无法悟明他干了些什么。忏悔那一刻就是新生的一刻。不仅如此，那也是一个人可以改变自己过去的方法。古希腊人认为这是不可能的。他们常在格言里指出："就连诸神也一样无法改变过去。"但基督向我们显明，即便最平凡的罪人照样有能力改变过去，这也是他们唯一有能力做的事。如果有人问基督，我肯定他会指出：就在浪子[1]跪下痛哭那一刻，他已经把他为妓女散尽钱财和与猪争吃豆荚的往事，提升为他人生中美好和神圣的事件。这是大多数人难以理解的观念。我敢说，这观念只有一个坐过牢的人才能理解。果真如此的话，坐牢便也是值得的了。

---

1 这里用了《圣经·路加福音》中"浪子回头"的典故：有一个小儿子硬要父亲分他家产，离家到处花天酒地，金钱散尽后饥寒交迫，沦落到为人放猪，但常常吃不饱，想要吃喂猪的豆荚。最后觉悟前非，回家认错，获得父亲原谅。

基督的最大特点是独一无二。当然，就像曙光出现前总是先有假曙光，就像冬日有时也会出现一片煦阳，骗得聪明的藏红花未到时节便先吐蕊，类似地，在基督之前便有过基督徒。我们应该为此感谢上天。不幸的是，自基督之后便再也没有基督徒。我愿意承认的唯一例外是阿西西的圣方济各。不过他会有这等能耐并不奇怪，因为上帝在他诞生时便给了他诗人的灵魂，而且他很年轻便娶了"贫穷"为新娘。既然有着诗人之魂和乞丐之体，他想找到通向至善至美之路便一点都不难。他了解基督，也让自己活得像基督。我们不需要靠《认证书》[1]才能知道圣方济各的人生是真正"效法基督"[2]的：如果说他的人生是一首诗，那以这四个字为书名的那本书只算一篇散文。

确实，在说过他的种种魅力之后，基督的真正魅力就在于他的独一无二。就此而言，他就像一件真正的艺术作品：因为他根本用不着教人什么，人只要被带到他面前便会得到成就。每个人都注定要被带到他的面前。每个人人

---

1 《认证书》(*Liber Conformitatum*)是一本十四世纪的书籍，由巴托洛梅乌斯神父(Fr. Bartholomaeus de Pisa)撰写。书中列举了基督和圣方济各的人生有哪些相同处。

2 《效法基督》(*Imitatio Christi*)是一部大为风行的基督教灵修书籍，写成于十五世纪初。

生中至少有一次会与基督同行至以马忤斯村[1]。

至于我说我想处理的另一个主题，即艺术家生命与为人处世的关系，你听了想必十分不解。人们指着雷丁监狱说："艺术家生命会把一个人带到此等地方来。"其实啊，艺术家生命还会把人带到更不堪的地方。对头脑机械化的人来说，人生要靠精明的计算，要权衡各种利害得失。这种人总是知道自己要往哪里去，也总是会到达。例如，如果他们想当教区助理，那么不管他们是什么身份地位，总当得上教区助理。不管一个人渴望成为一个自己本身以外的什么角色（比方说议员、生意兴隆的杂货店老板、著名律师、法官或诸如此类无聊乏味的角色），他们总是会如愿。这是惩罚。凡是想要一副面具的人都得终日戴上它。

但对那些有着蓬勃生命力，对那些想成为生命力化身的人来说，情况大不相同。那些只希冀自我实现的人从不会知道自己正在往哪里走。他们无从知道。当然，在某种意义上，我们必须（就像古希腊神谕所说的[2]）认识自己，因为这是知识的最初成就。但能明白人的灵魂无法认

_____

1 《圣经·路加福音》记载，耶稣复活当天，曾在路上向两个前往以马忤斯村的门徒显现自己，但他们认不出来。三人一起去到以马忤斯村，一起用晚餐，这时两个门徒突然眼睛明亮起来，认出他的身份。耶稣随后消失不见。
2 德尔斐阿波罗神殿大门的上方刻着"认识你自己"这句话。

识是"智慧"的最高成就。对任何人来说，他的最终秘密就是自己。即便你能称出太阳的重量，算出通往月亮要走几步，并绘制出银河中每一颗星星的地图，你仍然无法了解自己。又有谁能够计算出自己灵魂的轨道呢？当基士（Kish）的儿子[1]外出为父亲寻找走失的几头驴时，他又岂能知道上帝的使者已拿着加冕用的膏油正在等他，岂能知道自己的灵魂已成了王者的灵魂？

　　我希望足够长命，可以写出一部我能在寿尽时自豪地这样说的作品："是的，这就是或仅是艺术家生命可以把人带到之处。"我生平遇过最完美的两个生命是魏尔伦和克鲁泡特金[2]，而他们都坐过许多年牢。前者是但丁之后仅有的基督徒诗人，后者是拥有白人基督之魂的俄罗斯人。七八个月来，外面的世界虽然接二连三带给我极大烦恼，几乎从未间断，我却因为一些人和事得以与一个新来这监狱工作的人[3]发生直接接触。他带给我的帮助大得非笔墨所能形容。记得入狱的第一年，我在无力感和绝望中一蹶不振，只知成天绞着双手自言自语："全完了！多可怕的

1　"基士的儿子"指以色列第一任国王扫罗。据《圣经》记载，他有一天为父亲外出寻驴，却在路上遇到先知撒母耳，被册封为王。

2　克鲁泡特金：无政府主义理论家。

3　"新来这监狱工作的人"指雷丁监狱的新典狱长，他为王尔德提供了许多方便。

结局啊！"可如今我尽量要对自己说（有时还蛮由衷地）："多美好的开始啊！"也许这真的是事实，也许这真的会成为事实。果真如此的话，那我必须把许多功劳归于刚刚提到的那位先生，因为他改善了监狱里每一个人的处境。

物质本身殊少意义，甚至——我们得为形而上学教会我们这道理而至少感谢它这一次——并无真实性。唯有灵魂是重要的。因为监狱里最近所发生的改变让我明白，惩罚有时候也可以有疗愈性，而不是必然只会制造伤口（惩罚不得其法，就会像不得其法的施舍一样，让面包在受施者拿到手那一刻变成石头）。这段日子以来，监狱里的改变是多大啊（我不是指法规上的改变，不是，它们是硬性的，无可更改。我指的是执行这些法规时所采取的态度）。我跟你说过，我去年五月曾申请提早出狱，但如果当时申请成功，我将会是带着对这地方和它所有官员的深仇大恨离开，而因这深仇大恨，我的人生将会被毒化。因为没有申请成功，我待了下来。不过，随后人道精神降临了这地方，让每一个人受惠。如今，我知道在获释之后，我将会永远感念这里几乎每个人对我的好。出狱那天，我一定会找许多人道谢，并请他们务必记住我。

监狱制度是个天大和彻底的错误。出狱之后，我会想方设法让它发生改变。我想要试一试。不过，这世间没有什么错误是"爱"的精神或基督的精神（这基督不是住在教会里那个）所无法改变的——哪怕不是完全改正，也至少让它变得不会让人那么冤大仇深，变得可以忍耐。

我也知道，监狱外头有许多让人心旷神怡的事物在等着我：上至圣方济各口中的"风兄弟"和"雨姊妹"[1]（两者都是美好事物），下至商店橱窗和大城市的日落。如果要把这一类还属于我的东西列成清单，真不知道要列到何年何月。确实，上帝为我创造的世界和为任何人所创造的一样丰盛。说不定，等出狱时我已变了样子。毋庸说，道德革新就像神学革新[2]一样了无意义和庸俗。另一方面，虽说要求一个人变成好人是不科学的空想，但变成一个更深刻的人是吃苦者的特权。我认为我正在往这方向改变。是或不是，你可以自行判断。

出狱之后，要是有哪个朋友摆设筵席却不邀请我，我将一点都不介意。我光是独自一人过日子便其乐无穷。试问谁有了自由、书本、花朵和月亮之后还会不快活呢？何况，筵席已非我属意。它过去占去我太多心思。这方面的生活于我已经结束，而我敢说这是一大幸事。另一方面，待我出狱后，要是哪个朋友有哀痛却不让我分担，我将会

---

1 圣方济各把大自然的一切（包括风、雨、动物）视为自己的兄弟姊妹。
2 "道德革新"指道德上的洗心革面，"神学革新"指从不信上帝变为信徒。

无比难受。若是他把我拒之门外，我将会一次又一次折返求他准我进门，好让我分担我有权分担的。若是他认为我不配与他同哭，我将会视之为大辱而痛彻心扉。再没有更可怕的羞辱了。但这是不可能发生的，我有权分担悲哀。当一个人既能欣赏世界的美好，复能分担其悲哀并悟明两者的奇妙之处，此人可说是与圣界发生了直接接触，去了离上帝的秘密可能容许的最短距离内。

也许，除我的生命变得深刻以外，我的艺术也会变得更深刻，在激情上体现出更大的和谐，在冲动上体现出更大的直率。现代艺术真正在意的不是广度而是浓烈度。我们在艺术中关心的不再是典型，我们非创作不可的是例外。毋庸说，我不能把我所受过的种种苦放进它们过去的任何形式中。只有在模仿结束处才会有艺术的开端可言，但必须有某种不同于以前的东西进入我的作品：也许是更饱满的语言，也许是更丰富的节奏，也许是更奇特的色彩效果，也许是更简单的建筑结构——最起码是某种美学素质。

古希腊人说，玛耳绪阿斯被剥皮[1]之后（对这一幕，

---

1 玛耳绪阿斯是古希腊神话中小亚细亚的地方河神，传说他拾得雅典娜扔掉的芦笛后向擅弹七弦琴（类似竖琴）的太阳神阿波罗挑战，相约胜者可以任意处置败者。结果玛耳绪阿斯比输，被活生生剥皮而死。

但丁有塔西佗[1]笔法式的描绘："他的四肢从皮囊中被剥出"[2]），他的歌声止息了。七弦琴彻底打败了芦笛。但古希腊人大概弄错了，我在很多现代艺术作品里都听得到玛耳绪阿斯的歌声。这歌声在波德莱尔那里表现为苦涩，在拉马丁（Lamartine）那里表现为甜美和忧伤，在魏尔伦那里表现为神秘玄奥。它在肖邦的音乐里表现为和弦的延迟解决（deferred resolutions），在伯恩-琼斯的女性画像中表现为挥之不去的不满足情绪。即使是马修·阿诺德，他虽然借卡利克斯（Callicles）来歌颂"甜美动人的七弦琴声的胜利"[3]，但狐疑和焦虑的泛音仍流溢出来，透露出不少玛耳绪阿斯的歌声。阿诺德先后追随过歌德与华兹华斯，但这两位大诗人都无法真正疗愈他，所以，当他为"色希斯"哀悼或为"吉卜赛学者"[4]而歌时，他用以传达自己矛盾心情的乐器正是芦笛。但姑且勿论玛耳绪阿斯是否已经止声，我都不允许自己沉默。发声于我是必须的，一如树木的花叶必然会在风中摇曳。我的艺术与世界之间横

1　塔西佗：古罗马历史学家。

2　出自《神曲·天堂篇》第一首诗。

3　"甜美动人的七弦琴声的胜利"一语出自阿诺德的诗歌《恩培多克勒在埃特纳火山》（*Empedocles on Etna*）。卡利克斯是书中的竖琴手角色，他弹琴唱歌歌颂阿波罗对玛耳绪阿斯的胜利。

4　指《色希斯》（*Thyrsis*）和《吉卜赛学者》（*The Scholar Gipsy*）这两首诗。《色希斯》是阿诺德悼念亡友之作。

着一条鸿沟，但我与艺术之间没有任何间隙——至少我是这样希望的。

每个人分配到的命运各不相同。你的命运是自由、享乐和安逸的生活，哪怕你不配过那样的生活。我的命运却是当众受辱、长期监禁、可怜巴巴、毁灭和不光彩。这也是我不配过的生活，至少是还不配。记得我以前常常说，要是我遇上一出真正的悲剧，我想我承受得了——只要它是搭配着紫色的棺罩和一副肃穆的悲苦面具，我就承受得了。但现代性（modernity）的可怕之处在于，它会给悲剧披上一袭喜剧的外衣，由此把某些崇高事物降格为平庸、古怪可笑和缺乏格调的事物。这大概也是现实人生的写照。据说，一切殉道行为在旁观者眼中都不值一哂[1]。十九世纪并没有能跳出这条通则。

降临于我的那出悲剧处处都显得丑陋、卑贱、叫人恶心和缺乏格调，光是身上的衣服便丑怪得可笑。我们成了含悲的傻瓜，心碎的小丑；我们受到特殊装扮和摆弄，供别人调笑。一八九五年十一月十三日那天，我在未得到事先知会

1　"据说，一切殉道行为在旁观者眼中都不值一哂"这话出自爱默生的文章《论经验》（*Essay on Experience*）。王尔德在后文再次指出，在旁观者眼中，烧死一个殉教者"不过有如屠夫宰牛、制木炭人在森林里砍倒一棵树，或是割草人用镰刀砍下一朵花"。

的情况下被带离监狱医院，从伦敦被押解到这座监狱。为了等火车，我得在克拉珀姆交会站的中央站台从两点站到两点半。当时我穿着囚衣，戴着手铐，天底下就数我最丑最怪。人们看到我都笑了。每来一班火车，围观的人便愈多。没有什么可以让他们更快乐的了。他们起初当然不知道我是谁，随后知道了，便笑得更厉害。在那个灰蒙蒙的十一月的雨天，我就这样站了半小时，供一群暴民嗤笑。自此以后一整年，每天到了同一个钟点，我都会哭。其实，这种事没你想象的那么悲惨，因为对我们坐牢的人来说，以泪洗面只是家常便饭。一个人进牢后若是哪一天不哭了，只代表他的心变硬了，不代表他的心变快乐了。

不过呢，我现在开始觉得那些笑我的人比我自己更可悲。他们看到我的时候，我当然不是站在基座上[1]，而是套着颈手枷[2]。但一个人若是只对站在基座上的人感兴趣，那这个人非常缺乏想象力。基座有时可以非常虚幻不实，而颈手枷是铁一般的可怕事实。那些人本该学学怎样更好地诠释悲伤的。我说过，悲伤的背后总是只有悲伤。但更有智慧

---

1 王尔德这里是借用波西说过的话："你只要不是站在基座上便会没啥意思。"
2 颈手枷是套在犯人脖子和手腕上的刑具，用以锁起犯人示众。但王尔德说他"套着颈手枷"只是一种夸张的说法。

心本就是为破碎而设

The most terrible thing about it is not that it breaks one's heart — hearts are made to be broken — but that it turns one's heart to stone

的说法应该是：悲伤的背后总有一个灵魂。嘲笑一个痛苦的灵魂是件可怕的事，谁做了这等事谁的生命便会变得丑陋。这世间的经济法则简单得出奇：你付出什么便会得到什么回报。所以，那些想象力不足以穿透事物表面而又心生怜悯的人，他们除了鄙夷，还渴望得到什么回报呢？

我会叙述来这监狱的经过，只是为了让你明白，我要在我的惩罚中得到怨尤和绝望以外的东西，有多艰难卓绝。然而，这又是我非做到不可的，而我也终于做到可以不时地体验到片刻的顺服和接纳。光是一个花蕾便可藏着整个春天，而云雀在低地所筑的窝也可以预报许多玫瑰色破晓的来临，所以，我那些顺服和谦卑的片刻未尝不可能是表示，我未来的人生还有什么美好事物，等着我去取得。不管怎样，我都必须顺着我自身的路径演化，必须接纳一切曾发生在我身上的苦难羞辱，让自己配得上这一切。

人们常批评我太个人主义，但我必须努力让自己变得比从前更加个人主义。我必须比从前更多地向自己索取，更少地向世界索要。确实，我会身败名裂，并不是因为太过个人主义，而是不够个人主义。我人生中最不光彩、最不可原谅、永远值得鄙视的举动，就是我容许自己被迫求助于社会，以为社会的力量保护得了我，不受令尊侵害。

毋庸说，我一启动了社会的力量，社会便转过身对我说："你向来都视法律如无物，那你现在真的是要求助于法律的保护吗？真那样的话，你就得让法律尽情发挥——你必须接受它的约束。"结果就是我进了监牢。在打那三场官司的过程中，我常常痛感自己的立场有多可笑和丢人。我老是看到令尊跑东跑西，以期引起公众的注意，就像是担心会有人记不住他的马夫步态和马夫装束、他的O形腿、他抖个不停的手、他松垮垮的下唇和畜生般的傻笑。即便他不在现场，不在我眼前，我照样可以从法庭阴暗的四壁感觉到他的存在。就连空气本身也好像飘浮着无数张他那猿猴似的蠢脸。我毫无疑问是自作自受，用最不光彩的手段让自己摔了最不光彩的一跤。我在《道林·格雷的画像》里说过："人在选择敌人之时再小心都不为过。"当时我何曾想到，自己将会被一个贱民弄成贱民。

你怂恿我向社会求助，你逼我向社会求助——这既是我最鄙夷你的一点，又是我最鄙夷自己的一点（因为我任由自己屈从于你）。你不懂得欣赏我艺术家的一面还说得过去，那是气质使然，不是你能改变的。但你理应懂得欣赏我个人主义者的一面，因为这不需要文化修养便能办到。可你没有，反而把一种庸俗成分引入我的生命。庸俗成分之所以为庸俗，不在于它无法理解艺术。渔夫、牧羊人和农民之类的可爱庶民对艺术一窍不通，但他们是地上的盐[1]。真正的庸俗之辈是那些支持和襄助社会的盲目性和机械性力量的人，这种人无法从一个人或一个运动里面看出蓬勃的生命力。

听说我曾经招待一些勒索我的坏蛋吃晚餐，并以有他们做伴为乐，人们吓坏了。然而，从一个艺术家的角度来看，这些人是有启发性和刺激性的，可以带来快感。那就像是与虎豹共餐，一半的刺激来自其危险性。我有的感觉弄蛇人一定也有。想想看，用笛声把眼镜蛇从印花布或柳条筐里引出来，逗得它颈部愈鼓愈胀，逗得它像水草般在空气中前后摇摆，那感觉多过瘾、多刺激。生命中的邪恶事物对我来说就是色彩最斑斓的蛇，它们的毒性正是它们完美的一部分。我当时不知道，他们日后将会因为你的笛声和令尊的钱而攻击我。他们太有趣了，我一点不以与他们结交为耻。真正让我引以为耻的是你带给我那种可怕的庸俗氛围。作为艺术家，我理应与爱丽儿为伍，你却要我与卡利班角力[2]。结果，我没能创作出一些富于音色之美的艺术品（《莎乐美》《佛罗伦萨悲剧》或《圣妓》之类的戏剧），反而把时间浪费在给令尊写长长的律师信，被押

---

1 "地上的盐"典出《圣经·马太福音》，意指世界上最珍贵的东西。
2 "爱丽儿"和"卡利班"皆为莎士比亚剧作《暴风雨》中的角色。爱丽儿是个缥缈的精灵，卡利班是个粗野丑怪的奴隶。

着去向一直为我所不齿的社会求助。克利伯恩和阿特金斯[1]在勒索方面是行家里手，想招呼得了他们可得有两把刷子。换成大仲马、切利尼（Cellini）、戈雅（Goya）、爱伦·坡或波德莱尔与我易地而处，他们一样会乐于为之。让我厌烦的反而是你总拉着我去找我的律师汉弗莱斯，让我不得不坐在一间荒凉的办公室里，被一双阴森森的眼睛盯着，装出一本正经的模样向一个秃子撒些一本正经的谎。现在回顾你我交往的两年，我坐落的位置不偏不倚，刚好就在庸俗国的正中央，远离一切美好、奇妙和敢为人先的气质。到最后，我还得为了你的利益站出来，假装成"行不由心""清心寡欲"和"文以载道"理念的捍卫者。此乃走邪路之结果也！[2]

让我大惑不解的是你为什么偏偏要去模仿令尊的主要性格特征。我不明白，他明明是你的反面教材，你却把他引为榜样。除非这样解释：任何两个人会相恨，必然因为他们之间存在难兄难弟似的纽带，有某种共通之处。我猜想，你们会互相憎恨，是出于同类相斥的奇怪法

1　克利伯恩和阿特金斯两人都是勒索惯犯，但没有从王尔德身上勒索到什么。

2　出自巴尔扎克（Balzac）的小说《交际花盛衰记》（*Splendeurs et Misères des Courtisanes*）。

则，不是因为你们有许多差异，而是因为你们太相似。你在一八九三年六月离开牛津，没拿到学位却欠了一屁股债。你欠的只是很小的数目，但在令尊那样收入的人眼里可不得了。他为此写了一封粗俗、刻薄、凶恶的信把你骂了一顿。但你的回信处处有过之而无不及。这当然更不可原谅，你反而为此极端自豪。我清楚记得，你带着最自负的神情告诉我，你有本领在令尊"最拿手的行当"击败他。完全正确。但那是什么样的一种行当啊！是什么样的一种竞争啊！以前，你和令尊住在亲戚家时，你常常溜出来，为的是可以从邻近的旅馆写些脏话连篇的信骂他。你对我恰恰也是一样。有多少次，当我们在餐厅吃午餐时，你先是给我摆出一张臭脸或大吵大闹，吃过午餐后再跑到怀特俱乐部，写些不堪入目的信骂我。你和令尊不同的只有一点：派信差送过信几小时后就会跑到我房间来。但你不是来道歉的，而是问我在萨沃伊饭店订了晚餐没有；若我答没有，你便会问为什么没有。有时，你还会比你的骂人信先到。我记得，有一次你要我邀你两位朋友到皇家咖啡厅吃午餐，而其中一人我素未谋面。我照办了，还应你的要求订了一桌特别豪华的午餐。主厨是特别找来的，葡萄酒也分外讲究。可你非但没来用餐，反而派人送来了一封谩骂信，送达的时间精心安排在我于咖啡厅里等了你半小时之后。我读了第一行，明白了那是什么性质的信之后便放入口袋，然后对你两位朋友解释，说你突然病了，无法赴约，而信里主要是描述你的病情。事实上，我是到了那天傍晚要换衣服回泰特街吃晚饭时才把你的信拿出来读。那封信让我像是尝到了满嘴污泥，纳闷你是怎么写得出这种像是癫痫病人口吐白沫的文字。就在这时，仆人进来通报，说你正在门厅等候，急着要见我，说只会花我五分钟。我马上派仆人去请你上楼。你来了，样子非常慌张，脸色苍白。你求我帮你出主意和救救你，因为你听说有个从兰姆雷来的律师最近在卡多根广场一带打听你的下落。你担心是牛津时期的旧麻烦或什么新麻烦找上门来。我安慰你说（事情后来的发展证明我没猜错），那律师大概只是代表某个商家来向你讨一笔账款。我又让你留下来陪我一起吃晚饭，一起消磨那个晚上。你绝口不提早先写给我的谩骂信，我也绝口不提，只把它当成一种让人不快的个性所带来的一种让人不快的症状。这种事——先是在两点半写给我一封可憎的信，然后又在七点十五分飞跑来求我帮忙，求我同情——在你我的交往中司空见惯。你在这方面和其他方面都让令尊瞠乎其后。当他写给你的那些信在法庭上被公开宣读时，他理所当然地感到汗颜，不得不假装哭。不过，要是你写给他的那些信也被他的律师宣读出来的话，只怕在场每个人都会感受到更大的震惊和深恶痛绝。你不只文字风格上可以在令尊"最拿手的行当"击败他，还在攻击载体的多姿多彩方面让他望尘莫及。除写信以外，你还用了电报和明信片这一类公开化的信息传递方式。其实，你本应把这类骚扰别人的行径留给艾尔弗雷德·伍德[1]之流去干的，毕竟他是靠这个吃饭的，而你不是。恶语伤人对他而言是职业，对你却成了一种乐趣，一种很恶劣的乐趣。你迄今没有改掉写信骂人的可怕恶习，没有从这类信件把我害得多惨一事上吸取教训。你仍然把它看成你的一项成就，还用到了我的朋友身上，包括罗伯特·谢拉德和其他在我系狱期间关心我的人。你真够丢人现眼的。当罗伯特·谢拉德告诉你我不希望你在《法兰西信使报》发表文章（有没有附带发表我的信都一样），你本应感激他才是，因为他让你知道了我的意向，也让你不至于在不自知的情况下带给我更多伤害。要知道，你那种态度油滑而措辞庸俗的文章（说什么应给"一个被打倒的人"以"公平比赛"的机会）在英国的报纸还吃得开，因为英国报界的传统一向是把艺术家看扁，但在法国，这样的语气就会让我被嘲笑，让你被看不起。任何有关我的文

---

1 艾尔弗雷德·伍德：敲诈惯犯，曾因为握有一封王尔德写给波西的信敲诈到三十英镑。

章，要是我不知道其目的、格调和论述方式，都不可能同意让它发表。对艺术来说，立意良善一点价值也没有，所有烂作品都是良善立意的结果。

罗伯特·谢拉德也不是我的朋友中唯一遭你去信谩骂的。而你会骚扰他们，不过是因为他们认定你要发表有关我的文章、把诗集题献给我、刊登我的书信或典当我的礼物都应该先征得我同意。我知道你还骚扰或是企图骚扰过其他人。

你可曾想到过，过去两年的可怕牢狱生涯中，如果我只能指望你一人出于朋友之谊慰藉我，我的处境会有多凄惨？你有想过吗？对那些帮助我的朋友，你可曾有过一丝感激？他们毫无保留地关心我，对我竭尽忠诚，以对我付出为乐。他们努力开解我，一次又一次来看我，写来一些动人和充满同情的书信，为我处理各种事务，又为我出狱后的生活预做安排。虽然我被众人谩骂、奚落与羞辱，他们仍与我肩并肩站立。我每天都感谢主赐予我这些朋友。我欠他们的恩情多到数不完，就连我牢房里的书都是罗比掏腰包买的，我出狱时穿的衣服也将是由他惠赠。我不会耻于接受任何出于爱与情的赠予，反而会引而为傲。但你可曾有一刻思考过这些对我提供慰藉、帮助和同情的朋友——诸如莫尔·阿迪（More Adey）、罗比、罗伯特·谢拉德、弗兰克·哈里斯（Frank Harris）和亚瑟·克利夫顿（Arthur Clifton）——对我有何种意义？我猜你从来不明白。在我牢狱生涯中曾对我好的人除朋友外还有很多，包括那个会对我说"早安"或"晚安"的狱吏（这不是他的分内责任），包括那两个押送我往返破产法庭的普通警察（他们在我心烦意乱时设法用一些不怎么高明的方法安慰我），包括一个可怜的盗贼（他在旺兹沃思监狱放风时认出我，走过来用因为长期被迫沉默而变沙哑的囚犯嗓音低声对我说："我为你感到遗憾。这种苦日子对你比对我们这种人难熬。"）。如果你还多少有点想象力的话，就会知道，这些人中的任何一个若是允许你跪下擦去他们鞋上的污泥，你都应该感到光荣才对。

不知道你的想象力是否足以让你明白，碰上你们一家子对我而言是多么可怕的悲剧。其实，不管是谁，只要他有够高的身份地位和拥有任何够重要而绝不能失去的宝贝，碰上你们一家都会是天大的悲剧。你们家的年长者当中，没有一个不是促成我身败名裂的帮凶——珀西[1]除外，他是个大好人。

我先前曾带着怨气谈到令堂，而我现在也强烈建议

---

1 珀西：波西的二哥。

你（主要是为你好）把这信拿给她看。假如读一封指控她儿子的信让她痛苦，那就请她想想我的母亲吧。论才气，家母与伊丽莎白·巴雷特·布朗宁（Elizabeth Barrett Browning）相当；论历史地位，家母与罗兰夫人（Madame Roland）不相伯仲。但她是心碎而死。她会心碎，是因为她一向对儿子的才华和艺术引以为傲，一直认定儿子是显赫家名的合格传承人，没想到这儿子最后被判服苦役两年。你一定会问，令堂何以是促成我毁灭的帮凶。那我就来告诉你。就像你力图把你所有的不道德责任往我身上推，令堂也是力图把她对你应尽的所有道德责任往我身上推。她非但没有像一个为人母者应该做的那样，直接找你谈谈，反而老是私底下写信给我，又每次都诚惶诚恐地央求我不要让你知道她写过信。我被夹在你们母子之间，处境之为难、荒谬和可悲并不下于被夹在你和令尊之间。我和令堂就你的问题长谈过两次，时间分别是一八九二年的八月和十一月八日。我两次都问她为什么不直接找你摊开来谈，她两次都是一样的回答："我害怕。我一说，他就会大发脾气。"在第一次长谈中，我对你所知还甚少，所以不明白她的话，但到了第二次长谈，我对你已经了解甚深，所以完全明白她的意思（在这两次长谈中间，你曾黄疸病发，遵医嘱要到伯恩茅斯静养一周，而你因为讨厌孤单而找我做伴）。问题是，身为人母，第一个责任就是不能害怕找儿子开诚布公地谈话。要是在一八九二年七月的时候，令堂曾找你并把她在你身上看到的问题摊开来谈，让你对她吐露真情，那事情就会好办得多，而你俩最终也一定会更快乐。她鬼鬼祟祟向我诉说的做法是错误的。她写给我无数封的短信，每次信封上都注明是"私信"，信中不是求我不要太频繁地邀你吃晚餐就是求我不要给你任何钱，而且每封最后都会有一句殷切的附笔："任何情况下都不能让艾尔弗雷德知道我写过信给你。"这种通信能收到什么好处呢？你等过我邀你吃晚餐吗？从来没有。你把与我共进晚餐视为理所当然，不请自来。要是我说你几句，你总是顶嘴说："不跟你吃晚餐的话我要到哪儿吃去？难道你以为我会在家里吃？"这真是让人无言以对。每当我决绝地不让你与我共进晚餐，你都威胁说要干出什么蠢事来，而且说到做到。所以，令堂老是写信给我有什么用呢？唯一的作用不外是愚蠢而要命地把她该负的道德责任转嫁到我身上。许多事实都证明了，她的软弱和缺乏勇气不管对她自己、对你还是对我，都同样具有毁灭性。其间的种种细节就不必多说了，但有一点是毫无疑问的：当她听说令尊来过我家大吵大闹，让我当众出丑之后，她理应知道一个严重危机已迫在眉睫，必须采取行动加以化解。

但她唯一想得出来的，是派那个乔治·温德姆[1]来找我，以如簧之舌劝我"渐渐把你甩掉"！

要是我有法子"渐渐把你甩掉"就好了！我试过用尽一切方法结束你我的友谊，甚至离开英国，留下一个国外的假地址，希望可以一举斩断那个已经变得烦人、可憎和会毁了我的纽带。你以为我有法子"渐渐把你甩掉"吗？你以为那就足以让令尊满意吗？你知道不是这么回事。令尊真正想要的，不是你我中断友谊，而是让我成为天大丑闻的主角。那是他努力追求的。他的名字已经多年没有在报端出现，他看出自己有机会重新受到英国大众的注目，而且是以全新的形象出现：慈父。他的幽默感被唤醒。要是我真的跟你一刀两断，他将会无比失望，因为事实证明，他闹的二度离婚[2]官司不管始末和细节有多让人反胃，都只是为他赢得了小小的臭名。他追求大受欢迎，手段则是把自己打扮成纯洁世风的捍卫者——按照英国大众时下的水平，这是成为领一时风骚的英雄的不二法门。我在一出戏剧里说过，这个"大众"如果说上半年像卡利班，那下半年便像答尔丢夫[3]。令尊集这两种个性于一身，堪称英

1　乔治·温德姆：国会议员，与道格拉斯家有亲戚关系，写过好几本文学书。

2　昆士伯里侯爵与波西母亲离婚后再婚，但很快又离婚。

3　答尔丢夫：莫里哀笔下的伪君子和骗子。

国大众的化身，自然会被奉为清教徒主义最咄咄逼人和最典型的代表。所以，即使"渐渐把你甩掉"切实可行，对我一样于事无补。所以难道你现在还看不出来，令堂该做而未做的事是把你、我和令兄德拉姆兰里格[1]三人找来，毫不含糊地要求你我中断交往？真是那样的话，她将发现我会是她最热烈的附议者，而既然有我和令兄在场，她也不用害怕和你说话。但她不这样做，她害怕负责任，所以设法把它们推到我身上。没错，她是曾写给我一封短信，劝我不要对令尊发出律师信。她说得很对：我以为律师保护得了我，这想法极其荒谬。但不管她的信多么言之有理，它所可能产生的任何正面效果都会被那句一贯的附笔抵消无余："任何情况下都不能让艾尔弗雷德知道我写过信给你。"

一听说我继你之后也给令尊发出了律师信，你便乐不可支。我是受你怂恿才那么做的。我不能告诉你令堂非常反对这行动，因为她曾要我做出最庄严的承诺，保证绝不告诉你有关她写信的事，而我又愚不可及地信守承诺。你现在看得出来她没有找你摊开来谈是不对的吗？看得出来她老是暗地里找我谈话和偷偷摸摸给我写信都是不对的

---

1 指波西的长兄德拉姆兰里格（Drumlanrig）子爵法兰西斯·道格拉斯，他在一次打猎时因枪支走火身亡。

吗？谁都不应把该负的责任推给别人。任何推出去的责任终归会回到原该负责的人身上。你的人生观、你的哲学（这是假设你还有什么哲学可言）可以用一语道尽：不管你干了什么，都应该由别人买单。我不只是指你任何花费都要别人掏钱（这方面只是你的哲学在日常生活的一个应用），而是指你彻底地把一切责任转嫁到别人身上。你以此为信条。迄今为止，你这信条都很管用。你逼我采取法律行动，是因为知道我这么做了之后，令尊将会把炮口从你身上转移到我身上，而我将不得不扛起与他厮杀的责任。你的盘算很准，我和令尊真是照足你预想的剧本演出。尽管如此，你并非真的脱得了身。没错，你的"婴儿撒母耳"形象（为简洁起见姑且这么称之）在一般大众的接受度确实很高，哪怕伦敦颇有一些人嗤之以鼻，而牛津又有小部分人为之捧腹（因为这两个地方都有人认识你，而凡走过的必留下痕迹）。除这两个城市各一小圈子的人以外，世人都把你看成一个正派的年轻人，以为这年轻人差点受一个邪恶败德的艺术家引诱而误入歧途，幸赖慈父及时出手抢救，化险为夷。这故事听起来头头是道。但你知道你并未脱身。我说的"脱身"不是指你未能从其中一个愚蠢陪审员问的蠢问题中脱身（检察官和法官都没把他的问题当一回事，也没有谁会当一回事），我主要是就你的良心而言。总有一天，你会不由自主反省自己的所作所为，并对整件事情的演变结果无法心安理得；总有一天你会暗地里愧疚难当。戴着一副厚面具面对世界对你来说固然有莫大的必要，但每当四下无人，你总有些时候会把它脱下来一会儿——至少是为了呼吸而脱下来一会儿。不然，你真的可能会窒息而死。

出于同样的道理，令堂也必然总有些时候会对自己把责任推给别人的做法感到悔恨（何况那个人本身便有够多包袱要扛）。对于你，她可说是同时身兼父亲和母亲的职责，但她有充分尽到这两种职责的其中一种吗？如果说我已受够了你的坏脾气、粗鲁和吵闹，她想必也受够了。十四个月前，我最后一次与太太会面。我提醒她，从今以后，她将同时要对西里尔负起父亲和母亲的职责。我告诉了她令堂与你的相处之道（内容和这信提到的一样，只是更详细一些）。我又告诉她令堂以前为何会没完没了写一些信封上注明是"私信"的信件到泰特街（事实上，这些信是那么的源源不绝，以至我太太曾笑说我和令堂一定是正在合写一部社会小说）。我求太太无论如何不可以用令堂对待你的方式对待西里尔，我要她必须教导西里尔这个：日后他倘若让一个无辜之人流血，一定要回家告诉母亲，让她先帮他洁净双手，再教他如何通过忏悔或赔偿来洁净灵魂。我又说，若是她害怕为另一个人（哪怕这人是她儿子）的人生负责，她就应该找个监护人来帮忙。后来我高兴地知道，她照做了。她找了阿德里安·霍普（Adrian Hope）充当监护人（你和他在泰特街见过一面）。此人出身高贵、有教养且个性美好，有他当监护人，西里尔和维维安的未来人生将可望更光明。其实令堂也是一样：如果她害怕直接面对你，那她本该在亲戚之中挑个你也许会愿意听他说话的人来当你的监护人。但令堂从一开始本来就不应该害怕面对你。看看结果吧。你会说她对现在这样的结果感到满意和高兴吗？

我知道她把你的不长进归罪于我。我听说了——但不是从你认识的人那里听说的，而是从一些你不认识也不会想认识的人那里听说的。我听人说令堂喜欢说这类的话："年长者有责任对年轻人发挥影响力。"对你的不长进，这是她最喜欢采取的态度之一，这态度也迎合了公众的偏见和无知，因而备受肯定。我用不着问你，我对你产生过什么影响力，你知道我对你毫无影响力。这也是你最喜欢自夸的事情之一，而且是你唯一站得住脚的自夸。事实上，你有什么是我影响得了的呢？你的脑袋吗？它发育还不完全。你的想象力吗？它已经死掉。你的心吗？它还没有长出来。我生平遇过的所有人中，你是唯一我无法以任何方式加以影响的人，就连我因照顾你而病倒和发高烧的时候，我的影响力照样不足以让你为我拿杯牛奶，不足以让你张罗一个病人的各种必需品，也不足以让你坐马车到一两百码（编者注：一百码约合九十一米，王尔德此处意指书店不远）以外的书店用我的钱帮我买一本书。当我认真投入写作，创作着文采更胜康格里夫（Congreve）和哲理更胜小仲马的喜剧时，我的影响力并不足以让你不来打扰，留给一个艺术家他必需的清静。但我就是说不动你不来打扰我，不管我在什么地方写作，那地方都会成为你抽烟喝酒、废话连篇的休憩之所。"年长者有责任对年轻人发挥影响力"固然是漂亮理论，但我听了只想放声大笑。我猜你听了之后的反应也会是笑——得意的窃笑。你当然有权笑。我也听说令堂谈到了钱。她理直气壮地声称，她无数次恳求我不要给你钱花。我承认她说过。她写过无数封信给我，每封最后都有这句附笔："任何情况下都不能让艾尔弗雷德知道我写过信给你。"但我自己何尝高兴于为你支付从早晨的刮胡膏到半夜的马车费的每一项开支。我烦死了，并一再表示不满。我常常说："我讨厌你把我看成'有用'的人，因为没有艺术家喜欢被这样看待或对待。"艺术家就像艺术本身一样，是以无用为本质。听到这个你常生气。真话总是会让你生气。确实，真话是最不中听，也是最难启齿的。

但我说的真话并未改变你的观点或生活方式。每天我都得为你的每一笔消费掏钱，由早到晚。只有一个好到荒唐或愚蠢得不可思议的人才会那样做，我不幸集两者之大成。每次我指出令堂应该提供你一些所需的用度，你都会有一个很漂亮得体的回答。你说，令尊给她的钱（我相信是一年一千五百英镑左右）对她这种身份地位的女人是不够的，所以你不能在她已经给你的以外再向她要。你说得不错，令堂的收入确实与她的身份与品位极不相称，但你不应以此为借口，用我的钱花天酒地。正好相反，考虑到令堂收入不丰，你更应勉励自己过得节俭些才是。事实上，你原是个（我猜至今还是）典型的感伤主义者[1]。感伤主义者不过是这样一种人：既想要感受情绪上的痛快，又不想付出代价。你体贴令堂而不掏她腰包是高尚的情操，但你用我的钱包来支持这种情操是丑陋的行为。你以为人可以白白得到一种感情满足而不需要付出——没这回事。就连最美好、最自我牺牲的精神都是要付出的（说来奇怪，付出代价正是它们美好的原因）。芸芸众生的知性生活和感情生活都非常让人鄙夷：就像他们的观念净是从思想的流动图书馆借来（即从一个没灵魂时代的"时代精神"借来），一周

1　"感伤主义者"原是指那些读二三流催泪言情小说时会被逗哭的人，作者嘲笑他们感情廉价。

后再污渍斑斑地归还，他们也总是设法用挂账的方式获得感情，待收到账单时又拒绝付款。你应该走出你那种感伤主义的人生观。只有为一种感情付出过代价，你才会真正认识它的质量，并从这认识里得到长进。还要记住，感伤主义者骨子里总是个犬儒主义者[1]。确实，感伤主义只是犬儒主义的公假日罢了。而且不管犬儒主义在知性层面多么有趣，既然该主义已经爬出了大木盆而走进了俱乐部[2]，那它就只合当一个没灵魂的人的完美哲学。犬儒主义有它的社会价值（对艺术家来说，任何表现形式都是有趣的），但就其本身而言，这种主义是贫乏的，因为一个十足的犬儒主义者从不会悟明什么。

我想，只要你现在反省一下你是怎样看待令堂的收入，又是怎样看待我的收入，你将不会再自豪，而且说不定哪天会良心发现，告诉令堂你花我的钱之时从未问过我的意愿。你以为花我的钱就是表达了你对我的挚诚，这想法确实够古怪，花我的钱来表达，对我个人来说则是可悲之极。通过大钱小钱都向我要，你让你在自己眼中显得充

1　这里的"犬儒主义者"指不信人性有真善美可言，以讥笑态度对待一切的人。

2　相传犬儒主义的鼻祖第欧根尼（Diogenes）为了讽刺有钱人的奢华，睡觉时以一个大木盆为床。王尔德说"该主义已经爬出了大木盆而走进了俱乐部"是嘲讽波西的犬儒主义成色不纯。

满孩童的魅力；通过坚持要我替你的每项吃喝玩乐付账，你以为你找到了永远不用长大的诀窍。我承认，听到令堂对我的评论时，我感到痛苦。我也确信，你只要稍加反省，也一定会同意我说的：即便令堂不愿出于让我家庭破散而表示难过或后悔，更好的做法也毋宁是保持沉默。你不必把这信中谈我心理演化和我希望达到什么境界的那些部分给她过目，她不会感兴趣的。但如果我是你，就会把这信中那些纯粹与你生活有关的部分给她看。

事实上，如果我是你，就不会为了得到爱而用虚假装点门面。人没有理由把私生活公之于世，因为世界是不明事理的。但对于那些你想博得关爱的人，情况便另当别论了。前些时一个好朋友来看我（我们有十年的老交情）。他说他不相信我受到的任何一项指控是事实，说他肯定我是无辜的，是令尊丑陋阴谋的牺牲者。我听了泪如雨下，告诉他尽管令尊的许多指控是无中生有，是恶意陷害，但我从前的生活确实充满反常的欢愉和奇怪的激情。又说除非他接受这些事是事实，否则我将无法继续与他为友，甚至无法与他来往。他听了无比震撼。但我们既然是朋友，我便不想用假装的门面骗得他的友情。我说过，真话是难以启齿的，但被迫说谎会让人更痛苦。

我记得，在最后一场官司，当我坐在被告席上听着洛克伍德[1]历数我的罪状时（他的话骇人听闻，简直像是出自塔西佗和但丁的如椽之笔，又像是萨沃纳罗拉[2]在指控罗马教皇），我本来因为内心充满恐惧而昏昏沉沉。但我忽然想到："倘若正在挞伐我的人是我自己，那会是何等了不起！"在那一刹那，我明白了怎么说一个人并不重要，重要的是这些话是由谁所说。我毫不怀疑，当一个人跪倒在地，双手捶胸，把一生罪孽和盘托出之时，他正到达了他人生的最高点。这道理也适用于你。如果你能亲口告诉令堂一点你所过的生活，你一定会快乐一些。我在一八九三年十二月那次会面对她说了很多（有些事情当然不方便说，也有些只能说个梗概），但看来并未因此让她变得更有勇气。正好相反，她坚持要当鸵鸟，不过问你的生活。但事情如果是由你来告诉她，情况应当会大为不同。也许我说的许多话都让你觉得刺耳，但事实就是事实，无从否认。如果你读这信读得够仔细，就会与自己做过的事面对面。

我长篇大论写了这许多话，是为了让你悟明，在我入狱之前、在你我交往那致命的三年里，你是怎样对我的；

---

1 洛克伍德：内政部副检察长，王尔德第二次受审时的检察官。
2 萨沃纳罗拉：十五世纪佛罗伦萨修士，政治和宗教改革家，常在讲道时猛烈抨击当时的教皇。

是为了让你悟明，在我服刑期间（再两次月圆就刑满了），你是怎样对我的；也是为了让你悟明，我准备出狱后如何对待自己和对待别人。这信我无法重新构思，也无法重写，所以哪怕信中有很多地方被泪水弄脏，也有许多涂涂改改，你也只能照着它现有的样子读它，竭尽所能去理解。我之所以要涂涂改改，是为了把我的思想感情表达得绝对清楚，不致因为言过其实或词不达意而引起误解。就像小提琴一样，文字也是要调音的：歌声或琴弦不管是振动太多还是太少都会让音调有失真之虞，同样道理，文字太多或太少都会让信息有走样之虞。信里每句话都有它的确切用意，没半点修辞成分。不管乍看有多么不重要和钻牛角尖，信中的每处涂抹或改写都是为了努力传达我的真切感受，是为了找出我心境的精确对应语。最刻骨的感受总是最迟才能发为文字。

我承认这是封严厉的信，我下笔时没有留情。你确实可以抗议说，我连我最轻的一种悲伤和最小一项损失都拿来与你计较，这对你并不公平。没错，我确实是把你的个性一分一毫地拿来称，但别忘了，是你自己要爬到天平上去的。

你要晓得，哪怕只是拿你与我牢狱生涯的其中一刻相称量，你那一头的天平都会翘高到屋梁上去。虚荣心让你选择那一头，虚荣心让你死巴着那一头。这正是你我的友谊所包含的一个心理学性质的大错，即比例的完全失衡。你硬要闯进一个大得让你无法消受的生命：那生命的运行轨道既非你的目力可及，也非你的运行能力所能及；那生命的思想、激情和行动全都举足轻重、动见观瞻，可以带来最奇妙或最可怕的后果。你的小小生命连同它那些小小的任性和喜怒无常在你自己所属的界域里原是无伤大雅。例如，它们在牛津时便无伤大雅。在那里，你能碰到的最糟糕的体验不过是挨学监一顿训或挨院长一顿骂，最痛快的体验也不过是赛舟夺冠，然后在方院里筑篝火庆祝一番。离开牛津之后，你本该继续留在自己所属的界域里生活。只要一天留在这个界域内，你就会一天平安无事。你是一种非常现代的人类的典型，你错只错在跨入了我的界域。你无顾忌地挥霍生命并不是罪，因为挥霍原是青春的特权，但你逼我为你的挥霍买单是可耻的。你渴望找个朋友从早陪你到晚，这本身无可厚非，甚至几乎有点田园诗意。但被你巴着不放的朋友不应该是个文人和艺术家，因为你的持续出现会瘫痪他的创作机能，彻底摧毁美丽作品出现的可能。你严肃地认定，消磨一晚的最好方法是先在萨沃伊饭店喝香槟、吃晚餐，接着是到杂耍剧场开包厢看表演，最后是到威利斯餐厅喝香槟、吃消夜，为一晚画上完美句点。这种想法本无不妥。在伦敦，和你持相同观点的可爱年轻人车载斗量。你甚至不能称之为自以为是，因为那是怀特俱乐部的入会资格。但你无权要求我充当你这些享乐的包办人，而你那样做也显示你对我的才华缺乏真正的赏识。再者，你与令尊的争吵本该完全是你们两人间的事，你们应该把它拿到后院去吵才对（我相信，父子吵架通常都是到自家后院吵去），但你偏偏要闹得街知巷闻，要把它演成一出悲喜剧，要全世界的人当观众，又拿我当这场可耻竞赛的奖品。事实上，你恨令尊而令尊也恨你这件事，英国大众并不感兴趣。父子相恨在英国的家庭间司空见惯，它应该被局限在它该上演的地方，即家里。一出家庭范围它就会水土不服。这种逾越是一种冒犯。家务事不是一面应该拿到大街上挥舞的红旗，不是一把应该带到屋顶上吹响的号角。就像你把自己带出你应属的界域，你也把你家的家务事带出了它应属的界域。

那些走出他们应属界域的人改变了的只是环境，而非自己的本性。他们并不会获得与他们进入的那个新界域相适的思想或感情。他们力有不逮。正如我在《意图》（*Intentions*）一书里说过的，情绪力量就像物理能量一般，其范围或持续的时间都是有极限的。小个的杯子就只能装少量的酒，不能再多——这是个改变不了的事实，哪怕整

– 161 –

个勃艮第所有紫色酒桶都装满葡萄酒，或是西班牙所有葡萄园都堆满高及采收工膝盖的葡萄。最常见的误解莫过于以为那些大悲剧的制造者或旁观者会产生与悲剧气氛相恰的感情，也没有误解比这个更要致命了。那些披着"火之裳"[1]的殉教者也许会望见上帝的脸，但对那些负责堆放柴薪或弄松木头堆的人来说，整件事情不过有如屠夫宰牛、制木炭人在森林里砍倒一棵树，或是割草人用镰刀砍下一朵花。崇高的激情只会见于崇高的灵魂，而崇高的事件也只有高度与之相当的人能够理解。

若论艺术上的登峰造极，或论观察上的细致入微和饶富暗示意味，我看不出古往今来有哪出戏剧的笔力更胜莎士比亚对罗森克兰茨（Rosencrantz）和吉尔吉斯顿（Guildenstern）的描绘。他们是哈姆雷特大学时代的朋友，常常会一起回忆往日的快乐时光。剧中，当两人与哈姆雷特久别重聚时，后者正失魂落魄，承担着一个对他性情气质而言太沉重的责任：先前，他父亲的鬼魂身穿全副甲胄向他现身，强加给他一个于他而言既太伟大又太琐碎的任务[2]。哈姆雷特长于幻想，但父亲要求他去行动；他具有诗

---

1 "火之裳"指烈焰加身，语出十九世纪苏格兰诗人亚历山大·史密斯（Alexander Smith）的长诗《生活剧》（*A Life Drama*）。

2 莎士比亚剧作《哈姆雷特》中王子哈姆雷特的父王被其弟弟毒杀，化为鬼魂向儿子显现，要求儿子为他报仇。

人气质，却被要求去弄懂人间纠纷的前因后果。他被迫去面对人生的现实层面（他对这方面一无所知），而非人生的理想本质（这方面他倒是知之甚多）。他不知道该怎么办，只好装疯卖傻。布鲁图[1]是以装疯来隐藏行刺的匕首，但哈姆雷特装疯只是为了掩饰软弱。通过插科打诨，他争取到拖延的时间。就像艺术家对待艺术理论的态度总是半心半意，哈姆雷特对行动的态度也是半心半意。他老是在脑子里构想各种行动计划，又知道它们不过是"空话、空话、空话"。他不想成为缔造自己历史的英雄，只愿当自己悲剧的观众。他谁都不信任（包括不信任自己），但他的怀疑又帮助不了他，因为这怀疑不是出自怀疑主义，而是出自意志的犹豫不决。

对哈姆雷特所受的种种煎熬，罗森克兰茨和吉尔吉斯顿毫无察觉。他们唯一懂的是哈腰鞠躬，陪在哈姆雷特身边傻笑或微笑。两人就像唱双簧似的，一个说了什么，另一个便会以更谄媚的方式重说一遍。到最后，当哈姆雷特借助一出戏中戏"挖出国王内心的秘密"[2]，把倒霉的国王

---

1 布鲁图：罗马共和国贵族，刺杀恺撒的主谋。

2 "挖出国王内心的秘密"：这是哈姆雷特向罗森克兰茨和吉尔吉斯顿两人说过的话。当时他正安排用一出戏中戏，以探知他叔叔是否真的毒杀了他父亲。

吓得魂不附体，夹着尾巴离开之后，罗森克兰茨和吉尔吉斯顿还是对哈姆雷特的用心浑然不察，只认为他的举动破坏了宫廷礼仪，叫人难过。在"以相恰的感情谛视生命的风景"[1]一事上，这是他们所能达到的最高程度。他们与哈姆雷特心里藏着的秘密近在咫尺，却对其一无所知，明白告诉他们也是枉然。他们都是小小的杯子，只装得下少许，无法再多。在全剧快终场时，有文字暗示他们将会落入一个原为别人而设的圈套，将会（或是"也许将会"）死得很惨和很突然。不过，这么一种悲剧性下场并不是他们的真正下场。罗森克兰茨和吉尔吉斯顿永远不死，死的反倒是霍拉肖[2]。尽管戏文里说过，老天为了让霍拉肖可以"把哈姆雷特其人及其事迹向那些意犹未尽的人详细报告"，故意让他长命：

　　就暂且不让他享至福

　　留他在这个严酷世间继续受苦受难

1　"以相恰的感情谛视生命的风景"是华兹华斯的诗句，前文引用过。王尔德这里是说罗森克兰茨和吉尔吉斯顿完全无法"以相恰的感情谛视生命的风景"。

2　剧中的霍拉肖不但没死，反而是全剧主要角色中唯一能活到剧终的一位。所以王尔德后面才会说他没有"死在观众眼前"。

霍拉肖真的是死了，哪怕不是死在观众眼前，也没有留下兄弟。但罗森克兰茨和吉尔吉斯顿长生不死，不朽得就像安吉罗和答尔丢夫[1]，而且应该与后两人平起平坐。他们是现代生活对古典时代的友谊理想的贡献。凡有谁要写一篇新的《论友谊》[2]，都必须给罗森克兰茨和吉尔吉斯顿留个位置，以西塞罗的文风把两人讴歌一番。古往今来都不缺这类人，责难他们只会让自己显得缺乏鉴赏力。他们唯一的问题只在于逾越自己应属的界域，如此而已。灵魂的崇高性（sublimity）不具传染力，崇高的思想和崇高的情感就本质来说是孑然独立的。连奥菲莉亚[3]都不能弄明白的，罗森克兰茨和吉尔吉斯顿更不会领悟得了。我当然不是要拿他们两人和你相提并论。你们之间差别太大了：他们会是那样的人纯属命运安排，但你是刻意为之。你处心积虑和不请自来地闯入我的界域，在那里占住一个你既无权利也无资格占据的位子。凭着你那出奇的倔强劲儿，凭着没有一天不出现在我面前，你成功把我的整个人生吸走。你是吸走了，却不知道要拿它怎么用，火大之下把它

---

1 安吉罗为莎士比亚剧作《一报还一报》中的角色。前面提过，答尔丢夫是莫里哀笔下的角色，《伪君子》（*Tartuffe*）一剧主角。

2 《论友谊》：古罗马政治家和演说家西塞罗的作品，此作论述了理想的友谊应该是怎样的，表现了"古典时代的友谊理想"。

3 奥菲莉亚：哈姆雷特的爱人，她一直不理解哈姆雷特的奇怪言行。

砸得稀巴烂。以你的为人，会有这样的结果是很自然的。想想看，如果给一个小孩一件对他的小脑袋来说太神奇的玩具，或一件对他那双懵懂的眼睛来说太漂亮的玩具，结果只会有两种可能：如果是个任性小孩，就会把玩具给砸了；如果是个迟钝小孩，就会把玩具丢下，跑去找同伴玩耍。你就是这样。攫住我的生命之后，你并不知道怎么用它。你不可能知道。它太神奇了，让你不知所措。你本应把它丢下，跑去找同伴玩耍。不幸的是，你却出于任性把它给砸了。这也许就是一切发生过的事的最终秘密。因为秘密总是比它们的显相要小，所以，说不定只要抽掉一颗原子，这世界就会地动山摇。在"比例完全失衡"这事情上，我就像你一样难辞其咎，因为如果说你我的相识会对我构成危险，那你我相识的那个特定时刻对我更是致命：那时候你的人生充其量只是处于播种阶段，而我的人生处于大丰收阶段。

还有两件事是我必须说的。首先是我破产的事。前些天我听说（我承认这消息让我大为失望），即便你家人现在愿意代我还令尊钱也太迟了，这于法不合。换言之，我目前所处的痛苦破产地位将还要延续相当长的一段时间。哪怕只是出版一本书，都要先得到破产管理人的许可（我的所有账目也要上交给他）。另外，每逢我与一个剧院经理签约或制作一出戏剧，都得把收据交给令尊和其他几个债权人。我想，就算是你，现在也应该可以看出，你那个如意算盘（我破产可以让令尊"失分"）并不如你当初想象的那么高明，至少对我来说不高明。在把我弄得一贫如洗以前，你本不该以满足你的幽默感（一种刻薄和出人意表的幽默感）为首要考虑，而是应先考虑到我会多痛苦和屈辱。事实上，就像你逼我打那场官司一样，你任由我破产只是正中令尊下怀，如他所愿。若他只是单枪匹马、别无援手，本来绝对形成不了气候。拜你所赐（哪怕不是出于你的本心），他有了一个最有力的盟友。

我从莫尔·阿迪在夏天的来信中得知，你不止一次表示过，你想偿还我"一点我曾经为你花的钱"。不幸的是，我曾经为你花掉的是我的艺术、我的人生、我的名声和我的历史地位，所以，即便你家里坐拥天下的一切宝物，也偿还不了我被夺走的千万分之一，或补偿不了我流过的最小一滴眼泪。当然，一切债都是得还的，即便身处破产中的人亦不例外。看来你是以为，破产是赖债不还的便捷方法，甚至是让"债权人失分"的便捷方法。事实却是相反。如果继续借用你偏爱的语句来说，破产是债权人让债务人"失分"的好方法，因为通过宣布债务人破产，债权人可以动用法律来没收他所有的财产，然后才逼着他偿还每一笔欠款。要是这个人还不清，最后就会落得身无分文，穷得像是最穷的叫花子，不得不站在某个拱道里或大街上伸出手求人施舍（至少在英国，这个人是没脸那样做的）。法律夺走我拥有的一切，包括藏书、家具、油画、我所有书的著作权、我所有剧作的著作权（从《快乐王子》到《温夫人的扇子》），下至楼梯地毯和门前的踏垫。但法律不只夺走我原拥有的一切，还夺走我未来本该拥有的一切。例如，我在婚姻协议中占有的财产份额已经被卖掉。幸而，我后来通过一些朋友的名义把它们买了回来，要不然，万一我太太过世，两个小孩将会像我一样，一辈子不名一文。我猜想，我在我家爱尔兰庄园占有的份额（家父留给我的），将会是下一个被拍卖的项目。我为此非常痛心，但我必须认命。

欠令尊那七百便士（还是英镑？）也是我非还不可的。即便我原拥有和未来本该拥有的一切全都被夺走，只能以一个落魄破产者的身份走出监狱，我一样会想办法还清所有欠款。我用记账方式欠下的款项不少，包括了萨沃伊饭店的晚餐费（我还记得它那清澈的甲鱼汤，那包在皱皱葡萄叶子里的美味蒿雀，那色如琥珀而气味也几乎像琥珀的醇厚香槟——一八八〇年份的"达贡聂"是你的最爱，对否？）。再来还有威利斯餐厅的消夜费（我还记得它那些专为我们准备的特酿葡萄酒、那些从斯特拉斯堡直接进口的美妙馅饼，它那些妙不可言的干邑白兰地——这种白兰地总是斟在钟形大杯的杯底，好让真正的美食家可以更好地体会其精致绝伦的酒香）。对这些酒食账，我当然不能像赖债恶客那样拒不还钱。还有我送你那副精致的袖扣（由四颗镀银的心形月亮石构成，每颗边上镶着一圈相间的红宝石和钻石，样式是我亲自设计的，由刘易斯珠宝行负责打造，是为庆祝我第二出戏剧大获成功而送你的特别小礼物）。虽然我知道你几个月后便把它贱卖了，但我还是得归还欠店家的账款。总不能为了送你礼物而让珠宝行老板亏钱。所以你看到了，即使出了狱，我还有许多债要还。

欠钱是如此，人生方面的亏欠也是如此。人终归得为自己做过的每件事负责，这道理就连对你亦不例外。哪怕是你（你只想享受毫无责任拘束的绝对自由，坚持要别人供养你又拒绝回报以关爱、尊敬和感谢），都必然有一天会不由自主地反省自己做过的事，并设法做点什么（不管有多徒劳）当作赎罪。即便你始终缺乏反省能力，这本身便构成惩罚的一部分。别以为你洗洗手便可以推卸一切责任，以为耸耸肩或笑一笑便没你的事，以为这样做就可以再去交一个新朋友或铺开一桌新酒席。你无法把你给我造成的一切只当成一种茶余饭后偶尔品尝的感伤回忆，或当成只是廉价小旅馆墙上的旧挂毯，其作用在于作为现代舒适生活的陪衬。你固然可以靠一种新的酱汁或一瓶新的陈酿暂时忘忧，但酒筵终会散席，终会只剩下变馊的残羹和变苦的瓶底残酒。要么是今天，要么是明天，你总有一天非悟明不可。要是你至死不悟，你活过的人生将会是何等的委琐、贫乏和缺乏想象力。我在写给莫尔·阿迪的一封信中提出过一种可以帮助你的方法。他会告诉你是什么方法。弄懂它有助于培养你的想象力。记住我说过的，想象力可以让人同时懂得欣赏别人的理想状态和现实状态。如果你一个人悟明不了，就找个人来商议。我已经不得不直面我的过去，该轮到你来直面你的过去。静下来好好反省吧。最要不得的缺点莫过于浮浅。凡经过悟明的都会归正。找你兄长商量吧。不错，珀西确实是不二人选。让他读这封信，告诉他你我友谊的各种细节。得知整件事情的前因后果后，他一定可以提出最好的建议。要是早告诉他真相，我将会减少多少苦难和耻辱啊！记得吗，从阿尔及尔回到伦敦那个晚上，我曾提议这么做，但你断然反对。所以，当珀西在晚饭后来到之时，你我只能合演一出喜剧，指称令尊一定是疯了，才会满脑袋都是荒谬和难以解释的幻觉。那确实是出上乘的喜剧，一点都没有因为珀西信以为真和忧心忡忡而有所失色。不幸的是它的结局非常不堪。我在这信中谈到的种种惨状就是它的后果之一，而如果它们给你带来困扰，请别忘了它们曾带给我最深和无从逃避的耻辱。我别无选择，只能忍受。你也是一样。

第二件我要说的事是关于我们日后见面的条件、细节安排和地点。我从你去年夏初写给罗比的信里得知，你已经把我写给你的信和送给你的礼物（至少是还剩下的那些）封存为两包，急着要亲手还给我。你当然是有必要还给我的，因为你不明白我何以要写那些优美的信给你，一如不明白我何以要送你那些漂亮礼物。你不了解那些信的原意不是供你发表，那些礼物不是为了让你典当的。况且，它们是属于我人生一个逝去已久的部分，是属于一段你无法欣赏其真正价值的友谊。当你回首往事，看到你是如何把我的整个人生握在掌中，想必会不胜惊异。回首那段日子，我也是不胜惊异，只是除惊异以外还有着其他极为不同的情绪。

如果一切顺利，我将会在五月底获释，届时，我希望可以马上和罗比与莫尔·阿迪到国外某个滨海的小村住住。就像欧里庇得斯[1]在一出写伊菲革涅亚（Iphigenia）的

---

1 欧里庇得斯：古希腊三大悲剧家之一。王尔德引用的话出自《伊菲革涅亚在陶里斯》（*Iphigenia in Tauris*）。

戏剧中所说的：Θάλασσα κλύζει πάντα τ'ανθ ῶπων κακά
（大海可以涤去世界的污垢和创伤。）

我希望至少可以和两位朋友共度一个月，在他们有益身心和充满关爱的陪伴下，重获宁静和平衡，忘掉一些烦恼，获得较开朗的心境。对广大、单纯和原始的东西（大海是其中之一），我有一种深深的思慕。就像大地一样，大海对我而言不亚于母亲。我觉得，我们一向对自然都远观过甚，亲近得太不够。古希腊人的态度要明智太多。他们从来不会争论日落时的草影是不是真的紫红色。在他们眼中，大海是供人游泳的，沙地是供人奔跑的。他们喜爱树木是因为它的绿荫，喜欢树林是因为中午的幽静。最无用的东西到了他们手中都会变得有用：修剪葡萄藤的人懂得用常春藤编成发冠，戴在头上遮挡日晒；艺术家和运动员（我们从希腊人那里继承了这两大人物类型）戴的则是用味苦的桂叶和野百里香编成的桂冠——这两种植物对人类都原无用处。

我们自诩生活在重实用的时代，却什么都不会用。我们忘了水可用以洁净、火可用以精炼，而大地是众人之母。其结果是，我们的艺术沦为一种月亮艺术，只顾与影子嬉戏，而古希腊艺术是一种太阳艺术，着重与事物本身打交道。我切实感受到自然力中蕴含着净化的力量。我想要回到它们当中，住在它们旁边。当然，像我这般现代的人，像我这么一个"时代之子"，光是望向世界便能够感觉其可爱。想到出狱当天，花园里将会盛放着金链花和丁香花，我便高兴得簌簌发抖。届时我将会看到金链花在风中摇曳不停，流光溢彩；将会看到丁香花的淡紫色羽毛随风纷飞，为我在空中撒满清香。听说，当植物学家林奈（Linnaeus）在英格兰某处石南丛生的高地，第一次看到毫不起眼的荆豆花开得漫山遍野时，感动得跪倒在地，喜极而泣。我了解他的感觉，也知道有眼泪在某些玫瑰花的花瓣上等着我去流。花一直是我心之欢愉的一部分，从我孩提开始便是如此。花冠或贝壳纹路中潜藏着的任何色泽（它们以某种微妙的方式透露出万事万物的灵魂），都会引起我心性的深深共鸣。借戈蒂耶的话来说[1]，我是那种认定感官世界存在的人。

另一方面，自然的种种美固然让人满足，但我现在已意识到，它们的背后潜藏着某种精神力，而色彩斑斓的种种形状和形态，不过是这精神力的显相。我渴望与这精神力臻于和谐。我已经厌倦了述说诸般人和事。自然的大奥秘，即生命的大奥秘，才是我现在要寻索的，而说不定我

1　这话原是戈蒂耶用来形容《道林·格雷的画像》主角格雷之语。戈蒂耶：
　　法国诗人、小说家、评论家，与王尔德同为"唯美主义"运动的领袖人物。

可以在"音乐"的大交响曲里、在"悲伤"的启蒙中和在"大海"的深处找着它。我绝对有必要在某处找到它。

就像所有判刑都是死刑，所有审判都是对一个人一生的审判，我已经被审判过三次。第一次我在下了证人席后被逮捕，第二次我被带回拘留所，第三次我被送到监狱坐两年牢。社会将不会再有我的容身之处，也提供不出一处。但大自然（它的甜美雨水会同时分润给义人和不义之人[1]将提供岩缝让我藏身，提供无人知晓的河谷让我不受打扰，静静痛哭。它会在夜空张挂星星，让我不致被绊倒；会送风抹平我的脚印，让别人无法追踪我，加害我；还会用浩然之水洁净我，用苦口药草使我恢复完整。

在某个滨海村落住满一个月后，当六月的玫瑰全都肆意盛开之时，如果我觉得可行，将请罗比安排你我在某个宁静的外国小镇碰面。布鲁日会是理想地点，我多年前去过一次，它的青灰色民居、碧绿色运河和凉爽寂静的街道始终让我念念不忘。届时，你必须换个名字。如果你想见我，你就必须放弃那个让你无比得意的头衔[2]（它确实让你听起来像某种花）。我也必须放弃我的名字，哪怕它一度

1　典出《圣经·马太福音》五章四十五节："因为他叫日头照好人，也照歹人；降雨给义人，也给不义的人。"

2　指"百合花王子"。

在盛名之神口中显得饶富音乐性。与这个世纪所加之于我的重担相比，它是多么的委琐、狭隘和不充分啊！在我功成名就之时，它固然给了我一座金碧辉煌的宫殿，但在我含悲忍辱之际，它连一间容身的茅屋也不留给我。在中世纪，僧侣至少有兜帽可以盖头，而麻风病人也至少有脸巾可以遮脸，我却连这两样东西都不可得，唯一能做的只有改名换姓。

我希望，在发生过那么多事情之后，你我的会面会是它应有的样子。旧时，你我之间总横着一道鸿沟———道艺术成就和文化修养上的鸿沟。而现在，横在我们之间的鸿沟更宽了，而这条鸿沟的名字是"悲伤"。但只要心存谦卑，就没有什么是不可能的；只要心里有爱，世上就没有难成之事。

至于你的回信，内容长短随你喜欢。信封上写上"雷丁皇家监狱，典狱长收"，里面再用另一个信封（不封口的）放你写给我的那封信。如果你用的是很薄的信纸，就别两面写，因为那会不好读。我写这封信时是想到什么便写什么，无所顾忌，你也可以用同样的方式回信。你必须在信中告诉我，自前年八月到现在，你何以都不想给我写封信。特别是从去年五月起，即十一个月前，你明明已经向别人承认，我会这么惨是你害的，而我也知道是你害的，你却还是没有写信。我一个月又一个月等着你的信。就算我没有在等，而是已经铁了心对你关起门窗，你仍然应该知道，没有人可以对"爱"永远关起门窗。福音书里那个不公正的法官最终会做出公正判决，就是因为"公正"天天去敲他的门。同样，福音书里那个不肯夜间起床帮朋友忙的人（他心里没真正把对方当成朋友），最终也是禁不起对方"词恳情切的声声呼唤"而起了床。世界上没有一座监狱是"爱"无法破门而入的。若你不明白这个，就是完全不明白"爱"是何物。另外，你必须在回信中告诉我你为《法兰西信使报》写的那篇文章的内容。我听说了一点。你最好在信中引用一部分内容。别说你不记得了，那可是已经用铅字印成白纸黑字了。另外，告诉我你那本诗集的献词是怎样写的，我要它原原本本的模样：是散文体的话就给我散文体，是诗体的话就给我诗体。我毫不怀疑，这献词包含美的成分。我还要你老老实实告诉我你的生活状况、交友状况、在忙些什么、在看些什么书。告诉我你那本诗集的内容和读者的反应。你想替自己辩护就直说，不要害怕。我唯一介意的是你言不由衷。你信中若有什么弄虚作假之处，我会一眼看穿。我一辈子顶礼膜拜文学并不是白忙或瞎忙，因为它已把我练就为

一个小气鬼，对韵律和音节斤斤计较得

不下米达斯之于他的金币[1]

　　也别忘了我得重新认识你。大概你我都有必要重新认识彼此。

　　有关你，我只有最后一点要说。不要害怕过去。别相信"过去不可挽回"之说。在上帝眼中，过去、现在和未来不过是一瞬间罢了，而我们应该设法用上帝的眼光过生活。时间与空间，或连续与延展，不过是"思想"的偶然条件。想象力可以超越它们，把我们带入自由无碍的理想存在境界。何况，事物在本质上就是我们要它们怎样便怎样。一物是何物，取决于我们看待它的方式。布莱克（Blake）说过："别人看到的是黎明在山岭上展开，我却从中看到上帝子女的欢呼呐喊。"当我禁不起怂恿而对令尊提出诉讼，我的未来便在世人和我自己眼中看似无可挽回地丧失了（我敢说，其实我在更早之前便丧失了这未来）。这时，摆在我前面的只有我的过去。我必须使自己用不同的眼光看它，使世人用不同的眼光看它，使上帝用不同的眼光看它。要做到这个，我便不能忽略它、小

1　出自济慈的《论十四行诗的十四行诗》（*Sonnet on the Sonnet*）。米达斯：古希腊神话里有点石成金能力的国王。

看它、赞扬它或否定它，而只能把它看作我人生与个性演化中一个不可避免的部分，予以完全接纳。我必须对我承受过的所有苦难俯首顺服。我距离灵魂的本真气质还有多远，你从这封信变化不定的心境、它的冷嘲热讽、它的幡然醒悟却又未能活出这些醒悟可以清楚看见。但别忘了我是在一间多么可怕的学校里学这功课。哪怕我还不完全、还不完美，但你可以从我这里学到的也许仍然有很多。当初你走向我是为了学习生之欢愉和艺术之欢愉。不过，老天却看似暗中别有安排，挑了我来教你一些奇妙得多的事情：悲伤的意义和它的美。

你深情的朋友

奥斯卡·王尔德

Because Love is more beautiful than Hate.

Oscar Wilde

H.M. Prison, Reading

[January-March 1897]

Dear Bosie,

After long and fruitless waiting I have determined to write to you myself, as much for your sake as for mine, as I would not like to think that I had passed through two long years of imprisonment without ever having received a single line from you, or any news or message even, except such as gave me pain.

Our ill-fated and most lamentable friendship has ended in ruin and public infamy for me, yet the memory of our ancient affection is often with me, and the thought that loathing, bitterness and contempt should for ever take that place in my heart once held by love is very sad to me: and you yourself will, I think, feel in your heart that to write to me as I lie in the loneliness of prison-life is better than to publish my letters without my permission or to dedicate poems to me unasked, though the world will know nothing of whatever words of grief or passion, of remorse or indifference you may choose to send as your answer or your appeal.

I have no doubt that in this letter in which I have to write of your life and of mine, of the past and of the future, of sweet things changed to bitterness and of bitter things that may be turned into joy, there will be much that will wound your vanity to the quick. If it prove so, read the letter over and over again till it kills your vanity. If you find in it something of which you feel that you are unjustly accused, remember that one should be thankful that there is any fault of which one can be unjustly accused. If there be in it one single passage that brings tears to your eyes, weep as we weep in prison where the day no less than the night is set apart for tears. It is the only thing that can save you. If you go complaining to your mother, as you did with reference to the scorn of you I displayed in my letter to Robbie, so that she may flatter and soothe you back into self-complacency or conceit, you will be completely lost. If you find one false excuse for yourself, you will soon find a hundred, and be just what you were before. Do you still say, as you said to Robbie in your answer, that I *"attribute unworthy motives"* to you? Ah! you had no motives in life. You had appetites merely. A motive is an intellectual aim. That you were *"very young"* when our friendship began? Your defect was not that you knew so little about life, but that you knew so much. The morning dawn of boyhood with its delicate bloom, its clear pure light, its joy of innocence and expectation you had left far behind. With very swift and running feet you had passed from Romance to Realism. The gutter and the things that live in it had begun to fascinate you. That was the origin of the trouble in which you sought my aid, and I, so unwisely according to the wisdom of this world, out of pity and kindness gave it to you. You must read this letter right through, though each word may become to you as the fire or knife of the surgeon that makes the delicate flesh burn or bleed. Remember that the fool in the eyes of the gods and the fool in the eyes of man are very different. One who is entirely ignorant of the modes of Art in its revolution or the moods of thought in its progress, of the pomp of the Latin line or the richer music of the vowelled Greek, of Tuscan sculpture or Elizabethan song may yet be full of the very sweetest wisdom. The real fool, such as the gods mock or mar, is he who does not know himself. I was such a one too long. You have been such a one too long. Be so no more. Do not be afraid. The supreme vice is shallowness. Everything that is realised is right. Remember also that whatever is misery to you to read, is still greater misery to me to set down. To you the Unseen Powers have been very good. They have permitted you to see the strange and tragic shapes of Life as one sees shadows in a crystal. The head of Medusa that turns living men to stone, you have been allowed to look at in a mirror merely. You yourself have walked free among the flowers. From me the beautiful world of colour and motion has been taken away.

I will begin by telling you that I blame myself terribly. As I sit here in this dark cell in convict clothes, a disgraced and ruined man, I blame myself. In the perturbed and fitful nights of anguish, in the long monotonous days of pain, it is myself I blame. I blame myself for allowing an unintellectual friendship, a friendship whose primary aim was not the creation and contemplation of beautiful things, to entirely dominate my life. From the very first there was too wide a gap between us. You had been idle at your school, worse than idle at your university. You did not realise that an artist, and especially such an artist as I am, one, that is to say, the quality of whose work depends on the intensification of personality, requires for the development of his art the companionship of ideas, and intellectual atmosphere, quiet, peace, and solitude. You admired my work when it was finished: you enjoyed the brilliant successes of my first nights, and the brilliant banquets that followed them: you were proud, and quite naturally so, of being the intimate friend of an artist so distinguished: but you could not understand the conditions requisite for the production of artistic work. I am not speaking in phrases of rhetorical exaggeration but in terms of absolute truth to actual fact when I remind you that during the whole time we were together I never wrote one single line. Whether at Torquay, Goring, London, Florence or elsewhere, my life, as long as you were by my side, was entirely sterile and uncreative. And with but few intervals you were, I regret to say, by my side always.

I remember, for instance, in September '93, to select merely one instance out of many, taking a set of chambers, purely in order to work undisturbed, as I had broken my contract with John Hare for whom I had promised to write a play, and who was pressing me on the subject. During the first week you kept away. We had, not unnaturally indeed, differed on the question of the artistic value of your translation of *Salome*, so you contented yourself with sending me foolish letters on the subject. In that week I wrote and completed in every detail, as it was ultimately performed, the first act of *An Ideal Husband*. The second week you returned and my work practically had to be given up. I arrived at St James's Place every morning at 11.30, in order to have the opportunity of thinking and writing without the interruptions inseparable from my own household, quiet and peaceful as that household was. But the attempt was vain. At twelve o'clock you drove up, and stayed smoking cigarettes and chattering till 1.30, when I had to take you out to luncheon at the Café Royal or the Berkeley. Luncheon with its *liqueurs* lasted usually till 3.30. For an hour you retired to White's. At tea-time you appeared again, and stayed till it was time to dress for dinner. You dined with me either at the Savoy or at Tite Street. We did not separate as a rule till after midnight, as supper at Willis's had to wind up the entrancing day. That was my life for those three months, every single day, except during the four days when you went abroad. I then, of course, had to go over to Calais to fetch you back. For one of my nature and temperament it was a position at once grotesque and tragic.

You surely must realise that now? You must see

now that your incapacity of being alone: your nature so exigent in its persistent claim on the attention and time of others: your lack of any power of sustained intellectual concentration: the unfortunate accident—for I like to think it was no more—that you had not yet been able to acquire the "Oxford temper" in intellectual matters, never, I mean, been one who could play gracefully with ideas but had arrived at violence of opinion merely—that all these things, combined with the fact that your desires and interests were in Life not in Art, were as destructive to your own progress in culture as they were to my work as an artist? When I compare my friendship with you to my friendship with such still younger men as John Gray and Pierre Louÿs I feel ashamed. My real life, my higher life was with them and such as they.

Of the appalling results of my friendship with you I don't speak at present. I am thinking merely of its quality while it lasted. It was intellectually degrading to me. You had the rudiments of an artistic temperament in its germ. But I met you either too late or too soon, I don't know which. When you were away I was all right. The moment, in the early December of the year to which I have been alluding, I had succeeded in inducing your mother to send you out of England, I collected again the torn and ravelled web of my imagination, got my life back into my own hands, and not merely finished the three remaining acts of *An Ideal Husband*, but conceived and had almost completed two other plays of a completely different type, the *Florentine Tragedy* and *La Sainte Courtisane*, when suddenly, unbidden, unwelcome, and under circumstances fatal to my happiness you returned. The two works left then imperfect I was unable to take up again. The mood that created them I could never recover. You now, having yourself published a volume of verse, will be able to recognise the truth of everything I have said here. Whether you can or not it remains as a hideous truth in the very heart of our friendship. While you were with me you were the absolute ruin of my Art, and in allowing you to stand persistently between Art and myself I give to myself shame and blame in the fullest degree. You couldn't know, you couldn't understand, you couldn't appreciate. I had no right to expect it of you at all. Your interests were merely in your meals and moods. Your desires were simply for amusements, for ordinary or less ordinary pleasures. They were what your temperament needed, or thought it needed for the moment. I should have forbidden you my house and my chambers except when I specially invited you. I blame myself without reserve for my weakness. It was merely weakness. One half-hour with Art was always more to me than a cycle with you. Nothing really at any period of my life was ever of the smallest importance to me compared with Art. But in the case of an artist, weakness is nothing less than a crime, when it is a weakness that paralyses the imagination.

I blame myself again for having allowed you to bring me to utter and discreditable financial ruin. I remember one morning in the early October of '92 sitting in the yellowing woods at Bracknell with your mother. At that time I knew very little of your real nature. I had stayed from a Saturday to Monday with you at Oxford. You had stayed with me at Cromer for ten days and played golf. The conversation turned on you, and your mother began to speak to me about your character. She told me of your two chief faults, your vanity, and your being, as she termed it, *"all wrong about money."* I have a distinct recollection of how I laughed. I had no idea that the first would bring me to prison, and the second to bankruptcy. I thought vanity a sort of graceful flower for a young man to wear; as for extravagance—for I thought she meant no more than extravagance—the virtues of prudence and thrift were not in my own nature or my own race. But before our friendship was one month older I began to see what your mother really meant. Your insistence on a life of reckless profusion: your incessant demands for money: your claim that all your pleasures should be paid for by me whether I was with you or not: brought me after some time into serious monetary difficulties, and what made the extravagances to me at any rate so monotonously uninteresting, as your persistent grasp on my life grew stronger and stronger, was that the money was really spent on little more than the pleasures of eating, drinking, and the like. Now and then it is a joy to have one's table red with wine and roses, but you outstripped all taste and temperance. You demanded without grace and received without thanks. You grew to think that you had a sort of right to live at my expense and in a profuse luxury to which you had never been accustomed, and which for that reason made your appetites all the more keen, and at the end if you lost money gambling in some Algiers Casino you simply telegraphed next morning to me in London to lodge the amount of your losses to your account at your bank, and gave the matter no further thought of any kind.

When I tell you that between the autumn of 1892 and the date of my imprisonment I spent with you and on you more than £5000 in actual money, irrespective of the bills I incurred, you will have some idea of the sort of life on which you insisted. Do you think I exaggerate? My ordinary expenses with you for an ordinary day in London—for luncheon, dinner, supper, amusements, hansoms and the rest of it— ranged from £12 to £20, and the week's expenses were naturally in proportion and ranged from £80 to £130. For our three months at Goring my expenses (rent of course included) were £1340. Step by step with the Bankruptcy Receiver I had to go over every item of my life. It was horrible. *"Plain living and high thinking"* was, of course, an ideal you could not at that time have appreciated, but such extravagance was a disgrace to both of us. One of the most delightful dinners I remember ever having had is one Robbie and I had together in a little Soho café, which cost about as many shillings as my dinners to you used to cost pounds. Out of my dinner with Robbie came the first and best of all my dialogues. Idea, title, treatment, mode, everything was struck out at a 3 franc 50 c. *table-d'hôte*. Out of the reckless dinners with you nothing remains but the memory that too much was eaten and too much was drunk. And my yielding to your demands was bad for you. You know that now. It made you grasping often: at times not a little unscrupulous: ungracious always. There was on far too many occasions too little joy or privilege in being your host. You forgot—I will not say the formal courtesy of thanks, for formal courtesies will strain a close friendship—but simply the grace of sweet companionship, the charm of pleasant conversation, that τερπνόν κακόυ as the Greeks called it, and all those gentle humanities that make life lovely, and are an accompaniment to life as music might be, keeping things in tune and filling with melody the harsh or silent places. And though it may seem strange to you that one in the terrible position in which I am situated should find a difference between one disgrace and another, still I frankly admit that the folly of throwing away all this money on you, and letting you squander my fortune to your own hurt as well as to mine, gives to me and in my eyes a note of common profligacy to my Bankruptcy that makes me doubly ashamed of it. I was made for other things.

But most of all I blame myself for the entire ethical degradation I allowed you to bring on me. The basis of character is will-power, and my will-power became absolutely subject to yours. It sounds a grotesque thing to say, but it is none the less true. Those incessant scenes that seemed to be almost physically necessary to you, and in which your mind and body grew distorted and you became a thing as terrible to look at as to listen to: that dreadful mania you inherit from your father, the mania for writing revolting and loathsome letters: your entire lack of any control over your emotions as displayed in your long resentful moods of sullen silence, no less than in the sudden fits of almost epileptic rage: all these things in reference to which one of my letters to you, left by you lying about at the Savoy or some other hotel and so produced in Court by your father's Counsel, contained an entreaty not devoid of pathos, had you at that time been able to recognise pathos either in its elements or its expression:—these, I say, were the origin and causes of my fatal yielding to you in your daily increasing demands. You wore one out. It was the triumph of the smaller over the bigger nature. It was the case of that tyranny of the weak over the strong which somewhere in one of my plays I describe as being "the only tyranny that lasts."

And it was inevitable. In every relation of life with others one has to find some moyen de vivre. In your case, one had either to give up to you or to give you up. There was no other alternative. Through deep if misplaced affection for you: through great pity for your defects of temper and temperament: through my own proverbial good-nature and Celtic laziness: through an artistic aversion to coarse scenes and ugly words: through that incapacity to bear resentment of any kind which at that time characterised me: through my dislike of seeing life made bitter and uncomely by what to me, with my eyes really fixed on other things, seemed to be mere trifles too petty for more than a moment's thought or interest—through these reasons, simple as they may sound, I gave up to you always. As a natural result, your claims, your efforts at domination, your exactions grew more and more unreasonable. Your meanest motive, your lowest appetite, your most common passion, became to you laws by which the lives of others were to be guided always, and to which, if necessary, they were to be without scruple sacrificed. Knowing that by making a scene you could always have your way, it was but natural that you should proceed, almost unconsciously I have no doubt, to every excess of vulgar violence. At the end you did not know to what goal you were hurrying, or with what aim in view. Having made your own of my genius, my will-power, and my fortune, you required, in the blindness of an inexhaustible greed, my entire existence. You took it. At the one supremely and tragically critical moment of all my life, just before my lamentable step of beginning my absurd action, on the one side there was your father attacking me with hideous cards left at my club, on the other side there was you attacking me with no less loathsome letters. The letter I received from you on the morning of the day I let you take me down to the Police Court to apply for the ridiculous warrant for your father's arrest was one of the worst you ever wrote, and for the most shameful reason. Between you both I lost my head. My judgment forsook me. Terror took its place. I saw no possible escape, I may say frankly, from either of you. Blindly I staggered as an ox into the shambles. I had made a gigantic psychological error. I had always thought that my giving up to you in small things meant nothing: that when a great moment arrived I could reassert my will-power in its natural superiority. It was not so. At the great moment my willpower completely failed me. In life there is really no small or great thing. All things are of equal value and of equal size. My habit—due to indifference chiefly at first—of giving up to you in everything had become insensibly a real part of my nature. Without my knowing it, it had stereotyped my temperament to one permanent and fatal mood. That is why, in the subtle epilogue to the first edition of his essays, Pater says that "Failure is to form habits." When he said it the dull Oxford people thought the phrase a mere wilful inversion of the somewhat wearisome text of Aristotelian Ethics, but there is a wonderful, a terrible truth hidden in it. I had allowed you to sap my strength of character, and to me the formation of a habit had proved to be not Failure merely but Ruin. Ethically you had been even still more destructive to me than you had been artistically.

The warrant once granted, your will of course directed everything. At a time when I should have been in London taking wise counsel, and calmly considering the hideous trap in which I had allowed myself to be caught—the booby-trap as your father calls it to the present day—you insisted on my taking you to Monte Carlo, of all revolting places on God's earth, that all day, and all night as well, you might gamble as long as the Casino remained open. As for me—baccarat having no charms for me—I was left alone outside to myself. You refused to discuss even for five minutes the position to which you and your father had brought me. My business was merely to pay your hotel expenses and your losses. The slightest allusion to the ordeal awaiting me was regarded as a bore. A new brand of champagne that was recommended to us had more interest for you.

On our return to London those of my friends who really desired my welfare implored me to retire abroad, and not to face an impossible trial. You imputed mean motives to them for giving such advice, and cowardice to me for listening to it. You forced me to stay to brazen it out, if possible, in the box by absurd and silly perjuries. At the end, I was of course arrested and your father became the hero of the hour: more indeed than the hero of the hour merely: your family now ranks, strangely enough, with the Immortals: for with that grotesqueness of effect that is as it were a Gothic element in history, and makes Clio the least serious of all the Muses, your father will always live among the kind pure-minded parents of Sunday-school literature, your place is with the Infant Samuel, and in the lowest mire of Malebolge I sit between Gilles de Retz and the Marquis de Sade.

Of course I should have got rid of you. I should have shaken you out of my life as a man shakes from his raiment a thing that has stung him. In the most wonderful of all his plays Æschylus tells us of the great Lord who brings up in his house the lion-cub, the λέοντος ἶνιν, and loves it because it comes bright-eyed to his call and fawns on him for its food: φαιδϵ ωπὸς ποτὶ χεῖϑα, σαίνων τε γαστϵὸς ἀνάγκαις. And the thing grows up and shows the nature of its race, ἦθος τὸ πϵόσθε τοήων, and destroys the lord and his house and all that he possesses. I feel that I was such a one as he. But my fault was, not that I did not part from you, but that I parted from you far too often. As far as I can make out I ended my friendship with you every three months regularly, and each time that I did so you managed by means of entreaties, telegrams, letters, the interposition of your friends, the interposition of mine, and the like to induce me to allow you back. When at the end of March'93 you left my house at Torquay I had determined never to speak to you again, or to allow you under any circumstances to be with me, so revolting had been the scene you had made the night before your departure. You wrote and telegraphed from Bristol to beg me to forgive you and meet you. Your tutor, who had stayed behind, told me that he thought that at times you were quite irresponsible for what you said and did, and that most, if not all, of the men at Magdalen were of the same opinion. I consented to meet you, and of course I forgave you. On the way up to town you begged me to take you to the Savoy. That was indeed a visit fatal to me.

Three months later, in June, we are at Goring. Some of your Oxford friends come to stay from a Saturday to Monday. The morning of the day they went away you made a scene so dreadful, so distressing that I told you that we must part. I remember quite well, as we stood on the level croquet-ground with the pretty lawn all round us, pointing out to you that we were spoiling each other's lives, that you were absolutely ruining mine and that I evidently was not making you really happy, and that an irrevocable parting, a complete separation was the one wise philosophic thing to do. You went sullenly after luncheon, leaving one of your most offensive letters behind with the butler to be handed to me after your departure. Before three days had elapsed you were telegraphing from London to beg to be forgiven and allowed to return. I had taken the place to please you. I had engaged your own servants at your request. I was always terribly sorry for the hideous temper to which you were really a prey. I was fond of you. So I let you come back and forgave you. Three months later still, in September, new scenes occurred, the occasion of them being my pointing out the schoolboy faults of your attempted translation of *Salome*. You must by this time be a fair enough French scholar to know that the translation was as unworthy of you, as an ordinary Oxonian, as it was of the work it sought to render. You did not of course know it then, and in one of the violent letters you wrote to me on the point you said that you were under "*no intellectual obligation of any kind*" to me. I remember that when I read that statement, I felt that it was the one really true thing you had written to me in the whole course of our friendship. I saw that a less cultivated nature would really have suited you much better. I am not saying this in bitterness at all, but simply as a fact of companionship. Ultimately the bond of all companionship, whether in marriage or in friendship, is conversation, and conversation must have a common basis, and between two people of widely different culture the only common basis possible is the lowest level. The trivial in thought and action is charming. I had made it the keystone of a very brilliant philosophy expressed in plays and paradoxes. But the froth and folly of our life grew often very wearisome to me: it was only in the mire that we met: and fascinating, terribly fascinating though the one topic round which your talk invariably centred was, still at the end it became quite monotonous to me. I was often bored to death by it, and accepted it as I accepted your passion for going to music-halls, or your mania for absurd extravagances in eating and drinking, or any other of your to me less attractive characteristics, as a thing, that is to say, that one simply had to put up with, a part of the high price one paid for knowing you. When after leaving Goring I went to Dinard for a fortnight you were extremely angry with me for not taking you with me, and, before my departure there, made some very unpleasant scenes on the subject at the Albemarle Hotel, and sent me some equally unpleasant telegrams to a country house I was staying at for a few days. I told you, I remember, that I thought it was your duty to be with your own people for a little, as you had passed the whole season away from them. But in reality, to be perfectly frank with you, I could not under any circumstances have let you be with me. We had been together for nearly twelve weeks. I required rest and freedom from the terrible strain of your companionship. It was necessary for me to be a little by myself. It was intellectually necessary. And so I confess I saw in your letter, from which I have quoted, a very good opportunity for ending the fatal friendship that had sprung up between us, and ending it without bitterness, as I had indeed tried to do on that bright June morning at Goring, three months before. It was however represented to me—I am bound to say candidly by one of my own friends to whom you had gone in you difficulty—that you would be much hurt, perhaps almost humiliated at having your work sent back to you like a schoolboy's exercise; that I was expecting far too much intellectually from you; and that, no matter what you wrote or did, you were absolutely and entirely devoted to me. I did not want to be the first to check or discourage you in your beginnings in literature: I knew quite well that no translation, unless one done by a poet, could render the colour and cadence of my work in any adequate measure: devotion seemed to me, seems to me still, a wonderful thing, not to be lightly thrown away: so I took the translation and you back. Exactly three months later, after a series of scenes culminating in one more than usually revolting, when you came one Monday evening to my rooms accompanied by two of your friends, I found myself actually flying abroad next morning to escape from you, giving my family some absurd reason for my sudden departure, and leaving a false address with my servant for fear you might follow me by the next train. And I remember that afternoon, as I was in the railway-carriage whirling up to Paris, thinking what an impossible, terrible, utterly wrong state my life had got into, when I, a man of world-wide reputation, was actually forced to run away from England, in order to try and get rid of a friendship that was entirely destructive of everything fine in me either from the intellectual or ethical point of view: the person from whom I was flying being no terrible creature sprung from sewer or mire into modern life with whom I had entangled my days, but you yourself, a young man of my own social rank and position, who had been at my own college at Oxford, and was an incessant guest at my house. The usual telegrams of entreaty and remorse followed: I disregarded them. Finally you threatened that unless I consented to meet you, you would under no circumstances consent to proceed to Egypt. I had myself, with your knowledge and concurrence, begged your mother to send you to Egypt away from England, as you were wrecking your life in London. I knew that if you did not go it would be a terrible disappointment to her, and for her sake I did meet you, and under the influence of great emotion, which even you cannot have forgotten, I forgave the past; though I said nothing at all about the future.

On my return to London next day I remember sitting in my room and sadly and seriously trying to make up my mind whether or not you really were what you seemed to me to be, so full of terrible defects, so utterly ruinous both to yourself and to others, so fatal a one to know even or to be with. For a whole week I thought about it, and wondered if after all I was not unjust and mistaken in my estimate of you. At the end of the week a letter from your mother is handed in. It expressed to the full every feeling I myself had about you. In it she spoke of your blind exaggerated vanity which made you despise your home, and treat your elder brother—that candidissima anima—"as a Philistine:" of your temper which made her afraid to speak to you about your life, the life she felt, she knew, you were leading: about your conduct in money matters, so distressing to her in more ways than one: of the degeneration and change that had taken place in you. She saw, of course, that heredity had burdened you with a terrible legacy, and frankly admitted it, admitted it with terror: he is "the one of my children who has inherited the fatal Douglas temperament," she wrote of you. At the end she stated that she felt bound to declare that your friendship with me, in her opinion, had so intensified your vanity that it had become the source of all your faults, and earnestly begged me not to meet you abroad. I wrote to her at once, in reply, and told her that I agreed entirely with every word she had said. I added much more. I went as far as I could possibly go. I told her that the origin of our friendship was you in your undergraduate days at Oxford coming to beg me to help you in very serious trouble of a very particular character. I told her that your life had been continually in the same manner troubled. The reason of your going to Belgium you had placed to the fault of your companion in that journey, and your mother had reproached me with having introduced you to him. I replaced the fault on the right shoulders, on yours. I assured her at the end that I had not the smallest intention of meeting you abroad, and begged her to try to keep you there, either as an honorary *attaché*, if that were possible, or to learn modern languages, if it were not; or for any reason she chose, at least during two or three years, and for your sake as well as for mine.

In the meantime you are writing to me by every post from Egypt. I took not the smallest notice of any of your communications. I read them, and tore them up. I had quite settled to have no more to do with you. My mind was made up, and I gladly devoted myself to the Art whose progress I had allowed you to interrupt. At the end of three months, your mother, with that unfortunate weakness of will that characterises her, and that in the tragedy of my life has been an element no less fatal than your father's violence, actually writes to me herself—I have no doubt, of course, at your instigation—tells me that you are extremely anxious to hear from me, and in order that I should have no excuse for not communicating with you, sends me your address in Athens, which, of course, I knew perfectly well. I confess I was absolutely astounded at her letter. I could not understand how, after what she had written to me in December, and what I in answer had written to her, she could in any way try to repair or to renew my unfortunate friendship with you. I acknowledged her letter, of course, and again urged her to try and get you connected with some Embassy abroad, so as to prevent your returning to England, but I did not write to you, or take any more notice of your telegrams than I did before your mother had written to me. Finally you actually telegraphed to my wife begging her to use her influence with me to get me to write to you. Our friendship had always been a source of distress to her: not merely because she had never liked you personally, but because she saw how your continual companionship altered me, and not for the better: still, just as she had always been most gracious and hospitable to you, so she could not bear the idea of my being in any way unkind—for so it seemed to her—to any of my friends. She thought, knew indeed, that it was a thing alien to my character. At her request I did communicate with you. I remember the wording of my telegram quite well. I said that time healed every wound but that for many months to come I would neither write to you nor see you. You started without delay for Paris, sending me passionate telegrams on the road to beg me to see you once, at any rate. I declined. You arrived in Paris late on a Saturday night, and found a brief letter from me waiting for you at your hotel stating that I would not see you. Next morning I received in Tite Street a telegram of some ten or eleven pages in length from you. You stated in it that no matter what you had done to me you could not believe that I would absolutely decline to see you: you reminded me that for the sake of seeing me even for one hour you had travelled six days and nights across Europe without stopping once on the way: you made what I must admit was a most pathetic appeal, and ended with what seemed to me a threat of suicide, and one not thinly veiled. You had yourself often told me how many of your race there had been who had stained their hands in their own blood; your uncle certainly, your grandfather possibly; many others in the mad, bad line from which you come. Pity, my old affection for you, regard for your mother to whom your death under such dreadful circumstances would have been a blow almost too great for her to bear, the horror of the idea that so young a life, and one that amidst all its ugly faults had still promise of beauty in it, should come to so revolting an end, mere humanity itself—all these, if excuses be necessary, must serve as my excuse for consenting to accord you one last interview. When I arrived in Paris, your tears, breaking out again and again all through the evening, and falling over your cheeks like rain as we sat, at dinner first at Voisin's, at supper at Paillard's afterwards: the unfeigned joy you evinced at seeing me, holding my hand whenever you could, as though you were a gentle and penitent child: your contrition, so simple and sincere, at the moment: made me consent to renew our friendship. Two days after we had returned to London, your father saw you having luncheon with me at the Café Royal, joined my table, drank of my wine, and that afternoon, through a letter addressed to you, began his first attack on me.

It may be strange, but I had once again, I will not say the chance, but the duty of separating from you forced on me. I need hardly remind you that I refer to your conduct to me at Brighton from October 10th to 13th, 1894. Three years ago is a long time for you to go back. But we who live in prison, and in whose lives there is no event but sorrow, have to measure time by throbs of pain, and the record of bitter moments. We have nothing else to think of. Suffering—curious as it may sound to you—is the means by which we exist, because it is the only means by which we become conscious of existing; and the remembrance of suffering in the past is necessary to us as the warrant, the evidence, of our continued identity. Between myself and the memory of joy lies a gulf no less deep than that between myself and joy in its actuality. Had our life together been as the world fancied it to be, one simply of pleasure, profligacy and laughter, I would not be able to recall a single passage in it. It is because it was full of moments and days tragic, bitter, sinister in their warnings, dull or dreadful in their monotonous scenes and unseemly violences, that I can see or hear each separate incident in its detail, can indeed see or hear little else. So much in this place do men live by pain that my friendship with you, in the way through which I am forced to remember it, appears to me always as a prelude consonant with those varying modes of anguish which each day I have to realise; nay more, to necessitate them even; as though my life, whatever it had seemed to myself and to others, had all the while been a real Symphony of Sorrow, passing through its rhythmically-linked movements to its certain resolution, with that inevitableness that in Art characterises the treatment of every great theme.

I spoke of your conduct to me on three successive days, three years ago, did I not? I was trying to finish my last play at Worthing by myself. The two visits you had paid to me had ended. You suddenly appeared a third time bringing with you a companion whom you actually proposed should stay in my house. I (you must admit now quite properly) absolutely declined. I entertained you, of course; I had no option in the matter: but elsewhere, and not in my own home. The next day, a Monday, your companion returned to the duties of his profession, and you stayed with me. Bored with Worthing, and still more, I have no doubt, with my fruitless efforts to concentrate my attention on my play, the only thing that really interested me at the moment, you insist on being taken to the Grand Hotel at Brighton. The night we arrive you fall ill with that dreadful low fever that is foolishly called the influenza, your second, if not third attack. I need not remind you how I waited on you, and tended you, not merely with every luxury of fruit, flowers, presents, books, and the like that money can procure, but with that affection, tenderness and love that, whatever you may think, is not to be procured for money. Except for an hour's walk in the morning, an hour's drive in the afternoon, I never left the hotel. I got special grapes from London for you, as you did not care for those the hotel supplied, invented things to please you, remained either with you or in the room next to yours, sat with you every evening to quiet or amuse you.

After four or five days you recover, and I take lodgings in order to try and finish my play. You, of course, accompany me. The morning after the day on which we were installed I feel extremely ill. You have to go to London on business, but promise to return in the afternoon. In London you meet a friend, and do not come back to Brighton till late the next day, by which time I am in a terrible fever, and the doctor finds I have caught the influenza from you. Nothing could have been more uncomfortable for anyone ill than the lodgings turn out to be. My sitting-room is on the first floor, my bedroom on the third. There is no manservant to wait on one, not even anyone to send out on a message, or to get what the doctor orders. But you are there. I feel no alarm. The next two days you leave me entirely alone without care, without attendance, without anything. It was not a question of grapes, flowers, and charming gifts: it was a question of mere necessaries: I could not even get the milk the doctor had ordered for me: lemonade was pronounced an impossibility: and when I begged you to procure me a book at the bookseller's, or if they had not got whatever I had fixed on to choose something else, you never even take the trouble to go there. And when I was left all day without anything to read in consequence, you calmly tell me that you bought me the book and that they promised to send it down, a statement which I found out by chance afterwards to have been entirely untrue from beginning to end. All the while you are of course living at my expense, driving about, dining at the Grand Hotel, and indeed only appearing in my room for money. On the Saturday night, you having left me completely unattended and alone since the morning, I asked you to come back after dinner, and sit with me for a little. With irritable voice and ungracious manner you promise to do so. I wait till eleven o'clock and you never appear. I then left a note for you in your room just reminding you of the promise you had made me, and how you had kept it. At three in the morning, unable to sleep, and tortured with thirst, I made my way, in the dark and cold, down to the sitting-room in the hopes of finding some water there. I found *you*. You fell on me with every hideous word an intemperate mood, an undisciplined and untutored nature could suggest. By the terrible alchemy of egotism you converted your remorse into rage. You accused me of selfishness in expecting you to be with me when I was ill; of standing between you and your amusements; of trying to deprive you of your pleasures. You told me, and I know it was quite true, that you had come back at midnight simply in order to change your dress-clothes, and go out again to where you hoped new pleasures were waiting for you, but that by leaving for you a letter in which I had reminded you that you had neglected me the whole day and the whole evening, I had really robbed you of your desire for more enjoyments, and diminished your actual capacity for fresh delights. I went back upstairs in disgust, and remained sleepless till dawn, nor till long after dawn was I able to get anything to quench the thirst of the fever that was on me. At eleven o'clock you came into my room. In the previous scene I could not help observing that by my letter I had, at any rate, checked you in a night of more than usual excess. In the morning you were quite yourself. I waited naturally to hear what excuses you had to make, and in what way you were going to ask for the forgiveness that you knew in your heart was invariably waiting for you, no matter what you did; your absolute trust that I would always forgive you being the thing in you that I always really liked the best, perhaps the best thing in you to like. So far from doing that, you began to repeat the same scene with renewed emphasis and more violent assertion. I told you at length to leave the room: you pretended to do so, but when I lifted up my head from the pillow in which I had buried it, you were still there, and with brutality of laughter and hysteria of rage you moved suddenly towards me. A sense of horror came over me, for what exact reason I could not make out; but I got out of my bed at once, and bare-footed and just as I was, made my way down the two flights of stairs to the sitting-room, which I did not leave till the owner of the lodgings—whom I had rung for—had assured me that you had left my bedroom, and promised to remain within call, in case of necessity. After an interval of an hour, during which time the doctor had come and found me, of course, in a state of absolute nervous prostration, as well as in a worse condition of fever than I had been at the outset, you returned silently, for money: took what you could find on the dressing-table and mantelpiece, and left the house with your luggage. Need I tell you what I thought of you during the two wretched lonely days of illness that followed? Is it necessary for me to state that I saw clearly that it would be a dishonour to myself to continue even an acquaintance with such a one as you had showed yourself to be? That I recognised that the ultimate moment had come, and recognised it as being really a great relief? And that I knew that for the future my Art and Life would be freer and better and more beautiful in every possible way? Ill as I was, I felt at ease. The fact that the separation was irrevocable gave me peace. By Tuesday the fever had left me, and for the first time I dined downstairs. Wednesday was my birthday. Amongst the telegrams and communications on my table was a letter in your handwriting. I opened it with a sense of sadness over me. I knew that the time had gone by when a pretty phrase, an expression of affection, a word of sorrow would make me take you back. But I was entirely deceived. I had underrated you. The letter you sent to me on my birthday was an elaborate repetition of the two scenes, set cunningly and carefully down in black and white! You mocked me with common jests. Your one satisfaction in the whole affair was, you said, that you retired to the Grand Hotel, and entered your luncheon to my account before you left for town. You congratulated me on my prudence in leaving my sickbed, on my sudden flight downstairs. "*It was an ugly moment for you,*" you said, "*uglier than you imagine.*" Ah! I felt it but too well. What it had really meant I did not know: whether you had with you the pistol you had bought to try and frighten your father with, and that, thinking it to be unloaded, you had once fired off in a public restaurant in my company:

whether your hand was moving towards a common dinner-knife that by chance was lying on the table between us: whether, forgetting in your rage your low stature and inferior strength, you had thought of some specially personal insult, or attack even, as I lay ill there: I could not tell. I do not know to the present moment. All I know is that a feeling of utter horror had come over me, and that I had felt that unless I left the room at once, and got away, you would have done, or tried to do, something that would have been, even to you, a source of lifelong shame. Only once before in my life had I experienced such a feeling of horror at any human being. It was when in my library at Tite Street, waving his small hands in the air in epileptic fury, your father, with his bully, or his friend, between us, had stood uttering every foul word his foul mind could think of, and screaming the loathsome threats he afterwards with such cunning carried out. In the latter case he, of course, was the one who had to leave the room first. I drove him out. In your case I went. It was not the first time I had been obliged to save you from yourself.

You concluded your letter by saying: "*When you are not on your pedestal you are not interesting. The next time you are ill I will go away at once.*" Ah! what coarseness of fibre does that reveal! What an entire lack of imagination! How callous, how common had the temperament by that time become! "*When you are not on your pedestal you are not interesting. The next time you are ill I will go away at once.*" How often have those words come back to me in the wretched solitary cell of the various prisons I have been sent to. I have said them to myself over and over again, and seen in them, I hope unjustly, some of the secret of your strange silence. For you to write thus to me, when the very illness and fever from which I was suffering I had caught from tending you, was of course revolting in its coarseness and crudity; but for any human being in the whole world to write thus to another would be a sin for which there is no pardon, were there any sin for which there is none.

I confess that when I had finished your letter I felt almost polluted, as if by associating with one of such a nature I had soiled and shamed my life irretrievably.

I had, it is true, done so, but I was not to learn how fully till just six months later on in life. I settled with myself to go back to London on the Friday, and see Sir George Lewis personally and request him to write to your father to state that I had determined never under any circumstances to allow you to enter my house, to sit at my board, to talk to me, walk with me, or anywhere and at my time to be my companion at all. This done I would have written to you just to inform you of the course of action I had adopted; the reasons you would inevitably have realised for yourself. I had everything arranged on Thursday night, when on Friday morning, as I was sitting at breakfast before starting, I happened to open the newspaper and saw in it a telegram stating that your elder brother, the real head of the family, the heir to the title, the pillar of the house, had been found dead in a ditch with his gun lying discharged beside him. The horror of the circumstances of the tragedy, now known to have been an accident, but then stained with a darker suggestion; the pathos of the sudden death of one so loved by all who knew him, and almost on the eve, as it were, of his marriage; my idea of what your own sorrow would, or should be; my consciousness of the misery awaiting your mother at the loss of the one to whom she clung for comfort and joy in life, and who, as she told me once herself, had from the very day of his birth never caused her to shed a single tear; my consciousness of your own isolation, both your other brothers being out of Europe, and you consequently the only one to whom your mother and sister could look, not merely for companionship in their sorrow, but also for those dreary responsibilities of dreadful detail that Death always brings with it; the mere sense of the *lacrimae rerum*, of the tears of which the world is made, and of the sadness of all human things—out of the confluence of these thoughts and emotions crowding into my brain came infinite pity for you and your family. My own griefs and bitternesses against you I forgot. What you had been to me in my sickness, I could not be to you in your bereavement. I telegraphed at once to you my deepest sympathy, and in the letter that followed invited you to come to my house as soon as you were able. I felt that to abandon you at that particular moment, and formally through a solicitor, would have been too terrible for you.

On your return to town from the actual scene of the tragedy to which you had been summoned, you came at once to me very sweetly and very simply, in your suit of woe, and with your eyes dim with tears. You sought consolation and help, as a child might seek it. I opened to you my house, my home, my heart. I made your sorrow mine also, that you might have help in bearing it. Never, even by one word, did I allude to your conduct towards me, to the revolting scenes, and the revolting letter. Your grief, which was real, seemed to me to bring you nearer to me than you had ever been. The flowers you took from me to put on your brother's grave were to be a symbol not merely of the beauty of his life, but of the beauty that in all lives lies dormant and may be brought to light.

The gods are strange. It is not of our vices only they make instruments to scourge us. They bring us to ruin through what in us is good, gentle, humane, loving. But for my pity and affection for you and yours, I would not now be weeping in this terrible place.

Of course I discern in all our relations, not Destiny merely, but Doom: Doom that walks always swiftly, because she goes to the shedding of blood. Through your father you come of a race, marriage with whom is horrible, friendship fatal, and that lays violent hands either on its own life or on the lives of others. In every little circumstance in which the ways of our lives met; in every point of great, or seemingly trivial import in which you came to me for pleasure or for help; in the small chances, the slight accidents that look, in their relation to life, to be no more than the dust that dances in a beam, or the leaf that flutters from a tree, Ruin followed, like the echo of a bitter cry, or the shadow that hunts with the beast of prey. Our friendship really begins with your begging me in a most pathetic and charming letter to assist you in a position appalling to anyone, doubly so to a young man at Oxford: I do so, and ultimately through your using my name as your friend with Sir George Lewis, I begin to lose his esteem and friendship, a friendship of fifteen years' standing. When I was deprived of his advice and help and regard I was deprived of the one great safeguard of my life.

You send me a very nice poem, of the under-graduate school of verse, for my approval: I reply by a letter of fantastic literary conceits: I compare you to Hylas, or Hyacinth, Jonquil or Narcisse, or someone whom the great god of Poetry favoured, and hon-oured with his love. The letter is like a passage from one of Shakespeare's sonnets, transposed to a minor key. It can only be understood by those who have read the *Symposium* of Plato, or caught the spirit of a certain grave mood made beautiful for us in Greek marbles. It was, let me say frankly, the sort of letter I would, in a happy if wilful moment, have written to any graceful young man of either University who had sent me a poem of his own making, certain that he would have sufficient wit or culture to interpret rightly its fantastic phrases. Look at the history of that letter! It passes from you into the hands of a loathsome companion: from him to a gang of blackmailers: copies of it are sent about London to my friends, and to the manager of the theatre where my work is being performed: every construction but the right one is put on it: Society is thrilled with the absurd rumours that I have had to pay a huge sum of money for having written an infamous letter to you: this forms the basis of your father's worst attack: I produce the original letter myself in Court to show what it really is: it is denounced by your father's Counsel as a revolting and insidious attempt to corrupt Innocence: ultimately it forms part of a criminal charge: the Crown takes it up: the Judge sums up on it with little learning and much morality: I go to prison for it at last. That is the result of writing you a charming letter.

While I am staying with you at Salisbury you are terribly alarmed at a threatening communication from a former companion of yours: you beg me to see the writer and help you: I do so: the result is Ruin to me. I am forced to take everything you have done on my own shoulders and answer for it. When, having failed to take your degree, you have to go down from Oxford, you telegraph to me in London to beg me to come to you. I do so at once: you ask me to take you to Goring, as you did not like, under the circumstances, to go home: at Goring you see a house that charms you: I take it for you: the result from every point of view is Ruin to me. One day you come to me and ask me, as a personal favour to you, to write something for an Oxford undergraduate magazine, about to be started by some friend of yours, whom I had never heard of in all my life, and knew nothing at all about. To please you—what did I not do always to please you? —I sent him a page of paradoxes destined originally for the *Saturday Review*. A few months later I find myself standing in the dock of the Old Bailey on account of the character of the magazine. It forms part of the Crown charge against me. I am called upon to defend your friend's prose and your own verse. The former I cannot palliate; the latter I, loyal to the bitter extreme, to your youthful literature as to your youthful life, do very strongly defend, and will not hear of your being a writer of indecencies. But I go to prison, all the same, for your friend's undergraduate magazine, and "the Love that dares not tell its name." At Christmas I give you a "very pretty present," as you described it in your letter of thanks, on which I knew you had set your heart, worth some £40 or £50 at most. When the crash of my life comes, and I am ruined, the bailiff who seizes my library, and has it sold, does so to pay for the "very pretty present." It was for that the execution was put into my house. At the ultimate and terrible moment when I am taunted, and spurred-on by your taunts, to take an action against your father and have him arrested, the last straw to which I clutch in my wretched efforts to escape is the terrible expense. I tell the solicitor in your presence that I have no funds, that I cannot possibly afford the appalling costs, that I have no money at my disposal. What I said was, as you know, perfectly true. On that fatal Friday instead of being in Humphreys's office weakly consenting to my own ruin, I would have been happy and free in France, away from you and your father, unconscious of his loathsome card, and indifferent to your letters, if I had been able to leave the Avondale Hotel. But the hotel people absolutely refused to allow me to go. You had been staying with me for ten days: indeed you had ultimately, to my great and, you will admit, right-ful indignation, brought a companion of yours to stay with me also: my bill for the ten days was nearly £140. The proprietor said he could not allow my luggage to be removed from the hotel till I had paid the account in full. That is what kept me in London. Had it not been for the hotel bill I would have gone to Paris on Thursday morning.

When I told the solicitor I had no money to face the gigantic expense, you interposed at once. You said that your own family would be only too delighted to pay all the necessary costs: that your father had been an incubus to them all: that they had often discussed the possibility of getting him put into a lunatic asylum so as to keep him out of the way: that he was a daily source of annoyance and distress to your mother and to everyone else: that if I would only come forward to have him shut up I would be regarded by the family as their champion and their benefactor: and that your mother's rich relations themselves would look on it as a real delight to be allowed to pay all costs and ex-penses that might be incurred in any such effort. The solicitor closed at once, and I was hurried to the Police Court. I had no excuse left for not going. I was forced into it. Of course your family don't pay the costs, and, when I am made bankrupt, it is by your father, and *for* the costs—the meagre balance of them—some £700. At the present moment my wife, estranged from me over the important question of whether I should have £3 or £3.10 a week to live on, is preparing a divorce suit, for which, of course, entirely new evidence and an entirely new trial, to be followed perhaps by more serious proceedings, will be necessary. I, naturally, know nothing of the details. I merely know the name of the witness on whose evidence my wife's solicitors rely. It is your own Oxford servant, whom at your special request I took into my service for our summer at Goring.

But, indeed, I need not go on further with more instances of the strange Doom you seem to have brought on me in all things big or little. It makes me feel sometimes as if you yourself had been merely a puppet worked by some secret and unseen hand to bring terrible events to a terrible issue. But puppets themselves have passions. They will bring a new plot into what they are presenting, and twist the ordered issue of vicissitude to suit some whim or appetite of their own. To be entirely free, and at the same time entirely dominated by law, is the eternal paradox of human life that we realise at every moment; and this, I often think, is the only explanation possible of your nature, if indeed for the profound and terrible mysteries of a human soul there is any explanation at all, except one that makes the mystery more marvellous still.

Of course you had your illusions, lived in them indeed, and through their shifting mists and coloured veils saw all things changed. You thought, I remember quite well, that your devoting yourself to me, to the entire exclusion of your family and family life, was a proof of your wonderful appreciation of me, and your great affection. No doubt to you it seemed so. But recollect that with me was luxury, high living, unlimited pleasure, money without stint. Your family life bored you. The "cold cheap wine of Salisbury," to use a phrase of your own making, was distasteful to you. On my side, and along with my intellectual attractions, were the fleshpots of Egypt. When you could not find me to be with, the companions whom you chose as substitutes were not flattering.

You thought again that in sending a lawyer's letter to your father to say that, rather than sever your eternal friendship with me, you would give up the allowance of £250 a year which, with I believe deductions for your Oxford debts, he was then making you, you were realising the very chivalry of friendship, touching the noblest note of self-denial. But your surrender of your little allowance did not mean that you were ready to give up even one of your most superfluous luxuries, or most unnecessary extravagances. On the contrary. Your appetite for luxurious living was never so keen. My expenses for eight days in Paris for myself, you, and your Italian servant were nearly £150: Paillard alone absorbing £85. At the rate at which you wished to live, your entire income for a whole year, if you had taken your meals alone, and been especially economical in your selection of the cheaper form of pleasures, would hardly have lasted you for three weeks. The fact that in what was merely a pretence of bravado you had surrendered your allowance, such as it was, gave you at last a plausible reason for your claim to live at my expense, or what you thought a plausible reason: and on many occasions you seriously availed yourself of it, and gave the very fullest expression to it: and the continued drain, principally of course on me, but also to a certain extent, I know, on your mother, was never so distressing, because in my case at any rate, never so completely unaccompanied by the smallest word of thanks, or sense of limit.

You thought again that in attacking your own father with dreadful letters, abusive telegrams, and insulting postcards you were really fighting your mother's battles, coming forward as her champion, and avenging the no doubt terrible wrongs and sufferings of her married life. It was quite an illusion on your part; one of your worst indeed. The way for you to have avenged your mother's wrongs on your father, if you considered it part of a son's duty to do so, was by being a better son to your mother than you had been: by not making her afraid to speak to you on serious things: by not signing bills the payment of which devolved on her: by being gentler to her, and not bringing sorrow into her days. Your brother Francis made great amends to her for what she had suffered, by his sweetness and goodness to her through the brief years of his flower-like life. You should have taken him as your model. You were wrong even in fancying that it would have been an absolute delight and joy to your mother if you *had* managed through me to get your father put into prison. I feel sure you were wrong. And if you want to know what a woman really feels when her husband, and the father of her children, is in prison dress, in a prison cell, write to my wife and ask her. She will tell you.

I also had my illusions. I thought life was going to be a brilliant comedy, and that you were to be one of many graceful figures in it. I found it to be a revolting and repellent tragedy, and that the sinister occasion of the great catastrophe, sinister in its concentration of aim and intensity of narrowed will-power, was yourself, stripped of that mask of joy and pleasure by which you, no less than I, had been deceived and led astray.

You can now understand—can you not?—a little of what I am suffering. Some paper, the *Pall Mall Gazette* I think, describing the dress-rehearsal of one of my plays, spoke of you as following me about like my shadow: the memory of our friendship is the shadow that walks with me here: that seems never to leave me: that wakes me up at night to tell me the same story over and over till its wearisome iteration makes all sleep abandon me till dawn: at dawn it begins again: it follows me into the prison-yard and makes me talk to myself as I tramp round: each detail that accompanied each dreadful moment I am forced to recall: there is nothing that happened in those ill-starred years that I cannot recreate in that chamber of the brain which is set apart for grief or for despair: every strained note of your voice, every twitch and gesture of your nervous hands, every bitter word, every poisonous phrase comes back to me: I remember the street or river down which we passed, the wall or woodland that surrounded us, at what figure on the dial stood the hands of the clock, which way went the wings of the wind, the shape and colour of the moon.

There is, I know, one answer to all that I have said to you, and that is that you loved me: that all through those two and a half years during which the Fates were weaving into one scarlet pattern the threads of our divided lives you really loved me. Yes: I know you did. No matter what your conduct to me was I always felt that at heart you really did love me. Though I saw quite clearly that my position in the world of Art, the interest my personality had always excited, my money, the luxury in which I lived, the thousand and one things that went to make up a life so charmingly, so wonderfully improbable as mine was, were, each and all of them, elements that fascinated you and made you cling to me: yet besides all this there was something more, some strange attraction for you: you loved me far better than you loved anybody else. But you, like myself, have had a terrible tragedy in your life, though one of an entirely opposite character to mine. Do you want to learn what it was? It was this. In you Hate was always stronger than Love. Your hatred of your father was of such stature that it entirely outstripped, o'erthrew, and overshadowed your love of me. There was no struggle between them at all, or but little; of such dimensions was your Hatred and of such monstrous growth. You did not realise that there is no room for both passions in the same soul. They cannot live together in that fair carven house. Love is fed by the imagination, by which we become wiser than we know, better than we feel, nobler than we are: by which we can see Life as a whole: by which, and by which alone, we can understand others in their real as in their ideal relations. Only what is fine, and finely conceived, can feed Love. But anything will feed Hate. There was not a glass of champagne you drank, not a rich dish you ate of in all those years, that did not feed your Hate and make it fat. So to gratify it, you gambled with my life, as you gambled with my money, carelessly, recklessly, indifferent to the consequence. If you lost, the loss would not, you fancied, be yours.

If you won, yours, you knew, would be the exultation, and the advantages of victory.

Hate blinds people. You were not aware of that. Love can read the writing on the remotest star, but Hate so blinded you that you could see no further than the narrow, walled-in, and already lust-withered garden of your common desires. Your terrible lack of imagination, the one really fatal defect of your character, was entirely the result of the Hate that lived in you. Subtly, silently, and in secret, Hate gnawed at your nature, as the lichen bites at the root of some sallow plant, till you grew to see nothing but the most meagre interests and the most petty aims. That faculty in you which Love would have fostered, Hate poisoned and paralysed. When your father first began to attack me it was as your private friend, and in a private letter to you. As soon as I had read the letter, with its obscene threats and coarse violences, I saw at once that a terrible danger was looming on the horizon of my troubled days: I told you I would not be the catspaw between you both in your ancient hatred of each other: that I in London was naturally much bigger game for him than a Secretary for Foreign Affairs at Homburg: that it would be unfair to me to place me even for a moment in such a position: and that I had something better to do with my life than to have scenes with a man drunken, déclassé, and half-witted as he was. You could not be made to see this. Hate blinded you. You insisted that the quarrel had really nothing to do with me: that you would not allow your father to dictate to you in your private friendships: that it would be most unfair of me to interfere. You had already, before you saw me on the subject, sent your father a foolish and vulgar telegram, as your answer. That of course committed you to a foolish and vulgar course of action to follow. The fatal errors of life are not due to man's being unreasonable: an unreasonable moment may be one's finest moment. They are due to man's being logical. There is a wide difference. That telegram conditioned the whole of your subsequent relations with your father, and consequently the whole of my life. And the grotesque thing about it is that it was a telegram of which the commonest street-boy would have been ashamed.

From pert telegrams to priggish lawyers' letters was a natural progress, and the result of your lawyer's letters to your father was, of course, to urge him on still further. You left him no option but to go on. You forced it on him as a point of honour, or of dishonour rather, that your appeal should have the more effect. So the next time he attacks me, no longer in a private letter and as your private friend, but in public and as a public man. I have to expel him from my house. He goes from restaurant to restaurant looking for me, in order to insult me before the whole world, and in such a manner that if I retaliated I would be ruined, and if I did not retaliate I would be ruined also. Then surely was the time when you should have come forward, and said that you would not expose me to such hideous attacks, such infamous persecution, on your account, but would, readily and at once, resign any claim you had to my friendship? You feel that now, I suppose. But it never even occurred to you then. Hate blinded you. All you could think of (besides of course writing to him insulting letters and telegrams) was to buy a ridiculous pistol that goes off in the Berkeley, under circumstances that create a worse scandal than ever came to your ears. Indeed the idea of your being the object of a terrible quarrel between your father and a man of my position seemed to delight you. It, I suppose very naturally, pleased your vanity, and flattered your self-importance. That your father might have had your body, which did not interest me, and left me your soul, which did not interest him, would have been to you a distressing solution of the question. You scented the chance of a public scandal and flew to it. The prospect of a battle in which you would be safe delighted you. I never remember you in higher spirits than you were for the rest of that season. Your only disappointment seemed to be that nothing actually happened, and that no further meeting or fracas had taken place between us. You consoled yourself by sending him telegrams of such a character that at last the wretched man wrote to you and said that he had given orders to his servants that no telegram was to be brought to him under any pretence whatsoever. That did not daunt you. You saw the immense opportunities afforded by the open postcard, and availed yourself of them to the full. You hounded him on in the chase still more. I do not suppose he would ever really have given it up. Family instincts were strong in him. His hatred of you was just as persistent as your hatred of him, and I was the stalking-horse for both of you, and a mode of attack as well as a mode of shelter. His very passion for notoriety was not merely individual but racial. Still, if his interest had flagged for a moment your letters and postcards would soon have quickened it to its ancient flame. They did so. And he naturally went on further still. Having assailed me as a private gentleman and in private, as a public man and in public, he ultimately determines to make his final and great attack on me as an artist, and in the place where my Art is being represented. He secures by fraud a seat for the first night of one of my plays, and contrives a plot to interrupt the performance, to make a foul speech about me to the audience, to insult my actors, to throw offensive or indecent missiles at me when I am called before the curtain at the close, utterly in some hideous way to ruin me through my work. By the merest chance, in the brief and accidental sincerity of a more than usually intoxicated mood, he boasts of his intention before others. Information is given to the police, and he is kept out of the theatre. You had your chance then. Then was your opportunity. Don't you realise now that you should have seen it, and come forward and said that you would not have my Art, at any rate, ruined for your sake? You knew what my Art was to me, the great primal note by which I had revealed, first myself to myself, and then myself to the world; the real passion of my life; the love to which all other loves were as marshwater to red wine, or the glow-worm of the marsh to the magic mirror of the moon. Don't you understand now that your lack of imagination was the one really fatal defect of your character? What you had to do was quite simple, and quite clear before you, but Hate had blinded you, and you could see nothing. I could not apologise to your father for his having insulted me and persecuted me in the most loathsome manner for nearly nine months. I could not get rid of you out of my life. I had tried it again and again. I had gone so far as actually leaving England and going abroad in the hope of escaping from you. It had all been of no use. You were the only person who could have done anything. The key of the situation rested entirely with yourself. It was the one great opportunity you had of making some slight return to me for all the love and affection and kindness and generosity and care I had shown you. Had you appreciated me even at a tenth of my value as an artist you would have done so. But Hate blinded you. The faculty "by which, and by which alone, we can understand others in their real as in their ideal relations" was dead in you. You thought simply of how to get your father into prison. To see him "in the dock," as you used to say: that was your one idea. The phrase became one of the many scies of your daily conversation. One heard it at every meal. Well, you had your desire gratified. Hate granted you every single thing you wished for. It was an indulgent Master to you. It is so, indeed, to all who serve it. For two days you sat on a high seat with the Sheriffs, and feasted your eyes with the spectacle of your father standing in the dock of the Central Criminal Court. And on the third day I took his place. What had occurred? In your hideous game of hate together, you had both thrown dice for my soul, and you happened to have lost. That was all.

You see that I have to write your life to you, and you have to realise it. We have known each other now for more than four years. Half of the time we have been together: the other half I have had to spend in prison as the result of our friendship. Where you will receive this letter, if indeed it ever reaches you, I don't know. Rome, Naples, Paris, Venice, some beautiful city on sea or river, I have no doubt, holds you. You are surrounded, if not with all the useless luxury you had with me, at any rate with everything that is pleasurable to eye, ear, and taste. Life is quite lovely to you. And yet, if you are wise, and wish to find Life much lovelier still, and in a different manner, you will let the reading of this terrible letter—for such I know it is—prove to you as important a crisis and turning-point of your life as the writing of it is to me. Your pale face used to flush easily with wine or pleasure. If, as you read what is here written, it from time to time becomes scorched, as though by a furnace-blast, with shame, it will be all the better for you. The supreme vice is shallowness. Whatever is realised is right.

I have now got as far as the House of Detention, have I not? After a night passed in the Police Cells I am sent there in the van. You were most attentive and kind. Almost every afternoon, if not actually every afternoon till you go abroad, you took the trouble to drive up to Holloway to see me. You also wrote very sweet and nice letters. But that it was not your father but you who had put me into prison, that from beginning to end you were the responsible person, that it was through you, for you, and by you that I was there, never for one instant dawned upon you. Even the spectacle of me behind the bars of a wooden cage could not quicken that dead unimaginative nature. You had the sympathy and the sentimentality of the spectator of a rather pathetic play. That you were the true author of the hideous tragedy did not occur to you. I saw that you realised nothing of what you had done. I did not desire to be the one to tell you what your own heart should have told you, what it indeed

又有谁能够计算出自己灵魂的轨道呢?

...rn. With us time itself does not progress. It revolves. It seems to circle round one centre of pain

...g of the wonder of both, is in immediate contact with divine things, and has got as near to God's secret as anyone can ge...

...wn development, and by accepting all that has happened to me make myself worthy of it

...nd sorrow there is always. Sorrow. Pain, unlike pleasure, wears no mask

Suffering is one long moment. We cannot divide it by seasons. We can only record its moods, and chronicle

and he who can look at the loveliness of the world, and share its sorrow, and rea

I can, at any rate, merely proceed on th

Behind Joy and Laughter there may be a temperament, coarse, hard and cal would have told you if you had not let Hate harden it and make it insensate. Everything must come to one out of one's own nature. There is no use in telling a person a thing that they don't feel and can't understand. If I write to you now as I do it is because your own silence and conduct during my long imprisonment have made it necessary. Besides, as things had turned out, the blow had fallen upon me alone. That was a source of pleasure to me. I was content for many reasons to suffer, though there was always to my eyes, as I watched you, something not a little contemptible in your complete and wilful blindness. I remember your producing with absolute pride a letter you had published in one of the halfpenny newspapers about me. It was a very prudent, temperate, indeed commonplace production. You appealed to the *"English sense of fair play,"* or something very dreary of that kind, on behalf of *"a man who was down."* It was the sort of letter you might have written had a painful charge been brought against some respectable person with whom personally you had been quite unacquainted. But you thought it a wonderful letter.

You looked on it as a proof of almost quixotic chivalry. I am aware that you wrote other letters to other newspapers that they did not publish. But then they were simply to say that you hated your father. Nobody cared if you did or not. Hate, you have yet to learn, is, intellectually considered, the Eternal Negation. Considered from the point of view of the emotions it is a form of Atrophy, and kills everything but itself. To write to the papers to say that one hates someone else is as if one were to write to the papers to say that one had some secret and shameful malady: the fact that the man you hated was your own father, and that the feeling was thoroughly reciprocated, did not make your Hate noble or fine in any way. If it showed anything it was simply that it was an hereditary disease.

I remember again, when an execution was put into my house, and my books and furniture were seized and advertised to be sold, and Bankruptcy was impending, I naturally wrote to tell you about it. I did not mention that it was to pay for some gifts of mine to you that the bailiffs had entered the home where you had so often dined. I thought, rightly or wrongly, that such news might pain you a little. I merely told you the bare facts. I thought it proper that you should know them. You wrote back from Boulogne in a strain of almost lyrical exultation. You said that you knew your father was "hard up for money," and had been obliged to raise £1500 for the expenses of the trial, and that my going bankrupt was really a "splendid score" off him, as he would not then be able to get any of his costs out of me! Do you realise now what Hate blinding a person is? Do you recognise now that when I described it as an Atrophy destructive of everything but itself, I was scientifically describing a real psychological fact? That all my charming things were to be sold: my Burne-Jones drawings: my Whistler drawings: my Monticelli: my Simeon Solomons: my china: my Library with its collection of presentation volumes from almost every poet of my time, from Hugo to Whitman, from Swinburne to Mallarmé, from Morris to Verlaine; with its beautifully bound editions of my father's and mother's works; its wonderful array of college and school prizes, its *éditions de luxe*, and the like; was absolutely nothing to you. You said it was a great bore: that was all. What you really saw in it was the possibility that your father might ultimately lose a few hundred pounds, and that paltry consideration filled you with ecstatic joy. As for the costs of the trial, you may be interested to know that your father openly said in the Orleans Club that if it had cost him £20,000 he would have considered the money thoroughly well spent, he had extracted such enjoyment, and delight, and triumph out of it all. The fact that he was able not merely to put me into prison for two years, but to take me out for an afternoon and make me a public bankrupt was an extra-refinement of pleasure that he had not expected. It was the crowning-point of my humiliation, and of his complete and perfect victory. Had your father had no claim for his costs on me, you, I know perfectly well, would, as far as words go, at any rate have been most sympathetic about the entire loss of my library, a loss irreparable to a man of letters, the one of all my material losses the most distressing to me. You might even, remembering the sums of money I had lavishly spent on you and how you had lived on me for years, have taken the trouble to buy in some of my books for me. The best all went for less than £150: about as much as I would spend on you in an ordinary week. But the mean small pleasure of thinking that your father was going to be a few pence out of pocket made you forget all about trying to make me a little return, so slight, so easy, so inexpensive, so obvious, and so enormously welcome to me, had you brought it about. Am I right in saying that Hate blinds people? Do you see it now? If you don't, try to see it.

How clearly I saw it then, as now, I need not tell you. But I said to myself: *"At all costs I must keep Love in my heart. If I go into prison without Love what will become of my Soul?"* The letters I wrote to you at that time from Holloway were my efforts to keep Love as the dominant note of my own nature. I could if I had chosen have torn you to pieces with bitter reproaches. I could have rent you with maledictions. I could have held up a mirror to you, and shown you such an image of yourself that you would not have recognised it as your own till you found it mimicking back your gestures of horror, and then you would have known whose shape it was, and hated it and yourself for ever. More than that indeed. The sins of another were being placed to my account. Had I so chosen, I could on either trial have saved myself at his expense, not from shame indeed but from imprisonment. Had I cared to show that the Crown witnesses—the three most important—had been carefully coached by your father and his solicitors, not in reticences merely, but in assertions, in the absolute transference, deliberate, plotted, and rehearsed, of the actions and doings of someone else on to me, I could have had each one of them dismissed from the box by the Judge, more summarily than even wretched perjured Atkins was. I could have walked out of Court with my tongue in my cheek, and my hands in my pockets, a free man. The strongest pressure was put upon me to do so. I was earnestly advised, begged, entreated to do so by people whose sole interest was my welfare, and the welfare of my house. But I refused. I did not choose to do so. I have never regretted my decision for a single moment, even in the most bitter periods of my imprisonment. Such a course of action would have been beneath me. Sins of the flesh are nothing. They are maladies for physicians to cure, if they should be cured. Sins of the soul alone are shameful. To have secured my acquittal by such means would have been a life-long torture to me. But do you really think that you were worthy of the love I was showing you then, or that for a single moment I thought you were? Do you really think that at any period in our friendship you were worthy of the love I showed you, or that for a single moment I thought you were? I knew you were not. But Love does not traffic in a marketplace, nor use a huckster's scales. Its joy, like the joy of the intellect, is to feel itself alive. The aim of Love is to love: no more, and no less. You were my enemy: such an enemy as no man ever had. I had given you my life, and to gratify the lowest and most contemptible of all human passions, Hatred and Vanity and Greed, you had thrown it away. In less than three years you had entirely ruined me from every point of view. For my own sake there was nothing for me to do but to love you. I knew, if I allowed myself to hate you, that in the dry desert of existence over which I had to travel, and am travelling still, every rock would lose its shadow, every palm tree be withered, every well of water prove poisoned at its source. Are you beginning now to understand a little? Is your imagination wakening from the long lethargy in which it has lain? You know already what Hate is. Is it beginning to dawn on you what Love is, and what is the nature of Love? It is not too late for you to learn, though to teach it to you I may have had to go to a convict's cell.

After my terrible sentence, when the prison-dress was on me, and the prison-house closed, I sat amidst the ruins of my wonderful life, crushed by anguish, bewildered with terror, dazed through pain. But I would not hate you. Every day I said to myself, "*I must keep Love in my heart today, else how shall I live through the day.*" I reminded myself that you meant no evil, to me at any rate: I set myself to think that you had but drawn a bow at a venture, and that the arrow had pierced a King between the joints of the harness. To have weighed you against the smallest of my sorrows, the meanest of my losses, would have been, I felt, unfair. I determined I would regard you as one suffering too. I forced myself to believe that at last the scales had fallen from your long-blinded eyes. I used to fancy, and with pain, what your horror must have been when you contemplated your terrible handiwork. There were times, even in those dark days, the darkest of all my life, when I actually longed to console you. So sure was I that at last you had realised what you had done.

It did not occur to me then that you could have the supreme vice, shallowness. Indeed, it was a real grief to me when I had to let you know that I was obliged to reserve for family business my first opportunity of receiving a letter: but my brother-in-law had written to me to say that if I would only write once to my wife she would, for my own sake and for our children's sake, take no action for divorce. I felt my duty was to do so. Setting aside other reasons, I could not bear the idea of being separated from Cyril, that beautiful, loving, loveable child of mine, my friend of all friends, my companion beyond all companions, one single hair of whose little golden head should have been dearer and of more value to me than, I will not merely say you from top to toe, but the entire chrysolite of the whole world: was so indeed to me always, though I failed to understand it till too late.

Two weeks after your application, I get news of you. Robert Sherard, that bravest and most chivalrous of all brilliant beings, comes to see me, and amongst other things tells me that in that ridiculous *Mercure de France*, with its absurd affectation of being the true centre of literary corruption, you are about to publish an article on me with specimens of my letters. He asks me if it really was by my wish. I was greatly taken aback, and much annoyed, and gave orders that the thing was to be stopped at once. You had left my letters lying about for blackmailing companions to steal, for hotel servants to pilfer, for housemaids to sell. That was simply your careless want of appreciation of what I had written to you. But that you should seriously propose to publish selections from the balance was almost incredible to me. And which of my letters were they? I could get no information. That was my first news of you. It displeased me.

The second piece of news followed shortly afterwards. Your father's solicitors had appeared in the prison, and served me personally with a Bankruptcy notice, for a paltry £700, the amount of their taxed costs. I was adjudged a public insolvent, and ordered to be produced in Court. I felt most strongly, and feel still, and will revert to the subject again, that these costs should have been paid by your family. You had taken personally on yourself the responsibility of stating that your family would do so. It was that which had made the solicitor take up the case in the way he did. You were absolutely responsible. Even irrespective of your engagement on your family's behalf you should have felt that as you had brought the whole ruin on me, the least that could have been done was to spare me the additional ignominy of bankruptcy for an absolutely contemptible sum of money, less than half of what I spent on you in three brief summer months at Goring. Of that, however, no more here. I did through the solicitor's clerk, I fully admit, receive a message from you on the subject, or at any rate in connection with the occasion. The day he came to receive my depositions and statements, he leant across the table—the prison warder being present—and having consulted a piece of paper which he pulled from his pocket, said to me in a low voice: "Prince Fleur-de-Lys wishes to be remembered to you." I stared at him. He repeated the message again. I did not know what he meant. "The gentleman is abroad at present," he added mysteriously. It all flashed across me, and I remember that, for the first and last time in my entire prison-life, I laughed. In that laugh was all the scorn of all the world. Prince Fleur-de-Lys! I saw—and subsequent events showed me that I rightly saw—that nothing that had happened had made you realise a single thing. You were in your own eyes still the graceful prince of a trivial comedy, not the sombre figure of a tragic show. All that had occurred was but as a feather for the cap that gilds a narrow head, a flower to pink the doublet that hides a heart that Hate, and Hate alone, can warm, that Love, and Love alone, finds cold. Prince Fleur-de-Lys! You were, no doubt, quite right to communicate with me under an assumed name. I myself, at that time, had no name at all. In the great prison where I was then incarcerated I was merely the figure and letter of a little cell in a long gallery, one of a thousand lifeless numbers, as of a thousand lifeless lives. But surely there were many real names in real history which would have suited you much better, and by which I would have had no difficulty at all in recognising you at once? I did not look for you behind the spangles of a tinsel vizard only suitable for an amusing masquerade. Ah! had your soul been, as for its own perfection even it should have been, wounded with sorrow, bowed with remorse, and humble with grief, such was not the disguise it would have chosen beneath whose shadow to seek entrance to the House of Pain! The great things of life are what they seem to be, and for that reason, strange as it may sound to you, are often difficult to interpret. But the little things of life are symbols. We receive our bitter lessons most easily through them. Your seemingly casual choice of a feigned name was, and will remain, symbolic. It reveals you.

Six weeks later a third piece of news arrives. I am called out of the Hospital Ward, where I was lying wretchedly ill, to receive a special message from you through the Governor of the Prison. He reads me out a letter you had addressed to him in which you stated that you proposed to publish an article "on the case of Mr Oscar Wilde," in the Mercure de France ("a magazine", you added for some extraordinary reason, "corresponding to our English *Fortnightly Review*") and were anxious to obtain my permission to publish extracts and selections from—what letters? The letters I had written to you from Holloway Prison! The letters that should have been to you things sacred and secret beyond anything in the whole world! These actually were the letters you proposed to publish for the jaded *décadent* to wonder at, for the greedy *feuilletoniste* to chronicle, for the little lions of the *Quartier Latin* to gape and mouth at! Had there been nothing in your own heart to cry out against so vulgar a sacrilege you might at least have remembered the sonnet he wrote who saw with such sorrow and scorn the letters of John Keats sold by public auction in London and have understood at last the real meaning of my lines

I think they love not Art

Who break the crystal of a poet's heart

That small and sickly eyes may glare or gloat.

For what was your article to show? That I had been too fond of you? The Paris *gamin* was quite aware of the fact. They all read the newspapers, and most of them write for them. That I was a man of genius? The French understood that, and the peculiar quality of my genius, much better than you did, or could have been expected to do. That along with genius goes often a curious perversity of passion and desire? Admirable: but the subject belongs to Lombroso rather than to you. Besides, the pathological phenomenon in question is also found amongst those who have not genius. That in your war of hate with your father I was at once shield and weapon to each of you? Nay more, that in that hideous hunt for my life, that took place when the war was over, he never could have reached me had not your nets been already about my feet? Quite true: but I am told that Henri Bauër had already done it extremely well. Besides, to corroborate his view, had such been your intention, you did not require to publish my letters; at any rate those written from Holloway Prison.

Will you say, in answer to my questions, that in one of my Holloway letters I had myself asked you to try, as far as you were able, to set me a little right with some small portion of the world? Certainly, I did so. Remember how and why I am here, at this very moment. Do you think I am here on account of my relations with the witnesses on my trial? My relations, real or supposed, with people of that kind were matters of no interest to either the Government or Society. They knew nothing of them, and cared less. I am here for having tried to put your father into prison. My attempt failed of course. My own Counsel threw up their briefs. Your father completely turned the tables on me, and had me in prison, has me there still. That is why there is contempt felt for me. That is why people despise me. That is why I have to serve out every day, every hour, every minute of my dreadful imprisonment. That is why my petitions have been refused.

You were the only person who, and without in any way exposing yourself to scorn or danger or blame, could have given another colour to the whole affair: have put the matter in a different light: have shown to a certain degree how things really stood. I would not of course have expected, nor indeed wished you to have stated how and for what purpose you had sought my assistance in your trouble at Oxford: or how, and for what purpose, if you had a purpose at all, you had practically never left my side for nearly three years. My incessant attempts to break off a friendship that was so ruinous to me as an artist, as a man of position, as a member of society even, need not have been chronicled with the accuracy with which they have been set down here. Nor would I have desired you to have described the scenes you used to make with such almost monotonous recurrence: nor to have reprinted your wonderful series of telegrams to me with their strange mixture of romance and finance; nor to have quoted from your letters the more revolting or heartless passages, as I have been forced to do. Still, I thought it would have been good, as well for you as for me, if you had made some protest against your father's version of our friendship, one no less grotesque than venomous, and as absurd in its reference to you as it was dishonouring in its reference to me. That version has now actually passed into serious history: it is quoted, believed, and chronicled: the preacher has taken it for his text, and the moralist for his barren theme: and I who appealed to all the ages have had to accept my verdict from one who is an ape and a buffoon. I have said, and with some bitterness, I admit, in this letter that such was the irony of things that your father would live to be the hero of a Sunday-school tract: that you would rank with the infant Samuel: and that my place would be between Gilles de Retz and the Marquis de Sade. I dare say it is best so. I have no desire to complain. One of the many lessons that one learns in prison is that things are what they are, and will be what they will be. Nor have I any doubt but that the leper of mediaevalism, and the author of

Justine, will prove better company than *Sandford and Merton*.

But at the time I wrote to you I felt that for both our sakes it would be a good thing, a proper thing, a right thing not to accept the account your father had put forward through his Counsel for the edification of a Philistine world, and that is why I asked you to think out and write something that would be nearer the truth. It would at least have been better for you than scribbling to the French papers about the domestic life of your parents. What did the French care whether or not your parents had led a happy domestic life? One cannot conceive a subject more entirely uninteresting to them. What did interest them was how an artist of my distinction, one who by the school and movement of which he was the incarnation had exercised a marked influence on the direction of French thought, could, having led such a life, have brought such an action. Had you proposed for your article to publish the letters, endless I fear in number, in which I had spoken to you of the ruin you were bringing on my life, of the madness of moods of rage that you were allowing to master you to your own hurt as well as to mine, and of my desire, nay, my determination to end a friendship so fatal to me in every way, I could have understood it, though I would not have allowed such letters to be published: when your father's Counsel desiring to catch me in a contradiction suddenly produced in Court a letter of mine, written to you in March '93, in which I stated that, rather than endure a repetition of the hideous scenes you seemed to take such a terrible pleasure in making, I would readily consent to be "blackmailed by every renter in London," it was a very real grief to me that that side of my friendship with you should incidentally be revealed to the common gaze: but that you should have been so slow to see, so lacking in all sensitiveness, and so dull in apprehension of what is rare, delicate and beautiful, as to propose yourself to publish the letters in which, and through which, I was trying to keep alive the very spirit and soul of Love, that it might dwell in my body through the long years of that body's humiliation—this was, and still is to me, a source of the very deepest pain, the most poignant disappointment. Why you did so, I fear I know but too well. If Hate blinded your eyes, Vanity sewed your eyelids together with threads of iron. The faculty "by which, and by which alone, one can understand others in their real as in their ideal relations," your narrow egotism had blunted, and long disuse had made of no avail. The imagination was as much in prison as I was. Vanity had barred up the windows, and the name of the warder was Hate.

All this took place in the early part of November of the year before last. A great river of life flows between you and a date so distant. Hardly, if at all, can you see across so wide a waste. But to me it seems to have occurred, I will not say yesterday, but today. Suffering is one long moment. We cannot divide it by seasons. We can only record its moods, and chronicle their return. With us time itself does not progress. It revolves. It seems to circle round one centre of pain. The paralysing immobility of a life, every circumstance of which is regulated after an unchangeable pattern, so that we eat and drink and walk and lie down and pray, or kneel at least for prayer, according to the inflexible laws of an iron formula: this immobile quality, that makes each dreadful day in the very minutest detail like its brother, seems to communicate itself to those external forces the very essence of whose existence is ceaseless change. Of seed-time or harvest, of the reapers bending over the corn, or the grape-gatherers threading through the vines, of the grass in the orchard made white with broken blossoms, or strewn with fallen fruit, we know nothing, and can know nothing. For us there is only one season, the season of Sorrow. The very sun and moon seem taken from us. Outside, the day may be blue and gold, but the light that creeps down through the thickly-muffled glass of the small iron-barred window beneath which one sits is grey and niggard. It is always twilight in one's cell, as it is always midnight in one's heart. And in the sphere of thought, no less than in the sphere of time, motion is no more. The thing that you personally have long ago forgotten, or can easily forget, is happening to me now, and will happen to me again tomorrow. Remember this, and you will be able to understand a little of why I am writing to you, and in this manner writing.

A week later, I am transferred here. Three more months go over and my mother dies. You knew, none better, how deeply I loved and honoured her. Her death was so terrible to me that I, once a lord of language, have no words in which to express my anguish and my shame. Never, even in the most perfect days of my development as an artist, could I have had words fit to bear so august a burden, or to move with sufficient stateliness of music through the purple pageant of my incommunicable woe. She and my father had bequeathed me a name they had made noble and honoured not merely in Literature, Art, Archaeology and Science, but in the public history of my own country in its evolution as a nation. I had disgraced that name eternally. I had made it a low byword among low people. I had dragged it through the very mire. I had given it to brutes that they might make it brutal, and to fools that they might turn it into a synonym for folly. What I suffered then, and still suffer, is not for pen to write or paper to record.

My wife, at that time kind and gentle to me, rather than that I should hear the news from indifferent or alien lips, travelled, ill as she was, all the way from Genoa to England to break to me herself the tidings of so irreparable, so irredeemable a loss. Messages of sympathy reached me from all who had still affection for me. Even people who had not known me personally, hearing what a new sorrow had come into my broken life, wrote to ask that some expression of their condolence should be conveyed to me. You alone stood aloof, sent me no message, and wrote me no letter. Of such actions, it is best to say what Virgil says to Dante of those whose lives have been barren in noble impulse and shallow of intention: *"Non ragioniam di lor, ma guarda, e passa."*

Three more months go over. The calendar of my daily conduct and labour that hangs on the outside of my cell-door, with my name and sentence written upon it, tells me that it is Maytime. My friends come to see me again. I enquire, as I always do, after you. I am told that you are in your villa at Naples, and are bringing out a volume of poems. At the close of the interview it is mentioned casually that you are dedicating them to me. The tidings seemed to give me a sort of nausea of life. I said nothing, but silently went back to my cell with contempt and scorn in my heart. How could you dream of dedicating a volume of poems to me without first asking my permission? Dream, do I say? How could you dare to do such a thing? Will you give as your answer that in the days of my greatness and fame I had consented to receive the dedication of your early work? Certainly, I did so; just as I would have accepted the homage of any other young man beginning the difficult and beautiful art of literature. All homage is delightful to an artist, and doubly sweet when youth brings it. Laurel and bay leaf wither when aged hands pluck them. Only youth has a right to crown an artist. That is the real privilege of being young, if youth only knew it. But the days of abasement and infamy are different from those of greatness and of fame. You have yet to learn that Prosperity, Pleasure and Success may be rough of grain and common in fibre, but that Sorrow is the most sensitive of all created things. There is nothing that stirs in the whole world of thought or motion to which Sorrow does not vibrate in terrible if exquisite pulsation. The thin beaten-out leaf of tremulous gold that chronicles the direction of forces that the eye cannot see is in comparison coarse. It is a wound that bleeds when any hand but that of Love touches it and even then must bleed again, though not for pain.

You could write to the Governor of Wandsworth Prison to ask my permission to publish my letters in the Mercure de France, "corresponding to our English Fortnightly Review." Why not have written to the Governor of the Prison at Reading to ask my permission to dedicate your poems to me, whatever fantastic description you may have chosen to give of them? Was it because in the one case the magazine in question had been prohibited by me from publishing letters, the legal copyright of which, as you are of course perfectly well aware, was and is vested entirely in me, and in the other you thought that you could enjoy the wilfulness of your own way without my knowing anything about it till it was too late to interfere? The mere fact that I was a man disgraced, ruined, and in prison should have made you, if you desired to write my name on the fore-page of your work, beg it of me as a favour, an honour, a privilege. That is the way in which one should approach those who are in distress and sit in shame.

Where there is Sorrow there is holy ground. Some day you will realise what that means. You will know nothing of life till you do. Robbie, and natures like his, can realise it. When I was brought down from my prison to the Court of Bankruptcy between two policemen, Robbie waited in the long dreary corridor, that before the whole crowd, whom an action so sweet and simple hushed into silence, he might gravely raise his hat to me, as handcuffed and with bowed head I passed him by. Men have gone to heaven for smaller things than that. It was in this spirit, and with this mode of love that the saints knelt down to wash the feet of the poor, or stooped to kiss the leper on the cheek. I have never said one single word to him about what he did. I do not know to the present moment whether he is aware that I was even conscious of his action. It is not a thing for which one can render formal thanks in formal words. I store it in the treasury-house of my heart. I keep it there as a secret debt that I am glad to think I can never possibly repay. It is embalmed and kept sweet by the myrrh and cassia of many tears. When Wisdom has been profitless to me, and Philosophy barren, and the proverbs and phrases of those who have sought to give me consolation as dust and ashes in my mouth, the memory of that little lowly silent act of Love has unsealed for me all the wells of pity, made the desert blossom like a rose, and brought me out of the bitterness of lonely exile into harmony with the wounded, broken and great heart of the world. When you are able to understand, not merely how beautiful Robbie's action was, but why it meant so much to me, and always will mean so much, then, perhaps, you will realise how and in what spirit you should have approached me for permission to dedicate to me your verses.

It is only right to state that in any case I would not have accepted the dedication. Though, possibly, it would under other circumstances have pleased me to have been asked, I would have refused the request for *your* sake, irrespective of any feelings of my own. The first volume of poems that in the very springtime of his manhood a young man sends forth to the world should be like a blossom or flower of spring, like the white thorn in the meadow at Magdalen, or the cowslips in the Cumnor fields. It should not be burdened by the weight of a terrible, a revolting tragedy, a terrible, a revolting scandal. If I had allowed my name to serve as herald to the book it would have been a grave artistic error. It would have brought a wrong atmosphere round the whole work, and in modern art atmosphere counts for so much. Modern life is complex and relative. Those are its two distinguishing notes. To render the first we require atmosphere with its subtlety of *nuances*, of suggestion, of strange perspectives: as for the second we require background. That is why Sculpture has ceased to be a representative art; and why Music is a representative art; and why Literature is, and has been, and always will remain the supreme representative art.

Your little book should have brought with it Sicilian and Arcadian airs, not the pestilent foulness of the criminal dock or the close breath of the convict cell. Nor would such a dedication as you proposed have been merely an error of taste in Art; it would from other points of view have been entirely unseemly. It would have looked like a continuance of your conduct before and after my arrest. It would have given people the impression of being an attempt at foolish bravado: an example of that kind of courage that is sold cheap and bought cheap in the streets of shame. As far as our friendship is concerned Nemesis has crushed us both like flies. The dedication of verses to me when I was in prison would have seemed a sort of silly effort at smart repartee, an accomplishment on which in your old days of dreadful letter-writing—days never, I sincerely hope for your sake, to return—you used openly to pride yourself and about which it was your joy to boast. It would not have produced the serious, the beautiful effect which I trust—I believe indeed—you had intended. Had you consulted me, I would have advised you to delay the publication of your verses for a little; or, if that proved displeasing to you, to publish anonymously at first, and then when you had won lovers by your song—the only sort of lovers really worth the winning—you might have turned round and said to the world "These flowers that you admire are of my sowing, and now I offer them to one whom you regard as a pariah and an outcast, as my tribute to what I love and reverence and admire in him." But you chose the wrong method and the wrong moment. There is a tact in love, and a tact in literature: you were not sensitive to either.

I have spoken to you at length on this point in order that you should grasp its full bearings, and understand why I wrote at once to Robbie in terms of such scorn and contempt of you, and absolutely prohibited the dedication, and desired that the words I had written of you should be copied out carefully and sent to you. I felt that at last the time had come when you should be made to see, to recognise, to realise a little of what you had done. Blindness may be carried so far that it becomes grotesque, and an unimaginative nature, if something be not done to rouse it, will become petrified into absolute insensibility, so that while the body may eat, and drink, and have its pleasures, the soul, whose house it is, may, like the soul of Branca d'Oria in Dante, be dead absolutely. My letter seems to have arrived not a moment too soon. It fell on you, as far as I can judge, like a thunderbolt. You describe yourself, in your answer to Robbie, as being "deprived of all power of thought and expression." Indeed, apparently, you can think of nothing better than to write to your mother to complain. Of course, she, with that blindness to your real good that has been her ill-starred fortune and yours, gives you every comfort she can think of, and lulls you back, I suppose, into your former unhappy, unworthy condition; while as far as I am concerned, she lets my friends know that she is "very much annoyed" at the severity of my remarks about you. Indeed it is not merely to my friends that she conveys her sentiments of annoyance, but also to those—a very much larger number, I need hardly remind you—who are not my friends: and I am informed now, and through channels very kindly-disposed to you and yours, that in consequence of this a great deal of the sympathy that, by reason of my distinguished genius and terrible sufferings, had been gradually but surely growing up for me, has been entirely taken away. People say "Ah! he first tried to get the kind father put into prison and failed: now he turns round and blames the innocent son for his failure. How right we were to despise him! How worthy of contempt he is!" It seems to me that, when my name is mentioned in your mother's presence, if she has no word of sorrow or regret for her share— no slight one—in the ruin of my house, it would be more seemly if she remained silent. And as for you— don't you think now that, instead of writing to her to complain, it would have been better for you, in every way, to have written to me directly, and to have had the courage to say to me whatever you had or fancied you had to say? It is nearly a year ago now since I wrote that letter. You cannot have remained during that entire time "deprived of all power of thought and expression." Why did you not write to me? You saw by my letter how deeply wounded, how outraged I was by your whole conduct. More than that; you saw your entire friendship with me set before you, at last, in its true light, and by a mode not to be mistaken. Often in old days I had told you that you were ruining my life. You had always laughed. When Edwin Levy at the very beginning of our friendship, seeing your manner of putting me forward to bear the brunt, and annoyance, and expense even of that unfortunate Oxford mishap of yours, if we must so term it, in reference to which his advice and help had been sought, warned me for the space of a whole hour against knowing you, you laughed, as at Bracknell I described to you my long and impressive interview with him. When I told you how even that unfortunate young man who ultimately stood beside me in the Dock had warned me more than once that you would prove far more fatal in bringing me to utter destruction than any even of the common lads whom I was foolish enough to know, you laughed, though not with such sense of amusement. When my more prudent or less well-disposed friends either warned me or left me, on account of my friendship with you, you laughed with scorn.

You laughed immoderately when, on the occasion of your father writing his first abusive letter to you about me, I told you that I knew I would be the mere cats-paw of your dreadful quarrel and come to some evil between you. But every single thing had happened as I had said it would happen, as far as the result goes. You had no excuse for not seeing how all things had come to pass. Why did you not write to me? Was it cowardice? Was it callousness? What was it? The fact that I was outraged with you, and had expressed my sense of the outrage, was all the more reason for writing. If you thought my letter just, you should have written. If you thought it in the smallest point unjust, you should have written. I waited for a letter. I felt sure that at last you would see that, if old affection, much-protested love, the thousand acts of ill-requited kindness I had showered on you, the thousand unpaid debts of gratitude you owed me—that if all these were nothing to you, mere duty itself, most barren of all bonds between man and man, should have made you write. You cannot say that you seriously thought I was obliged to receive none but business communications from members of my family. You knew perfectly well that every twelve weeks, Robbie was writing to me a little budget of literary news. Nothing can be more charming than his letters, in their wit, their clever concentrated criticism, their light touch: they are real letters: they are like a person talking to one: they have the quality of a French *causerie intime*: and in his delicate modes of deference to me, appealing at one time to my judgment, at another to my sense of humour, at another to my instinct for beauty or to my culture, and reminding me in a hundred subtle ways that once I was to many an arbiter of style in Art, the supreme arbiter to some, he shows how he has the tact of love as well as the tact of literature. His letters have been the little messengers between me and that beautiful unreal world of Art where once I was King, and would have remained King, indeed, had I not let myself be lured into the imperfect world of coarse uncompleted passions, of appetite without distinction, desire without limit, and formless greed. Yet, when all is said, surely you might have been able to understand, or conceive, at any rate, in you own mind, that, even on the ordinary grounds of mere psychological curiosity, it would have been more interesting to me to hear from *you* than to learn that Alfred Austin was trying to bring out a volume of poems, or that Street was writing dramatic criticisms for the *Daily Chronicle*, or that by one who cannot speak a panegyric without stammering Mrs Meynell had been pronounced to be the new Sibyl of Style.

Ah! had *you* been in prison—I will not say through any fault of mine, for that would be a thought too terrible for me to bear—but through fault of your own, error of your own, faith in some unworthy friend, slip in sensual mire, trust misapplied, or love ill-bestowed, or none, or all of these—do you think that I would have allowed you to eat your heart away in darkness and solitude without trying in some way, however slight, to help you to bear the bitter burden of your disgrace? Do you think that I would not have let you know that if you suffered, I was suffering too: that if you wept, there were tears in my eyes also: and that if you lay in the house of bondage and were despised of men, I out of my very griefs had built a

- *288* -

house in which to dwell until your coming, a treasury in which all that men had denied to you would be laid up for your healing, one hundredfold in increase? If bitter necessity, or prudence, to me more bitter still, had prevented my being near you, and robbed me of the joy of your presence, though seen through prison-bars and in a shape of shame, I would have written to you in season and out of season in the hope that some mere phrase, some single word, some broken echo even of Love might reach you. If you had refused to receive my letters, I would have written none the less, so that you should have known that at any rate there were always letters waiting for you. Many have done so to me. Every three months people write to me, or propose to write to me. Their letters and communications are kept. They will be handed to me when I go out of prison. I know that they are there. I know the names of the people who have written them. I know that they are full of sympathy, and affection, and kindness. That is sufficient for me. I need to know no more. Your silence has been horrible. Nor has it been a silence of weeks and months merely, but of years; of years even as they have to count them who, like yourself, live swiftly in happiness, and can hardly catch the gilt feet of the days as they dance by, and are out of breath in the chase after pleasure. It is a silence without excuse; a silence without palliation. I knew you had feet of clay. Who knew it better? When I wrote, among my aphorisms, that it was simply the feet of clay that made the gold of the image precious, it was of you I was thinking. But it is no gold image with clay feet that you have made of yourself. Out of the very dust of the common highway that the hooves of horned things pash into mire you have moulded your perfect semblance for me to look at, so that, whatever my secret desire might have been, it would be impossible for me now to have for you any feeling other than that of contempt and scorn, for myself any feeling other than that of contempt and scorn either. And setting aside all other reasons, your indifference, your worldly wisdom, your callousness, your prudence, whatever you may choose to call it, has been made doubly bitter to me by the peculiar circumstances that either accompanied or followed my fall.

Other miserable men, when they are thrown into prison, if they are robbed of the beauty of the world, are at least safe, in some measure, from the world's most deadly slings, most awful arrows. They can hide in the darkness of their cells, and of their very disgrace make a mode of sanctuary. The world, having had its will, goes its way, and they are left to suffer undisturbed. With me it has been different. Sorrow after sorrow has come beating at the prison doors in search of me. They have opened the gates wide and let them in. Hardly, if at all, have my friends been suffered to see me. But my enemies have had full access to me always. Twice in my public appearances at the Bankruptcy Court, twice again in my public transferences from one prison to another, have I been shown under conditions of unspeakable humiliation to the gaze and mockery of men. The messenger of Death has brought me his tidings and gone his way, and in entire solitude, and isolated from all that could give me comfort, or suggest relief, I have had to bear the intolerable burden of misery and remorse that the memory of my mother placed upon me, and places on me still. Hardly has that wound been dulled, not healed, by time, when violent and bitter and harsh letters come to me from my wife through her solicitor. I am, at once, taunted and threatened with poverty. That I can bear. I can school myself to worse than that. But my two children are taken from me by legal procedure. That is and always will remain to me a source of infinite distress, of infinite pain, of grief without end or limit. That the law should decide, and take upon itself to decide, that I am one unfit to be with my own children is something quite horrible to me. The disgrace of prison is as nothing compared to it. I envy the other men who tread the yard along with me. I am sure that their children wait for them, look for their coming, will be sweet to them.

The poor are wiser, more charitable, more kind, more sensitive than we are. In their eyes prison is a tragedy in a man's life, a misfortune, a casualty, something that calls for sympathy in others. They speak of one who is in prison as of one who is "*in trouble*" simply. It is the phrase they always use, and the expression has the perfect wisdom of Love in it. With people of our rank it is different. With us prison makes a man a pariah. I, and such as I am, have hardly my right to air and sun. Our presence taints the pleasures of others. We are unwelcome when we reappear. To revisit the glimpses of the moon is not for us. Our very children are taken away. Those lovely links with humanity are broken. We are doomed to be solitary, while our sons still live. We are denied the one thing that might heal us and help us, that might bring balm to the bruised heart, and peace to the soul in pain.

And to all this has been added the hard, small fact that by your actions and by your silence, by what you have done and by what you have left undone, you have made every day of my long imprisonment still more difficult for me to live through. The very bread and water of prison fare you have by your conduct changed. You have rendered the one bitter and the other brackish to me. The sorrow you should have shared you have doubled, the pain you should have sought to lighten you have quickened to anguish. I have no doubt that you did not mean to do so. I know that you did not mean to do so. It was simply that "one really fatal defect of your character, your entire lack of imagination."

And the end of it all is that I have got to forgive you. I must do so. I don't write this letter to put bitterness into your head, but to pluck it out of mine. For my own sake I must forgive you. One cannot always keep an adder in one's breast to feed on one, nor rise up every night to sow thorns in the garden of one's soul. It will not be difficult at all for me to do so, if you help me a little. Whatever you did to me in old days I always readily forgave. It did you no good then. Only one whose life is without stain of any kind can forgive sins. But now when I sit in humiliation and disgrace it is different. My forgiveness should mean a great deal to you now. Some day you will realise it. Whether you do so early or late, soon or not at all, my way is clear before me. I cannot allow you to go through life bearing in your heart the burden of having ruined a man like me. The thought might make you callously indifferent, or morbidly sad. I must take the burden from you and put it on my own shoulders.

I must say to myself that neither you nor your father, multiplied a thousand times over, could possibly have ruined a man like me: that I ruined myself: and that nobody, great or small, can be ruined except by his own hand. I am quite ready to do so. I am trying to do so, though you may not think it at the present moment. If I have brought this pitiless indictment against you, think what an indictment I bring without pity against myself. Terrible as what you did to me was, what I did to myself was far more terrible still.

I was a man who stood in symbolic relations to the art and culture of my age. I had realised this for myself at the very dawn of my manhood, and had forced my age to realise it afterwards. Few men hold such a position in their own lifetime and have it so acknowledged. It is usually discerned, if discerned at all, by the historian, or the critic, long after both the man and his age have passed away. With me it was different. I felt it myself, and made others feel it. Byron was a symbolic figure, but his relations were to the passion of his age and its weariness of passion. Mine were to something more noble, more permanent, of more vital issue, of larger scope.

The gods had given me almost everything. I had genius, a distinguished name, high social position, brilliancy, intellectual daring: I made art a philosophy, and philosophy an art: I altered the minds of men and the colours of things: there was nothing I said or did that did not make people wonder: I took the drama, the most objective form known to art, and made it as personal a mode of expression as the lyric or the sonnet, at the same time that I widened its range and enriched its characterisation: drama, novel, poem in rhyme, poem in prose, subtle or fantastic dialogue, whatever I touched I made beautiful in a new mode of beauty: to truth itself I gave what is false no less than what is true as its rightful province, and showed that the false and the true are merely forms of intellectual existence. I treated Art as the supreme reality, and life as a mere mode of fiction: I awoke the imagination of my century so that it created myth and legend around me: I summed up all systems in a phrase, and all existence in an epigram.

Along with these things, I had things that were different. I let myself be lured into long spells of senseless and sensual ease. I amused myself with being a *flâneur*, a dandy, a man of fashion. I surrounded myself with the smaller natures and the meaner minds. I became the spendthrift of my own genius, and to waste an eternal youth gave me a curious joy. Tired of being on the heights I deliberately went to the depths in the search for new sensations. What the paradox was to me in the sphere of thought, perversity became to me in the sphere of passion. Desire, at the end, was a malady, or a madness, or both. I grew careless of the lives of others. I took pleasure where it pleased me and passed on. I forgot that every little action of the common day makes or unmakes character, and that therefore what one has done in the secret chamber one has some day to cry aloud on the housetops. I ceased to be Lord over myself. I was no longer the Captain of my Soul, and did not know it. I allowed you to dominate me, and your father to frighten me. I ended in horrible disgrace. There is only one thing for me now, absolute Humility: just as there is only one thing for you, absolute Humility also. You had better come down into the dust and learn it beside me.

I have lain in prison for nearly two years. Out of my nature has come wild despair; an abandonment to grief that was piteous even to look at; terrible and impotent rage: bitterness and scorn: anguish that wept aloud: misery that could find no voice: sorrow that was dumb. I have passed through every possible mood of suffering. Better than Wordsworth himself I know what Wordsworth meant when he said:

Suffering is permanent, obscure, and dark

And has the nature of Infinity.

But while there were times when I rejoiced in the idea that my sufferings were to be endless, I could not bear them to be without meaning. Now I find hidden away in my nature something that tells me that nothing in the whole world is meaningless, and suffering least of all. That something hidden away in my nature, like a treasure in a field, is Humility.

It is the last thing left in me, and the best: the ultimate discovery at which I have arrived: the starting-point for a fresh development. It has come to me right out of myself, so I know that it has come at the proper time. It could not have come before, nor later. Had anyone told me of it, I would have rejected it. Had it been brought to me, I would have refused it. As I found it, I want to keep it. I must do so. It is the one thing that has in it the elements of life, of a new life, a Vita Nuova for me. Of all things it is the strangest. One cannot give it away, and another may not give it to one. One cannot acquire it, except by surrendering everything that one has. It is only when one has lost all things, that one knows that one possesses it.

Now that I realise that it is in me, I see quite clearly what I have got to do, what, in fact, I must do. And when I use such a phrase as that, I need not tell you that I am not alluding to any external sanction or command. I admit none. I am far more of an individualist than I ever was. Nothing seems to me of the smallest value except what one gets out of oneself. My nature is seeking a fresh mode of self-realisation. That is all I am concerned with. And the first thing that I have got to do is to free myself from any possible bitterness of feeling against you.

I am completely penniless, and absolutely homeless. Yet there are worse things in the world than that. I am quite candid when I tell you that rather than go out from this prison with bitterness in my heart against you or against the world I would gladly and readily beg my bread from door to door. If I got nothing at the house of the rich, I would get something at the house of the poor. Those who have much are often greedy Those who have little always share. I would not a bit mind sleeping in the cool grass in summer, and when winter came on sheltering myself by the warm closethatched rick, or under the penthouse of a great barn, provided I had love in my heart. The external things of life seem to me now of no importance at all. You can see to what intensity of individualism I have arrived, or am arriving rather, for the journey is long, and "where I walk there are thorns."

Of course I know that to ask for alms on the high-way is not to be my lot, and that if ever I lie in the cool grass at night-time it will be to write sonnets to the Moon. When I go out of prison, Robbie will be waiting for me on the other side of the big iron-studded gate, and he is the symbol not merely of his own affection, but of the affection of many others besides. I believe I am to have enough to live on for about eighteen months at any rate, so that, if I may not write beautiful books, I may at least read beautiful books, and what joy can be greater? After that, I hope to be able to recreate my creative faculty. But were things different: had I not a friend left in the world: were there not a single house open to me even in pity: had I to accept the wallet and ragged cloak of sheer penury: still as long as I remained free from all resentment, hardness, and scorn, I would be able to face life with much more calm and confidence than I would were my body in purple and fine linen, and the soul within it sick with hate. And I shall really have no difficulty in forgiving you. But to make it a pleasure for me you must feel that you want it. When you really want it you will find it waiting for you.

I need not say that my task does not end there. It would be comparatively easy if it did. There is much more before me. I have hills far steeper to climb, valleys much darker to pass through. And I have to get it all out of myself. Neither Religion, Morality, nor Reason can help me at all.

Morality does not help me. I am a born antinomian. I am one of those who are made for exceptions, not for laws. But while I see that there is nothing wrong in what one does, I see that there is something wrong in what one becomes. It is well to have learned that.

Religion does not help me. The faith that others give to what is unseen, I give to what one can touch, and look at. My Gods dwell in temples made with hands, and within the circle of actual experience is my creed made perfect and complete: too complete it may be, for like many or all of those who have placed their Heaven in this earth, I have found in it not merely the beauty of Heaven, but the horror of

Hell also. When I think about Religion at all, I feel as if I would like to found an order for those who cannot believe: the Confraternity of the Fatherless one might call it, where on an altar, on which no taper burned, a priest, in whose heart peace had no dwelling, might celebrate with unblessed bread and a chalice empty of wine. Everything to be true must become a religion. And agnosticism should have its ritual no less than faith. It has sown its martyrs, it should reap its saints, and praise God daily for having hidden Himself from man. But whether it be faith or agnosticism, it must be nothing external to me. Its symbols must be of my own creating. Only that is spiritual which makes its own form. If I may not find its secret within myself, I shall never find it. If I have not got it already, it will never come to me.

Reason does not help me. It tells me that the laws under which I am convicted are wrong and unjust laws, and the system under which I have suffered a wrong and unjust system. But, somehow, I have got to make both of these things just and right to me. And exactly as in Art one is only concerned with what a particular thing is at a particular moment to oneself, so it is also in the ethical evolution of one's character. I have got to make everything that has happened to me good for me. The plank-bed, the loathsome food, the hard ropes shredded into oakum till one's fingertips grow dull with pain, the menial offices with which each day begins and finishes, the harsh orders that routine seems to necessitate, the dreadful dress that makes sorrow grotesque to look at, the silence, the solitude, the shame—each and all of these things I have to transform into a spiritual experience. There is not a single degradation of the body which I must not try and make into a spiritualising of the soul.

I want to get to the point when I shall be able to say, quite simply and without affectation, that the two great turning-points of my life were when my father sent me to Oxford, and when society sent me to prison. I will not say that it is the best thing that could have happened to me, for that phrase would savour of too great bitterness towards myself. I would sooner say, or hear it said of me, that I was so typical a child of my age that in my perversity, and for that perversity's sake, I turned the good things of my life to evil, and the evil things of my life to good. What is said, however, by myself or by others matters little. The important thing, the thing that lies before me, the thing that I have to do, or be for the brief remainder of my days one maimed, marred, and incomplete, is to absorb into my nature all that has been done to me, to make it part of me, to accept it without complaint, fear, or reluctance. The supreme vice is shallowness. Whatever is realised is right.

When first I was put into prison some people advised me to try and forget who I was. It was ruinous advice. It is only by realising what I am that I have found comfort of any kind. Now I am advised by others to try on my release to forget that I have ever been in a prison at all. I know that would be equally fatal. It would mean that I would be always haunted by an intolerable sense of disgrace, and that those things that are meant as much for me as for anyone else— the beauty of the sun and the moon, the pageant of the seasons, the music of daybreak and the silence of great nights, the rain falling through the leaves, or the dew creeping over the grass and making it silver— would all be tainted for me, and lose their healing power and their power of communicating joy. To reject one's own experiences is to arrest one's own development. To deny one's own experiences is to put a lie into the lips of one's own life. It is no less than a denial of the Soul. For just as the body absorbs things of all kinds, things common and unclean no less than those that the priest or a vision has cleansed, and converts them into swiftness or strength, into the play of beautiful muscles and the moulding of fair flesh, into the curves and colours of the hair, the lips, the eye: so the Soul, in its turn, has its nutritive functions also, and can transform into noble moods of thought, and passions of high import, what in itself is base, cruel, and degrading: nay more, may find in these its most august modes of assertion, and can often reveal itself most perfectly through what was intended to desecrate or destroy.

The fact of my having been the common prisoner of a common gaol I must frankly accept, and, curious as it may seem to you, one of the things I shall have to teach myself is not to be ashamed of it. I must accept it as a punishment, and if one is ashamed of having been punished, one might just as well never have been punished at all. Of course there are many things of which I was convicted that I had not done, but then there are many things of which I was convicted that I had done, and a still greater number of things in my life for which I never was indicted at all. And as for what I have said in this letter, that the gods are strange, and punish us for what is good and humane in us as much as for what is evil and perverse, I must accept the fact that one is punished for the good as well as for the evil that one does. I have no doubt that it is quite right one should be. It helps one, or should help one, to realise both, and not to be too conceited about either. And if I then am not ashamed of my punishment, as I hope not to be, I shall be able to think, and walk, and live with freedom.

Many men on their release carry their prison along with them into the air, hide it as a secret disgrace in their hearts, and at length like poor poisoned things creep into some hole and die. It is wretched that they should have to do so, and it is wrong, terribly wrong, of Society that it should force them to do so. Society takes upon itself the right to inflict appalling punishments on the individual, but it also has the supreme vice of shallowness, and fails to realise what it has done. When the man's punishment is over, it leaves him to himself: that is to say it abandons him at the very moment when its highest duty towards him begins. It is really ashamed of its own actions, and shuns those whom it has punished, as people shun a creditor whose debt they cannot pay, or one on whom they have inflicted an irreparable, an irredeemable wrong. I claim on my side that if I realise what I have suffered, Society should realise what it has inflicted on me: and that there should be no bitterness or hate on either side.

Of course I know that from one point of view things will be made more difficult for me than for others; must indeed, by the very nature of the case, be, made so. The poor thieves and outcasts who are imprisoned here with me are in many respects more fortunate than I am. The little way in grey city or green field that saw their sin is small: to find those who know nothing of what they have done they need go no further than a bird might fly between the twilight before dawn and dawn itself: but for me "the world is shrivelled to a handsbreadth," and everywhere I turn my name is written on the rocks in lead. For I have come, not from obscurity into the momentary notoriety of crime, but from a sort of eternity of fame to a sort of eternity of infamy, and sometimes seem to myself to have shown, if indeed it required showing, that between the famous and the infamous there is but one step, if so much as one.

Still, in the very fact that people will recognise me wherever I go, and know all about my life, as far as its follies go, I can discern something good for me. It will force on me the necessity of again asserting myself as an artist, and as soon as I possibly can. If I can produce even one more beautiful work of art I shall be able to rob malice of its venom, and cowardice of its sneer, and to pluck out the tongue of scorn by the roots. And if life be, as it surely is, a problem to me, I am no less a problem to Life. People must adopt some attitude towards me, and so pass judgment both on themselves and me. I need not say I am not talking of particular individuals. The only people I would care to be with now are artists and people who have suffered: those who know what Beauty is, and those who know what Sorrow is: nobody else interests me. Nor am I making any demands on Life. In all that I have said I am simply concerned with my own mental attitude towards life as a whole: and I feel that not to be ashamed of having been punished is one of the first points I must attain to, for the sake of my own perfection, and because I am so imperfect.

Then I must learn how to be happy. Once I knew it, or thought I knew it, by instinct. It was always springtime once in my heart. My temperament was akin to joy. I filled my life to the very brim with pleasure, as one might fill a cup to the very brim with wine. Now I am approaching life from a completely new standpoint, and even to conceive happiness is often extremely difficult for me. I remember during my first term at Oxford reading in Pater's Renaissance—that book which has had such a strange influence over my life—how Dante places low in the Inferno those who wilfully live in sadness, and going to the College Library and turning to the passage in the Divine Comedy where beneath the dreary marsh lie those who were "sullen in the sweet air," saying for ever through their sighs:

Tristi fummo

nell'aer dolce che dal sol s'allegra.

I knew the Church condemned accidia, but the whole idea seemed to me quite fantastic, just the sort of sin, I fancied, a priest who knew nothing about real life would invent. Nor could I understand how Dante, who says that "sorrow remarries us to God," could have been so harsh to those who were enamoured of melancholy, if any such there really were. I had no idea that some day this would become to me one of the greatest temptations of my life.

While I was in Wandsworth Prison I longed to die. It was my one desire. When after two months in the Infirmary I was transferred here, and found myself growing gradually better in physical health, I was filled with rage. I determined to commit suicide on the very day on which I left prison. After a time that evil mood passed away, and I made up my mind to live, but to wear gloom as a King wears purple: never to smile again: to turn whatever house I entered into a house of mourning: to make my friends walk slowly in sadness with me: to teach them that melancholy is the true secret of life: to maim them with an alien sorrow: to mar them with my own pain. Now I feel quite differently. I see it would be both ungrateful and unkind of me to pull so long a face that when my friends came to see me they would have to make their faces still longer in order to show their sympathy, or, if I desired to entertain them, to invite them to sit down silently to bitter herbs and funeral baked meats. I must learn how to be cheerful and happy.

The last two occasions on which I was allowed to see my friends here I tried to be as cheerful as possible, and to show my cheerfulness in order to make them some slight return for their trouble in coming all the way from town to visit me. It is only a slight return, I know, but it is the one, I feel certain, that pleases them most. I saw Robbie for an hour on Saturday week, and I tried to give the fullest possible expression to the delight I really felt at our meeting. And that, in the views and ideas I am here shaping for myself, I am quite right is shown to me by the fact that now for the first time since my imprisonment I have a real desire to live.

There is before me so much to do that I would regard it as a terrible tragedy if I died before I was allowed to complete at any rate a little of it. I see new developments in Art and Life, each one of which is a fresh mode of perfection. I long to live so that I can explore what is no less than a new world to me. Do you want to know what this new world is? I think you can guess what it is. It is the world in which I have been living.

Sorrow, then, and all that it teaches one, is my new world. I used to live entirely for pleasure. I shunned sorrow and suffering of every kind. I hated both. I resolved to ignore them as far as possible, to treat them, that is to say, as modes of imperfection. They were not part of my scheme of life. They had no place in my philosophy. My mother, who knew life as a whole, used often to quote to me Goethe's lines— written by Carlyle in a book he had given her years ago—and translated, I fancy, by him also:

Who never ate his bread in sorrow,

Who never spent the midnight hours

Weeping and waiting for the morrow,

He knows you not, ye Heavenly Powers.

They were the lines that noble Queen of Prussia, whom Napoleon treated with such coarse brutality, used to quote in her humiliation and exile: they were lines my mother often quoted in the troubles of her later life: I absolutely declined to accept or admit the enormous truth hidden in them. I could not understand it. I remember quite well how I used to tell her that I did not want to eat my bread in sorrow, or to pass any night weeping and watching for a more bitter dawn. I had no idea that it was one of the special things that the Fates had in store for me; that for a whole year of my life, indeed, I was to do little else. But so has my portion been meted out to me; and during the last few months I have, after terrible struggles and difficulties, been able to comprehend some of the lessons hidden in the heart of pain. Clergymen, and people who use phrases without wisdom, sometimes talk of suffering as a mystery. It is really a revelation. One discerns things that one never discerned before. One approaches the whole of history from a different standpoint. What one had felt dimly through instinct, about Art, is intellectually and emotionally realised with perfect clearness of vision and absolute intensity of apprehension.

I now see that sorrow, being the supreme emotion of which man is capable, is at once the type and test of all great Art. What the artist is always looking for is that mode of existence in which soul and body are one and indivisible: in which the outward is expressive of the inward: in which Form reveals. Of such modes of existence there are not a few: youth and the arts preoccupied with youth may serve as a model for us at one moment: at another, we may like to think that, in its subtlety and sensitiveness of impression, its suggestion of a spirit dwelling in external things and making its raiment of earth and air, of mist and city alike, and in the morbid sympathy of its moods, and tones and colours, modern landscape art is realising for us pictorially what was realised in such plastic perfection by the Greeks. Music, in which all subject is absorbed in expression and cannot be separated from it, is a complex example, and a flower or a child a simple example of what I mean: but Sorrow is the ultimate type both in life and Art.

Behind Joy and Laughter there may be a temperament, coarse, hard and callous. But behind Sorrow there is always Sorrow. Pain, unlike Pleasure, wears no mask. Truth in Art is not any correspondence between the essential idea and the accidental existence; it is not the resemblance of shape to shadow, or of the form mirrored in the crystal to the form itself: it is no Echo coming from a hollow hill, any more than it is the well of silver water in the valley that shows the Moon to the Moon and Narcissus to Narcissus. Truth in Art is the unity of a thing with itself: the outward rendered expressive of the inward: the soul made incarnate: the body instinct with spirit. For this reason there is no truth comparable to Sorrow. There are times when Sorrow seems to me to be the only truth. Other things may be illusions of the eye or the appetite, made to blind the one and cloy the other, but out of Sorrow have the worlds been built, and at the birth of a child or a star there is pain.

More than this, there is about Sorrow an intense, an extraordinary reality. I have said of myself that I was one who stood in symbolic relations to the art and culture of my age. There is not a single wretched man in this wretched place along with me who does not stand in symbolic relations to the very secret of life. For the secret of life is suffering. It is what is hidden behind everything. When we begin to live, what is sweet is so sweet to us, and what is bitter so bitter, that we inevitably direct all our desires towards pleasure, and seek not merely for "a month or twain to feed on honeycomb," but for all our years to taste no other food, ignorant the while that we may be really starving the soul.

I remember talking once on this subject to one of the most beautiful personalities I have ever known: a woman, whose sympathy and noble kindness to me both before and since the tragedy of my imprisonment have been beyond power and description: one who has really assisted me, though she does not know it, to bear the burden of my troubles more than anyone else in the whole world has: and all through the mere fact of her existence: through her being what she is, partly an ideal and partly an influence, a suggestion of what one might become, as well as a real help towards becoming it, a soul that renders the common air sweet, and makes what is spiritual seem as simple and natural as sunlight or the sea, one for whom Beauty and Sorrow walk hand in hand and have the same message. On the occasion of which I am thinking I recall distinctly how I said to her that there was enough suffering in one narrow London lane to show that God did not love man, and that wherever there was any sorrow, though but that of a child in some little garden weeping over a fault that it had or had not committed, the whole face of creation was completely marred. I was entirely wrong. She told me so, but I could not believe her. I was not in the sphere in which such belief was to be attained to. Now it seems to me that Love of some kind is the only possible explanation of the extraordinary amount of suffering that there is in the world. I cannot conceive any other explanation. I am convinced that there is no other, and that if the worlds have indeed, as I have said, been built out of Sorrow, it has been by the hands of Love, because in no other way could the Soul of man for whom the worlds are made reach the full stature of its perfection. Pleasure for the beautiful body, but Pain for the beautiful Soul.

When I say that I am convinced of these things I speak with too much pride. Far off, like a perfect pearl, one can see the city of God. It is so wonderful that it seems as if a child could reach it in a summer's day. And so a child could. But with me and such as I am it is different. One can realise a thing in a single moment, but one loses it in the long hours that follow with leaden feet. It is so difficult to keep "heights that the soul is competent to gain." We think in Eternity, but we move slowly through Time: and how slowly time goes with us who lie in prison I need not speak again, nor of the weariness and despair that creep back into one's cell, and into the cell of one's heart, with such strange insistence that one has, as it were, to garnish and sweep one's house for their coming, as for an unwelcome guest, or a bitter master, or a slave whose slave it is one's chance or choice to be. And, though at present you may find it a thing hard to believe, it is true none the less that for you, living in freedom and idleness and comfort, it is more easy to learn the lessons of Humility than it is for me, who begin the day by going down on my knees and washing the floor of my cell. For prison-life, with its endless privations and restrictions, makes one rebellious. The most terrible thing about it is not that it breaks one's heart— hearts are made to be broken—but that it turns one's heart to stone. One sometimes feels that it is only with a front of brass and a lip of scorn that one can get through the day at all. And he who is in a state of rebellion cannot receive grace, to use the phrase of which the Church is so fond—so rightly fond, I dare say—for in life, as in Art, the mood of rebellion closes up the channels of the soul, and shuts out the airs of heaven. Yet I must learn these lessons here, if I am to learn them anywhere, and must be filled with joy if my feet are on the right road, and my face set towards the "gate which is called Beautiful," though I may fall many times in the mire, and often in the mist go astray.

This new life, as through my love of Dante I like sometimes to call it, is, of course, no new life at all, but simply the continuance, by means of development, and evolution, of my former life. I remember when I was at Oxford saying to one of my friends—as we were strolling round Magdalen's narrow bird-haunted walks one morning in the June before I took my degree—that I wanted to eat of the fruit of all the trees in the garden of the world, and that I was going out into the world with that passion in my soul. And so, indeed, I went out, and so I lived. My only mistake was that I confined myself so exclusively to the trees of what seemed to me the sungilt side of the garden, and shunned the other side for its shadow and its gloom. Failure, disgrace, poverty, sorrow, despair, suffering, tears even, the broken words that come from the lips of pain, remorse that makes one walk in thorns, conscience that condemns, self-abasement that punishes, the misery that puts ashes on its head, the anguish that chooses sackcloth for its raiment and into its own drink puts gall— all these were things of which I was afraid. And as I had determined to know nothing of them, I was forced to taste each one of them in turn, to feed on them, to have for a season, indeed, no other food at all. I don't regret for a single moment having lived for pleasure. I did it to the full, as one should do everything that one does to the full. There was no pleasure I did not experience. I threw the pearl of my soul into a cup of wine. I went down the primrose path to the sound of flutes. I lived on honeycomb. But to have continued the same life would have been wrong because it would have been limiting. I had to pass on. The other half of the garden had its secrets for me also.

Of course all this is foreshadowed and prefigured in my art. Some of it is in "The Happy Prince:" some of it is in "The Young King," notably in the passage where the Bishop says to the kneeling boy, "Is not He who made misery wiser than thou art?" a phrase which when I wrote it seemed to me little more than a phrase: a great deal of it is hidden away in the note of Doom that like a purple thread runs through the gold cloth of *Dorian Gray*: in "The Critic as Artist" it is set forth in many colours: in *The Soul of Man* it is written down simply and in letters too easy to read: it is one of the refrains whose recurring *motifs* make *Salome* so like a piece of music and bind it together as a ballad: in the prose-poem of the man who from the bronze of the image of the "Pleasure that liveth for a Moment" has to make the image of the "Sorrow that abideth for Ever" it is incarnate. It could not have been otherwise. At every single moment of one's life one is what one is going to be no less than what one has been. Art is a symbol, because man is a symbol.

It is, if I can fully attain to it, the ultimate realisation of the artistic life. For the artistic life is simple self-development. Humility in the artist is his frank acceptance of all experiences, just as Love in the artist is simply that sense of Beauty that reveals to the world its body and its soul. In *Marius the Epicurean* Pater seeks to reconcile the artistic life with the life of religion in the deep, sweet and austere sense of the word. But Marius is little more than a spectator: an ideal spectator indeed, and one to whom it is given "to contemplate the spectacle of life with appropriate emotions," which Wordsworth defines as the poet's true aim: yet a spectator merely, and perhaps a little too much occupied with the comeliness of the vessels of the Sanctuary to notice that it is the Sanctuary of Sorrow that he is gazing at.

I see a far more intimate and immediate connection between the true Life of Christ and the true life of the artist, and I take a keen pleasure in the reflection that long before Sorrow had made my days her own and bound me to her wheel I had written in *The Soul of Man* that he who would lead a Christ-like life must be entirely and absolutely himself, and had taken as my types not merely the shepherd on the hillside and the prisoner in his cell but also the painter to whom the world is a pageant and the poet for whom the world is a song. I remember saying once to André Gide, as we sat together in some Paris café, that while Metaphysics had but little real interest for me, and Morality absolutely none, there was nothing that either Plato or Christ had said that could not be transferred immediately into the sphere of Art, and there find its complete fulfilment. It was a generalisation as profound as it was novel.

Nor is it merely that we can discern in Christ that close union of personality with perfection which forms the real distinction between classical and romantic Art and makes Christ the true precursor of the romantic movement in life, but the very basis of his nature was the same as that of the nature of the artist, an intense and flamelike imagination. He realised in the entire sphere of human relations that imaginative sympathy which in the sphere of Art is the sole secret of creation. He understood the leprosy of the leper, the darkness of the blind, the fierce misery of those who live for pleasure, the strange poverty of the rich. You can see now—can you not?—that when you wrote to me in my trouble, "When you are not on your pedestal you are not interesting. The next time you are ill I will go away at once," you were as remote from the true temper of the artist as you were from what Matthew Arnold calls "the secret of Jesus." Either would have taught you that whatever happens to another happens to oneself, and if you want an inscription to read at dawn and at night-time and for pleasure or for pain, write up on the wall of your house in letters for the sun to gild and the moon to silver "*Whatever happens to another happens to oneself*," and should anyone ask you what such an inscription can possibly mean you can answer that it means "Lord Christ's heart and Shakespeare's brain."

Christ's place indeed is with the poets. His whole conception of Humanity sprang right out of the imagination and can only be realised by it. What God was to the Pantheist, man was to him. He was the first to conceive the divided races as a unity. Before his time there had been gods and men. He alone saw that on the hills of life there were but God and Man, and, feeling through the mysticism of sympathy that in himself each had been made incarnate, he calls himself the Son of the One or the son of the other, according to his mood. More than anyone else in history he wakes in us that temper of wonder to which Romance always appeals. There is still something to me almost incredible in the idea of a young Galilean peasant imagining that he could bear on his own shoulders the burden of the entire world: all that had been already done and suffered, and all that was yet to be done and suffered: the sins of Nero, of Caesar Borgia, of Alexander VI., and of him who was Emperor of Rome and Priest of the Sun: the sufferings of those whose name is Legion and whose dwelling is among the tombs, oppressed nationalities, factory children, thieves, people in prison, outcasts, those who are dumb under oppression and whose silence is heard only of God: and not merely imagining this but actually achieving it, so that at the present moment all who come in contact with his personality, even though they may neither bow to his altar nor kneel before his priest, yet somehow find that the ugliness of their sins is taken away and the beauty of their sorrow revealed to them.

I have said of him that he ranks with the poets. That is true. Shelley and Sophocles are of his company. But his entire life also is the most wonderful of poems. For "pity and terror" there is nothing in the entire cycle of Greek Tragedy to touch it. The absolute purity of the protagonist raises the entire scheme to a height of romantic art from which the sufferings of "Thebes and Pelops' line" are by their very horror excluded, and shows how wrong Aristotle was when he said in his treatise on the Drama that it would be impossible to bear the spectacle of one blameless in pain. Nor in Æschylus or Dante, those stern masters of tenderness, in Shakespeare, the most purely human of all the great artists, in the whole of Celtic myth and legend where the loveliness of the world is shown through a mist of tears, and the life of a man is no more than the life of a flower, is there anything that for sheer simplicity of pathos wedded and made one with sublimity of tragic effect can be said to equal or approach even the last act of Christ's Passion. The little supper with his companions, one of whom had already sold him for a price: the anguish in the quiet moonlit olive-garden: the false friend coming close to him so as to betray him with a kiss: the friend who still believed in him and on whom as on a rock he had hoped to build a House of Refuge for Man denying him as the bird cried to the dawn: his own utter loneliness, his submission, his acceptance of everything: and along with it all such scenes as the high priest of Orthodoxy rending his raiment in wrath, and the Magistrate of Civil Justice calling for water in the vain hope of cleansing himself of that stain of innocent blood that makes him the scarlet figure of History: the coronation-ceremony of Sorrow, one of the most wonderful things in the whole of recorded time: the crucifixion of the Innocent One before the eyes of his mother and of the disciple whom he loved: the soldiers gambling and throwing dice for his clothes: the terrible death by which he gave the world its most eternal symbol:

and his final burial in the tomb of the rich man, his body swathed in Egyptian linen with costly spices and perfumes as though he had been a King's son— when one contemplates all this from the point of view of Art alone one cannot but be grateful that the supreme office of the Church should be the playing of the tragedy without the shedding of blood, the mystical presentation by means of dialogue and costume and gesture even of the Passion of her Lord, and it is always a source of pleasure and awe to me to remember that the ultimate survival of the Greek Chorus, lost elsewhere to art, is to be found in the servitor answering the priest at Mass.

Yet the whole life of Christ—so entirely may Sorrow and Beauty be made one in their meaning and manifestation—is really an idyll, though it ends with the veil of the temple being rent, and the darkness coming over the face of the earth, and the stone rolled to the door of the sepulchre. One always thinks of him as a young bridegroom with his companions, as indeed he somewhere describes himself, or as a shepherd straying through a valley with his sheep in search of green meadow or cool stream, or as a singer trying to build out of music the walls of the city of God, or as a lover for whose love the whole world was too small. His miracles seem to me as exquisite as the coming of Spring, and quite as natural. I see no difficulty at all in believing that such was the charm of his personality that his mere presence could bring peace to souls in anguish, and that those who touched his garments or his hands forgot their pain: or that as he passed by on the highway of life people who had seen nothing of life's mysteries saw them clearly, and others who had been deaf to every voice but that of Pleasure heard for the first time the voice of Love and found it as "musical as is Apollo's lute:" or that evil passions fled at his approach, and men whose dull unimaginative lives had been but a mode of death rose as it were from the grave when he called them: or that when he taught on the hillside the multitude forgot their hunger and thirst and the cares of this world, and that to his friends who listened to him as he sat at meat the coarse food seemed delicate, and the water had the taste of good wine, and the whole house became full of the odour and sweetness of nard.

Renan in his *Vie de Jésus*—that gracious Fifth Gospel, the Gospel according to St Thomas one might call it—says somewhere that Christ's great achievement was that he made himself as much loved after his death as he had been during his lifetime. And certainly, if his place is among the poets, he is the leader of all the lovers. He saw that love was that lost secret of the world for which the wise men had been looking, and that it was only through love that one could approach either the heart of the leper or the feet of God.

And, above all, Christ is the most supreme of Individualists. Humility, like the artistic acceptance of all experiences, is merely a mode of manifestation. It is man's soul that Christ is always looking for. He calls it "God's Kingdom"—ἡ βασιλεία τοῦ θεοῦ —and finds it in everyone. He compares it to little things, to a tiny seed, to a handful of leaven, to a pearl. That is because one only realises one's soul by getting rid of all alien passions, all acquired culture, and all external possessions be they good or evil.

I bore up against everything with some stubbornness of will and much rebellion of nature till I had absolutely nothing left in the world but Cyril. I had lost my name, my position, my happiness, my freedom, my wealth. I was a prisoner and a pauper. But I had still one beautiful thing left, my own eldest son. Suddenly he was taken away from me by the law. It was a blow so appalling that I did not know what to do, so I flung myself on my knees, and bowed my head, and wept and said "The body of a child is as the body of the Lord: I am not worthy of either." That moment seemed to save me. I saw then that the only thing for me was to accept everything. Since then—curious as it will no doubt sound to you—I have been happier.

It was of course my soul in its ultimate essence that I had reached. In many ways I had been its enemy, but I found it waiting for me as a friend. When one comes in contact with the soul it makes one simple as a child, as Christ said one should be. It is tragic how few people ever "possess their souls"

Love

can

read

爱 可 以 让 人 读 出 最 遥 远 星 星 的 信 息

the   writing

on

the

remotest   star

is no more
The aim of Love to love and
You no less
already
know what beginning
to
I Hate is it dawn
on you Love
Is is is what
myself and wha
nature the
knew hate that in of Love I
I to allowed dry of
if you the over desert existence
write letter which I had
don't this into to to travel
I bitterness your head but pluck am and
put it out own travellin
of mine every still
For my sake rock
to must would
I you One cannot I keep adder lose
forgive rise always an in be every shadov
feed nor up breast one's palm
night in the of withered tree
to on one every garden one's water every
The sow soul prove well of
thorns is poisoned at it
are strange It source of
gods beautiful our
must Because Love more than not vices only
is they
freedom make
books Hate instruments
With the
flowers scourge
moon not be happy to
and The who could They us
final mystery the
is oneself weighed
one has
When balance us bring
sun in a to ruir
and
measured the steps of through
mapped the moon and
out the what
the star in the
seven us the
heavens his soul orbit
own of
in my there is good
heart star still remains gentle
by humane
oneself Who loving
can calculate

before they die. "Nothing is more rare in any man," says Emerson, "than an act of his own." It is quite true. Most people are other people. Their thoughts are someone else's opinions, their life a mimicry, their passions a quotation. Chris was not merely the supreme Individualist, but he was the first in History. People have tried to make him out an ordinary Philanthropist, like the dreadful philanthropists of the nineteenth century, or ranked him as an Altruist with the unscientific and sentimental. But he was really neither one nor the other. Pity he has, of course, for the poor, for those who are shut up in prisons, for the lowly, for the wretched, but he has far more pity for the rich, for the hard Hedonists, for those who waste their freedom in becoming slaves to things, for those who wear soft raiment and live in Kings' houses. Riches and Pleasure seemed to him to be really greater tragedies than Poverty and Sorrow. And as for Altruism, who knew better than he that it is vocation not volition that determines us, and that one cannot gather grapes off thorns or figs from thistles?

To live for others as a definite self-conscious aim was not his creed. It was not the basis of his creed. When he says "Forgive your enemies," it is not for the sake of the enemy but for one's own sake that he says so, and because Love is more beautiful than Hate. In his entreaty to the young man whom when he looked on he loved, "Sell all that thou hast and give it to the poor," it is not of the state of the poor that he is thinking but of the soul of the young man, the lovely soul that wealth was marring. In his view of life he is one with the artist who knows that by the inevitable law of self-perfection the poet must sing, and the sculptor think in bronze, and the painter make the world a mirror for his moods, as surely and as certainly as the hawthorn must blossom in Spring, and the corn burn to gold at harvest-time, and the Moon in her ordered wanderings change from shield to sickle, and from sickle to shield.

But while Christ did not say to men, "Live for others," he pointed out that there was no difference at all between the lives of others and one's own life. By this means he gave to man an extended, a Titan personality. Since his coming the history of each separate individual is, or can be made, the history of the world. Of course Culture has intensified the personality of man. Art has made us myriad-minded. Those who have the artistic temperament go into exile with Dante and learn how salt is the bread of others and how steep their stairs: they catch for a moment the serenity and calm of Goethe, and yet know but too well why Baudelaire cried to God:

O Seigneur, donnez-moi la force et le courage

De contempler mon corps et mon cœur sans dégoût.

Out of Shakespeare's sonnets they draw, to their own hurt it may be, the secret of his love and make it their own: they look with new eyes on modern life because they have listened to one of Chopin's nocturnes, or handled Greek things, or read the story of the passion of some dead man for some dead woman whose hair was like threads of fine gold and whose mouth was as a pomegranate. But the sympathy of the artistic temperament is necessarily with what has found expression. In words or in colour, in music or in marble, behind the painted masks of an Æschylean play or through some Sicilian shepherd's pierced and jointed reeds the man and his message must have been revealed.

To the artist, expression is the only mode under which he can conceive life at all. To him what is dumb is dead. But to Christ it was not so. With a width and wonder of imagination, that fills one almost with awe, he took the entire world of the inarticulate, the voiceless world of pain, as his kingdom, and made of himself its eternal mouthpiece. Those of whom I have spoken, who are dumb under oppression and "whose silence is heard only of God," he chose as his brothers. He sought to become eyes to the blind, ears to the deaf, and a cry on the lips of those whose tongue had been tied. His desire was to be to the myriads who had found no utterance a very trumpet through which they might call to Heaven. And feeling, with the artistic nature of one to whom Sorrow and Suffering were modes through which he could realise his conception of the Beautiful, that an idea is of no value till it becomes incarnate and is made an image, he makes of himself the image of the Man of Sorrows, and as such has fascinated and dominated Art as no Greek god ever succeeded in doing.

For the Greek gods, in spite of the white and red of their fair fleet limbs, were not really what they appeared to be. The curved brow of Apollo was like the sun's disk crescent over a hill at dawn, and his feet were as the wings of the morning, but he himself had been cruel to Marsyas and had made Niobe childless: in the steel shields of the eyes of Pallas there had been no pity for Arachne: the pomp and peacocks of Hera were all that was really noble about her: and the Father of the Gods himself had been too fond of the daughters of men. The two deep suggestive figures of Greek mythology were, for religion, Demeter, an earth-goddess, not one of the Olympians, and, for art, Dionysus, the son of a mortal woman to whom the moment of his birth had proved the moment of her death also.

But Life itself from its lowliest and most humble sphere produced one far more marvellous than the mother of Proserpina or the son of Semele. Out of the carpenter's shop at Nazareth had come a personality infinitely greater than any made by myth or legend, and one, strangely enough, destined to reveal to the world the mystical meaning of wine and the real beauty of the lilies of the field as none, either on Cithaeron or at Enna, had ever done it.

The song of Isaiah, "*He is despised and rejected of men, a man of sorrows and acquainted with grief: and we hid as it were our faces from him,*" had seemed to him to be a prefiguring of himself, and in him the prophecy was fulfilled. We must not be afraid of such a phrase. Every single work of art is the fulfilment of a prophecy. For every work of art is the conversion of an idea into an image. Every single human being should be the fulfilment of a prophecy. For every human being should be the realisation of some ideal, either in the mind of God or in the mind of man. Christ found the type, and fixed it, and the dream of a Virgilian poet, either at Jerusalem or at Babylon, became in the long progress of the centuries incarnate in him for whom the world was waiting. "His visage was marred more than any man's, and his form more than the sons of men," are among the signs noted by Isaiah as distinguishing the new ideal, and as soon as Art understood what was meant it opened like a flower at the presence of one in whom truth in Art was set forth as it had never been before. For is not truth in Art, as I have said, "that in which the outward is expressive of the inward; in which the soul is made flesh, and the body instinct with spirit: in which Form reveals"?

To me one of the things in history the most to be regretted is that the Christ's own renaissance which had produced the Cathedral of Chartres, the Arthurian cycle of legends, the life of St Francis of Assisi, the art of Giotto, and Dante's Divine Comedy, was not allowed to develop on its own lines but was interrupted and spoiled by the dreary classical Renaissance that gave us Petrarch, and Raphael's frescoes, and Palladian architecture, and formal French tragedy, and St Paul's Cathedral, and Pope's poetry, and everything that is made from without and by dead rules, and does not spring from within through some spirit informing it. But wherever there is a romantic movement in Art, there somehow, and under some form, is Christ, or the soul of Christ. He is in *Romeo and Juliet*, in the *Winter's Tale*, in Provencal poetry, in "The Ancient Mariner," in "La Belle Dame sans Merci," and in Chatterton's "Ballad of Charity."

We owe to him the most diverse things and people. Hugo's *Les Misérables*, Baudelaire's *Fleurs du Mal*, the note of pity in Russian novels, the stained glass and tapestries and quattrocento work of Burne-Jones and Morris, Verlaine and Verlaine's poems, belong to him no less than the Tower of Giotto, Lancelot and Guinevere, Tannhäuser, the troubled romantic marbles of Michael Angelo, pointed architecture, and the love of children and flowers— for both of whom, indeed, in classical art there was but little place, hardly enough for them to grow or play in, but who from the twelfth century down to our own day have been continually making their appearance in art, under various modes and at various times, coming fitfully and wilfully as children and flowers are apt to do.

And it is the imaginative quality of Christ's own nature that makes him this palpitating centre of romance. The strange figures of poetic drama and ballad are made by the imagination of others, but out of his own imagination entirely did Jesus of Nazareth create himself. The cry of Isaiah had really no more to do with his coming than the song of the nightingale has to do with the rising of the moon— no more, though perhaps no less. He was the denial as well as the affirmation of prophecy. For every expectation that he fulfilled, there was another that he destroyed. In all beauty, says Bacon, there is "some strangeness of proportion," and of those who are born of the spirit, of those, that is to say, who like himself are dynamic forces, Christ says that they are like the wind that "bloweth where it listeth and no man can tell whence it cometh or whither it goeth." That is why he is so fascinating to artists. He has all the colour-elements of life: mystery, strangeness, pathos, suggestion, ecstasy, love. He appeals to the temper of wonder, and creates that mood by which alone he can be understood.

And it is to me a joy to remember that if he is "of imagination all compact," the world itself is of the same substance. I said in *Dorian Gray* that the great sins of the world take place in the brain, but it is in the brain that everything takes place. We know now that we do not see with the eye or hear with the ear. They are merely channels for the transmission, adequate or inadequate, of sense-impressions. It is in the brain that the poppy is red, that the apple is odorous, that the skylark sings.

Of late I have been studying the four prose-poems about Christ with some diligence. At Christmas I managed to get hold of a Greek Testament, and every morning, after I have cleaned my cell and polished my tins, I read a little of the Gospels, a dozen verses taken by chance anywhere. It is a delightful way of opening the day. To you, in your turbulent, ill-disciplined life, it would be a capital thing if you would do the same. It would do you no end of good, and the Greek is quite simple. Endless repetition, in and out of season, has spoiled for us the *naïveté*, the freshness, the simple romantic charm of the Gospels. We hear them read far too often, and far too badly, and all repetition is anti-spiritual. When one returns to the Greek it is like going into a garden of lilies out of some narrow and dark house.

And to me the pleasure is doubled by the reflection that it is extremely probable that we have the actual terms, the *ipissima verba*, used by Christ. It was always supposed that Christ talked in Aramaic. Even Renan thought so. But now we know that the Galilean peasants, like the Irish peasants of our own day, were bilingual, and that Greek was the ordinary language of intercourse all over Palestine, as indeed all over the Eastern world. I never liked the idea that we only knew of Christ's own words through a translation of a translation. It is a delight to me to think that as far as his conversation was concerned, Charmides might have listened to him, and Socrates reasoned with him, and Plato understood him: that he really said ἐγώ εἰμί ὁ καλός: that when he thought of the lilies of the field, and how they neither toil nor spin, his absolute expression was καταμα θετε τὰ κθίνα τοῦ ἀγροῦ πῶς ανξάνει οὐ κοπιᾶ οὐδὲ νήθει, and that his last word when he cried out "My life has been completed, has reached its fulfillment, has been perfected," was exactly as St John tells us it was: τετέλεσται: no more.

And while in reading the Gospels—particularly that of St John himself, or whatever early Gnostic took his name and mantle—I see this continual assertion of the imagination as the basis of all spiritual and material life, I see also that to Christ imagination was simply a form of Love, and that to him Love was Lord in the fullest meaning of the phrase. Some six weeks ago I was allowed by the Doctor to have white bread to eat instead of the coarse black or brown bread of ordinary prison fare. It is a great delicacy. To you it will sound strange that dry bread could possibly be a delicacy to anyone. I assure you that to me it is so much so that at the close of each meal I carefully eat whatever crumbs may be left on my tin plate, or have fallen on the rough towel that one uses as a cloth so as not to soil one's table: and do so not from hunger— I get now quite sufficient food—but simply in order that nothing should be wasted of what is given to me. So one should look on love.

Christ, like all fascinating personalities, had the power not merely of saying beautiful things himself, but of making other people say beautiful things to him; and I love the story St Mark tells us about the Greek woman—the γυνὴ ῾Ελληνίς—who, when as a trial of her faith he said to her that he could not give her the bread of the children of Israel, answered him that the little dogs—κυνάρια, "little dogs" it should be rendered—who are under the table eat of the crumbs that the children let fall. Most people live for love and admiration. But it is by love and admiration that we should live. If any love is shown us we should recognise that we are quite unworthy of it. Nobody is worthy to be loved. The fact that God loves man shows that in the divine order of ideal things it is written that eternal love is to be given to what is eternally unworthy. Or if that phrase seems to you a bitter one to hear, let us say that everyone is worthy of love, except he who thinks that he is. Love is a sacrament that should be taken kneeling, and *Domine, non sum dignus* should be on the lips and in the hearts of those who receive it. I wish you would sometimes think of that. You need it so much.

If I ever write again, in the sense of producing artistic work, there are just two subjects on which and through which I desire to express myself: one is "Christ, as the precursor of the Romantic movement in life:" the other is "the Artistic life considered in its relation to Conduct." The first is, of course, intensely fascinating, for I see in Christ not merely the essentials of the supreme romantic type, but all the accidents, the wilfulnesses even, of the romantic temperament also. He was the first person who ever said to people that they should live "flower-like" lives. He fixed the phrase. He took children as the type of what people should try to become. He held them up as examples to their elders, which I myself have always thought the chief use of children, if what is perfect should have a use. Dante describes the soul of man as coming from the hand of God "weeping and laughing like a little child," and Christ also saw that the soul of each one should be "*a guisa di fanciulla, che piangendo e ridendo pargoleggia.*" He felt that life was changeful, fluid, active, and that to allow it to be stereotyped into any form was death. He said that people should not be too serious over material, common interests: that to be unpractical was a great thing: that one should not bother too much over affairs. "The birds didn't, why should man?" He is charming when he says, "Take no thought for the morrow. Is not the soul more than meat? Is not the *body* more than raiment?" A Greek might have said the latter phrase. It is full of Greek feeling. But only Christ could have said both, and so summed up life perfectly for us.

His morality is all sympathy, just what morality should be. If the only thing he had ever said had been "Her sins are forgiven her because she loved much," it would have been worth while dying to have said it. His justice is all poetical justice, exactly what justice should be. The beggar goes to heaven because he had been unhappy. I can't conceive a better reason for his being sent there. The people who work for an hour in the vineyard in the cool of the evening receive just as much reward as those who had toiled there all day long in the hot sun. Why shouldn't they? Probably no one deserved anything. Or perhaps they were a different kind of people. Christ had no patience with the dull lifeless mechanical systems that treat people as if they were things, and so treat everybody alike: as if anybody, or anything for that matter, was like aught else in the world. For him there were no laws: there were exceptions merely.

That which is the very keynote of romantic art was to him the proper basis of actual life. He saw no other basis. And when they brought him one taken in the very act of sin and showed him her sentence written in the law and asked him what was to be done, he wrote with his finger on the ground as though he did not hear them, and finally, when they pressed him again and again, looked up and said "Let him of you who has never sinned be the first to throw the stone at her." It was worth while living to have said that.

Like all poetical natures, he loved ignorant people. He knew that in the soul of one who is ignorant there is always room for a great idea. But he could not stand stupid people, especially those who are made stupid by education—people who are full of opinions not one of which they can understand, a peculiarly modern type, and one summed up by Christ when he describes it as the type of one who has the key of knowledge, can't use it himself, and won't allow other people to use it, though it may be made to open the gate of God's Kingdom. His chief war was against the Philistines. That is the war every child of light has to wage. Philistinism was the note of the age and community in which he lived. In their heavy inaccessibility to ideas, their dull respectability, their tedious orthodoxy, their worship of vulgar success, their entire preoccupation with the gross materialistic side of life, and their ridiculous estimate of themselves and their importance, the Jew of Jerusalem in Christ's day was the exact counterpart of the British Philistine of our own. Christ mocked at the "whited sepulchers" of respectability, and fixed that phrase for ever. He treated worldly success as a thing to be absolutely despised. He saw nothing in it at all. He looked on wealth as an encumbrance to a man. He would not hear of life being sacrificed to any system of thought or morals. He pointed out that forms and ceremonies were made for man, not man for forms and ceremonies. He took Sabbatarianism as a type of the things that should be set at nought. The cold philanthropies, the ostentatious public charities, the tedious formalisms so dear to the middle-class mind, he exposed with utter and relentless scorn. To us, what is termed Orthodoxy is merely a facile unintelligent acquiescence, but to them, and in their hands, it was a terrible and paralysing tyranny. Christ swept it aside. He showed that the spirit alone was of value. He took a keen pleasure in pointing out to them that though they were always reading the Law and the Prophets they had not really the smallest idea of what either of them meant. In opposition to their tithing of each separate day into its fixed routine of prescribed duties, as they tithed mint and rue, he preached the enormous importance of living completely for the moment.

Those whom he saved from their sins are saved simply for beautiful moments in their lives. Mary

Magdalen, when she sees Christ, breaks the rich vase of alabaster that one of her seven lovers had given her and spills the odorous spices over his tired, dusty feet, and for that one moment's sake sits for ever with Ruth and Beatrice in the tresses of the snow-white Rose of Paradise. All that Christ says to us by way of a little warning is that *every* moment should be beautiful, that the soul should *always* be ready for the coming of the Bridegroom, always waiting for the voice of the Lover. Philistinism being simply that side of man's nature that is not illumined by the imagination, he sees all the lovely influences of life as modes of Light: the imagination itself is the world-light, τὸ φῶς τοῦ κοσμοῦ: the world is made by it, and yet the world cannot understand it: that is because the imagination is simply a manifestation of Love, and it is love, and the capacity for it, that distinguishes one human being from another.

But it is when he deals with the Sinner that he is most romantic, in the sense of most real. The world had always loved the Saint as being the nearest possible approach to the perfection of God. Christ, through some divine instinct in him, seems to have always loved the sinner as being the nearest possible approach to the perfection of man. His primary desire was not to reform people, any more than his primary desire was to relieve suffering. To turn an interesting thief into a tedious honest man was not his aim. He would have thought little of the Prisoners' Aid Society and other modern movements of the kind. The conversion of a Publican into a Pharisee would not have seemed to him a great achievement by any means. But in a manner not yet understood of the world he regarded sin and suffering as being in themselves beautiful, holy things, and modes of perfection. It sounds a very dangerous idea. It is so. All great ideas are dangerous. That it was Christ's creed admits of no doubt. That it is the true creed I don't doubt myself.

Of course the sinner must repent. But why? Simply because otherwise he would be unable to realise what he had done. The moment of repentance is the moment of initiation. More than that. It is the means by which one alters one's past. The Greeks thought that impossible. They often say in their gnomic aphorisms "Even the Gods cannot alter the past." Christ showed that the commonest sinner could do it. That it was the one thing he could do. Christ, had he been asked, would have said—I feel quite certain about it—that the moment the prodigal son fell on his knees and wept he really made his having wasted his substance with harlots, and then kept swine and hungered for the husks they ate, beautiful and holy incidents in his life. It is difficult for most people to grasp the idea. I dare say one has to go to prison to understand it. If so, it may be worth while going to prison.

There is something so unique about Christ. Of course, just as there are false dawns before the dawn itself, and winter-days so full of sudden sunlight that they will cheat the wise crocus into squandering its gold before its time, and make some foolish bird call to its mate to build on barren boughs, so there were Christians before Christ. For that we should be grateful. The unfortunate thing is that there have been none since. I make one exception, St Francis of

Assisi. But then God had given him at his birth the soul of a poet, and he himself when quite young had in mystical marriage taken Poverty as his bride; and with the soul of a poet and the body of a beggar he found the way to perfection not difficult. He understood Christ, and so he became like him. We do not require the *Liber Conformitatum* to teach us that the life of St Francis was the true *Imitatio Christi*: a poem compared to which the book that bears that name is merely prose. Indeed, that is the charm about Christ, when all is said. He is just like a work of art himself. He does not really teach one anything, but by being brought into his presence one becomes something. And everybody is predestined to his presence. Once at least in his life each man walks with Christ to Emmaus.

As regards the other subject, the relation of the artistic life to conduct, it will no doubt seem strange to you that I should select it. People point to Reading Gaol, and say "There is where the artistic life leads a man." Well, it might lead one to worse places. The more mechanical people, to whom life is a shrewd speculation dependent on a careful calculation of ways and means, always know where they are going, and go there. They start with the desire of being the Parish Beadle, and, in whatever sphere they are placed, they succeed in being the Parish Beadle and no more. A man whose desire is to be something separate from himself, to be a Member of Parliament, or a successful grocer, or a prominent solicitor, or a judge, or something equally tedious, invariably succeeds in being what he wants to be. That is his punishment. Those who want a mask have to wear it.

But with the dynamic forces of life, and those in whom those dynamic forces become incarnate, it is different. People whose desire is solely for self-re-alisation never know where they are going. They can't know. In one sense of the word it is, of course, necessary, as the Greek oracle said, to know oneself. That is the first achievement of knowledge. But to recognise that the soul of a man is unknowable is the ultimate achievement of Wisdom. The final mystery is oneself. When one has weighed the sun in a balance, and measured the steps of the moon, and mapped out the seven heavens star by star, there still remains oneself. Who can calculate the orbit of his own soul? When the son of Kish went out to look for his father's asses, he did not know that a man of God was waiting for him with the very chrism of coronation, and that his own soul was already the Soul of a King.

I hope to live long enough, and to produce work of such a character, that I shall be able at the end of my days to say, "Yes: this is just where the artistic life leads a man." Two of the most perfect lives I have come across in my own experience are the lives of Verlaine and of Prince Kropotkin: both of them men who passed years in prison: the first, the one Christian poet since Dante, the other a man with the soul of that beautiful white Christ that seems coming out of Russia. And for the last seven or eight months, in spite of a succession of great troubles reaching me from the outside world almost without intermission, I have been placed in direct contact with a new spirit working in this prison through men and things, that has helped me beyond any possibility of expression in words; so that while for the first year of my imprisonment I did nothing else, and can remember doing nothing else, but wring my hands in impotent despair, and say "What an ending! What an appalling ending!" Now I try to say to myself, and sometimes when I am not torturing myself do really and sincerely say, "What a beginning! What a wonderful beginning!" It may really be so. It may become so. If it does, I shall owe much to this new personality that has altered every man's life in this place.

Things in themselves are of little importance, have indeed—let us for once thank Metaphysics for something that she has taught us—no real existence. The spirit alone is of importance. Punishment may be inflicted in such a way that it will heal, not make a wound, just as alms may be given in such a manner that the bread changes to a stone in the hands of the giver. What a change there is—not in the regulations, for they are fixed by iron rule, but in the spirit that uses them as its expression—you can realise when I tell you that had I been released last May, as I tried to be, I would have left this place loathing it and every official in it with a bitterness of hatred that would have poisoned my life. I have had a year longer of imprisonment, but Humanity has been in the prison along with us all, and now when I go out I shall always remember great kindnesses that I have received here from almost everybody, and on the day of my release will give my thanks to many people and ask to be remembered by them in turn.

The prison-system is absolutely and entirely wrong. I would give anything to be able to alter it when I go out. I intend to try. But there is nothing in the world so wrong but that the spirit of Humanity, which is the spirit of Love, the spirit of the Christ who is not in Churches, may make it, if not right, at least possible to be borne without too much bitterness of heart.

I know also that much is waiting for me outside that is very delightful, from what St Francis of Assisi calls *"my brother the wind"* and *"my sister the rain,"* lovely things both of them, down to the shop-windows and sunsets of great cities. If I made a list of all that still remains to me, I don't know where I should stop: for, indeed, God made the world just as much for me as for anyone else. Perhaps I may go out with something I had not got before. I need not tell you that to me Reformations in Morals are as meaningless and vulgar as Reformations in Theology. But while to propose to be a better man is a piece of unscientific cant, to have become a *deeper* man is the privilege of those who have suffered. And such I think I have become. You can judge for yourself.

If after I go out a friend of mine gave a feast, and did not invite me to it, I shouldn't mind a bit. I can be perfectly happy by myself. With freedom, books, flowers, and the moon, who could not be happy? Besides, feasts are not for me any more. I have given too many to care about them. That side of life is over for me, very fortunately I dare say. But if, after I go out, a friend of mine had a sorrow, and refused to allow me to share it, I should feel it most bitterly. If he shut the doors of the house of mourning against me I would come back again and again and beg to be admitted, so that I might share in what I was entitled to share in.

If he thought me unworthy, unfit to weep with him, I should feel it as the most poignant humiliation, as the most terrible mode in which disgrace could be inflicted on me. But that could not be. I have a right to share in Sorrow, and he who can look at the loveliness of the world, and share its sorrow, and realise something of the wonder of both, is in immediate contact with divine things, and has got as near to God's secret as anyone can get.

Perhaps there may come into my art also, no less than into my life, a still deeper note, one of greater unity of passion, and directness of impulse. Not width but intensity is the true aim of modern Art. We are no longer in Art concerned with the type. It is with the exception we have to do. I cannot put my sufferings into any form they took, I need hardly say. Art only begins where Imitation ends. But something must come into my work, of fuller harmony of words perhaps, of richer cadences, of more curious colour-effect, of simpler architectural-order, of some aesthetic quality at any rate.

When Marsyas was "torn from the scabbard of

his limbs"— *dalla vagina delle membre sue*, to use one of Dante's most terrible, most Tacitean phrases—he had no more song, the Greeks said. Apollo had been victor. The lyre had vanquished the reed. But perhaps the Greeks were mistaken. I hear in much modern Art the cry of Marsyas. It is bitter in Baudelaire, sweet and plaintive in Lamartine, mystic in Verlaine. It is in the deferred resolutions of Chopin's music. It is in the discontent that haunts the recurrent faces of Burne-Jones's women. Even Matthew Arnold, whose song of Callicles tells of "the triumph of the sweet persuasive lyre," and the "famous final victory," in such a clear note of lyrical beauty—even he, in the troubled undertone of doubt and distress that haunts his verse, has not a little of it. Neither Goethe nor Wordsworth could heal him, though he followed each in turn, and when he seeks to mourn for "Thyrsis" or to sing of "the Scholar Gipsy," it is the reed that he has to take for the rendering of his strain. But whether or not the Phrygian Faun was silent, I cannot be. Expression is as necessary to me as leaf and blossom are to the black branches of the trees that show themselves above the prison wall and are so restless in the wind. Between my art and the world there is now a wide gulf, but between Art and myself there is none. I hope at least that there is none.

To each of us different fates have been meted out. Freedom, pleasure, amusements, a life of ease have been your lot, and you are not worthy of it. My lot has been one of public infamy, of long imprisonment, of misery, of ruin, of disgrace, and I am not worthy of it either—not yet, at any rate. I remember I used to say that I thought I could bear a real tragedy if it came to me with purple pall and a mask of noble sorrow, but that the dreadful thing about modernity was that it put Tragedy into the raiment of Comedy, so that the great realities seemed commonplace or grotesque or lacking in style. It is quite true about modernity. It has probably always been true about actual life. It is said that all martyrdoms seemed mean to the looker-on. The nineteenth century is no exception to the general rule.

Everything about my tragedy has been hideous, mean, repellent, lacking in style. Our very dress makes us grotesques. We are the zanies of sorrow. We are clowns whose hearts are broken. We are specially designed to appeal to the sense of humour. On November 13th 1895 I was brought down here from London. From two o'clock till half-past two on that day I had to stand on the centre platform of Clapham Junction in convict dress and handcuffed, for the world to look at. I had been taken out of the Hospital Ward without a moment's notice being given to me. Of all possible objects I was the most grotesque. When people saw me they laughed. Each train as it came up swelled the audience. Nothing could exceed their amusement. That was of course before they knew who I was. As soon as they had been informed, they laughed still more. For half an hour I stood there in the grey November rain surrounded by a jeering mob. For a year after that was done to me I wept every day at the same hour and for the same space of time. That is not such a tragic thing as possibly it sounds to you. To those who are in prison, tears are a part of every day's experience. A day in prison on which one does not weep is a day on which one's heart is hard, not a day on which one's heart is happy.

Well, now I am really beginning to feel more regret for the people who laughed than for myself. Of course when they saw me I was not on my pedestal. I was in the pillory. But it is a very unimaginative nature that only cares for people on their pedestals. A pedestal may be a very unreal thing. A pillory is a terrific reality. They should have known also how to interpret sorrow better. I have said that behind Sorrow there is always Sorrow. It were still wiser to say that behind sorrow there is always a soul. And to mock at a soul in pain is a dreadful thing. Unbeautiful are their lives who do it. In the strangely simple economy of the world people only get what they give, and to those who have not enough imagination to penetrate the mere outward of things and feel pity, what pity can be given save that of scorn?

I have told you this account of the mode of my being conveyed here simply that you should realise how hard it has been for me to get anything out of my punishment but bitterness and despair.

I have however to do it, and now and then I have moments of submission and acceptance. All the spring may be hidden in a single bud, and the low ground-nest of the lark may hold the joy that is to herald the feet of many rose-red dawns, and so perhaps whatever beauty of life still remains to me is contained in some moment of surrender, abasement and humiliation. I can, at any rate, merely proceed on the lines of my own development, and by accepting all that has happened to me make myself worthy of it.

People used to say of me that I was too individualistic. I must be far more of an individualist than I ever was. I must get far more out of myself than I ever got, and ask far less of the world than I ever asked. Indeed my ruin came, not from too great individualism of life, but from too little. The one disgraceful, unpardonable, and to all time contemptible action of my life was my allowing myself to be forced into appealing to Society for help and protection against your father.

Of course once I had put into motion the forces

of Society, Society turned on me and said, "Have you been living all this time in defiance of my laws, and do you now appeal to those laws for protection? You shall have those laws exercised to the full. You shall abide by what you have appealed to." The result is I am in gaol. And I used to feel bitterly the irony and ignominy of my position when in the course of my three trials, beginning at the Police Court, I used to see your father bustling in and out in the hopes of attracting public attention, as if anyone could fail to note or remember the stableman's gait and dress, the bowed legs, the twitching hands, the hanging lower lip, the bestial and half-witted grin. Even when he was not there, or was out of sight, I used to feel conscious of his presence, and the blank dreary walls of the great Court-room, the very air itself, seemed to me at times to be hung with multitudinous masks of that apelike face. Certainly no man ever fell so ignobly, and by such ignoble instruments, as I did. I say, in *Dorian Gray* somewhere, that "a man cannot be too careful in the choice of his enemies." I little thought that it was by a pariah that I was to be made a pariah myself.

This urging me, forcing me to appeal to Society for help, is one of the things that make me despise you so much, that make me despise myself so much for having yielded to you. Your not appreciating me as an artist was quite excusable. It was temperamental. You couldn't help it. But you might have appreciated me as an Individualist. For that no culture was required. But you didn't, and so you brought the element of Philistinism into a life that had been a complete protest against it, and from some points of view a complete annihilation of it. The Philistine element in life is not the failure to understand Art. Charming people such as fishermen, shepherds, ploughboys, peasants and the like know nothing about Art, and are the very salt of the earth. He is the Philistine who upholds and aids the heavy, cumbrous, blind mechanical forces of Society, and who does not recognise the dynamic force when he meets it either in a man or a movement.

People thought it dreadful of me to have entertained at dinner the evil things of life, and to have found pleasure in their company. But they, from the point of view through which I, as an artist in life, approached them, were delightfully suggestive and stimulating. It was like feasting with panthers. The danger was half the excitement. I used to feel as the snake-charmer must feel when he lures the cobra to stir from the painted cloth or reed-basket that holds it, and makes it spread its hood at his bidding, and sway to and fro in the air as a plant sways restfully in a stream. They were to me the brightest of gilded snakes. Their poison was part of their perfection. I did not know that when they were to strike at me it was to be at your piping and for your father's pay. I don't feel at all ashamed of having known them. They were intensely interesting. What I do feel ashamed of is the horrible Philistine atmosphere into which you brought me. My business as an artist was with Ariel. You set me to wrestle with Caliban. Instead of making beautiful coloured, musical things such as *Salome*, and the *Florentine Tragedy*, and *La Sainte Courtisane*, I found myself forced to send long lawyer's letters to your father and constrained to appeal to the very things against which I had always protested. Clibborn and Atkins were wonderful in their infamous war against life. To entertain them was an astounding adventure. Dumas père, Cellini, Goya, Edgar Allan Poe, or Baudelaire, would have done just the same. What is loathsome to me is the memory of interminable visits paid by me to the solicitor Humphreys in your company, when in the ghastly glare of a bleak room you and I would sit with serious faces telling serious lies to a bald man, till I really groaned and yawned with *ennui*. *There* is where I found myself after two years' friendship with you, right in the centre of Philistia, away from everything that was beautiful, or brilliant, or wonderful, or daring. At the end I had to come forward, on your behalf, as the champion of Respectability in conduct, of Puritanism in life, and of Morality in Art. *Voilà où mènent les mauvais chemins!*

And the curious thing to me is that you should have tried to imitate your father in his chief characteristics. I cannot understand why he was to you an exemplar, where he should have been a warning, except that whenever there is hatred between two people there is bond or brotherhood of some kind. I suppose that, by some strange law of the antipathy of similars, you loathed each other, not because in so many points you were so different, but because in some you were so like. In June 1893 when you left Oxford, without a degree and with debts, petty in themselves, but considerable to a man of your father's income, your father wrote you a very vulgar, violent and abusive letter. The letter you sent him in reply was in every way worse, and of course far less excusable, and consequently you were extremely proud of it. I remember quite well your saying to me with your most conceited air that you could beat your father "at his own trade." Quite true. But what a trade! What a competition! You used to laugh and sneer at your father for retiring from your cousin's house where he was living in order to write filthy letters to him from a neighbouring hotel. You used to do just the same to me. You constantly lunched with me at some public restaurant, sulked or made a scene during luncheon, and then retired to White's Club and wrote me a letter of the very foulest character. The only difference between you and your father was that after you had dispatched your letter to me by special messenger, you would arrive yourself at my rooms some hours later, not to apologise, but to know if I had ordered dinner at the Savoy, and if not, why not. Sometimes you would actually arrive before the offensive letter had been read. I remember on one occasion you had asked me to invite to luncheon at the Café Royal two of your friends, one of whom I had never seen in my life. I did so, and at your special request ordered beforehand a specially luxurious luncheon to be prepared. The chef, I remember, was sent for, and particular instructions given about the wines. Instead of coming to luncheon you sent me at the Café an abusive letter, timed so as to reach me after we had been waiting half an hour for you. I read the first line, and saw what it was, and putting the letter in my pocket, explained to your friends that you were suddenly taken ill, and that the rest of the letter referred to your symptoms. In point of fact I did not read the letter till I was dressing for dinner at

Tite Street that evening. As I was in the middle of its mire, wondering with infinite sadness how you could write letters that were really like the froth and foam on the lips of an epileptic, my servant came in to tell me that you were in the hall and were very anxious to see me for five minutes. I at once sent down and asked you to come up. You arrived, looking I admit very frightened and pale, to beg my advice and assistance, as you had been told that a man from Lumley, the solicitor, had been enquiring for you at Cadogan Place, and you were afraid that your Oxford trouble or some new danger was threatening you. I consoled you, told you, what proved to be the case, that it was merely a tradesman's bill probably, and let you stay to dinner, and pass your evening with me. You never mentioned a single word about your hideous letter, nor did I. I treated it as simply an unhappy symptom of an unhappy temperament. The subject was never alluded to. To write to me a loathsome letter at 2.30, and fly to me for help and sympathy at 7.15 the same afternoon, was a perfectly ordinary occurrence in your life. You went quite beyond your father in such habits, as you did in others. When his revolting letters to you were read in open Court he naturally felt ashamed and pretended to weep. Had your letters to him been read by his own Counsel still more horror and repugnance would have been felt by everyone. Nor was it merely in style that you "beat him at his own trade," but in mode of attack you distanced him completely. You availed yourself of the public telegram, and the open postcard. I think you might have left such modes of annoyance to people like Alfred Wood whose sole source of income it is. Don't you? What was a profession to him and his class was a pleasure to you, and a very evil one. Nor have you given up you horrible habit of writing offensive letters, after all that has happened to me through them and for them. You still regard it as one of your accomplishments, and you exercise it on my friends, on those who have been kind to me in prison like Robert Sherard and others. That is disgraceful of you. When Robert Sherard heard from me that I did not wish you to publish any article on me in the Mercure de France, with or without letters, you should have been grateful to him for having ascertained my wishes on the point, and for having saved you from, without intending it, inflicting more pain on me than you had done already. You must remember that a patronising and Philistine letter about "fair play" for a "man who is down" is all right for an English newspaper. It carries on the old traditions of English journalism in regard to their attitude towards artists. But in France such a tone would have exposed me to ridicule and you to contempt. I could not have allowed any article till I had known its aim, temper, mode of approach and the like. In art good intentions are not of the smallest value. All bad art is the result of good intentions.

Nor is Robert Sherard the only one of my friends to whom you have addressed acrimonious and bitter letters because they sought that my wishes and my feelings should be consulted in matters concerning myself, the publication of articles on me, the dedication of your verses, the surrender of my letters and presents, and such like. You have annoyed or sought to annoy others also.

Does it ever occur to you what an awful position I would have been in if for the last two years, during my appalling sentence, I had been dependent on you as a friend? Do you ever think of that? Do you ever feel any gratitude to those who by kindness without stint, devotion without limit, cheerfulness and joy in giving, have lightened my black burden for me, have visited me again and again, have written to me beautiful and sympathetic letters, have managed my affairs for me, have arranged my future life for me, have stood by me in the teeth of obloquy, taunt, open sneer or insult even? I thank God every day that he gave me friends other than you. I owe everything to them. The very books in my cell are paid for by Robbie out of his pocket-money. From the same source are to come clothes for me, when I am released. I am not ashamed of taking a thing that is given by love and affection. I am proud of it. But do you ever think of what my friends such as More Adey, Robbie, Robert Sherard, Frank Harris, and Arthur Clifton, have been to me in giving me comfort, help, affection, sympathy and the like? I suppose that has never dawned on you. And yet—if you had any imagination in you— you would know that there is not a single person who has been kind to me in my prison-life, down to the warder who may give me a good-morning or a good-night that is not one of his prescribed duties— down to the common policemen who in their homely rough way strove to comfort me on my journeys to and fro from the Bankruptcy Court under conditions of terrible mental distress—down to the poor thief who, recognising me as we tramped round the yard at Wandsworth, whispered to me in the hoarse pris- on-voice men get from long and compulsory silence: *"I am sorry for you: it is harder for the likes of you than it is for the likes of us"*—not one of them all, I say, the very mire from whose shoes you should not be proud to be allowed to kneel down and clean.

Have you imagination enough to see what a fearful tragedy it was for me to have come across your family? What a tragedy it would have been for anyone at all, who had a great position, a great name, anything of importance to lose? There is hardly one of the elders of you family—with the exception of Percy, who is really a good fellow—who did not in some way contribute to my ruin.

I have spoken of your mother to you with some bitterness, and I strongly advise you to let her see this letter, for your own sake chiefly. If it is painful to her to read such an indictment against one of her sons, let her remember that my mother, who intellectually ranks with Elizabeth Barrett Browning, and historically with Madame Roland, died broken-hearted because the son of whose genius and art she had been so proud, and whom she had regarded always as a worthy continuer of a distinguished name, had been condemned to the treadmill for two years. You will ask me in what way your mother contributed to my destruction. I will tell you. Just as you strove to shift onto me all your immoral responsibilities, so your mother strove to shift on to me all her moral responsibilities with regard to you. Instead of speaking directly to you about your life, as a mother should, she always wrote privately to me with earnest, frightened entreaties not to let you know that she was writing to me. You see the position in which I was placed between you and your mother. It was one as false, as absurd, and as tragic as the one in which I was placed between you and your father. In August 1892, and on the 8th of November in the same year, I had two long interviews with your mother about you. On both occasions I asked her why she did not speak directly to you herself. On both occasions she gave the same answer: "*I am afraid to: he gets so angry when he is spoken to.*" The first time, I knew you so slightly that I did not understand what she meant. The second time, I knew you so well that I understood perfectly. (During the interval you had had an attack of jaundice and been ordered by the doctor to go for a week to Bournemouth, and had induced me to accompany you as you hated being alone.) But the first duty of a mother is not to be afraid of speaking seriously to her son. Had your mother spoken seriously to you about the trouble she saw you were in in July 1892 and made you confide in her it would have been much better, and much happier ultimately for both of you. All the underhand and secret communications with me were wrong. What was the use of your mother sending me endless little notes, marked "Private" on the envelope, begging me not to ask you so often to dinner, and not to give you any money, each note ending with an earnest postscript *"On no account let Alfred know that I have written to you"*? What good could come of such a correspondence? Did you ever wait to be asked to dinner? Never. You took all your meals as a matter of course with me. If I remonstrated, you always had one observation: *"If I don't dine with you, where am I to dine? You don't suppose that I am going to dine at home?"* It was unanswerable. And if I absolutely refused to let you dine with me, you always threatened that you would do something foolish, and always did it. What possible result could there be from letters such as your mother used to send me, except that which did occur, a foolish and fatal shifting of the moral responsibility on to my shoulders? Of the various details in which your mother's weakness and lack of courage proved so ruinous to herself, to you, and to me, I don't want to speak any more, but surely, when she heard of your father coming down to my house to make a loathsome scene and create a public scandal, she might then have seen that a serious crisis was impending, and taken some serious steps to try and avoid it? But all she could think of doing was to send down plausible George Wyndham with his pliant tongue to propose to me—what? That I should "gradually drop you"!

As if it had been possible for me to gradually drop you! I had tried to end our friendship in every possible way, going so far as actually to leave England and give a false address abroad in the hopes of break- ing at one blow a bond that had become irksome, hateful, and ruinous to me. Do you think that I *could* have "gradually dropped" you? Do you think that would have satisfied your father? You know it would not. What your father wanted, indeed, was not the cessation of our friendship, but a public scandal. That is what he was striving for. His name had not been in the papers for years. He saw the opportunity of appearing before the British public in an entirely new character, that of the affectionate father. His sense of humour was roused. Had I severed my friendship with you it would have been a terrible disappointment to him, and the small notoriety of a second divorce suit, however revolting its details and origin, would have proved but little consolation to him. For what he was aiming at was popularity, and to pose as a champion of purity, as it is termed, is, in the present condition of the British public, the surest mode of becoming for the nonce a heroic figure. Of this public I have said in one of my plays that if it is Caliban for one half of the year, it is Tartuffe for the other, and your father, in whom both characters may be said to have become incarnate, was in this way marked out as the proper representative of Puritanism in its aggressive and most characteristic form. No gradual dropping of you would have been of any avail, even had it been practicable. Don't you feel now that the only thing for your mother to have done was to have asked me to come to see her, and had you and your brother present, and said definitely that the friendship must absolutely cease? She would have found in me her warmest seconder, and with Drumlanrig and myself in the room she need not have been afraid of speaking to you. She did not do so. She was afraid of her responsibilities, and tried to shift them on to me. One letter she did certainly write to me. It was a brief one, to ask me not to send the lawyer's letter to your father warning him to desist. She was quite right. It was ridiculous my consulting lawyers and seeking their protection. But she nullified any effect her letter might have produced by her usual postscript: *"On no account let Alfred know that I have written to you."*

You were entranced at the idea of my sending lawyers' letters to your father, as well as yourself. It was your suggestion. I could not tell you that your mother was strongly against the idea, for she had bound me with the most solemn promises never to tell you about her letters to me, and I foolishly kept my promise to her. Don't you see that it was wrong of her not to speak directly to you? That all the backstairs-interviews with me, and, the area-gate correspondence were wrong? Nobody can shift their responsibilities on anyone else. They always return ultimately to the proper owner. Your one idea of life, your one philosophy, if you are to be credited with a philosophy, was that whatever you did was to be paid for by someone else: I don't mean merely in the financial sense—that was simply the practical application of your philosophy to everyday life— but in the broadest, fullest sense of transferred responsibility. You made that your creed. It was very successful as far as it went. You forced me into taking the action because you knew that your father would not attack your life or yourself in any way, and that I would defend both to the utmost, and take on my own shoulders whatever would be thrust on me. You were quite right. Your father and I, each from different motives of course, did exactly as you counted on our doing. But somehow, in spite of everything, you have not really escaped. The "infant Samuel theory," as for brevity's sake one may term it, is all very well as far as the general world goes. It may be a good deal scorned in London, and a little sneered at in Oxford, but that is merely because there are a few people who know you in each place, and because in each place you left traces of you passage. Outside of a small set in those two cities, the world looks on you as the good young man who was very nearly tempted into wrong-doing by the wicked and immoral artist, but was rescued just in time by his kind and loving father. It sounds all right. And yet, you know you have not escaped. I am not referring to a silly question asked by a silly juryman, which was of course treated with contempt by the Crown and by the Judge. No one cared about that. I am referring perhaps principally to yourself. In your own eyes, and some day you will have to think of your conduct, you are not, cannot be quite satisfied at the way in which things have turned out. Secretly you must think of yourself with a good deal of shame. A brazen face is a capital thing to show the world, but now and then when you are alone, and have no audience, you have, I suppose, to take the mask off for mere breathing purposes. Else, indeed, you would be stifled.

And in the same manner your mother must at times regret that she tried to shift her grave responsibilities on someone else, who already had enough of a burden to carry. She occupied the position of both parents to you. Did she really fulfil the duties of either? If I bore with your bad temper and your rudeness and your scenes, she might have borne with them too. When last I saw my wife— fourteen months ago now—I told her that she would have to be to Cyril a father as well as a mother. I told her everything about your mother's mode of dealing with you in every detail as I have set it down in this letter, only of course far more fully. I told her the reason of the endless notes with "Private" on the envelope that used to come to Tite Street from your mother, so constantly that my wife used to laugh and say that we must be collaborating in a society novel or something of that kind. I implored her not to be to Cyril what your mother was to you. I told her that she should bring him up so that if he shed innocent blood he would come and tell her, that she might cleanse his hands for him first, and then teach him how by penance or expiation to cleanse his soul afterwards. I told her that if she was frightened of facing the responsibility of the life of another, though her own child, she should get a guardian to help her. That she has, I am glad to say, done. She has chosen

Adrian Hope, a man of high birth and culture and fine character, her own cousin, whom you met once at Tite Street, and with him Cyril and Vyvyan have a good chance of a beautiful future. Your mother, if she was afraid of talking seriously to you, should have chosen someone amongst her own relatives to whom you might have listened. But she should not have been afraid. She should have had it out with you and faced it. At any rate, look at the result. Is she satisfied and pleased?

I know she puts the blame on me. I hear of it, not from people who know you, but from people who do not know you, and do not desire to know you. I hear of it often. She talks of the influence of an elder over a younger man, for instance. It is one of her favourite attitudes towards the question, and it is always a successful appeal to popular prejudice and ignorance. I need not ask you what influence I had over you. You know I had none. It was one of your frequent boasts that I had none, and the only one indeed that was well-founded. What was there, as a mere matter of fact, in you that I could influence? Your brain? It was undeveloped. Your imagination? It was dead. Your heart? It was not yet born. Of all the people who have ever crossed my life you were the one, and the only one, I was unable in my way to influence in any direction. When I lay ill and helpless in a fever caught from tending on you, I had not sufficient influence over you to induce you to get me even a cup of milk to drink, or to see that I had the ordinary necessaries of a sickroom, or to take the trouble to drive a couple of hundred yards to a bookseller's to get me a book at my own expense. When I was actually engaged in writing, and penning comedies that were to beat Congreve for brilliancy, and Dumas fils for philosophy, and I suppose everybody else for every other quality, I had not sufficient influence with you to get you to leave me undisturbed as an artist should be left. Wherever my writing room was, it was to you an ordinary lounge, a place to smoke and drink hock-and-seltzer in, and chatter about absurdities. The "influence of an elder over a younger man" is an excellent theory till it comes to my ears. Then it becomes grotesque. When it comes to your ears, I suppose you smile—to yourself. You are certainly entitled to do so. I hear also much of what she says about money. She states, and with perfect justice, that she was ceaseless in her entreaties to me not to supply you with money. I admit it. Her letters were endless, and the postscript *"Pray do not let Alfred know that I have written to you"* appears in them all. But it was no pleasure to me to have to pay every single thing for you from your morning shave to your midnight hansom. It was a horrible bore. I used to complain to you again and again about it. I used to tell you—you remember, don't you?—how I loathed your regarding me as a *"useful"* person, how no artist wishes to be so regarded or so treated; artists, like art itself, being of their very essence quite useless. You used to get very angry when I said it to you. The truth always made you angry. Truth, indeed, is a thing that is most painful to listen to and most painful to utter. But it did not make you alter your views or your mode of life. Every day I had to pay for every single thing you did all day long. Only a person of absurd good nature or of indescribable folly would have done so. I unfortunately was a complete combination of both. When I used to suggest that your mother should supply you with the money you wanted, you always had a very pretty and graceful answer. You said that the income allowed her by your father—some £1500 a year I believe—was quite inadequate to the wants of a lady of her position, and that you could not go to her for more money than you were getting already. You were quite right about her income being one absolutely unsuitable to a lady of her position and tastes, but you should not have made that an excuse for living in luxury on me: it should on the contrary have been a suggestion to you for economy in your own life. The fact is that you were, and are I suppose still, a typical sentimentalist. For a sentimentalist is simply one who desires to have the luxury of an emotion without paying for it. To propose to spare your mother's pocket was beautiful. To do so at my expense was ugly. You think that one can have one's emotions for nothing. One cannot. Even the finest and the most self-sacrificing emotions have to be paid for. Strangely enough, that is what makes them fine. The intellectual and emotional life of ordinary people is a very contemptible affair. Just as they borrow their ideas from a sort of circulating library of thought—the *Zeitgeist* of an age that has no soul—and send them back soiled at the end of each week, so they always try to get their emotions on credit, and refuse to pay the bill when it comes in. You should pass out of that conception of life. As soon as you have to pay for an emotion you will know its quality, and be the better for such knowledge. And remember that the sentimentalist is always a cynic at heart. Indeed sentimentality is merely the bank holiday of cynicism. And delightful as cynicism is from its intellectual side, now that it has left the Tub for the Club, it never can be more than the perfect philosophy for a man who has no soul. It has its social value, and to an artist all modes of expression are interesting, but in itself it is a poor affair, for to the true cynic nothing is ever revealed.

I think that if you look back now to your attitude towards you mother's income, and your attitude towards my income, you will not feel proud of yourself, and perhaps you may some day, if you don't show your mother this letter, explain to her that your living on me was a matter in which my wishes were not consulted for a moment. It was simply a peculiar, and to me personally most distressing, form that your devotion to me took. To make yourself dependent on me for the smallest as well as the largest sums lent you in your own eyes all the charm of childhood, and in the insisting on my paying for every one of your pleasures you thought that you had found the secret of eternal youth. I confess that it pains me when I hear of your mother's remarks about me, and I am sure that on reflection you will agree with me that if she has no word of regret or sorrow for the ruin your race has brought on mine it would be better if she remained silent. Of course there is no reason she should see any portion of this letter that refers to any mental development I have been going through, or to any point of departure I hope to attain to. It would not be interesting to her. But the parts concerned purely with your life I should show her if I were you.

If I were you, in fact, I would not care about being

loved on false pretences. There is no reason why a man should show his life to the world. The world does not understand things. But with people whose affection one desires to have it is different. A great friend of mine—a friend of ten years' standing—came to see me some time ago and told me that he did not believe a single word of what was said against me, and wished me to know that he considered me quite innocent, and the victim of a hideous plot concocted by your father. I burst into tears at what he said, and told him that while there was much amongst your father's definite charges that was quite untrue and transferred to me by revolting malice, still that my life had been full of perverse pleasures and strange passions, and that unless he accepted that fact as a fact about me and realised it to the full, I could not possibly be friends with him any more, or ever be in his company. It was a terrible shock to him, but we are friends, and I have not got his friendship on false pretences. I have said to you that to speak the truth is a painful thing. To be forced to tell lies is much worse.

I remember as I was sitting in the dock on the

occasion of my last trial listening to Lockwood's appalling denunciation of me—like a thing out of Tacitus, like a passage in Dante, like one of Savonarola's indictments of the Popes at Rome—and being sickened with horror at what I heard. Suddenly it occurred to me, *"How splendid it would be, if I was saying all this about myself!"* I saw then at once that what is said of a man is nothing. The point is, who says it. A man's very highest moment is, I have no doubt at all, when he kneels in the dust, and beats his breast, and tells all the sins of his life. So with you. You would be much happier if you let your mother know a little at any rate of your life from yourself. I told her a good deal about it in December 1893, but of course I was forced into reticences and generalities. It did not seem to give her any more courage in her relations with you. On the contrary, She avoided looking at the truth more persistently than ever. If you told her yourself it would be different. My words may perhaps be often too bitter to you. But the facts you cannot deny. Things were as I have said they were, and if you have read this letter as carefully as you should have done you have met yourself face to face.

I have now written, and at great length, to you in order that you should realise what you were to me before my imprisonment, during those three years' fatal friendship: what you have been to me during my imprisonment, already within two moons of its completion almost: and what I hope to be to myself and to others when my imprisonment is over. I cannot reconstruct my letter, or rewrite it. You must take it as it stands, blotted in many places with tears, in some with the signs of passion or pain, and make it out as best you can, blots, corrections and all. As for the corrections and errata, I have made them in order that my words should be an absolute expression of my thoughts, and err neither through surplusage nor through being inadequate. Language requires to be tuned, like a violin: and just as too many or too few vibrations in the voice of the singer or the trembling of the string will make the note false, so too much or too little in words will spoil the message. As it stands, at any rate, my letter has its definite meaning behind every phrase. There is in it nothing of rhetoric.

Wherever there is erasion or substitution, however slight, however elaborate, it is because I am seeking to render my real impression, to find for my mood its exact equivalent. Whatever is first in feeling comes always last in form.

I will admit that it is a severe letter. I have not spared you. Indeed you may say that, after admitting that to weigh you against the smallest of my sorrows, the meanest of my losses, would be really unfair to you, I have actually done so, and made scruple by scruple the most careful assay of your nature. That is true. But you must remember that you put yourself into the scales.

You must remember that, if when matched with one mere moment of my imprisonment the balance in which you lie kicks the beam, Vanity made you choose the balance, and Vanity made you cling to it. *There* was the one great psychological error of our friendship, its entire want of proportion. You forced your way into a life too large for you, one whose orbit transcended your power of vision no less than your power of cyclic motion, one whose thoughts, passions and actions were of intense import, of wide interest, and fraught, too heavily indeed, with wonderful or awful consequence. Your little life of little whims and moods was admirable in its own little sphere. It was admirable at Oxford, where the worst that could happen to you was a reprimand from the Dean or a lecture from the President, and where the highest excitement was Magdalen becoming head of the river, and the lighting of a bonfire in the quad as a celebration of the august event. It should have continued in its own sphere after you left Oxford. In yourself, you were all right. You were a very complete specimen of a very modern type. It was simply in reference to me that you were wrong. Your reckless extravagance was not a crime. Youth is always extravagant. It was your forcing me to pay for your extravagances that was disgraceful. Your desire to have a friend with whom you could pass your time from morning to night was charming. It was almost idyllic. But the friend you fastened on should not have been a man of letters, an artist, one to whom your continual presence was as utterly destructive of all beautiful work as it was actually paralysing to the creative faculty. There was no harm in your seriously considering that the most perfect way of passing an evening was to have a champagne dinner at the Savoy, a box at a Music-Hall to follow, and a champagne supper at Willis's as a bonne-bouche for the end. Heaps of delightful young men in London are of the same opinion. It is not even an eccentricity. It is the qualification for becoming a member of White's. But you had no right to require of me that I should become the purveyor of such pleasures for you. It showed your lack of any real appreciation of my genius. Your quarrel with your father, again, whatever one may think about its character, should obviously have remained a question entirely between the two of you. It should have been carried on in a backyard. Such quarrels, I believe, usually are. Your mistake was in insisting on its being played as a tragi-comedy on a high stage in History, with the whole world as the audience, and myself as the prize for the victor in the contemptible contest. The fact that your father loathed you, and that you loathed your father, was not a matter of any interest to the English public. Such feelings are very common in English domestic life, and should be confined to the place they characterise: the home. Away from the home-circle they are quite out of place. To translate them is an offence. Family-life is not to be treated as a red flag to be flaunted in the streets, or a horn to be blown hoarsely on the housetops. You took Domesticity out of its proper sphere, just as you took yourself out of your proper sphere.

And those who quit their proper sphere change their surroundings merely, not their natures. They do not acquire the thoughts or passions appropriate to the sphere they enter. It is not in their power to do so. Emotional forces, as I say somewhere in *Intentions*, are as limited in extent and duration as the forces of physical energy. The little cup that is made to hold so much can hold so much and no more, though all the purple vats of Burgundy be filled with wine to the brim, and the treaders stand knee-deep in the gathered grapes of the stony vineyards of Spain.

There is no error more common than that of thinking that those who are the causes or occasions of great tragedies share in the feelings suitable to the tragic mood: no error more fatal than expecting it of them. The martyr in his "shirt of flame" may be looking on the face of God, but to him who is piling the faggots or loosening the logs for the blast the whole scene is no more than the slaying of an ox is to the butcher, or the felling of a tree to the charcoal-burner in the forest, or the fall of a flower to one who is mowing down the grass with a scythe. Great passions are for the great of soul, and great events can be seen only by those who are on a level with them.

I know of nothing in all Drama more incomparable from the point of view of Art, or more suggestive in its subtlety of observation, than Shakespeare's drawing of Rosencrantz and Guildenstern. They are Hamlet's college friends. They have been his companions. They bring with them memories of pleasant days together. At the moment when they come across him in the play he is staggering under the weight of a burden intolerable to one of his temperament. The dead have come armed out of the grave to impose on him a mission at once too great and too mean for him. He is a dreamer, and he is called upon to act. He has the nature of the poet and he is asked to grapple with the common complexities of cause and effect, with life in its practical realisation, of which he knows nothing, not with life in its ideal essence, of which he knows much. He has no conception of what to do, and his folly is to feign folly. Brutus used madness as a cloak to conceal the sword of his purpose, the dagger of his will, but to Hamlet madness is a mere mask for the hiding of weakness. In the making of mows and jests he sees a chance of delay. He keeps playing with action, as an artist plays with a theory. He makes himself the spy of his proper actions, and listening to his own words knows them to be but "words, words, words." Instead of trying to be the hero of his own history, he seeks to be the spectator of his own tragedy. He disbelieves in everything, including himself, and yet his doubt helps him not, as it comes not from scepticism but from a divided will.

Of all this, Guildenstern and Rosencrantz realise nothing. They bow and smirk and smile, and what the one says the other echoes with sicklier iteration. When at last, by means of the play within the play and the puppets in their dalliance, Hamlet "catches the conscience" of the King, and drives the wretched man in terror from his throne, Guildenstern and Rosencrantz see no more in his conduct than a rather painful breach of court-etiquette. That is as far as they can attain to in "the contemplation of the spectacle of life with appropriate emotions." They are close to his very secret and know nothing of it. Nor would there be any use in telling them. They are the little cups that can hold so much and no more. Towards the close it is suggested that, caught in a cunning springe set for another, they have met, or may meet with a violent and sudden death. But a tragic ending of this kind, though touched by Hamlet's humour with something of the surprise and justice of comedy, is really not for such as they. They never die. Horatio who, in order to "report Hamlet and his cause aright to the unsatisfied,"

Absents him from felicity a while

And in this harsh world draws his breath in pain,

dies, though not before an audience, and leaves no brother. But Guildenstern and Rosencrantz are as immortal as Angelo and Tartuffe, and should rank with them. They are what modern life has contributed to the antique ideal of friendship. He who writes a new *De Amicitia* must find a niche for them and praise them in Tusculan prose. They are types fixed for all time. To censure them would show a lack of appreciation. They are merely out of their sphere: that is all. In sublimity of soul there is no contagion. High thoughts and high emotions are by their very existence isolated. What Ophelia herself could not understand was not to be realised by "Guildenstern and gentle Rosencrantz," by "Rosencrantz and gentle Guildenstern." Of course I do not propose to compare you. There is a wide difference between you. What with them was chance, with you was choice. Deliberately and by me uninvited you thrust yourself into my sphere, usurped there a place for which you had neither right nor qualifications, and having by curious persistence, and by the rendering of your very presence a part of each separate day, succeeded in absorbing my entire life, could do no better with that life than break it in pieces. Strange as it may sound to you, it was but natural that you should do so. If one gives to a child a toy too wonderful for its little mind, or too beautiful for its but halfawakened eyes, it breaks the toy, if it is wilful; if it is listless it lets it fall and goes its way to its own companions. So it was with you. Having got hold of my life, you did not know what to do with it. You couldn't have known. It was too wonderful a thing to be in your grasp. You should have let it slip from your hands and gone back to your own companions at their play. But unfortunately you were wilful, and so you broke it. That, when everything is said, is perhaps the ultimate secret of all that has happened. For secrets are always smaller than their manifestations. By the displacement of an atom a world may be shaken. And that I may not spare myself any more than you I will add this: that dangerous to me as my meeting with you was, it was rendered fatal to me by the particular moment in which we met. For you were at that time of life when all that one does is no more than the sowing of the seed, and I was at that time of life when all that one does is no less than the reaping of the harvest.

There are some few things more about which I must write to you. The first is about my Bankruptcy. I heard some days ago, with great disappointment I admit, that it is too late now for your family to pay your father off, that it would be illegal, and that I must remain in my present painful position for some considerable time to come. It is bitter to me because I am assured on legal authority that I cannot even publish a book without the permission of the Receiver to whom all the accounts must be submitted. I cannot enter into a contract with the manager of a theatre, or produce a play without the receipts passing to your father and my few other creditors. I think that even you will admit now that the scheme of "scoring off" your father by allowing him to make me a bankrupt has not really been the brilliant all-round success you imagined it was going to turn out. It has not been so to me at any rate, and my feelings of pain and humiliation at my pauperism should have been consulted rather than your own sense of humour, however caustic or unexpected. In point of actual fact, in permitting my Bankruptcy, as in urging me on to the original trial, you really were playing right into your father's hands, and doing just what he wanted. Alone, and unassisted, he would from the very outset have been powerless. In you—though you did not mean to hold such a horrible office—he has always found his chief ally.

I am told by More Adey in his letter that last summer you really did express on more than one occasion your desire to repay me "a little of what I spent" on you. As I said to him in my answer, unfortunately I spent on you my art, my life, my name, my place in history, and if your family had all the marvellous things in the world at their command, or what the world holds as marvellous, genius, beauty, wealth, high position and the like, and laid them all at my feet, it would not repay me for one tithe of the smallest things that have been taken from me, or one tear of the least tears that I have shed. However, of course everything one does has to be paid for. Even to the Bankrupt it is so. You seem to be under the impression that Bankruptcy is a convenient means by which a man can avoid paying his debts, a "score off his creditors" in fact. It is quite the other way. It is the method by which a man's creditors "score off" him, if we are to continue your favourite phrase, and by which the Law by the confiscation of all his property forces him to pay every one of his debts, and if he fails to do so leaves him as penniless as the commonest mendicant who stands in an archway, or creeps down a road, holding out his hand for the alms for which, in England at any rate, he is afraid to ask. The Law has taken from me not merely all that I have, my books, furniture, pictures, my copyright in my published works, my copyright in my plays, everything in fact from *The Happy Prince* and *Lady Windermere's* Fan down to the staircarpets and door-scraper of my house, but also all that I am ever going to have. My interest in my marriage-settlement, for instance, was sold. Fortunately I was able to buy it in through my friends. Otherwise, in case my wife died, my two children during my lifetime would be as penniless as myself. My interest in our Irish estate, entailed on me by my own father, will I suppose have to go next. I feel very bitterly about its being sold, but I must submit.

Your father's seven hundred pence—or pounds is it?—stand in the way, and must be refunded. Even when I am stripped of all have, and am ever to have, and am granted a discharge as a hopeless Insolvent, I have still got to pay my debts. The Savoy dinners— the clear turtle-soup, the luscious ortolans wrapped in their crinkled Sicilian vine-leaves, the heavy amber-coloured, indeed almost amber-scented champagne—Dagonet 1880, I think, was your favourite wine?—all have still to be paid for. The suppers at Willis's, the special *cuvée* of Perrier-Jouet reserved always for us, the wonderful *pâtés* procured directly from Strasburg, the marvellous *fine champagne* served always at the bottom of great bell-shaped glasses that its bouquet might be the better savoured by the true epicures of what was really exquisite in life—these cannot be left unpaid, as bad debts of a dishonest client. Even the dainty sleeve-links—four heart-shaped moonstones of silver mist, girdled by alternate ruby and diamond for their setting—that I designed, and had made at Henry Lewis's as a special little present to you, to celebrate the success of my second comedy—these even—though I believe you sold them for a song a few months afterwards—have to be paid for. I cannot leave the jeweller out of pocket for the presents I gave you, no matter what you did with them. So, even if I get my discharge, you see I have still my debts to pay.

And what is true of a bankrupt is true of everyone else in life. For every single thing that is done someone has to pay Even you yourself—with all your desire for absolute freedom from all duties, your insistence on having everything supplied to you by others, your attempts to reject any claim on your affection, or regard, or gratitude—even you will have some day to reflect seriously on what you have done, and try, however unavailingly, to make some attempt at atonement. The fact that you will not be able really to do so will be part of your punishment. You can't wash your hands of all responsibility, and propose with a shrug or a smile to pass on to a new friend and a freshly spread feast. You can't treat all that you have brought upon me as a sentimental reminiscence to be served up occasionally with the cigarettes and *liqueurs*, a picturesque background to a modem life of pleasure like an old tapestry hung in a common inn. It may for the moment have the charm of a new sauce or a fresh vintage, but the scraps of a banquet grow stale, and the dregs of a bottle are bitter. Either today, or tomorrow, or some day you have got to realise it. Otherwise you may die without having done so, and then what a mean, starved, unimaginative life you would have had. In my letter to More I have suggested one point of view from which you had better approach the subject as soon as possible. He will tell you what it is. To understand it you will have to cultivate your imagination. Remember that imagination is the quality that enables one to see things and people in their real as in their ideal relations. If you cannot realise it by yourself, talk to others on the subject. I have had to look at my past face to face. Look at your past face to face. Sit down quietly and consider it. The supreme vice is shallowness. Whatever is realised is right. Talk to your brother about it. Indeed the proper person to talk to is Percy. Let him read this letter, and know all the circumstances of our friendship. When things are clearly put before him, no judgment is better. Had we told him the truth, what a lot would have been saved to me of suffering and disgrace! You remember I proposed to do so, the night you arrived in London from Algiers. You absolutely refused. So when he came in after dinner we had to play the comedy of your father being an insane man subject to absurd and unaccountable delusions. It was a capital comedy while it lasted, none the less so because Percy took it all quite seriously. Unfortunately it ended in a very revolting manner. The subject on which I write now is one of its results, and if it be a trouble to you, pray do not forget that it is the deepest of my humiliations, and one I must go through. I have no option. You have none either.

The second thing about which I have to speak to you is with regard to the conditions, circumstances, and place of our meeting when my term of imprisonment is over. From extracts from your letter to Robbie written in the early summer of last year I understand that you have sealed up in two packages my letters and my presents to you—such at least as remain of either—and are anxious to hand them personally to me. It is, of course, necessary that they should be given up. You did not understand why I wrote beautiful letters to you, any more than you understood why I gave you beautiful presents. You failed to see that the former were not meant to be published, any more than the latter were meant to be pawned. Besides, they belong to a side of life that is long over, to a friendship that somehow you were unable to appreciate at its proper value. You must look back with wonder now to the days when you had my entire life in your hands. I too look back to them with wonder, and with other, with far different, emotions.

I am to be released, if all goes well with me, towards the end of May, and hope to go at once to some little seaside village abroad with Robbie and More Adey. The sea, as Euripides says in one of his plays about Iphigenia, washes away the stains and wounds of the world, Θάλασσα κλύζει πάντα τ'ανθϱ ῶπων κακά.

I hope to be at least a month with my friends, and to gain, in their healthful and affectionate company, peace, and balance, and a less troubled heart, and a sweeter mood. I have a strange longing for the great simple primeval things, such as the Sea, to me no less of a mother than the Earth. It seems to me that we all look at Nature too much, and live with her too little. I discern great sanity in the Greek attitude. They never chattered about sunsets, or discussed whether the shadows on the grass were really mauve or not. But they saw that the sea was for the swimmer, and the sand for the feet of the runner. They loved the trees for the shadow that they cast, and the forest for its silence at noon. The vineyard-dresser wreathed his hair with ivy that he might keep off the rays of the sun as he stooped over the young shoots, and for the artist and the athlete, the two types that Greece gave us, they plaited into garlands the leaves of the bitter laurel and of the wild parsley which else had been of no service to man.

We call ourselves a utilitarian age, and we do not know the uses of any single thing. We have forgotten that Water can cleanse, and Fire purify, and that the Earth is mother to us all. As a consequence our Art is of the Moon and plays with shadows, while Greek art is of the Sun and deals directly with things. I feel sure that in elemental forces there is purification, and I want to go back to them and live in their presence. Of course, to one so modern as I am, *enfant* de mon siècle, merely to look at the world will be always lovely. I tremble with pleasure when I think that on the very day of my leaving prison both the laburnum and the lilac will be blooming in the gardens, and that I shall see the wind stir into restless beauty the swaying gold of the one, and make the other toss the pale purple of its plumes so that all the air shall be Arabia for me. Linnaeus fell on his knees and wept for joy when he saw for the first time the long heath of some English upland made yellow with the tawny aromatic blossoms of the common furze, and I know that for me, to whom flowers are part of desire, there are tears waiting in the petals of some rose. It has always been so with me from my boyhood. There is not a single colour hidden away in the chalice of a flower, or the curve of a shell, to which, by some subtle sympathy with the very soul of things, my nature does not answer. Like Gautier I have always been one of those *pour qui le monde visible existe*.

Still, I am conscious now that behind all this Beauty, satisfying though it be, there is some Spirit hidden of which the painted forms and shapes are but modes of manifestation, and it is with this Spirit that I desire to become in harmony. I have grown tired of the articulate utterances of men and things. The Mystical in Art, the Mystical in Life, the Mystical in Nature—this is what I am looking for, and in the great symphonies of Music, in the initiation of Sorrow, in the depths of the Sea I may find it. It is absolutely necessary for me to find it somewhere.

All trials are trials for one's life, just as all sentences are sentences of death, and three times have I been tried. The first time I left the box to be arrested, the second time to be led back to the House of Detention, the third time to pass into a prison for two years. Society, as we have constituted it, will have no place for me, has none to offer; but Nature, whose sweet rains fall on unjust and just alike, will have clefts in the rocks where I may hide, and secret valleys in whose silence I may weep undisturbed. She will hang the night with stars so that I may walk abroad in the darkness without stumbling, and send the wind over my footprints so that none may track me to my hurt: she will cleanse me in great waters, and with bitter herbs make me whole.

At the end of a month, when the June roses are in all their wanton opulence, I will, if I feel able, arrange through Robbie to meet you in some quiet foreign town like Bruges, whose grey houses and green canals and cool still ways had a charm for me, years ago. For the moment you will have to change your name. The little title of which you were so vain—and indeed it made your name sound like the name of a flower—you will have to surrender, if you wish to see me; just as my name, once so musical in the mouth of Fame, will have to be abandoned by me, in turn. How narrow, and mean, and inadequate to its burdens is this century of ours! It can give to Success its palace of porphyry, but for Sorrow and Shame it does not keep even a wattled house in which they may dwell: all it can do for me is to bid me alter my name into some other name, where even mediaevalism would have given me the cowl of the monk or the face-cloth of the leper behind which I might be at peace.

I hope that our meeting will be what a meeting between you and me should be, after everything that has occurred. In old days there was always a wide chasm between us, the chasm of achieved Art and acquired culture: there is a still wider chasm between us now, the chasm of Sorrow: but to Humility there is nothing that is impossible, and to Love all things are easy.

As regards your letter to me in answer to this, it may be as long or as short as you choose. Address the envelope to "The Governor, H.M. Prison, Reading." Inside, in another, and an open envelope, place your own letter to me: if your paper is very thin do not write on both sides, as it makes it hard for others to read. I have written to you with perfect freedom. You can write to me with the same. What I must know from you is why you have never made any attempt to write to me, since the August of the year before last, more especially after, in the May of last year, eleven months ago now, you knew, and admitted to others that you knew, how you had made me suffer, and how I realised it. I waited month after month to hear from you. Even if I had not been waiting but had shut the doors against you, you should have remembered that no one can possibly shut the doors against Love for ever. The unjust judge in the Gospels rises up at length to give a just decision because Justice comes knocking daily at his door; and at night-time the friend, in whose heart there is no real friendship, yields at length to his friend "because of his importunity." There is no prison in any world into which Love cannot force an entrance. If you did not understand that, you did not understand anything about Love at all. Then, let me know all about your article on me for the *Mercure de France*. I know something of it. You had better quote from it. It is set up in type. Also, let me know the exact terms of your Dedication of your poems. If it is in prose, quote the prose; if in verse, quote the verse. I have no doubt that there will be beauty in it. Write to me with full frankness about yourself: about you life: your friends: your occupations: your books. Tell me about your volume and its reception. Whatever you have to say for yourself, say it without fear. Don't write what you don't mean: that is all. If anything in your letter is false or counterfeit I shall detect it by the ring at once. It is not for nothing, or to no purpose, that in my lifelong cult of literature I have made myself

> Miser of sound and syllable, no less
>
> Than Midas of his coinage.

Remember also that I have yet to know you. Perhaps we have yet to know each other.

For yourself, I have but this last thing to say. Do not be afraid of the past. If people tell you that it is irrevocable, do not believe them. The past, the present and the future are but one moment in the sight of God, in whose sight we should try to live. Time and space, succession and extension, are merely accidental conditions of Thought. The Imagination can transcend them, and move in a free sphere of ideal existences. Things, also, are in their essence what we choose to make them. A thing is, according to the mode in which one looks at it. "Where others," says Blake, "see but the Dawn coming over the hill, I see the sons of God shouting for joy." What seemed to the world and to myself my future I lost irretrievably when I let myself be taunted into taking the action against your father: had, I dare say, lost it really long before that. What lies before me is my past. I have got to make myself look on that with different eyes, to make the world look on it with different eyes, to make God look on it with different eyes. This I cannot do by ignoring it, or slighting it, or praising it, or denying it. It is only to be done by fully accepting it as an inevitable part of the evolution of my life and character: by bowing my head to everything that I have suffered. How far I am away from the true temper of soul, this letter in its changing, uncertain moods, its scorn and bitterness, its aspirations and its failure to realise those aspirations, shows you quite clearly. But do not forget in what a terrible school I am sitting at my task. And incomplete, imperfect, as I am, yet from me you may have still much to gain. You came to me to learn the Pleasure of Life and the Pleasure of Art. Perhaps I am chosen to teach you something much more wonderful, the meaning of Sorrow, and its beauty.

Your affectionate friend

OSCAR WILDE

哪里有悲伤，哪里就有圣所

图书在版编目（CIP）数据

自深深处：汉文、英文 /（英）奥斯卡·王尔德（Oscar Wilde）著；梁永安译 . -- 长沙：湖南文艺出版社，2025. 1. -- ISBN 978-7-5726-2174-1

I. I561.64

中国国家版本馆 CIP 数据核字第 2024K9H044 号

ZI SHEN SHEN CHU: HANWEN、YINGWEN
自深深处：汉文、英文

著　者：[英]奥斯卡·王尔德（Oscar Wilde）
译　者：梁永安
出 版 人：陈新文
责任编辑：吕苗莉
监　制：邢越超
策划编辑：王　迪　刘　筝
特约编辑：尹　晶
营销支持：文刀刀
装帧设计：陈　杰
内文排版：百朗文化
出　版：湖南文艺出版社
　　　　（长沙市雨花区东二环一段 508 号　邮编：410014）
网　址：www.hnwy.net
印　刷：北京中科印刷有限公司
开　本：855 mm × 1040 mm　1/32
字　数：229 千字
印　张：13.5
版　次：2025 年 1 月第 1 版
印　次：2025 年 1 月第 1 次印刷
书　号：ISBN 978-7-5726-2174-1
定　价：69.00 元

若有质量问题，请致电质量监督电话：010-59096394
团购电话：010-59320018